FORBIDDEN

FORBIDDEN

KICK | USE | BREAK

CD REISS

Flip City Media Inc

PART I

KICK

Chapter 1

My ankles were shackled. The chain between them clicked when I rolled over, and the steel bit my anklebones when I rested my feet together.

My brain chemistry had been set for arousal at the touch of hard metal edges on my skin, and even though I felt a growing swirl of lust when I pressed my legs together, I was preoccupied. Deacon hadn't put the leg irons on me, nor had I squeezed them tighter than I should, just to feel them holding me while he played me like a musician at an instrument.

I didn't know what had happened.

The last thing I remembered was rain.

No. The last thing I remembered was being in scene with Deacon and entering subspace, outside of myself, where pleasure and pain merged.

No.

Nuzzling Snowcone as he huffed and clopped his hoof on the stable floor, I held his bit. I thought, *he's slow, it's over, he's slow, he's old, it's over, he won't take the bit, he's slow.* My thoughts repeated as if they were stuck.

The last thing I remembered was hanging from the ceiling, listening to rain on the windows. It never rained in Los Angeles—unless it did, and then it rained like a holy hail of fuck yous.

The last thing I remembered was wet thighs. Feeling so sore I couldn't sit. Thinking about fucking. Finding someone to fuck.

There was so much fucking.

The last thing I remembered was snorting a line of flake off Amanda's tits.

And then?

Nothing.

Anxiety sat in my chest like a kinetic weight, but I wasn't scared. I knew I wasn't thinking right, that I was little more than a jumble of emotions and half sentences. I thought in colors, and saw in bursts of silence. The aggressive white light above illuminated the angles of the corners. The tight space and soft white walls were the product of some kind of regulating entity. Was I in prison? A hospital? Was I even in the United States? When would Deacon come for me?

Soon.

He'd come soon, and everything would be in control again.

Until then, I'd submit to the fog of my half-formed thoughts and nothing would go wrong.

▭

"DO YOU KNOW WHERE YOU ARE?"

His voice was so gentle in powder blues and jazzy notes, but he was a stranger. I'd never heard a voice like that—thick and soft as heavy cream, a satin sheet on a bed of sand. I opened my eyes to bright white fog and a charcoal blur that must have been attached to the voice. Not a cop. Not a lawyer. Not an ER doc.

"No," I croaked.

"I'm going to ask you some questions. All right?"

I nodded. I didn't realize how quiet it was until the noise of the sheet rubbing against my ear sounded like an electric guitar amp set to eleven.

"Can you tell me your name?"

It wasn't loud, that voice. Like Deacon's, it had its own kind of authority, but unlike my master's, it was gentle.

I cleared the frog from my throat. "Fiona."

"Hi, Fiona. My name is Doctor Chapman. But you can call me Elliot."

My eyes cleared a little. The charcoal smear turned into a beige oval with two green-grey dots for eyes and non-committally colored hair. His skin wrinkled around the eyes, but his mouth was young. He was either in his late twenties, or forty-ish, like Deacon. Or maybe somewhere in between.

"Good," he said, crouching to meet my gaze. "How old are you?"

"Twenty-three."

"Where do you live?"

That was a hard question, with its own complexity.

"The first thing that comes to mind," the doctor said.

"Number three, Maundy Street."

He nodded, so my answer must have been satisfactory. "Get cleaned up, get something to eat, then we can talk."

I nodded, and the noise in my ear was less shocking. He stood and went for the white door with the little window at eye level.

"Where am I?" I asked.

"Westonwood Acres."

THEY FED me in my room from a metal tray. I didn't eat much. I was shown to a small bathroom, where I was expected to clean up and change out of one light blue jumpsuit into another. I had never been squeamish about germs or ickiness, but in the soft cotton of my mind, something seemed inherently wrong with the space, the room, the clothes.

Deacon would find me. He was probably in some office right now, demanding my release from the mental ward. He had a way of sniffing me out, even when I snuck away, as if he and I were connected by a vibrating fiber. No matter how far I went, no matter how fast, he knew. If there was anyone in the world I could count on, it was him. He was coming. All I had to do was behave long enough for him to arrive.

Just thinking of him, the bones of his wrist, the tendons tight on his forearms when he gripped my body, his growl—*mine mine mine*—sent a wave of pleasure between my legs.

I knew who I was. I was a celebrity without talent. I was an heiress. I was a whore. I was a party waiting to happen. I was an addict. I was his, and in that last definition—that I was owned by Deacon I knew my place in the chaos.

Sitting on the edge of my bed, the headache came like slowly tightening wrenches clamped to my temples and the back of my neck. As the pain bloomed, my mind cleared. Though I couldn't remember shit any better than before, I gained the good sense to worry about it. I gained details. Cast-iron grates on the windows in a decorative pattern. No doorknob. Walls of suede microfiber. Cork floors. Soft wood bed with Egyptian cotton sheets.

There were people around me, but I felt more than saw them. Intuited their presence. How long had I been walking through plasma? Where was the other side?

The last thing I remembered… What was the last thing I remembered? It was Deacon in the kitchen of number three, sweatpants and no shirt, with his arms out. He was saying something. Pleading. He was telling me I had to kick. Kick? What did that mean? And was it the kitchen or the stables? Whatever space he was in was plagued by his raw pain. He was mad and resigned at the same time, two things I'd never seen from him.

Was that the last thing I remembered? Whatever it was must have landed me here.

There had been a dream with red and blue lights.

There had been a party, possibly before the lights, maybe after. I was on my hands and knees. I was high, so high, flooded with endorphins and knocking around subspace. My ache was dulled to pleasure, and I wanted something desperately.

I couldn't put it all together. Maybe I'd gone just a little heavy on the flake. Deacon would be pissed. I'd apologize. We'd do a knotting, and I'd get better.

The last thing… Deacon had gone away. He'd put his face in my neck, and I was surrounded by peppermint and sandalwood. He'd gotten in the limo, and I watched it glide down the hill and past the gate of the private road, splashing in the rushing water of the drainage dip. Maundy Street. Left turn past Debbie and Martin's place, and away.

Christmas. He said he'd be back for Christmas.

The house had seemed big, and I'd thought about spending the week at home in Bel-Air. Avoid Debbie. Avoid Martin. Their eyes and their temptations pressed against me. I could handle it. I could handle anything. I was strong.

Was that decision even worth remembering? What was the last thing that had *happened*?

I only remembered stuff from long ago. A knotting, the last one, my favorite. Deacon had laced me to hooks in the ceiling with patterns of knotted rope, turning my body into a work of art. I was upside down, naked, falling from the sky, and he crouched on the floor, caressing my head and shoulders. I always felt at peace when he knotted me, but that time, when he became part of the work, my very identity and all the anxiety that came with it melted away.

Something about a horse, but I must have been dreaming. I hadn't touched a horse in months. Years, maybe.

And the last party. The knots of skin and fluid.

A stinging drip in my nose.

When? Yesterday? Last month? Never?

Now. Here. In Westonwood.

Fuck.

Chapter 2

Having eaten a meal in a tiny pale grey room, and walked down wide, pale grey hallway, showered in a white-tiled stall, and gotten into a stainless steel elevator, I found the office jarring. It could have been my headache that grew more potent by the moment, or it could have been the presence of actual colors.

Pale blue curtains drawn against the rain pounding the window. Green lantern. Rich brown wainscoting and desk. Burgundy carpets. I squinted. Even the light from the desk lamp felt intentionally painful.

"Thanks, Bernie," Dr. Chapman said from the corner of the room.

He wore a grey jacket and a sage-green sweater over a white shirt. His voice didn't hurt my head, though when Bernie, the orderly, clicked the door behind him, I felt as if someone had hit my temple with a crowbar.

"Headache?" the doctor asked. I nodded, and he sighed. "For what you pay to be here, you think they'd be on the ball with the analgesics." He slid open a desk drawer and removed a bottle of over-the-counter medicine. "Let me get you some water."

I held out my hand. "Don't need it."

He shook two into my palm. I kept my hand out then spread my fingers wider. He shook out two more. I kept my hand out.

"That's plenty," he said.

I threw them to the back of my throat and swallowed. One caught on the back of my tongue, releasing a wave of sour and bitter, but I took it all.

"Would you like to sit?" He put the bottle back and slid the drawer closed.

"Is that a question? About what I like?"

"It's a suggestion phrased as a question."

A padded leather chair in soft green and worn dark wood sat to my left. I touched the brass studs that kept the leather attached and sat down. Doctor Chapman sat behind the desk, settling his right elbow on the arm of the chair. I didn't know if I was supposed to start with questions about what had happened or why I was there. I didn't know if I should rattle off a list of what I remembered and didn't, or ask just how much trouble I was in, or when Deacon was coming to get me out.

But he saved me the trouble. "Can you tell me the last thing you remember?"

I stiffened. My mouth locked up. I couldn't tell him. "When can I leave?"

"Do you think you should leave?"

"Do you think I should leave?"

"It's more important to know what you think," he said.

"It's more important for *you* to know what I think, and it's more important for me to know what you think. So you first."

He rubbed his upper lip with his middle finger, an odd gesture, then dropped his hand. "You're here for your own protection, at the great expense and effort of your family. I have seventy-two hours to report on whether or not you're a danger to yourself or others."

"How am I a danger?"

"You don't remember?"

"You know I don't."

He put his elbows on the desk and looked right into my eyes. I wanted to know what he saw, other than what everyone saw—a party girl with a permanent smile and spread legs. A balls-to-the-wall princess with an entourage and two wrecked Bentleys in the garage. But more than that, I wanted to know how old he was. He looked so young and so wise at the same time.

"If I tell you why you're here," he said with that gentle voice, "I want to warn you, that you've probably blocked it because it's painful to you."

"Okay." I didn't believe him, but I let him think I'd blocked it. The reason I didn't know was because I'd been drunk or high. Whatever sweet chemicals I'd taken had kept my neurons from connecting.

It must have been bad, and I could never feel guilty about it because I didn't remember it. I'd had a drunk driving accident. I'd given someone bad pills. I'd been gang-fucked and dumped in an alley. I'd killed some random paparazzi. One of the entourage had turned on me. All the things Mom had listed as a fear and Dad had implied with his look.

"You're making me nervous," I whispered even though my headache abated.

"Do you know Deacon Bruce?"

I heard his last name so infrequently, sometimes I forgot he even had one. "Yes."

"Do you remember what he is to you?"

"Yes." I refused to clarify further. He was my safety. My control. The hub on the wheel of my life. Without him, the spokes didn't meet.

And he was coming for me. All I had to do was stall.

"It would help if you told me the last thing you remember."

"I don't remember anything."

"Do you remember going to the Branwyn Stables yesterday?"

"I haven't been to the stables in years." As if the back of my face had a surface all its own, it tingled. A corset tightened around my chest. I was going to cry, and I had no idea why. "I need you to just tell me, Doctor."

"Call me Elliot."

"Fucking tell me right now!"

"Can you stay calm?"

I swallowed a golf ball of cry gunk. "Yes. I'm fine. Yes."

Seconds passed. He watched me as if casually observing a churning barrel of worry.

"I'm fine," I said. "You can tell me. I'll be cool."

"We don't know what happened exactly. There are details missing. Mister Bruce isn't well enough to be interviewed."

I tried to hold myself together, but my fingers gripped the edge of the chair. He saw my knuckles turn white. I knew it, but I had nowhere else for the tension to go.

"Go on," I said.

"There are some things that are known for sure, and some questions. If you remember any portion of what I'm telling you, please stop me."

"Is Deacon okay?"

He cleared his throat and looked away before turning back to me. I realized he didn't want to tell me at all, and that barrel of worry filled up with panic.

"You stabbed him in the chest."

Chapter 3

I woke up strapped to the bed with a brain full of fog. Then they took me to a room with a balding doctor and a nurse whose face I couldn't make out through my drug-induced lethargy.

The doctor clucked and groaned as he read things off to the nurse. I could barely sort through what he was saying, and I could barely remember what had happened a few hours ago. Had I attacked someone? The therapist? I'd apologize. He seemed nice. I hoped I didn't hurt him. What had he said to make me freak out? Something about something I did. The reason I was here.

I was in incredible physical shape—I knew that because suspending a woman from the ceiling in rough hemp ropes took hours of work, days of practice, and stamina and strength from both parties. And Deacon, Master Deacon, did not fuck around. I had to get off the flake, reduce the alcohol, and sleep eight hours a day, even if they were when the sun was out. He'd had to watch me sometimes to make sure I ate right, stretched, and stayed off substances, but it was worth it.

Except I was here.

Had Deacon been away?

If he'd been around, I wouldn't have done whatever it was I'd done to land in Westonwood. He'd come and…something. Something was wrong. Something about Deacon. I couldn't find the specifics, but it was something huge and upsetting. My heart beat faster when I tried to think of it. I got impatient with the nurse as she moved my wrist and said a bunch of gibberish as if I wasn't there. She was keeping me from thinking the things I needed to think. Facts lay a layer under the sand, and I was trying to dig them up, but the bitch kept taking my shovel.

The doctor looked at my teeth and poked a molar. A shot of pain cut through me, and I pushed him away so hard he crashed into a tray of torture devices.

Fucking meds. I was going to have to detox again. Once I was curled up in my bed again, I would get the itchy skin, the broken lethargy, the attacks of consciousness that cut into my thoughtless reflections on my sensory space. I'd spent a lot of time trying to get away from my thoughts. Most of my days, actually. I had it down to a science. I never thought about a damn thing.

Or more accurately, I thought plenty and drowned it however I could. When the therapist had told me I'd done something so terrible, such an anathema to me, and I didn't have a substance or an orgasm to drape over the news, I did things without thinking. My determination to be good had gone out the window, and I'd lunged for that lying doctor. I remembered being hauled away screaming, strapped down, and I remembered the injection.

It wasn't until I woke up secured to the bed in a mental ward that I knew what it was like to be distanced from my brain. I could separate the drug thoughts from the real-me thoughts. The drug thoughts were blank and foggy, and the real-me thoughts were black holes where information should have been. Things floated by as if someone was changing the station from a comedy to a thriller to a terror fest to colored bars that went *eeeeeee*.

I'd stabbed Deacon.

No, it was a lie.

You know it's true.

Not.

Yes.

Not.

You did it.

Never.

I turned my head. Nothing in that room could upset me, because the space was absent of stimuli. The room was still grey, still bathed in light, and in the corner, a silver disk got lost in the vents and alarms dotting the ceiling.

A camera.

If I screamed—and I believed I could—they'd know, and they'd come for me. Or not. I wasn't ready to find out.

I'd been strapped to beds for long periods of time, usually with my legs spread farther than they were now, often with my knees bent. When I was left in that position, it was so I couldn't press my legs closed and give myself an orgasm. By the time Deacon came in, I was wet with anticipation and ready for anything he dished out.

In the hospital, my ankles and wrists were bound so I couldn't hurt myself. I was wet all over again. I tried to close my legs and couldn't. And no one was coming to slap or fuck me. Not even one of Deacon's friends. Not even Debbie. I wasn't strapped down so I could stew in my own lust. I was strapped down because after Elliot had told me I'd stabbed Deacon, my mind had gone white hot.

Fuck.

Even as I got angry at myself over this forgotten thing, I felt the bloat of arousal.

You're swelled, kitten.

Swelled didn't mean horny. That was easy enough. Swelled meant I needed it. Sex. Hot and dirty fucking. Masturbating couldn't stop a swell. Rubbing my cunt on the pillow, vibrators, dildos, eggs, none of them chased away a swell. Only penetration, anywhere, by a warm-blooded man, took care of it. Until that happened, I couldn't function.

It had never been a problem. I took what I wanted, made no commitments, found willing participants wherever, whenever I needed it. I was on three forms of birth control, for fuck's sake. I got tested weekly. I wrapped it up. Past that, my first priority to a swell was getting rid of it, and I was mindless in my pursuit. For Deacon, it became a challenge—to know when I would need it, predict it, and put me in a position where he could withhold penetration. He created the unique torture of being tied in knots, naked, cunt out, ready as he tugged the rope and I begged him to take me.

"I need to finish, kitten. How would it be to have people arrive to a party without the table set?"

He'd hurt me to forestall satisfaction, leaving my ass a deep shade of pink and my little tits sore, putting me on the edge and keeping me there for hours, until I wept.

Had I killed Deacon? My master? Why? How? Oh God, what had I done?

The holes in my mind closed, filled with the thick caulk of sex. I needed it. I needed to feel good. I needed my mind to go blank with pleasure for a second or two, to clear the pain out like a firehose. I could be in for a swell. I needed to feel good. Needed.

"Now!" I cried. "Bathroom!"

Bernie, a big, dark-skinned guy with a kind face, came through the door seconds later. "Hi, Miss Drazen."

He smelled of man, and though he wasn't the best looking guy ever, I was painfully aware of the cock under his blue cotton pants.

"Bernie."

"Yes, ma'am?"

"Do you know anything? About my case?"

"No, ma'am."

He unstrapped me. When his hands touched my wrist, the feeling went right between my legs. I tried to catch his gaze, but his eyes wouldn't meet mine, and I noticed he was trying to avoid touching me. It was as if he knew.

"Thank you." Despite everything, I said it in my softest, most inviting voice.

He let me in the bathroom without another word or touch. When the door snapped shut, I stripped out of the jumpsuit and hitched my leg over the sink. The cold porcelain edge lay hard against my cunt, and I shuddered, clasping my left hand on the faucet, and my right on the edge in front of me.

"Let me come, Sir," I whispered so it wouldn't echo, and I called to mind our first knotting.

THE TWENTY-TWO YEAR OLD ME, the taste of flake a bitter, recent memory, kneels on the wood floor his loft with light pouring in the windows. I am naked but for simple panties. He says that when he ties me naked, he's taking me. We haven't fucked, though our relationship is intensely sexual. He's worth waiting for, this delicious man with his scorching eyes and knowing smirk. I want to obey the rules for him. I feel right when I take care of myself for him.

When Deacon returned from Africa, he sailed, and when he sailed, he knotted mast ropes and women. He'd been led to what Westerners called shibari. In its ancient form, it was the art of binding prisoners to maximize pain and humiliation. In its modern form, it is the art of patterning rope around a subject for an aesthetic—drawing the lengths around the body to create patterns, to press against erogenous zones, to provide a sexual partner with a compliant, accessible body. The black and white photographs of his work are erotic and sublime, and I knew as soon as he showed me them that I wanted to be part of it.

He puts my hands behind my back and begins. He handles me roughly, moving my body to tie it. There will be no suspension today. Just me, on the floor. It's too soon to risk suspension. I'm not practiced enough. And he won't put anything through my nipple rings until he's sure I can stay still. He's still keeping it simple—teaching me how to hold my hands, checking my reactions, my ability to take instruction, my commitment to safety.

He touches me more than he ever has, and though I'd promised many men I'd be their fuckdoll, for the first time, I actually feel like one. My arms twist behind my back, hands clasping elbows, wrists facing away from the ropes, protected from the pressure. I'm to tell him if anything tingles or feels wrong, but so far, everything is exactly right.

He loops the rope around my ponytail, yanking it so the short rope can be tied to my ankles, and he's done. I'm immobilized, calves to the floor, back arched, forced to look at the hooks in the ceiling from the pressure on the back of my head.

I've never been so aroused. From the tips of my toes to the beating of my heart, my tranquility vibrates with awakening. I feel him standing over me, cutting off the light.

"You doing all right?" he asks.

I open my eyes halfway. He's down to his bare feet and trousers. Shirtless, magnificent Deacon. I can't make words, but my smile answers in the affirmative. He kneels and puts his fingers to my lips. I part them, and he slides them in.

"I'll gag you next time," he says. "The cloth will go around the ropes."

I wet his finger with my tongue. I usually have a ton of dirty talk at my disposal, but I'm so high from this, I can't even speak.

"You'll only be able to grunt, but I'll understand you, kitten. You and I, we're going to speak without speaking."

Lightly, so very lightly, his fingers stroke inside my thigh. I feel my spit drying on them.

"I'm going to tie you and fuck you breathless." He slides my panties aside and runs his finger along the length of my slit. "I've never seen a girl so wet. You really want to fuck."

"I need it." I whisper the only three words I have at the moment.

He gathers the wetness at my tingling opening and moistens me all over, asshole to clit. His pressure is perfect, delicate, gentle. He's not trying to get me to come; he's trying to get me turned on. He slides two fingers in my cunt so slowly, I feel my soul go to heaven.

"You like my fingers?"

I swallow in response. He pulls them out, slowly again, then touches the hood of my clit, shifting it slightly. The effect is hypnotic.

"Look at you," he says, his face close enough to mine that I can smell his peppermint breath. "You're a slave to me right now." He runs his fingers back to my opening, and to my clit, with just the tip, in circles. "Your discomfort is getting crowded out by pleasure. You want to come so bad. This isn't even pleasure. It's the expectation of release. Do you know how long I can keep you going like this? Do you know what I can do to your body? As long as you need that release, I can take you to the breaking point. What wouldn't you do for me?"

He circles a wet finger around my asshole then back to my clit, which feels explosive, engorged, hot to the touch.

"Show me what a kitten you are. Meow for me."

I mewl, wiggling my hips to get a little more pressure on my cunt when he puts his fingers in me. But he and the ropes have complete control.

"Not like that. Don't be saucy. Do it like a real kitten."

"Oh God, just let me—"

He squeezes my clit, and I cry out, because it hurts, and it's just about as close to an orgasm as possible.

He slaps the inside of my thigh. "Easy, girl. The more you demand, the longer I'll keep you on the edge."

I'm sweating, leaking fluid everywhere. I don't have a brain. I don't even want to fuck. I just want to come.

"Meow for me," he says.

A kitten. What does a kitten sound like? A real mewl. No M sound, just a vowel. I make it. I mewl for him as he runs his fingertip over my hood, shifting it just enough. I mewl again. It's humiliating, to make animal sounds while tied and bent over, but it gives me something to concentrate on. This isn't the first time I've enjoyed being debased.

"Good girl. You're such a good girl. Do you want to come?"

"Yes."

"Yes, what?"

"Yes, please. Please. God, let me come for you."

With his free hand, he grabs the hair on the top of my head, yanking it against the ties to my ankles. "Don't move. Just meow."

He slides a finger in my asshole, and my mewl turns to a cry of pleasure. When he presses his thumb to my clit, hard, I lose my breath. He rotates the thumb, and I explode. My asshole pulses around him, my cunt tightens, and the rush of release comes out of my mouth in grunts that I can't concentrate on enough to make the kitten sounds he likes.

His thumb drifts off me halfway then presses again, and I explode all over, wiggling in the confines of the ropes. The orgasm is eternal, like an electrical pulse arching my back, my fingers gripping my forearms. He does it again, leaning forward and shoving two fingers in my ass. My back arches farther, and the ropes press into my ribs.

Time happens for someone else, but not me. The orgasm goes on and on under this madass bastard's hands.

I open my eyes, and I see him through my hair as he fucks me with his fingers again. His face is intense, as if he's reining in a hotblood, and I gear up for another explosion.

I need to breathe. I need to think. It's almost painful to come this much. But I can't move. I'm going to die, and live, and crack into a thousand fleshy pieces.

"Stop," I say. "Please stop."

"One more, kitten," he growls. And he gets it.

I RODE the Westonwood sink on the tips of my right toes, sliding my wet pussy against it. I came in four pushes, legs tingling, back arching, mouth open. Knowing less than the sum of what I remembered and forgot, only blank, preciously empty but for pleasure.

Chapter 4

Margie, three years out of law school, was already boring. I couldn't stand her, but I loved her for sitting in the visitation room in a pale green suit, her red hair in a sensible bob.

Before I even had my butt in my chair, she said, "He's alive."

"How alive?"

"He's too weak to talk. You got the hoof knife between two ribs—"

"A hoof knife? My God—" Hoof knives didn't have a point, though mine was sharp on the tip. How hard had I been at him to get that to even puncture?

"You missed his heart by an eighth of an inch and just scraped a lung. There'll be a nice scar to show the grandkids."

"Was it me? I did it? Are you sure?"

"You called the cops and said you did, and you attacked them when they got there."

"I don't… There's no way I could have." I was utterly baffled. Why would I do that? I'd done crazy shit, but stab Deacon? That was the craziest of crazyfuckshit I'd ever heard. "Where? We weren't on Maundy Street. Couldn't have been."

"The stables. Then you tried to slit your own throat. You really don't remember?"

"You think I'm putting it on?"

"I wouldn't put anything past you." She held her face firm as if daring me to get offended.

"You don't have to represent me if you don't want to," I said. "I know you find me repulsive."

"I don't."

"You do. You've never understood me."

"That's not the same as finding you repulsive," Margie said. "Let's face it. *You* don't even understand you. The difference between us is that I happen to love you."

I had no answer. I just fixed my jaw and felt like more of a recalcitrant child than I ever did in front of Mom.

"Fiona, do you want to talk about this? Should I come back tomorrow? Or not at all? Daddy's trying to get me pulled off the case."

"Why?"

"He says I'm not experienced enough. I don't know the real reason." She shook her head. "Point is—"

I grabbed her hand over the table. "It has to be you. Don't leave me."

"Tell me what happened. I know you don't remember, but what was with you two? Did he cheat on you? Did he hit you? What would have made you snap?"

I rubbed my eyes with the heels of my hands. She didn't understand us. No one would.

"Drazen pledge," I said.

"I'm your lawyer. Anything you say is under attorney-client privilege."

I held up my hand. "Are you opening pledge or not?"

"Fine." She held up her hand. "Pledge open."

I relaxed. Between myself and my seven siblings, six sisters and one brother, opening a pledge meant nothing said could be repeated and only the truth could be spoken.

"This is so hard to explain," I said.

"It'll get easier after the first ten times."

"I don't know where to start."

She crossed her arms. "Start by not stalling. Assume I know you use drugs. Assume I know you've had more sex in the past three years than I've had in my life."

"We had an open-ish relationship."

"Okay."

"The ish part is that…" I swallowed. "Up until a few months ago, my other partners were limited to people we knew, at parties he threw." I didn't mention the knottings. I wasn't ready to tell her I had been a fuckable art object, because I'd have to explain that I'd never been in such control of my sexuality as I was in this open-ish relationship.

"And why did that change?"

There was a relief in her question, because it didn't judge the excesses, only the switch to normalcy.

"We fell in love." The blade of those words cut through the dullness of the meds, and snot and tears flooded my face.

"No," Margie said. "You stop right now."

I tried to tell her I couldn't, but I was beyond speaking, beyond using my mouth for anything but breathing thick cry gunk. I could barely breathe without croaking—how could I speak a whole sentence? "I couldn't have hurt him."

"Fuck." Margie had always been impatient with outbursts, yet she always knew what to do about them. She swung her chair to my side of the table as if she was flinging it in a bar fight and sat next to me, putting her arm over my shoulder. I fell into her. She said nothing and stroked my hair.

"He went away, and I couldn't keep it together," I croaked. "I have a hard time without sex. I need it. But he understands me. We worked on ways to make it work. Why would I stab him?"

"He's not saying. Is it possible he came after you, and you stabbed him in self-defense? Maybe he surprised you at the stables?"

"I don't remember. I swear I don't. What I was even doing there? I haven't been to Branwyn in forever."

"You have a chipped molar. Do you remember when that happened?" she asked.

"No."

"The exam showed nerve damage in your wrist. Did he ever grab you there?"

I shook my head as if I was emptying change out of the bottom of a piggy bank. Nerve damage to the wrist could be caused by an improper knotting, but Deacon would never, ever make that mistake, and I would have called it out if I'd felt a tingling.

"Margie, I'm so confused. It's like my brain isn't working right. I have to see him. I have to talk to him." I didn't know how I'd calmed enough to make sentences, but I had. I wiped my nose and smeared my tears over my eyelids with the backs of my hands.

"That's the least of your worries," she said. "You have to get released first. Your therapist has seventy-two hours to determine if you're a danger to yourself or others. So no more lunging over the desk to kill the good doctor. If you do get out, you'll get taken in for questioning or arrested, depending on what the DA feels he has and, to be honest, whatever Dad decides he wants to do. He's got every judge in L.A. in his pocket, but the media loves rich girls and violence. If you walk, it'll look like we've gotten away with attempted murder. And just so you know, we've got some problems at home."

"What?"

"Jonathan's girlfriend disappeared from a party at Sheila's last night. His car's gone."

"He had a girlfriend?" I tapped my fingers against my thumb, counting. When did my baby brother turn sixteen? How long had I been high on flake and fucking? Shit, he was old enough to *drive*?

"Theresa's friend Rachel."

Theresa was my sister, and Rachel was, indeed, her friend. She hung around a lot. I'd never given her a thought.

As if reading my mind, Margie continued. "I didn't know about her and Jon either. So that's why I'm here and not Quentin."

"I just want to talk to Deacon."

"I know. But maybe what you want isn't what you need." She took my hand. "When we're done here, you're having your orientation meeting with the hospital admin. Be nice. Be good. Okay?"

"Will being nice get me out?"

"It'll increase the odds."

"Then I'm all over it."

Chapter 5

The administrator smiled. She seemed genuine enough, but she was probably genuine with everyone, which made the whole act as fake as shit. Her brown hair was straight, but at the ends, I could see it was naturally curly. A little patch of eyebrow had begun to grow at the top of her nose. She wore a little wreath with a bell hanging from it on her lapel.

"I'm Doctor Frances Ramone, but you can just call me Frances."

Apparently, we were all on a first-name basis in Westonwood.

"You can call me Miss Drazen."

My joke had no effect on her that I could see. Being blind with a headache, who knew what was happening in my peripheral vision. On the other side of the glass walls, people played checkers and some asshole grumbled in a wheelchair. More windows decoratively barred against escape. Lightweight plastic chairs, great for throwing but not hurting. A television permanently set to beautiful scenes of nature, flowers, butterflies. And that was how rich kids disappeared into Westonwood. No TV. No internet. No phone.

"That's fine, Miss—"

"I was kidding. Fiona's fine."

"Are you okay, Fiona?"

Was I okay? What kind of question was that?

"I have a headache, and I'm a little grouchy, if you don't mind."

"Your medication's worn off."

Was her smile smug? Or just a smile?

"I need you to hear this and retain it, so I preferred you have all your faculties. Okay?" she said.

"Okay."

"You're here so we can determine if you're fit to be questioned for attempted murder, and if you had your faculties about you when you committed the act."

Though my crying was silent and controlled, Frances flipped me a tissue. I dabbed my eyes.

"Allegedly," I said.

"Allegedly. You have a lawyer you can discuss this with further."

"Yes."

She put a piece of paper in front of me. There was a list on it with little boxes to the left of each item, and she ticked them off as she spoke. "We don't allow you to use the phones or fax except to talk to lawyers. Even family calls come through us. We have some rules here, and the rules are tailored specifically for you. Everyone's comfort here is important. You will be provided everything you need from medicine to meals. You are not allowed any of your own. This is to prevent substance abuse. Do you understand?"

"Yes."

She ticked one of the boxes with her pen. I pressed my legs together and jammed my hands between my knees. I was so tense. I wanted to be in the common room having a goddamn conversation with the backgammon set.

"You will have two sessions per day with Doctor Chapman. He's agreed to keep seeing you, despite your attack this morning."

I nodded. I didn't like what I'd done. Not the attack on Deacon or Dr. Chapman. It wasn't *me*.

"Violence won't fly a second time. We don't like to use our solitary rooms, but we will if we think you're a danger to yourself or others. You're a compulsory patient, but we can send you to a state facility."

I looked her in the eye for the first time. Their color was

indeterminate, somewhere between light brown and blue and green. She held my gaze.

"Is that what you told my father?" I considered telling her I'd go wherever my father wanted me, and if he wanted me in Westonwood, then that was where I'd stay. You didn't cross Daddy. Period.

She changed the subject. "There's a light switch in your room. It doesn't work after lights out at ten. Most residents go to bed earlier." Tick. "You will be given medication according to a schedule. You must take it as directed." Tick.

"I'd like an Advil or something." I needed a Vicodin, but I knew asking for it would get marked on my paper, and I wanted out, even if it meant getting questioned by the gestapo.

"After we're done here, I'll get you something for the headache." She tapped her pen, asking for attention to her list. "You will not touch any of the patients or staff." Tick. "Your bedroom door must remain open during the day unless your doctors or staff ask that it be closed." Tick. "You must get to your sessions on time. We consider punctuality a sign of your commitment to the process here. Two late appearances mean you are not fully committed." Tick. "And your performance in the bathroom this morning will not be repeated."

"What performance?"

"Specific to you, there will be no masturbation."

I laughed. "Are you *fucking* with me?"

"Next time we hear you through the door, we're coming in. We are a private institution. Accredited, yes, but we do get to custom-tailor the Westonwood experience to each patient. In your case, sex is a distraction that is strictly forbidden."

"Lady, I can make myself come by breathing a certain way, okay? And shame's not my thing. Privacy isn't a prerequisite; I'll come right in front of you. So that rule is a fucking joke."

"I assure you, it's not a joke." She slid back her chair. "Your meals are scheduled. Mark will take you to the dining hall."

MARK, the orderly, was one of those guys who was trouble outside his job. He had on the same pale blue uniform as the rest of the orderlies, but his goatee was fingered to a point and his hair was shaved over the ears. The top flopped down, but I knew he made it stick up on the weekends. I tried not to look too closely, but I couldn't help it. He had an empty piercing hole in his nostril. He glanced at me, and I turned away.

I held my tray in the center of the dining room, trying to decide between seats that all looked the same. The room was done up in modern grey and white, same as everything else. Even the Christmas decorations were simple brushed-chrome snowflakes hanging from the windows. The linoleum shined, the paint scuffs were removed nightly, and the chairs were Scandinavian, but it still looked and smelled like a mental ward.

A group of three ate on the patio. It rained on the other side of the overhang. They laughed and smoked cigarettes as if they were at the Wilshire Country Club, not Westonwood. They were my age, more or less, with smooth skin and trim bodies. One girl saw me and waved me over. I stood in the doorway.

"Fiona Drazen," she said. "Heard you were here."

They all looked at me. I waved. Their faces seemed familiar. The girl in question had her bare feet curled on the chair and a lit cigarette in the fingers that rested on her knee.

"Hey." One of the young men, with tight curly hair and a knowing slouch, raised his hand to me. "Good to see you again."

I didn't know him. Had I fucked him? Was I supposed to remember? I couldn't even remember the last two days.

"Hey." I nodded at him, then the rest.

The girl's shirt buckled under her crouch, and I saw the curve of her breast. I remembered her. It had been a weekend in her mother's time share—two days in an ocean of skin. I barely remembered their three faces from that party. Karen. Karen Hinnley. Her mother was a producer.

"Ojai," I said. "Fuck, man. What a weekend."

"It was…" She rolled her eyes as if at a loss for words.

"Beautiful," I finished for her.

"Damn," said the guy with the curly hair, "we should do it again."

"Yeah." Karen nodded to a boy with blond hair who couldn't have been a day over fifteen. "You gotta come this time."

Everyone concurred except me. I couldn't bear another minute. I didn't know why.

"Nice and quiet here," I said.

"Christmas," Karen said. "Everyone gets sprung for a couple of days. Except I don't want to go home to look at the buffet. Gross. After New Year's, there'll be a line for the tri-tip."

Too-Young shook his head. Curly Hair laughed. Warren. That was his name. Warren Chilton, son of the actor.

"I'm going inside," I said. "Call me when we're all out of here."

There was agreement, but no discussion about whether or not I would serve time, even though my situation must have been public knowledge. People like us didn't serve time. Even the suggestion meant that my lawyer wasn't connected well enough.

I wasn't hungry, so I drifted into the common room, where the TV screen showed nature in all its high-definition glory. It was compelling in its way. I sat on the grey leather couch and watched, staring at daisies fluttering in the breeze. I felt too weak for a walk. Frances had given me a cocktail of pills for the headache, some of which I recognized, and they dulled the pain and the brain.

I'd stabbed Deacon. What would make me do such a thing? What could he have done? Beat me? I laughed to myself, because beat me was what he did on any given day. I rubbed my eyes as if I wanted to erase the lids and see what I'd done.

My body tipped a quarter of a degree when someone sat next to me. I glanced toward my right. He had short-cropped hair and pink lips, and he smiled and blinked slowly. I could fuck him. No reason not to, besides the no touching rule and Deacon, who wasn't dead. I'd betrayed him enough already.

"*Bellis perennis*," he said, tilting his head toward the nature show. "Common daisy, often confused with their more tightly petaled family members, *Arctotis*. You're Fiona Drazen, aren't you?"

"Yeah."

"Jack Kent. Carlton Prep. I was a year below you. You were a celebrity even then. What are you in for?"

I didn't have a chance to answer before a nurse came close, and Jack pointed at the TV.

"*Arctotis stoechadifolia*, nearly extinct in its native South Africa, and now a weed pest in Southern California," he said.

"Attempted murder," I said when the nurse passed, "but I don't remember it."

"Car?"

"Knife."

"Wow. Trust you to do it big."

I wished I remembered this guy half as much as he remembered me.

"No, wait. I remember you," I said. "Nerd."

"Not totally unfuckable, I think. But yeah."

"What are you in for?"

"Being an embarrassment, unofficially. But officially, bipolar disorder."

"Picked up in a manic phase?" I asked.

"Totes manic. I came up with a new way to process *ricinus communis* in a hundred forty-seven steps. No one in their right mind could get past the seventy-fifth."

"Why did you?"

"Because I could. And the high? Woke out of it with my underwear full of jizz."

I nodded. I knew how he felt.

"You voluntary?" he asked.

I shook my head. The flowers changed from yellow to pink.

"Fifty-one-fiftied?"

"Yeah. I supposedly tried to stab a cop. Resisted arrest. Turned the knife on myself. Yada yada. I'm screwed."

"Who's your psych?" he asked.

"Chapman."

Jack puffed out his cheeks and released slowly, an expression of overwhelming sympathy.

"What?"

"Hardass."

"Really? Seems nice enough."

He shifted on the couch until he faced me, one leg bent on the cushions, the other with toes tensed against the floor. "It's his job to be nice. Listen. Do you want out or in?"

"Out, of course. What person in their right mind would want to stay here?"

"The question kind of answers itself. But if you want out, you have to do it in the seventy-two-hour window, six therapy sessions, or shit gets indefinite. Like, they keep you in thirty-day increments and revisit, and it gets less and less likely you'll get out unless your parents start making a stink. In my case, they won't, so I can stay as long as I want."

He didn't look at me for the last sentence, as if he couldn't bear the shame. I didn't blame him. I'd be ashamed too, if I had any.

"I'll convince him I'm sane."

Which meant I'd face charges. If I convinced him I was nuts, I'd be stuck in Westonwood with their no touching rule and scheduled meals. If I faced charges, would I get to see Deacon? Or would I just be out and arrested and as separate from him as I was in the hospital? Only he knew what happened. Only he could say what I'd done and hadn't done.

Staying in, staring at a flat screen of flowers with bars on the windows between Deacon and me, wasn't going to cut it. I had to take my chances with the real world, which meant no more tantrums. No more attacks on the doctor or anyone else. For the next two days, I would be a model citizen.

Chapter 6

"How was your morning?" Doctor Chapman—no, Elliot—asked. He had a tiny scratch on his left eyelid. Otherwise, he looked no worse for the wear.

"Fine," I said. "Sorry about attacking you. I'm not usually like that."

"You're repressing a slew of emotions and memories. Stuff can only stay in lockdown so long."

"Speaking of lockdown..." I curled my lip to the side. Elliot's hands were folded in front of him, and his attention was fully on me. I didn't know if anyone outside of Deacon had ever paid me such razor-sharp attention. "Is it even legal to have solitary confinement in a hospital?"

"I told Frances you needed an hour of restraints so you didn't hurt yourself. I didn't know how the tranq would affect you. Where did you get the idea of solitary?"

"She mentioned it. Like a threat. Not a fan of threats."

"What about the thought of it scares you?" he asked.

"I didn't say I was scared."

"Okay. Why bring it up? I'm sure she told you plenty of rules. Why does that stick out?"

"Because it's a legal issue."

"Is it?"

"According to Amnesty International and a whole bunch of entities who think it's wrong."

"We're a private institution serving a specific segment of society. We get some leeway," he said.

"Meaning there's enough money getting passed around that you can do what you want."

"Money flows both ways. But if you need reassurances, and you might, it's not something I'd sign off on for you." He watched me, reading me, observing me like a thing in a cage.

I wiggled in my seat, as if that would throw him off, but it didn't. The grip of his gaze only got tighter.

"You're making me uncomfortable," I said.

"You're not here to be comfortable."

How many times had Deacon said that when the backs of my knees bordered my face? Or when I didn't sit right at breakfast and he straightened me out?

"I hear you're a hardass," I said.

"As long as you contribute to your treatment, you'll have nothing negative to say about me. If you shut down or fail to participate fully, I will take note."

"That's hardassy."

He smiled, and his face curved from chin to forehead. Somehow, those two words had either delighted him or thwarted his expectations. I didn't know how to respond to his smile except to fidget and suppress my own grin.

"It's the world outside your bubble, Fiona. What you call hardass, other people call real."

"Where are you from, Doctor?"

"Elliot."

"Elliot. Tough Loveland? Toobad City? A mile outside Hardscrabble?"

"Menlo Park."

"Oh, sweet. Tech geek?" I asked.

"My dad actually knows how a microchip works. It's fascinating and utterly boring at the same time. I ran as fast as I could."

"To Los Angeles."

I could imagine him on the train in the middle of the night, running from a world where people found practical applications for calculus. He'd fail as a writer/actor/musician and put himself through school as a therapist, finding a hidden talent, yet always yearning to spend his nights with that one creative task that fulfilled him.

"Pasadena," he said.

"What's in Pasadena?"

"I went to school there. Let's get back to you."

He was evading. It had been all over his face since he mentioned the city where his school was. Would he lie? Were therapists allowed to do that? I didn't know if making our session about him would hurt my chances of release, but I wanted him to know if I could hold a conversation, act sane, function.

"Okay. Back to me," I said. "I've been to Pasadena. I was screwing a skate kid who ollied the six sets at Cal Arts. Did we meet then?"

"No."

"Pepperdine?"

"No."

"Four Twenty College?" I mentioned the name of the pot school, where one could learn how to deal marijuana legally, with a lilt in my voice.

He took a deep breath then, as if resigned, said, "Fuller."

"Fuller? That's a seminary."

"That a problem for you?"

"Did my father pick you personally?"

Elliot laughed again, rubbing the arm of his chair. "No. At least, I don't think so. But I'm aware that your family is, if not religious, Catholic in a way that's in the blood. I have no idea where you stand on it."

"I'm a C and E." I knew he'd know the term for Christmas and Easter Catholics.

"Why bother?"

"It's nice to touch base twice a year. Jump the hoops. You know, show face. So you're a priest? Or did you just say no to celibacy?"

"I'm Episcopalian, first off, so celibacy isn't on the table. And I just haven't been ordained."

"Why not?"

"This is really all going to be about me, isn't it?" he said.

"If you tell me why you're not ordained, I'll tell you something dirty I did."

I felt the weight of my mistake instantly.

He got dead serious. "I know that's how you're used to being valued, but that's not what you're here for."

"Sorry," I said. "It came out before I thought about it."

"That's allowed. There was some discussion with the board about whether or not you should have a male therapist, but from what we could understand, it wouldn't matter."

"So I got the hardass, unordained priest who knows I'm bisexual."

"You got the guy with the MDiv and PsyD who spent three years in a hospital chaplaincy in Compton. After that, I go where I'll do the most good, not where I get the most authority."

"Ah. Compton. You must have seen some bad shit."

"Very bad shit."

"Then why are you at the rich kids' retreat?"

"I can do good here as well as there." He wasn't thrown. Not an inch. I respected that.

"I need you to do some good for me," I said, feeling suddenly less vulnerable. "I want to go home."

"To Maundy Street?"

Trick question? Maybe. Deacon was on that private road. Second house to the right. First house on the right, his shibari students. Only house on the left was where the parties were. Where the art was made. Where I surrendered to whomever my master allowed, and my hunger was sated for days at a time.

"I figure I'll stay with my parents for a few weeks, then decide. I mean, unless the prosecutor decides for me."

"Will you try to see Deacon?"

"Why?"

"It could be dangerous."

"Dangerous?"

"I don't know if it's safe for you."

How much longer was this session? Because it would take me that long to describe how fucking off base he was. Despite needing to get the fuck out of Westonwood, despite wanting to appear sane and stable, I couldn't for the life of me let Elliot Chapman misunderstand my lover.

"I'm more afraid of you than I am of Deacon," I said. "I'm more afraid of this chair. The sky would fall before he'd hurt me more than I could take. He is the only man, the only person in the world who has made me safe. And I mean, not safe from some boogeyman or earthquakes or random shit happening. I mean I had a place. I had things I had to do. I had rules. He was in control, and the only time things got fucked up was when I disobeyed him because I just had to fly off the fucking handle. And before you ask, and you will, he tied me up good. He gagged me and hit me. He made me cry a hundred times, and he wiped my tears and I thanked him for breaking me. I. Thanked. Him."

I expected my speech to disgust him, to give him cause to judge me, call me sick and out of control. Instead, he waited, expressionless.

"Do you want to remember what happened?" he finally asked.

"Yes."

"You might not be ready to remember."

"I don't feel right in my head. There are black spaces where feelings should be. Like someone came and erased stuff. I don't know if it was the drugs or the Librium you people put me on or what. I can't put stuff together. It's like I have the horse and I can see the track, but she's bucking, and the tack's in pieces all over the barn. Does that make sense?"

He sat back, putting an ankle on a knee, elbows on the arms of the chair. He rubbed his lip with his middle finger. "Have you ever been hypnotized?"

"You're joking."

"Best case scenario, you recall enough to release some of the pain you're in. Worst case scenario, you create a false memory that includes a unicorn and Jim Morrison in drag."

I laughed. I couldn't help it. That was the most ridiculous thing, and anything more ridiculous than what was actually happening deserved a laugh.

"Do I have to sit on the couch?" I indicated the long, uncomfortable divan behind me.

"Yes."

I didn't move.

"Come on," he said, standing. "It'll be fun."

"Are you going to make me cluck like a chicken?"

"It's just a relaxation technique. No more."

I took three steps to cross the room and sat on the couch.

He stood over me. "Lie back."

I looked up at him, a twisted smile on my face. I could fuck him. It should have occurred to me sooner. I was suddenly ready for sex, all tingling skin and hyper aware. I could sense his cock, its taste, its scent, its pink skin sliding against the silk of my thigh as it found its way home. It would feel so good, and if anyone needed to feel good, it was me.

"Lie back," he said again with a voice so devoid of desire, my own need collapsed.

I put my feet up and my head back. He sat next to me on the edge of the couch.

"I want you to recall the last time you were at the stables, okay?" He held up a pen, and I watched the angles of his fingers on the instrument. He didn't have a wedding ring. "Now focus on the tip of the pen." He moved the pen back and forth, and I fell into the rhythm of his breathing. His voice, a velvet mask of gentleness, said, "I'm going to count backward from five."

I FEEL a pressure on my hand. It's Deacon, slipping his hand into mine. The gesture, in its adolescent simplicity, creates a rush of emotions I can't hold back. I run out to the empty patio. There are candles everywhere from the cocktail hour, still flickering their last heated breaths. I've been without him for a week while he was on assignment, and now that he's back, he's a scary jar of emotion with a poorly threaded lid.

"Are you all right?" he asks, closing the glass door behind him.

"I'm fine, it's just…" I'm not good at expressing myself unless I'm angry, and I'm not angry. I'm just about everything else.

He takes me by the waist with his right arm. He's so tall, so handsome. His body moves like a leopard on the African plain. "Tell me."

"I don't think we should see each other anymore."

He smirks. He knows I'm not serious. He knows I'm broaching painful subjects by running away first.

"I'll be more than happy to blindfold you." He brushes his lips on my cheek. "But my eyes stay open. I want to see you beg for me later."

"I miss you when you're gone," I say. "I can't take it."

"Ten years ago, I'd have been gone for six months at a stretch."

When he says things like that, he reminds me of our age difference. Ten years ago, I was thirteen and he was almost thirty. I've never asked him what he sees in someone so young, because that would imply we have something more than a semi-casual open-hot-regular-fuck.

"Deacon, I'm sorry. I think now is a bad time, with everyone here." I push him off me and turn away from the strip of twinkling lights that disappears into the black of the sea. "We can talk later." I collect myself to pull him back to the glass doors.

I want to do a hundred crazy things. I want to grab a champagne bottle and down it. I want to stand on the railing and play at falling into the canyon. I want to get into my car and crash the gates. But he inspires me to be better than my impulses, and that's why I need him.

He yanks me back. "We talk now."

"You have guests."

"They don't need me. I can take you to the studio right now and knot you up and they'd be fine." His face gets hard. He becomes the man who spent years photographing the horror of central Africa, who took pictures and walked away. The man kept behind a rock for three months while he was negotiated out. That man, like a real face behind a mask, or a mask on real face, I can't disobey. "Talk,"

He doesn't have to threaten me. There's not a consequence in the world that would be stronger than his simple command. I don't fear him. He makes me strong. He makes me dare.

"I'm not one of those girls who's going to ask you where we are in a relationship," I say. "Because I'm not stupid. What we have is exactly what I want. I have you when you're here, which is most of the time. But if I want to fuck someone else, I just do it, no questions asked."

"As long as you stay fit and safe, kitten."

"My problem is, I'm starting to feel guilty about it."

He nods and looks down at our clasped hands. "I see."

"That's not the deal. We agreed. It's all clear, and it all works. But when you picked me up tonight…" I press my lips together and look out into the sparkling black skyline. "I wanted to run into your arms. I wanted to promise you my body and soul. Forsake all others. Beg you to make a commitment. And I wanted to run the other way and get high. Call Earl. Call Amanda. Fuck anything that walked. Fly to China to search for real opium."

"I can get you that."

"But you won't."

"Never."

"Why are we even this far?"

He laughs a little to himself then put his eyes back on my hand. "You…" He looks back up at me, eyes lit from one side by the light through the door and the other by the candles. "I'm not a jealous man. I've seen too much. And you, it was always a choice to share you or not have you."

"I know and—"

He cuts me off with a finger to my lips. "You did something to me. I was functioning, but I was in absolute despair. And you bang on my car window." He shakes his head. "You breathed life into me again. You gave me hope that everything on this waste of a planet isn't shit. You gave me permission to enjoy myself for the sake of it. I needed it. I needed you for that, and now, things have changed. We'd be crazy to pretend it's the same as it was two months ago even."

I know what he's asking. I want to sit, just to relieve the ache in my heart that's traveled all over my body, but I'm afraid to move.

"You want to do this?" I ask.

"Do you?"

Did I? What reason would I have to take him up on a promise of fidelity? What was in it for me, except *him*? "I've never been faithful to anyone in my life. I'm not built for it."

He laughs. "You're built for a lot of things, kitten."

"I want you, Deacon. I want you so bad."

"I think we need this."

"I won't fail you," I say, believing it from fingertips to core. I believe I can be exclusive to him.

"I know."

He leans in to kiss me, his breath a draft of mint and the floral bloom of gin. I melt into his lips. My face scrunches, and the ache in my body slams back into my chest. I'm thrown by a bucking memory.

Fucking brain. Goddamn brain won't let me kiss him. I'm on my bed in my stupid condo, weeping uncontrollably, and my sheets stink to heaven of fucking.

Fiona. I'm not going to wake you. I'm going to count to three. On three, think of your happiest moment.

I claw at the sheets until they rip.

One.

He is not the indestructible Dom. He's just a man. I want to destroy the sheets, the bed, the room. In the middle of my self-loathing, a weight between my legs grows, a siren call to forgetfulness and obliteration. I throw a leg over the bed's footboard and ride it.

Two.

I cry out, and that cry is drowned out by the breaking dam of my orgasm.

Three.

I'm on a small plane, on my back. Charlie fucks me, and Amanda's face is right before me. Her tits brush my shoulder, her blond hair in my face. She smiles. She is beautiful. I open my mouth because I'm going to come. Charlie puts his lips on my cheek, grinding his sweet cock. Amanda's eyelids drop when I put my wet fingers on her clit. I'm high, on some delicious drug that lets me feel the connection between us three, our surrender, the tightening and expanding space between us, the puzzle pieces of cocks and cunts and asses, how we all fit together like one big universe forever and ever, amen.

⸺

I BREATHED as if my lungs had been vacuum-packed into my rib cage. Elliot moved to face me as I gulped air.

"I've never seen anyone have such an intense experience," he said.

"That's me. Intense experience girl." I grabbed his hand because I still felt as though I was falling.

He brought his other hand over mine. "You still don't remember."

"No. I'm tired."

His green-grey eyes looked at me as if they were peeling me open. "What are you feeling?"

"Tiredness."

"Don't shut down."

"I'm tired, and I want to…" I took a deep breath.

"You want to use."

"Yes. But I got it. It's not a problem."

"You're so sure? You haven't promised yourself this before? That you would stop using drugs or having sex to keep from feeling?"

"Don't push me. Please."

"It's my job to push you."

I leaned back and closed my eyes. I shut him out. He may have said something. I felt his presence in the room, his breath, his existence, his virility, and I closed myself to it completely.

Chapter 7

I didn't sleep in the dark.

I didn't really sleep, period.

I wasn't a *woe is me* kind of girl, because it wasn't as though I actually had problems. I didn't pretend I was ever going to live under a bridge. I didn't pretend bad shit didn't exist. I didn't pretend I didn't live in some wider world. I got it. I had a television. I had the internet. But what was I supposed to do? Devote my life to serving the poor? Take away all the suffering in the world?

But usually the minutes before sleep was when the woe-is-me cantered in, and if it was dark and I couldn't see something to focus on, they got bad. I hated them.

Your best friend died. You're in a mental ward. You nearly killed the only man who ever understood you. Half your life floated in a grey blur. Big fucking deal. Buck up. Fuck everyone. There was nothing they could do to me I wouldn't do to myself first.

Assholes.

Fucktards.

Animals feeding at a trough of fucking bile.

I didn't even know who I was cursing anymore, but fuck them.

I was fine. And when I got out, I was going to bathe in hundred-dollar bills and cocaine just to prove it.

I crossed my legs and blacked into an orgasm that was flat and rageful and over too soon. In the aftermath, I wept, because my best friend died, and I was in a mental ward, and I'd nearly killed the only man who cared for me.

Fuck me.

———————————————

Chapter 8

———————————————

"Your parents are in the waiting room," Elliot said when I entered.

"Should I go see them?"

"After the session."

"Making my dad wait?" I said, lying on the couch. "You're a brave man."

He seemed unimpressed with himself. "I want you to start with something pleasant," Elliot said, getting into the seat behind me.

I wanted to turn and look at him. Without seeing his face, the calm, dusty timbre of his voice was without flaw, and it soothed me, which made me anxious. I didn't trust my soothed, unregulated self. "I can just tell you about stuff. We don't have to do the hypnosis."

"Do you not want to?"

"Well, what do you want?"

"You have to make your own decision about how this goes."

I didn't trust my ability to make a decision. That had been my problem from the get-go. I could have just said that, but I was starting to think he didn't trust me any more than I trusted myself.

"Can you tell me why you like the hypnosis?" I asked.

"You have an anxiety disorder. We're medicating it, but the hypnosis backs up the relaxation without making you tired. And there's a time

43

limit on how long you can be in here. I think we need to do whatever we can to move this along."

"I like all that."

"Okay, you can stop any time you want by saying a word."

"Like what? Like a safeword?" I wondered if he could see me smile.

"Sure. A safeword."

"Pinkerton."

"Pinkerton? The assassins of the old west?"

"The assassin of the 405." I didn't elaborate, because despite the slurry of medicine in my blood, I was going to cry.

"Okay," he said after I sniffled audibly. "I'm counting back from five, and start with something pleasant."

▭

I'M HORNY.

The feeling hits like a freight train between my legs, before a scene or setting even comes into my mind. The swelling rush of blood to my clit begs for release. And then, the preoccupation. I have to get it. I don't care where it comes from. I need arms and legs all over me. I need to smell sweat, cunt, and sticky sperm.

This is the last thing you remember? Can you take me back a minute or two? What happened before?

Elliot's voice, in its pure perfection, doesn't break the reverie, but the realization that I was speaking aloud about the bite of my arousal certainly does. I tell him no. I'm not going backward, because the smell of wet cock and the subtle sting of cocaine fills my face. At this point, I have no idea what I'm narrating and what I'm keeping to myself, and I have no feelings about it either way.

I'm sitting on a toilet in a tiny club bathroom stall. Everything is marble and glass, but a bathroom stall is a bathroom stall. I hear the *thump thump* of music. The Pompeii Room. I look up. Earl. He's all right. Six-foot-four of pure stupid. Easy pickings. His dick is dusted with a fine powder.

"More," I say.

"Greedy bitch." He smiles and holds a baggie of coke over his erection. He taps a line onto it while I hold it level.

"I'm worth it," I say before I snort the line off his cock. Ah, that's just right, just that rush. The feeling of unmotivated pleasure exploding heart-to-brain-to-toes. I'm totally in control of everything in my line of sight, especially this fucker. "I'm going to suck your cock so hard your daddy's gonna come."

"Touch your pussy, baby," he growls.

But I don't. I won't ever touch myself, and this dumbass never remembers. I swallow his dick before he can ask again.

"Oh, fuck, baby—"

The music suddenly gets louder as the bathroom door opens, smacking Earl in the ass.

"Excuse me," the man in the dark suit says. He's halfway to closing the door.

"No problem," Earl says.

I look at the intruder in that fucking suit. He's really not a problem. He's more than good. More than tall. More than perfect. Dark hair and blue eyes. Rugged like a dock worker and refined like a prince. I have to stop him from leaving.

"Loosen that tie and get your cock out," I say. "I'm enough woman for two."

He smirks. "Sorry. I'm too much man for half a woman."

The door shuts, and the music goes back to a dulled *thump thump*.

"Snap," Earl says, aiming his dick at my lips again. "That was cold."

I have two choices: finish sucking off Earl and let him get me off, or not.

"Suck it yourself," I say, standing.

He grabs me by the neck. "Hey."

I look him in the eye. "Don't fuck with me, Earl. I say what goes and when. Jerk it off and make more." I leave before he can object, pulling my shirt together as I pass a short guy washing his hands.

The club is thick with humanity. The dance floor stinks. The voices are like a bag of broken glass. The music is a throbbing heartbeat. And the man is gone.

I put my hands on bare, sweaty skin, pushing through. Amanda finds me, blond hair stuck to her forehead, lipstick fading. Her bodyguard, Joel, is two steps behind her with his dark glasses and firearm. She kisses me on the lips. I push her away.

"You see a guy in a suit? Tall? Hair like this?" I make a motion with my fingers.

"Hot?"

"Hot."

She points at the exit with a wink. I smack a kiss on her lips and continue pushing through. She calls my name as I walk away, but I pretend I don't hear her. I have a man to find.

Nothing like coke to make the impossible seem within reach, or to make it within your rights to shove, growl, and curse through a crowd just to get a look at some hot stranger. Nothing like that expansion of the ego to make it okay to push some squealing teenybopper out of your way when she screams "Fiona Drazen! You're Fiona Drazen!" as if your name alone is front page fucking news.

Of course, they wait outside in a cluster, pressing against the red velvet ropes. Paparazzi don't care about the weather, which is rainy and cold for Los Angeles. Lights flash. They call my name as if I even answer to it anymore. Let them get their pictures. I have him in my sights.

He hands the valet a tip and takes the keys to a black Range Rover.

He is a thoroughbred, and twenty assholes with cameras are between him and me, which is too bad, because I have to have him.

I put my knuckles out to them, both middle fingers extended for all they're worth. I have rings on top of rings, and I know the lights will glint on them in the pictures. I'm going to look like a flashy rich bitch, and the coke tells me I don't give a fucking shit what Daddy thinks.

I turn to the doorman, a skinny ex-cop with a pencil moustache. He looks at my chest then at my face. I know Irv. He's a hustler. He keeps these assholes off us, but he takes their cash to let them know when Amanda and I show up.

"Irv! What the fuck?"

"I got it," he says.

"Outta my way, cocksuckers!" I plow through them with Irv's help.

They back off for him in a way they'd never do for me. I know they'd chew me up, spit me out, and photograph me crawling to the hospital. I get to the Range Rover and pound on the passenger-side window. It's tinted. The car doesn't move, and the window stays up. Do I have the right one?

"Fiona Drazen!"

They're behind me, and I'm on the curb, out of Irv's field of influence. If he comes to get me, he's leaving the door, and that's not cool. I pound on the window again. Bursts of light flash on it.

I'm about to get mobbed.

"Hey, asshole," I shout.

The window rolls down so slowly, I feel as if I'm in a movie about falling.

And there he is. My heart jumps out of my chest.

"Hi," I say, sticking my head in. I feel them behind me. I hear them calling my name, over and over. "You took something of mine outta the bathroom."

"Really?" He's older than I thought, and that makes him more attractive then humanly possible. "What?"

Fiona.

"My heart." It's a stupid come on, but I'm a girl. I can get away with it.

I'm going to count backward from three. At one, you'll open your eyes feeling rested and relaxed.

"Ah. I thought maybe your shirt buttons."

For the first time, he glances at my chest, and I feel that my breasts are chilled. My shirt is wide open, diamond-studded nipple rings glistening. Fucking Earl with his octopus hands.

Three.

"Don't make me turn around," I say. "They already got enough pictures."

Two.

He takes a second to think about it, looking me straight in the face. A little smirk plays on the perfect line of his lips, and I think I just might die.

One.

Chapter 9

I was barely in the Westonwood waiting room before Mom hugged me fiercely, all defiance and no affection. It was amazing how much strength was in that tiny little bag of bones.

"It's fine, Ma." I looked over her shoulder at Dad, his Drazen-trademark red hair just beginning to turn grey.

His hands were in his pockets and his shoulder was against the wall. I rolled my eyes at him, but he just turned to look out the window. He always tried so hard, and I always failed him.

Everything in the room was designed to avoid upsetting the patients and their families. Round table in pale blue Formica with matching water pitcher and three plastic glasses. White molded plastic chairs with chrome legs. The windows were barred in the same decorative pattern overlooking the expanse of the Topanga Canyon, which was covered in grey, misty rain. The seasonal decorations were non-denominational. The best seat in the house, for the benefit of the people writing the checks.

Mom squeezed me, and I felt something hard and breakable between us. She pulled back and handed me a wrapped gift. Dancing snowmen. Gold ribbon.

"I had it in case you came to the house."

I popped the tape and unfolded the paper, revealing a framed photo.

"Snowcone." I pulled it from the wrapping completely. I stood in my riding gear, all of fifteen, next to my beautiful grey stallion. "Thanks, Mom."

"Lindy says you haven't been to the stables in a long time, at least not before the other day."

I hadn't ridden Snowcone in how long? Was it measured in years already? The last time I'd gone to the stables, I'd gone with two guys I'd promised to fuck on a hay bale. I was so high, Lindy kicked me out. Told me I wasn't worthy of the labor animals. I cursed her, knowing she was right.

"We're going to get you cleared of all this," Mom whispered. She looked me in the eye, squeezing my shoulders. "Ten years ago, we could have made it go away. But the internet—" She shook her head. "You're a good girl. Your father and I know you didn't do this."

Daddy didn't look so sure.

"Thanks, Mom. I'm fine."

"We're going to get everyone on this. This man? This Deacon Bruce? We'll get so much dirt on him, pressing charges would ruin him."

"Eileen," Dad said, "it's not like pushing a button."

She turned to Dad, giving him the fire-eye. The power struggle between my parents had always been epic. One day, one of them would die in a pile of crushed bone shards and twisted skin.

"What's it like then?" snarled Mom.

"Quentin's dealing with the other matter right now—"

"He can do both."

"No."

A staring contest ensued. I didn't know if they were going to kiss or scratch each other's eyes out.

"Guys?" I said, but I had no effect on their stare. "I'm going to get out in a few days. Can we—"

Without breaking their staring contest, Dad said, "Don't bet on getting out."

"But—"

"She's getting out, Declan," Mom said. "I'm calling Franco. If you want to handle it that way, I'll handle it that way."

"You won't. She doesn't need the kind of help you're offering."

I didn't know what they were talking about, but I knew that if Mom wanted to call Franco, whoever that was, she was calling Franco. My part in the conversation was pretty much over. "Thanks, guys. Nice visit. Merry fucking Christmas."

I turned on my soft, suede heel and strode out. Halfway down the hall, Dad caught up to me.

"Thanks for defending me," I said. "I think."

"Hold up." He stepped in front of me, blocking my path.

The security guard stood from his station. My father looked at the two-hundred-pound refrigerator of a man, who carried a gun, and with just a look, made him sit the fuck back down.

Dad turned his blue eyes to me. "This pleases you? What you're doing?"

"I'm not here to shame you."

"The effect is the same, but I know that was never much of a concern for you."

"Just tell me what you want."

He held his hand up before I could finish. "Your life is out of control. You've wrecked more cars than I've bought. You've used your body shamelessly. I can only imagine what your blood is actually made of. And you've never faced a single consequence. You have a classic case of affluenza."

I crossed my arms. I didn't know if he was making a joke or not. "You're saying I'm a bad person."

"You're dissolute, and you don't care."

"And you do?" I stiffened, and my extremities tingled. You didn't challenge Daddy. You just didn't. If I never faced any consequences in the outside world, inside his fiefdom, I certainly did. Yet there I was, feeling safe enough to do just that.

"I do. This family, Fiona, this ten-person unit, is all that matters. How we're perceived is important. How we act is important. And if you don't get control of yourself, I'm taking control."

That was close, too close. I heard his words in Deacon's voice, and I squirmed.

He continued, poking at my core insecurity. "Whether or not you ever leave here can very easily be up to me."

"I'm of age," I whispered, but I knew I had no way of enforcing my emancipation.

"Indeed you are. Something to think about. The dew is off the petal, and you've gone from wild child to aged curiosity. There are younger and wilder taking your place as we speak."

Maybe my medication was wearing off or maybe I was raw from recalling my first meeting with Deacon, but something about him calling me old and washed up frightened me. Something about the look on his face, as if he'd stepped in a hot mess on the sidewalk. I respected my father, respected his opinions and beliefs even if I didn't follow them. I had consistently thwarted his will, and he'd consistently bailed me out because I had such respect for him. What would happen if that respect went away? Would he stop protecting me?

"What about you?" I shouted, though he never flinched. "What about what *you did*? You shamed this family with Mom."

"I married her. No one's marrying you." He didn't bat a fucking eyelash.

The only reason I didn't lunge for him was he was telling me the truth.

Instead, I walked toward the hall. Like a cat, he moved so quickly and silently, I was surprised when I felt a yank at the back of my collar. The security guard did exactly nothing when Daddy took my jaw in his hands.

He whispered in my ear, "When are we going to stop playing at this same drama, Fiona? It's tiresome. And I don't like disruption."

There was only one answer.

"Yes, Daddy."

"We understand each other then?"

"Yes."

"You will get control of your life?"

"Yes."

"Good, because if you don't, I will. And you will not like it."

—

I COULDN'T BEAR the common room, the patio, the garden. Couldn't stand a conversation. My parents confused me. I always left their company wondering what the fuck had just happened. So I took my meds as prescribed and went to lie down.

You're controlled by your cunt. Who controls your cunt, controls you.

The ceiling of my grey and white little room was a dull shade of neutral. The shade was drawn over the open window, and when the breeze came, it slapped against the sill as if angry.

I control my cunt.

Deacon in his suit, smiling that godawful devil of a smile, looked at my face even though I was naked and tied to hooks in the wall. He didn't believe me. He was right. In the battle for control of my life, my cunt won every time.

I'll control it, kitten. And you're welcome. He put the riding crop to my lips, and I kissed it. *It's three days. You'll be good, or this is what you're getting.*

I put my eyes all over his handsome face, which I wasn't supposed to do. I was supposed to look at the floor as a symbol of my submission. He drew the crop back and whacked the side of my face with it. The sting felt wet and deep.

That's to keep you in the house. He said it without cruelty or emotion, then backhanded the crop over my breasts. *That's for looking me in the eye.*

The next ten came down in a rain of blows over my belly, my hips, the tops of my thighs. Then, with an underhanded swat, he slapped my clit with the leather. I ground my teeth. I wasn't supposed to scream.

That's three days of control I expect.

I remembered the welts when he touched them, the way they burned as he unhooked me and threw me on the bed, lashing me face down to the bedposts so that the mattress rubbed them when he fucked me. I remembered the orgasm spilling out of me, and the welts bleeding over the next three days, reminding me of how hard I'd come that day. And how without him, I had no control over my cunt.

You can touch yourself if you want, but that's it.

He smirked like Satan. I didn't even address the joke of it, I was so aroused. I didn't touch myself for pleasure, even when he tormented me by giving me that as my only option.

Thinking of him in my Westonwood bed, my clit felt like a hot, throbbing marble. I crossed my legs under the covers, listening to the rain in the palm trees outside. I played the memory over again and again. The pain all over my body, the sweat in the wounds as I danced at Dabney's with who-even-knows. Earl's fingers digging in them as he fucked me from behind. I took his friend Tammy's pussy in my mouth, the sting of flake hot on my tongue. I knew he'd punish me when he got back.

When Master Deacon came home three days later, the beating had been relentless, and joyful in its way. He'd tugged and twisted on my nipple rings until I came, then made me come again and again. It was the beginning, and a game. Our hearts hadn't dropped out of us yet.

Yet.

I pressed my thighs together, rotating my hips slightly. It would take forever to come, but I wasn't going anywhere. My lips parted, and heat washed over my hips, my heart beat between my legs, and I felt that relief, that joy, that release.

———————————————————

Chapter 10

———————————————————

Lunch.

I felt as though I was being fattened for the Easter feast. It was Asian today. Dumpling soup, fried rice, Korean beef, some lightly sautéed green leafy vegetable with a name I couldn't recall.

"It's low-sodium soy sauce," said Karen from the seat across from me. She'd had her face buried in her journal while her soup got cold. "I guess they figure you're on so many meds the sodium might spike your pressure?" She dumped a stream of soy sauce on her fried rice. Her hair was twisted up in a quick knot, and her swan-length neck had a fresh hickey blossoming on its base.

"You wanna cover up the suck stain?" I touched my neck.

She looked shocked then tried to look at her own neck, as if that was possible.

"There's a mirror right over there," I suggested.

"No, I got it." She took her hair down.

Seeing her hair against her face and her forearms up, I realized how thin she was. Jesus, I must have been stoned on scrips yesterday. She fiddled with her fork and glanced at Mark, the orderly who moonlit as a nose-ring-wearing punk. I noticed from that he had a tattoo creeping onto his neck from under his collar. He looked at her and spun his finger as if telling her to get to it. She picked up her fork. I knew from the way she handled it that no food was landing in her mouth. I'd seen that particular twirl before.

"I'm sorry I didn't make Amanda's funeral," she said. "There was so much going on. My sister was there. Tanya. She went. Said it rained. Like a movie." She rolled her eyes.

"It's all right. Nothing really happened. You know. Closed casket from the accident. She didn't zombie." I raised my arm and curled it at the wrist, making an ugly zombie face, because what better way to pretend I didn't give a shit?

"I heard about the party after," Karen said.

"Yeah." I cleared my throat. "Wow. Days. It was the best sendoff I could have given her." I felt bad scooping food into my face in front of someone who was obviously anorexic, but I was hungry. "We had a line of limos up the hill. Man, there was so much flake."

I stopped chewing and pushed my tray away. The flake had been the problem. At that point, Deacon didn't care that I'd had multiple partners. He cared that he didn't know them. He cared that there had been drugs on Maundy Street, where he wanted things quiet and unimpeachable, and he cared that I'd taken them. He wouldn't knot me until it was out of my system and then some. That week had been torture. Amanda's death had weighed on me fully, and Deacon withheld every coping mechanism I had.

"I spent a week in the corner drooling after that," I said as if it was a joke.

But it hadn't been. I'd felt like the bottom was going to fall out of me until Deacon picked me up and knotted me from the ceiling. Things had changed after Amanda died. It was as if we needed each other, he and I. As if it pained him to see me take such poor care of myself. It wasn't too long after that we decided to own each other.

"Hey," Warren said, sitting across from me. "Rain just stopped. Creek's flooding up to the bench."

"There's a creek?"

Warren and Karen glanced at each other.

She pushed her tray forward and shot a look at Mark before standing. "Let's give Fiona a tour. Our tour."

Warren looked me up and down, as if seeing my body through the light blue cotton uniform. "Can I trust you?"

"You can take your tour and stick it."

"You want this tour," Karen said. "It's worth it. Almost as good as freedom."

"I don't need to prove I'm trustworthy. I ate you out in Ojai, and you"—I turned to Warren—"licked flake off my tits. That was my coke, and you never gave me shit in return but numb nipples."

"Point taken," Warren said as he guided me out the door.

The outside had been designed, manicured, and planted to the teeth. The verdant garden was dotted with wood benches—places to reflect on your mental sickness, eat yourself with regret, and chew on your shortcomings. Jack crouched over a bed of wildflowers, rubbing the yellow petals.

"Hey, Jack," Warren said as he slapped the not totally unfuckable nerd so hard on the ass he nearly fell over.

"Ow!"

"Not cool, Warren," I said, helping Jack up. "You all right?"

"I'm fine." He glared at Warren.

I brushed Jack's shoulders even though there was nothing there.

"Sorry, man." Warren made a fist as if to punch Jack in the arm.

Jack flinched. I liked Warren less and less with each passing second.

"We're checking out the holes. You coming?" Warren asked.

"Nah. I'm good."

"Can we go?" Karen asked, walking backward toward the gardens. "I have a session in fifteen minutes." She indicated the clock on the highest part of the common building.

Our personal effects had been taken, including watches. The clocks dotting the facility were the only way we had to keep time.

"Me too," I said.

Warren jogged ahead of us and spread his arms. He looked handsome in the deep foliage, like a Greek god of abundance. "There are cameras everywhere." He pointed upward.

I didn't look directly, but with a sidelong glance, I saw the shiny glass at the crook of a tree branch.

"But there are some corners they don't get to. Holes in their vision matrix." Even in his silly mental ward uniform, Warren carried himself as if he was entitled to the known universe. He stood with his back to an old oak. "Like here. Hole. Right here. They might find you if they're walking around, but the cameras can't see shit until they prune this shit back. Follow me." Like the docent of sneaky spaces, he pointed out three more places where a patient couldn't be seen by the cameras.

"But they know where the holes are, too," Karen interjected. "If they see you go out of range, and don't see you come out, they come and check."

"If they're paying attention," Warren said. "Which is a crap shoot. Let's go to the creek."

We walked down a winding path. I heard cars speeding somewhere past a hedge, but it didn't sound like a major road. The sound of moving water added to the white noise, and past a line of trees, we came to a swelling creek. A chain-link fence separated us from it.

"Is that PCH?" I asked, referring to the water. I followed them along the fence to a hole cut into it.

"Not even close." Warren pulled the cut fence open. "We're in the middle of nowhere."

We crept through. Karen put her journal on a fallen tree trunk and kicked off her shoes. She rolled up her pants.

"Go on, sweetheart," Warren said as Karen stepped into the water. "I'm sitting this out."

"Why?" I followed Karen's lead, rolling up my pants.

"The thing with my kid brother."

"What thing?" I put my toe in. The water was ice cold, even in the sun, and the bed was made up of small, rounded rocks.

"I waterboarded him." He said it as if he'd helped the kid color or taught him how to play a video game. "They catch me in water, and my dad's gonna kill me."

"If it's morning, they can't see much once you're in the water. The lenses get condensation on them, and the cameras get wet. If it's just rained, the leaves are heavy and block the cameras." Karen held her hands out and put her face to the sky. "I love the holes."

"If you're ever looking for Karen," Warren called from the edge, "check the holes."

There was something freeing about not being seen by the hospital staff, but with Warren's eyes on me, I didn't feel safe.

"What are you looking at?" I said.

"You got Chapman?"

"Yeah."

Warren craned his neck to see the clock at the top of the common building. "Next set of sessions starts in five."

Fuck. I hopped out of the water and got my cold feet back into my shoes.

"You know how to get back?" Karen shouted, but I was already past the chain link.

Chapter 11

Doctor Chapman looked tired as he closed the blinds against the sun.

"Why did you stop me last time?" My feet ached from the cold water, and I was trying to hide that I was winded from the run over. "There was a good part coming up."

"The session was over." He glanced out the window and back at me so quickly, I might have missed it if the Adderall hadn't made me hyper vigilant.

"Really?"

"Why do you ask?"

"Because we had five minutes of small talk after that. So, you know, I kind of left thinking about what happened after. In Deacon's car."

"You can tell me." He rubbed his upper lip again.

I saw his watch peek past his cuff, hanging on his wrist. He had nice wrists, angled and wide. Masculine. I narrowed my eyes, willing his cuff back so I could see more.

"I don't want to tell you now. Your loss," I said.

"Your parents came to visit last night. How did that go?"

I shrugged.

"Your father's an interesting guy."

"How so?"

"He married your mother quite young."

I sat ramrod straight, and I felt my hand want to go up, as if fending him off. That was sacred territory. He could psychoanalyze me all he wanted, but my family was off limits. "They're still married eight children later. I don't see the problem."

He said nothing. As much as I wanted to scrape his pretty little face off for it, I wanted to prove myself even more.

"You going to hypnotize me again?" I asked.

"If you found it helpful last time."

"You ever going to take a stand on something you want, Doctor?"

He stood. "Not in this room, no. In this room, you're the boss."

Well, if that was how it was going to be, I would take it. I could be the boss of this tiny, half-lit room. I threw myself on the couch. Elliot followed and sat behind me. I heard the rustle of him crossing his legs.

"Counting backward from five," he said.

"Okay."

"Five."

▭

HIS CAR IS HUGE, and he smells like peppermint. He doesn't say anything, and my chest winds up with tension. Is this a mistake? He doesn't look like a serial killer, but maybe he's not interested in me. Earl is a good enough fuck in a pinch; that would be better than nothing.

"Got a name?" I ask, trying to get my shirt buttoned.

"Yes."

"My name's Fiona."

"I figured that out." He turns his head a little. "I'm Deacon." His eyes drift down to my exposed tits then back to the road.

"Should I bother buttoning up?"

"Yes."

I shake as I finger the buttons. That wasn't the answer I expected, and I'm suddenly ashamed. But when he flattens his hand on the wheel and turns it with pressure on the heel, my nipples harden through the white shirt, and the rings piercing them stretch the fabric.

"So," I say, "where we going?"

"Away from a crowd of paparazzi." He stops at a light and turns toward me. "How do you live like that? All these people around all the time?"

I shrug. "At first, I got upset when they misunderstood something or printed me kissing a Brent Ogilve when I was dating Gerald. That sucked. But then, Gerald was kind of a dick, so they did me a favor."

I don't want to talk about paparazzi. I want this guy. I put my hand on his thigh and slide it between his legs. He's all muscle. He puts his hand on mine and moves it back to my lap.

"Are you gay?" I ask.

"No."

"Look, if you don't want to do it, that's fine. Just drop me off."

"Take it easy," he says, squeezing my hand before he lets it go.

But I'm uncomfortable, unhappy. The car feels too small, and this man expands like a balloon, as if his psychic space crowds me. Suddenly, I don't want to have sex at all. Not with him, not with anyone. I just want to feel like I have everything under control again.

I open the door enough for the hood light to go on. We're not going fast, and I know he'll slow down. But he doesn't. He stretches over me and pulls the seat belt across my body. His peppermint smell is layered with sandalwood, and I want to fall inside it at the same time as I want out of this fucking car.

Snap. He clicks the belt. "You're in the arts district. It's late, and everyone's drunk. There's no need to take unnecessary risks."

I'm pissed. Really pissed. Because he's right.

I look at him as he drives a few blocks. I hate him, and I'm attracted to him, and in my rage, I want to fuck again. I feel the swell between my legs as I remember shit I'm trying to forget—that windshield kiss, and me in the passenger seat inches from a dead girl's pussy, and it smells like sex.

I'm not thinking about that.

I am *not* thinking about that.

Fiona, do you want to stop? You're crying.

I say something. Something about Pinkerton never failing when Amanda drove. And no, I don't want to fucking stop. I want to remember Deacon with this level of clarity and beauty. Something about the way he smells and the texture of his jacket in the lamplight. Something about his hands. The way they're completely still when he isn't using them. I'd forgotten that.

I feel Elliot's fingers on my wrist and hear the soft curtain of his voice.

All right. You're mixing things up. Amanda Westin died after you met Deacon. You don't have to think about the accident if you don't want to. You're in control.

Deacon turns right then right again onto a cobblestone loading dock. We're in an unlit alley downtown. He turns on the dome light.

"So," I say, "what do you want? You going to tie me up and kill me?"

He laughs, and my anger melts off me.

"I'm assuming that wasn't your boyfriend."

I shrug. "Just a Thursday night."

I undo the seatbelt to see if he'll let me. He makes no move to restrain me again. I turn around and kneel on the warm leather, the small of my back to the dashboard, to get a good look at this guy. Older. Late thirties, early forties maybe. Little beard happening. Strong chin. Dark hair. Eyes blue and lit from within.

I know he can see my tits through my shirt. I go braless pretty often because I'm small, somewhere between an A and a B. I call it A plus. My light pink nipples are standing on end from him looking at me.

"You like what you see?" I ask.

"Yes, quite a bit. Do you always walk around half naked?"

"Only when I chase gorgeous men out of bathrooms."

"And why did you do that?"

"Impulse and instinct. It's how I do everything."

"You're very beautiful," he says.

"Thanks, hon. You don't need to flatter me to get under my skirt."

"I'm still trying to decide if it would be worthwhile."

"Oh, I promise…" I reach out to touch him, but he grabs my wrist.

"Put them behind you, on the dash."

Oh. A bossy one.

"You came into the bathroom," I say. "Do you still have to pee?"

"I'm good."

"Uh, huh. I don't know what you're into, but I've done that."

"You let someone piss on you?"

"It was a give and take."

"And how was it?"

I shrug without moving my hands off the leather dash. "Scratched it off my bucket list."

He takes half a pause before he laughs so hard and deep I can see his chest moving. I can't help but smile. Pleasing him does something for me.

"How old are you?" he asks.

"Old enough."

He's perturbed by that answer, and he snaps up my bag.

"Hey!"

"Hands on the dash," he says while looking in my bag.

He flips past my packet of birth control pills and extracts my wallet. I'm nervous, like Sister Elizabeth is standing over me with a napkin and I have a wad of gum in my mouth.

"This your kink?" I say. "Looking in a girl's bag?"

He flips my wallet open. "You seem quite willing to let me use your body, but you don't want me to look in your bag. I don't know if the boundary differences are cultural or generational, but the fact is, I want to keep myself out of jail if you don't mind." He rifles through the wad of hundreds to the stack of cards. The Amex Black has a quarter inch of white dust on the edge. He presses his thumb to my driver's license and pushes it out. "Twenty-two."

"My birthday's Groundhog Day."

He tucks my license back and puts the wallet back in my bag. "What else is on that bucket list of yours?" He tosses the bag aside.

I bite my bottom lip. "Getting nailed in an alley downtown."

"A real one."

I would have gotten bored with this shit already, but I want to impress him. I want him to *like* me. "Ride dressage in the Olympics."

"Dressage? I would have taken you for a dancer."

"What's that supposed to mean?"

"It wasn't meant as an insult. You have a gymnast's body, but the discipline that takes would keep you out of club bathrooms. So I went to dancer. Dressage wouldn't have occurred to me, even if I knew you rode."

"I was the only rider at Stanford with an Arabian. And I ride him Prix St. George." My answer is defensive, not sexy. He's implied that I'm an out-of-control little girl with a flat chest and muscular legs. Normally a man's little insults are met with backhanded returns ending in ammunition for dirty hatefuck talk. But I want this man to respect me.

"Calm, forward, straight," he says, putting his thumb to my cheek. "And submission to the bit."

"You've ridden?"

"I spent a few years overseas with a certain crowd."

I turn my head and take his thumb between my lips, letting it slip past my teeth and over my tongue. He smiles when I suck it on the way out.

"I'm going to be honest," he says.

"Uh-huh." I take his thumb again.

"I'm not looking for a sex partner."

"Then what were you doing at Pompeii?" I take his middle and ring finger down my throat, all the way, and watch his face change. He may have just wanted to help a celebutante in distress, but his ideas of what to do with her are expanding by the second. I see it in his willing, wet fingers and the dilation of his pupils.

"Meeting the owner. We're scheduling an event," he says.

"What kind of event?"

"Something you might enjoy."

And my brain, in its super-relaxed state, fell into his smiling blue eyes. At that event in the house on Maundy Street, I would be on my knees with an expert tongue in my asshole, a vibrating object in my cunt, and my mouth on a cock. So happy, content, satisfied, that when the orgasms came, I felt as if I'd transcended my own skin.

I WOKE with my back arched, out of breath, with Elliot pressed two fingers to the inside of my wrist.

"I'm sorry," I said, panting.

"Don't be." He stared at his watch another second then put my hand down. "You're taching at one-fourteen."

"I wasn't trying to make you uncomfortable."

"You're going to have to work harder than that to make me uncomfortable." His smile was so relaxed, I believed him.

I wanted to work hard enough to make him uncomfortable, just to see what he looked like. "I'll remember that."

"Just lie back and relax."

We didn't say anything for a few minutes. I breathed slowly, trying to slow my racing heart.

"Was that your first encounter with Deacon?"

"Yes."

"When did you see him again?"

"He invited me to that party through Paolo, the owner of the club. I wasn't going to go, but Charlie heard it was at Maundy Street and went nuts. I figured I'd see Deacon again. Which I didn't."

"No?"

"He's known for not showing to his own parties. But he found me, like, a week later at Lucien's. Bought the whole table dinner from across the room then tried to slip out."

"What did you do?"

I huffed a sarcastic little laugh. "Chased his ass. He was waiting for me in the parking lot, like he knew I'd come after him. And he wouldn't let me touch him. Even back at his place. He said touching him was a privilege that was earned. I didn't understand. I thought he was just being a dick."

"Many dominants don't like to be touched. At least not before there's trust."

"Yeah, well, I didn't know that. How do *you* know?"

"I'm treating you. I've stayed up late doing a lot of research."

"'Research,' huh? With a box of tissues by the computer, I bet."

He didn't answer.

"Sorry," I said.

"When did he let you touch him?"

"I don't know. I keep thinking, if I stabbed him, he must have been tied down or something. But how? He'd been tied down in Congo, so he's not turned on getting tied up. He's anti-aroused. So maybe I ran up and jabbed him?" I shook my head slowly. "The last thing I remember is a jumble of shit."

"What kind of shit?"

"Pills and sex. And some rope work. I think I was suspended for part of whatever it was. Which means Deacon was there, and I was the one tied up."

"No one else ever tied you?" Elliot asked.

"I got tied up plenty, before we were exclusive, but the real rope work, the art, the shibari? That was all Deacon. He wouldn't let anyone else do it. And that was from the beginning."

"So in a way, you were exclusive from day one."

"In a way." I hadn't thought of it that way, and I swelled with a childish pride. "Even Martin and Debbie weren't allowed."

"Who are they?"

"They live in number two. They're his top trainees. Debbie's great. She only ties men. She does beautiful things, and she's really methodical, even for how young she is. Martin's talented, but Deacon says he'll never really get it." I shrugged. "Even if I was so stoned I'd let them knot me, well, Debbie wouldn't have disobeyed, and Martin was in New York. So I don't know."

Elliot shifted a pen on his desk as if it was a lever he needed to flip, then he shifted in his seat. Why was his every movement so interesting to me? Why did I watch him? It could have been because he had so much power over me, or it could have been because he expressed himself with his motions, as if a shade of what he was about to say existed in his body before it came alive verbally.

"I think we're going to find out soon," he said. "Mister Bruce has been found well enough to be interviewed. So if you have anything to tell me, the police, or your lawyer, you should do so."

He was well enough to be interviewed. He was getting better. I swallowed hard and took a deep breath. "Thank God."

"You're not afraid of what he's going to say?"

"No."

"He may implicate you."

"I'm not worried about it."

"What are you worried about?" he asked.

"How long have you been working here?"

"That's not relevant right now. Not as relevant as you changing the subject."

"My point is, no matter what he says, we have lawyers. Our lawyers have lawyers. If Hitler needed to walk, Hitler would walk. What I'm worried about isn't the law. Deacon is my law. He's the only one I have to obey. I'm worried about what I *did*. How it affected *him*. Us."

"You have a very strange sense of entitlement."

"I'm told it's affluenza."

He smiled ruefully. "Session over. See you tomorrow."

Chapter 12

I could have eaten in my room, but I wasn't good at alone time, and I'd already had a bit too much of it. So when Jack sat next to me, I was relieved by the human contact. At the same time, I didn't know what to do with it.

"Last day is tomorrow," he said, breaking his artisanal bread and dunking it in his sweet whipped butter. "What's your guess?"

"I think they're going to let me out."

"You'll get picked up before you're out the door."

I shrugged. "They'll set bail. I'll go home, and then we'll see."

Split pea soup with hand-cut bits of ham. Grilled vegetables. Marinated tri-tip. All the meals had been like that, and by "like that," I meant the very worst of what I'd ever had in my life, unless I was deliberately slumming or in a neighborhood south of the 10.

I pushed my tray away. "This food sucks."

I wanted something, but it wasn't on my tray. The roil of anxiety built in my chest. I had no relief for it, at least not in the pills they were feeding me. Not in the therapy or hypnosis. I had ways to manage myself, and they had all been taken away.

"They're going to expect me to be sober when I get out, aren't they?" I asked.

"Probably. But whatever. Just get someone else to drive, and they'll never know the difference. No one gives a shit what you do as long as you're not hurting some middle-class honor student. Then you're up shit creek."

The way he rubbed his bread around his bowl, as if he was just flipping off some commentary, should have told me he didn't mean it personally. He wasn't trying to jab at me. He wasn't trying to twist my sore places. But he did, and I decided it was careless and cruel.

"What's that supposed to mean?" I said.

He barely stopped eating. "Means we can get away with self-destruction until we hurt someone who doesn't have anything. Then it's off with our heads." He drew his finger across his throat. "Seriously, I'm in here because I sold an ounce of sky gum to a teacher. The news was all about how much my dad made versus how much she made. And I'm like, seriously? I sold four grams to Rolf Wente, and I got crickets." He stopped chewing. "Why are you looking at me like that?"

"People cared about Amanda."

"No. You cared. The rest of them were slowing down to see the blood on the road."

There had been plenty of it. Rich blood. Blue blood if you counted Charlie's cut head. Amanda's flowed with the webbed lines of windshield cracks as I sat in the passenger seat in a half daze. I thought she looked like a cartoon character sticking her head through a wall, and she'd just pull it out and make a goofy face. I put my hand on her ass and patted it, whispering, "Tight and sweet, baby. Tight and sweet. You're going to be okay."

"You're not going to cry," Jack said, incredulous. "You're not allowed to have problems, sweet tits. Sorry."

I didn't know what was going on with Jack. Something must have been happening in his world, because he was ornery and defensive, but I didn't care. The thought that no one had cared about Amanda dying, even though it had been in all the papers and her parents turned people away from the funeral, pulled at my heart. He was right. No one cared about her.

And how did you make people care? Amanda Westin died in a drunk-driving accident, and the driver walked away because his dad was a duke in some tiny European backwater, and the news vans came, and the flowers were imported from India, but how could I make them care? Tell them who she was? That she made me laugh when I was sad? That she loved her dogs? That she gave me the last of her flake when I needed it? Or that she stood by me the million times I bailed on her to get laid?

"She was a good person," I said. "One of the best."

"Sure." He shrugged.

That little knot of anxiety grew into something bigger, something without boundaries. It was larger than me. Wider than the expanse of my chest, with an energy all its own.

It was that force inside me, but not *me*, that flung my tray. Flinging it felt good, because it made a little room inside me, a tiny corner without anxiety. I flung Jack's tray. I swept my hand over the table and knocked over the condiments, and then I got up on the table. When I flung myself off it, the motherfuckers were already there to catch me. Bernie, good old Bernie, looked intent on not letting me fall, and Frances already had a needle.

Chapter 13

I woke up strapped to the bed. Elliot sat by me, marking something on a chart.

"Oh, God," I said, trying to put my hand over my eyes and failing.

Elliot got up and turned off the overhead, flicking on the soft table lamp over my photo of Snowcone. "Do you have any muscle pain or weakness?"

"What drugs did you give me? I can't feel anything."

"Do you promise not to get violent?"

"Fuck. You're never going to let me out now. I'm stuck here. Why did I do that?" My face crunched up. I was going to cry right there in front of Elliot, every tear another nail in the coffin of my sanity. When he freed my right hand, I put it over my face.

"I'm not an MD, so I don't dispense your meds, I only suggest. But it looks like you got a little too much slap and not enough tickle," he said.

"What?"

He laughed. "I'm sorry. It's late. My sense of humor shorts out when I'm tired." He freed my left arm and went to the foot of the bed.

"Nice you have one that's wired at all."

He smiled as he unstrapped my feet. "I'll contraindicate the Paxil."

He got my ankles free, and I sat up. The world swam a little, and I gripped the edge of the bed. The room righted itself.

"Are you going to let me go?" I asked.

"I have another day of observation. You want to go?"

"Please."

He sat next to me. "Deacon Bruce, by his own admission, fell on the hoof knife."

"He what?"

"Fell on the thing twice, apparently."

Any relaxation I'd gotten from the meds molted off me like a skin I'd never owned. "He's protecting me."

"The district attorney doesn't believe him either. But in the end, it'll be hard to make a case. You're a lucky girl." His green-grey eyes looked at me as if they were peeling me open. "You don't look relieved."

"I'm relieved."

"Don't start packing yet. Okay?"

"I don't have much to pack. A picture, and I guess there were clothes? I mean, who knows with me, right?" I held my hand out for the picture, and like a father intuiting what his toddler wanted, Elliot gave it to me.

"You're going to have to continue some sort of program once you're out," he said. "I know you guys have ways of getting around it, but for your own good, I hope this is the bottom for you."

I barely heard him. I was looking at myself with my new horse. I'd gotten Snowcone as a surprise from Daddy, and my delight in my new black-and-white dressage gear was all over my face. Snowcone was pulling away from the odd, smiling creature at his feet.

"How old are you in that picture?" Elliot asked, sitting in the chair by the bed.

"I'd just turned fifteen. Mom didn't want me to have him. She thought I was too irresponsible. I swore I was going to prove her wrong."

"Did you?"

"I did, until recently. When Amanda died, I kind of left him to the stable. Fuck. He was mine; I trained him. He was so good. Perfect temperament, moving off my legs easily, finding the bit like a champ.

And I just abandoned him as if he didn't even matter. And I want people to care about me? Fuck, I am worthless."

Elliot handed me a box of tissues, and I had to laugh through my tears.

"Fucking therapists," I said.

"What?"

"Like the most important thing in the world is giving me a place to put my snot."

He leaned forward, elbows on his knees. "The most important thing is that, by doing that, I show you you're not worthless."

I blew my nose. I felt so bad, as if a rotting, twisting ball of blackness curled inside me was getting bigger by the minute. I knew how to push it back. I knew how to manage it, and watching Elliot's fingers woven together between his knees, I started wondering how to get him into bed. When his hand touched my forearm, a blazing heat fell between us.

"You were out for the morning session. So our last one's in an hour."

He needed to stop touching me. He needed to back the fuck off. I had to swallow my reaction to him like a horse pill.

"Okay," I said, not looking at him.

I knew his eyes would be warm and inviting, and his lips curved like a promise. He smelled of musk and desire. His fingers slid a quarter inch over my skin when he removed his hand. When he walked out, he took the air with him.

Oh God.

I was swelled.

I needed it.

If I went into Elliot's office like this, I would do something stupid. I would lose control. Touch him. Get close to him. Show him my body. And that would be it. I'd be stuck in Westonwood, because despite the heat I felt in his touch, he was a professional. A therapeutic fuck wasn't on the table. My brain might have been high on fuckjuice, but that didn't make me stupid.

An hour. I had an hour to get unswelled. I was in a mixed-gender ward with sixty minutes to find willing, slightly sane cock. How hard could it be?

In two days, I'd gotten the hang of the schedule, more or less. I went into the rec room. It was off hours, meaning most of the residents had therapy or visits. Jack wasn't in front of the TV cataloging flowers. Karen was outside, scribbling in her journal as if homework was due.

"Looking for something?"

I spun around. Frances stood behind me with her hands behind her.

"I was. Uh, Jack's usually hanging around here?"

"You might check his room."

"Yeah, thanks." I stepped back.

"Miss Drazen," Frances said.

"Yeah?"

"The doors stay open."

"Yes, ma'am."

I scuttled off toward the hall that led to the rooms. After I made the first turn, I doubled back to the garden. The rain had disappeared for a full day, and rainy-ass Los Angeles was sunny-ass Los Angeles again. I looked for someone, anyone. I drifted over to the creek, thinking maybe Jack was picking up nettles or something. He wasn't, but Warren Chilton was. His eyes cut through me from the other side of the fence.

"Hi," I said. "Whatcha doing?"

"What's it look like?"

"Jerking around." I poked my head through the hole in the gate. "Want help?"

I came out on the other side just as Warren tossed a rock into the creek. It got lost in the rushing swells without even a splash.

"They kill you with boredom in this shithole," he said.

"Got a cure for that," I said, taking his hand.

I put it on my breast, which was usually a non-event, considering their size. But Warren, without missing a beat, grabbed the nipple and pinched.

"These were pierced," he said.

"They took everything. You know that."

He twisted. God, it felt good. I didn't like the guy, but I liked how he was making me feel.

"I'm going to fuck you so hard you're going to have to stay here another ten years."

"Get to it, preppy."

He searched my face for a second, as if discerning whether or not I was looking to trap or double-cross him. I moved my hand to his cock, which was at least half hard. God, I hoped his meds didn't make him unable to do it, because I had no time to work him. He grabbed me by the neck and pushed me against the fence.

"Wa…" I couldn't finish the word, such was the pressure on my throat.

I didn't like it, and I wanted to tell him to stop. When I tried to push his arm away, he ignored it and yanked at my pants.

"Keep still," he said, fingering my cleft under the standard-issue panties. "Oh, you're ready."

His grip on my neck moved to my upper chest when he got his dick out. I breathed.

"No choking, Warren." I pulled one pant leg down. "I'm warning you."

"Sure."

"Hey." The voice wasn't loud, just firm.

Fuck. A guard stood behind us. Warren jumped back as if his hand had been in the cookie jar, but I could have told him he hadn't even gotten the lid off yet.

"What are you doing on that side of the fence?"

"It was her." Warren pointed at me, the fleshy rod swinging from above his waistband making a lie of his participation.

"Chilton, get the fuck out of here," the guard said. "Don't make me write your ass up again." He got out his walkie-talkie, observing the hole in the fence. "Hey, Ned," he said into the radio. "There's a breach at four-seven-two."

Warren ran through the hole and past the grove of trees. The guard glanced at me after I'd gotten my pants up.

"Go on inside," he said. "You get a pass this time. Go on."

He indicated the building, and I hustled. I had forty-five minutes left. My clit rubbed on my inner thighs when I hustled back inside, swelled to pain and wanting release so bad it swallowed my brain. All I could think about was fucking. Fucking swell. I hated my needs. For the first time, they seemed more of a burden than an indelible character trait.

Warren was a dead issue. That asshole was going to mark me and get me in trouble. He must have been the source of Karen's mark.

When I got back to the residents' hall, I realized I had no idea where Jack's room was. Fuck. Fuck fuck fuckity fuck. Was he even in his room? And what if I couldn't find him? I was starting to think about Elliot in ways I shouldn't. Ways that would come out in hypnosis. He'd touch me again, and I'd say something like, "Hey…let's—"

I ran down the halls, looking in each room. All the doors were open. Most of the rooms were empty, or being cleaned, or occupied by strangers. In forty minutes, I'd be in front of a man, and he had a dick, and I could maybe convince him to fuck me.

But I kept thinking about being tied to the ceiling, the knots in the rope rubbing my skin, and Deacon's cock sliding against the back of my thigh.

Tell me how badly you want it, beautiful kitten.

Bad bad bad bad….

My ass. My poor ass as he'd paddled it, holding back the avalanche of need. I lost days to his ministrations. I needed him. I had no control without him.

And I'd stabbed him.

I didn't believe his denials for a minute. His refusal to implicate me only meant one thing: I'd done it. I'd stabbed him.

What the fuck?

What the actual *fuck?*

"Hi, Fiona."

I spun. Jack was standing in the hall with a paper towel of yellow petals.

"Jack, I was looking for you."

"Job well done, then. You found me."

I stepped close to him so I could say something without being overheard. "You said you weren't completely unfuckable."

"I'd like to think so. Why?"

It was as if the cues and clues I'd given men my entire sexual life were a foreign code to this guy. Normally I'd reveal some part of my body, but we were on camera.

So I tilted my head and pressed my lips together before whispering, "I want to show you how fuckable you are."

His bottom jaw went slack, and his eyes widened. He made a little tick in the back of his throat as if an attempt to swallow had failed. I took that as a good sign.

"Do you want to touch my tits? The nipples are hard already. I know places we can go to do it, where they can't see. I can put your cock down my throat so deep I can lick your balls. And I'll swallow your load, every drop."

He didn't say anything, and when I went to touch his arm, he dropped his paper towel, sending yellow petals adrift.

"Jack?"

He ran down the hall as if his ass was on fire.

I guessed I had that coming. It was a mental ward, after all. But talking dirty had made the swell worse. I had thirty minutes to release it, and I didn't even have a damn vibrator. I was going to just going to have to take care of myself and hope for the best.

My room was a few doors down. I ran in and closed the door. The window was still open, and the shade blew in, slapping back against the window when the breeze went out. I went into the bathroom. Frances didn't want to hear me, I got that. I knew I could be quiet. I'd done it for Deacon a hundred times.

Slipping out of my crazy-proof cotton pants and shoes, I eyed the sink again, its smooth texture and cold surface. It was good in a pinch, but this wasn't a pinch. This was something else entirely. I wanted warm skin and a fullness, a filled feeling.

There were reasons I didn't touch myself. Good reasons.

That pleases you, Fiona? What you're doing?

That was old stuff. Dad catching me in the chair by the window.

Because it's disgusting.

He'd been behind me, arms crossed, having watched the whole thing in the reflection of the window. I was spread-eagled on the chair, seeing how long I could make myself go. I was fifteen, and so unsure about the power of my feelings and my bursts of uninitiated arousal.

I knew one of you would be like this. Out of seven, the odds…

I hadn't reached orgasm yet when he let himself be seen, and when I jumped up in the chair at the sound of his voice, I was still aroused.

Outside the bathroom, the shade slapped against that open widow.

A hundred years ago, you'd have been married off before you shamed this whole family. But now? Now I can't do a damned thing. I'd like to sew it shut.

I didn't think about the other thing.

The thing where he was erect.

I couldn't forget it, but I didn't think about it. I kept it in some nether-place where it existed without me actually seeing it or letting it come to me in words.

I sat on the toilet and opened my legs, angling my body so the pressure of the lid rubbed on me. That wasn't going to work. Fuck. I wanted my fingers, their warmth, their shape, their knowing touch.

I could put a tampon in without trouble, and I could groom and wash myself. But I hadn't touched myself to orgasm since Daddy had walked out of the room, shaking his head. He'd never lectured me afterward, and I never found out if he mentioned it to Mom. Mom, as if sensing something was amiss, stayed close, and defended me from any and all consequences. But he could pit us against each other. I became the one my sisters should avoid emulating. The bad example. The dissolute one. I lived it joyfully, believing they all envied me.

But God, straddling that stupid toilet, I just wanted to fuck. So bad. And there was no one in this shithole. Elliot would know; he'd see the swell on me. I'd do something impulsive, and I'd have to stay.

But I needed it, and I wasn't using the word "need" loosely.

I was about to get up and just go figure it out when I decided to give in to impulse. I slid my middle finger over my clit.

I gasped. The shade slapped against the window again, and something fell. I'd forgotten how good that was, how electric. My finger and my clit reacted at the same time, and I was blindsided by it.

The bathroom door opened. I jerked my hand up and opened my eyes.

Mark, the orderly with the tattoo, said, "Whatcha doing?"

"I'm in the bathroom, asshole."

He stood there, taking up the doorframe. He had Jack's paper towel in his hand, a few yellow petals poking out. "Bedroom door was closed."

"Maybe you know why now?"

"Sure do." He still didn't move

My eyes drifted where they always did when I felt that constant throb between my legs. He had a cock, and if it wasn't hard, I'd be a monkey's uncle. I could take that thing. It would have to be a secret for all of how many hours? I'd go to my session, clear shit up, get rubberstamped, and get the fuck over to Deacon, aye-sap.

"There aren't cameras in the bathrooms, are there?"

He looked me up and down, eyes lingering on my bare legs and the triangle where they met. "On the doorway. Everything up to the toilet."

"Too bad. I was feeling like a fuckdoll." Newly emboldened, I stroked my belly with an extended finger.

"Five minutes, pretty thing."

"Three's all I got."

He winked at me. "Stay right where you are." He clicked the door shut behind him.

I had twenty minutes. Maybe I could be two minutes late to the session. I had no idea who reported lateness or at what point they'd come looking for me. I wasn't interested in getting found with Mark.

I sat back and let my fingers rediscover pleasure. I didn't think about anything, just focused on what I was feeling. I teased the swell out so that when a real living, breathing cock entered the room, I could get the job done. I needed it, and with every pulse of need, I shifted my finger over my clit. Sweet, overwhelming delight. Thoughtless anticipation, the tremble of life, a precipice into the chasm of forgetting.

And he was back.

"What did you do?"

"My buddy's at the monitors." He closed the door. "Get down, psycho."

He took me by the back of the head and pulled me to my knees. I yanked his waistband down and pulled out his cock. It smelled antiseptic and stung my tongue when I licked it.

"Oh God, yes, you little fucking whore. Take it all."

I looked up at him, making my eyes big and wide. I let him slide his dick over my tongue and down my open throat. He held me there a second longer than I thought I could stand it.

I stood up. "Just fuck me. Use me. I'll be your horny slut. Your fuckdoll whore."

He turned me and pushed me against the toilet. I braced myself on the tank. He got a condom on while I stared at the tiles. I hoped he didn't try anal. That was always nice, but I wouldn't come without help, and I suspected he wasn't a big helper. He jammed it in my pussy and held onto my hips, pumping in and out. I angled my body so his shaft rubbed my clit, and I felt the orgasm coming.

"Oh, fuck you, you little rich slut. You like it like this, don't you? You like it when I fuck you like this."

"I'm a whore. Fuck me like a whore. Yes, fuck me like a rich little whore." I knew I was saying the right things. They turned me on, and they made him slam me harder. I felt the swirl of my climax.

Everything was there. Skin on skin. Tick. Prone, exposed to a stranger. Tick. No commitments, no intimacy. Tick. A little risk thrown in for good measure. Tick, tick, tick.

There was the thing I'd forgotten.

The boredom. The space between the hunt for sex and the orgasm, and even the orgasm, half the time. Tedious.

I wanted to come and get it the fuck over with. The seconds in between were not savored but reviled. They were an unworthy means to a worthy end. His grunts were annoying. His dirty talk held no meaning. I didn't want to look at him, so I bent over. He thought I was a slut, so he called me a slut. Boring.

I pushed against him. "Harder, fucker. Bury it. Break it off."

He slapped my ass and pounded me. "Shut up, bitch."

His balls slapped my clit, and his dick plowed against it. I was going to come. I felt it in my muscles, and when they tensed and clenched, it was a release, not a joy. Just a job well done.

He came with an *oof,* and I rolled my eyes.

He stroked my back from neck to ass. "Baby—"

"Get out. I have shit to do."

"Why's it gotta be like that?" He got the condom off and rolled it up in toilet paper.

I stood up. "How else should it be?"

"You don't want me to be nice?"

"You thought you were the one using me? Funny."

"You some kinda weirdo?"

"You're in a mental ward, dude. Come on. Get the fuck out of my bathroom."

Condom stowed in his pocket, pants zipped, girl disinterested, he got the hint and opened the door. He was almost out, but being a man, he needed the last word.

"Slut."

Chapter 14

"Last session," Elliot said. "How do you feel?"

He looked relaxed, clean-shaven, happy. I hadn't realized how troubled he'd looked during our last session.

"I'm okay. Are you going to let me go?"

"I can only make a recommendation. After this session, I'll type it up, and we'll meet with Frances and your lawyer. Give me an hour after we're done. Your mother and lawyer are already here."

I sit on the couch. "Are we doing hypnosis again today?"

He shrugged. "Sure, if you're up for it. I'd like to try to find more recent memories. Track back to the last thing you remember."

I laid back. "We tried this before."

"Maybe things have changed." He sat next to me and got out his pen.

I wished I could have met him under different circumstances. When he was a seminarian, before I was a happy little fuckdoll, when things could have been kind of normal. That absurd sense of humor would drive me insane while my affluenza frustrated him.

"Things have changed," I said, though I couldn't define them.

"Keep your eyes on the tip of the pen."

Forbidden

ARE YOU RELAXED?

I am. I feel a freedom I hadn't felt before. I feel hopeful and generous, sweet and melancholy. Emboldened and encouraged, ready to start a new journey, a life after this incident.

I want you to think about the ride here, to Westonwood. Can you remember that?

I don't. It's not even a blur; it's blank.

Go back a little further. To the stables. You were given a shot. Do you remember the pain in your arm?

The black goes grey, and I feel something in my arm, as if I'm being poked with a rigid finger. I feel something else, a pounding in my chest, a confusion that I'm separate from. I can't tell what's happening, besides the feeling of being restrained.

Go back further. Before the shot.

I don't want to. I feel the resistance binding me to my forgetfulness, the comfort of not knowing. If I lean into it, just a little, maybe I can see what happened without feeling it. Maybe I can observe coldly, like a reporter noting facts for relevance, not profundity. If I let myself accept that fear, I'll know. So I relax into where the rope of my fear pulls and binds me, dropping into some unknown graphite-colored place in my head. I expect to go back in my memory a minute, two minutes, half an hour, but intuitively, though I can't tell the whens and wheres, I know I've gone back further.

His breath falls on my cheek, and a pain in my arm runs from my wrist to the sensitive side of my bicep.

"You did not," he says from deep in his throat. He's naked, stunning, the stink of sex and blood on him. He pins me to the wall, the friction screaming against the open skin on my ass.

Regret. Pounds of it. Miles wide. Regret to the depth of my broken spirit.

"I'm sorry." Am I? Or am I just saying it?

"Why?"

My wrist hurts. He's pressing it so hard against the wall, as if I'd leave, as if I'd ever turn my back on him. Yet I want to get away, to run, to show him that I can abandon him the way he abandons me.

I wiggle, but he only presses harder and demands, "Why?"

83

"Get off me!"

"Tell me why!" His eyes are wider, his teeth flashing as if he wants to rip out my throat. "Why?"

"I need it!"

The words come out before I think, and they're poison to him. Before I expect it, he slaps me in the mouth. He lets me go, and I fall to the floor. When I look at him, he's cradling the lower half of his face as if he can't believe what he's done. He's slapped me plenty, but not in anger. Not without me halfway in subspace and high on dopamine. Never outside a scene.

But that's nothing compared to what he does next. The ropes of my fear try to pull me away, back to safety, and I let them.

What is it? What does he do?

I must have been silent too long. I must have watched Deacon's face, frozen in my memory, for a second too many. The sense that he is going to do something terrible is all I have, but I don't remember what it is. When Elliot asks from the present what Deacon does, I stay to see it.

"I'm sorry," Deacon says.

I don't say anything. My face hurts, and I taste liquid copper. We stay like that forever, or time is stretched in my memory. This is the moment I can tell him it's okay, or the moment I can be angry, or I can have a reaction that will make him not do what he's going to do.

But I don't do anything. Not a word or gesture.

He walks out.

I don't know why there's a finality to it that I haven't ever felt before, but there is. When the bedroom door clicks behind him, that's it.

I want to wake up. I don't want to observe my emotions, even as a time-traveling bystander.

You're fidgeting.

Pinkerton Pinkerton Pinkerton

Okay, on three, you'll wake rested and happy.

Amanda's next to her hot pink Bugattti. Pinkerton, before it became the assassin of the 405. She tips, holds herself straight, smiles at me. Oh, no. I don't think so.

One.

I snap the keys from her and give them to Charlie. I open the passenger door in the front, even though it's her car. Let her sit in the back. I don't want her puking on Charlie when he's driving.

Two.

I'm not in the mood to die.

Three.

"YOU ASSOCIATE THOSE TWO THINGS," Elliot said. "Amanda dying, and Deacon hitting you."

"He hit me all the time. It was a turn-on."

"Hard enough to break a molar?"

I heard him shift in his chair. I wanted to sit upright, but my body felt like the inside of a broken egg.

"Did you usually sit in the back of Pinkerton?"

"If Charlie was driving and it's Amanda's car, I should be in the back. That's just social mores. But Amanda got aggressive when she drank too much, and she was doing God knows what else. I just didn't feel like worrying about her having a psychotic break while Charlie was driving, because it wasn't like he was in much better shape."

"And Deacon hitting you?"

"He left. That was the painful part."

"Why did he leave?"

I sighed. It had been the sore point between us. Our thing. "He went away for a few days to hang a show in San Diego. And I swelled, so I needed to fuck, and I got it where I could. I tried not to. I tried to be good, but I failed, okay? And he found out, which was lying on top of cheating. I packed my shit and left. That was the last time I saw him. Until the stables, which I still don't remember."

"So you feel responsible for him leaving?"

"I was. We stopped sharing and fucking around. We agreed."

"I think you need some therapy after you leave here. I don't think you've worked through your feelings. We haven't had time to touch on anything in your past."

"Sure, Elliot. Sure."

"And I know you don't have access to the outside world in here, but the press is being unkind is probably the nicest way to put it. You're going to need somewhere to go to talk about it."

"I'm sure I can find someone."

"It's been nice talking to you, Fiona. I'm pretty sure I know what you think of yourself, but I want you to know that you don't have to believe it."

I twisted around until I could see him. He looked the same as always, relaxed and confident, middle finger on his upper lip as if he couldn't think without it.

"Believe what?" I asked.

"That you're useless."

"You don't know what you're talking about."

"You're sensitive. You're bright. You're brave. Can you believe that?"

He pissed me off. He had no right to tell me about me, not after three days. But if I argued with him, if I put him in his place, it would be another reason to let me rot in that grey room.

"Thanks, Doc."

He stood and opened the door. "I want you to remember that when you see your mother. She's in visiting."

Chapter 15

Margie caught me in the foyer, on the way to the visiting room.

"Have you seen Mom?" I asked.

"I have no idea what she's doing here. I told her to stay home. Jonathan's a wreck over his girlfriend, and Theresa's no better. They're mad at Dad, but won't say why, which is fucking typical Drazen bullshit. You sure you don't want to stay in here?"

"I'm sure."

"Between you and Jonathan, the press is going apeshit."

"Fuck them."

"I wish I could get myself committed. " Her phone dinged, and she tapped it. "Hang on, this came from the prosecutor." She scanned the email. "Provided you're cleared to leave here, you agree not to contest the charge and waive the preliminary hearing. We accept aggravated assault. Community service. I'm inclined to tell him to fuck off. Deacon's denying it all, so bail and a grand jury appearance is my guess."

"What does the press want?"

"They want you turning on a spit."

"Take the plea."

"As your attorney, I wouldn't advise it."

I shrugged. "I'd rather not have this over my head. Or have Deacon change his mind after I see him and beg forgiveness. Just take it and be done. A little community service won't kill me."

"As your sister, I approve."

I sneered at her playfully, and she hid her smile.

THE GARLAND and lights were gone from the visiting room, as if Christmas had been mentioned once and wiped away. Mom paced in front of the window, a wisp of a thing with a bent neck, tapping her finger on her chin.

"Hi, Mom."

When she faced me, I knew she wasn't there to join me for the therapist's recommendation. Her eyes were on fire, her jaw set. She sat down like it was her job.

"What's happening?" I asked.

"How are you?"

"I'm f—"

"Did your father ever touch you?"

"Mom!"

"Answer me!" She slammed her palm on the table.

I held my hands up and sat back. It was too much. I needed time to think, to talk to people. To breathe, for Chrissakes.

"Fiona, tell me. I'll protect you. I'll put myself between you and anything. But just tell me. Did he ever touch you in a way that made you uncomfortable?"

"No, Mom. He never touched me inappropriately."

"Your sisters?"

"Why now? I'm twenty-three years old. What happened?"

She sighed then pursed her lips, a series of facial tics that meant she was holding in an emotion, any emotion. I said nothing. My heart was pounding too fast.

"There's talk that he'd had a relationship with the girl who just died."

"Jonathan's girlfriend?"

"Previous to that, when she was a bit younger, but yes. Your brother didn't know until recently, and he's not happy with it. So." She sat up straighter. "Did he ever touch one of your sisters?"

I wished for time, and my wish was not granted. The clock still moved. Things had been said in pledge. We'd held our hands up and made promises, and though I'd broken plenty of promises in life, I'd never broken pledge. None of us had. We had a code of silence, and inside of it sat our denials, our shame, our bonds.

"I can't say," I said. "Not directly."

Mom's face melted, constricting, as if her tears shrunk and crinkled it. I snapped up the ubiquitous box of tissues and put it in front of her.

"So it's true," she spit out before the sob choked her.

"It's complicated, Mom. It's not what you think, but I can't say. It's not my place."

"You think you're protecting someone, but have you thought that the way you all are… that you hurt each other with this wall you put up?"

"Yeah, I've thought about it."

"What are you all afraid of?"

Afraid? I wasn't afraid of being cut off from their money. I had more than I needed, and it couldn't be touched. I wasn't afraid of being cut off from my siblings, because we were strung together with strong twine.

I was afraid of Dad.

Dad had a way of making things happen. He had a way of using his relationships and his money to create chaos or order, as he saw fit.

But Mom was in distress, and how much worse could it all get? I was already up a creek; what would be the difference if I threw my paddle in the rushing billows of shit?

"You should talk to Carrie," I said, instantly regretting it, yet feeling the release of something I hadn't realized I was holding so close.

"It was Carrie?" she squeaked.

"Talk to her."

She wiped her eyes, but her tears barely abated. "God damn that big house." She folded and refolded the tissue. "God damn the corners. You can't see what's happening. You can't hear. We avoid each other. Did you see how that happened? How we went to the far corners?"

"There were eight kids, Mom. You needed a big house. What were you supposed to do?"

"Pay attention. I was supposed to pay attention!"

Mom looked up and behind me. I followed her gaze.

Margie stood in the doorway. "What's going on?"

"Nothing," I said. "Mom thinks I'm a disappointment and a failure." I may have been ready to break pledge, but I wasn't ready to get busted for it. "Let's get this done. You're buying me dinner at Roberto's. I'm hungry, and I need a drink."

"You're too young to need a drink," Margie said, getting out of the way of the exit.

"Well, I need something."

"How about a job?" she replied, putting her arm around Mom.

I stuck my tongue out at her.

Chapter 16

We waited.

On the hard, squared-off modern couch in the common room, we waited. I imagined Elliot typing, his middle finger rubbing his upper lip. I waited for Mom to come back from the parking lot and throttle me into saying what I knew, which was nothing. I swear, I knew nothing except that Carrie had talked to Deirdre and Sheila about something in pledge. That was it. Nothing I could build a case on.

I shook a little. I was getting out. The press was out to skewer me and possibly my brother. My little coterie of fuckbuddies and hangers-on were going to steer clear of me and the media attention I dragged behind me. My relationship with Deacon was in a sick holding pattern. Amanda was still dead. I'd broken, or at least fractured, a lifelong bond of trust between me and my sisters and brother.

A little community service would go a long way to distracting me.

Bored, yet jumpy and upset, I went into the cafeteria. Dinner was starting. The staff placed trays of deluxe meals into the steam trays. I'd never see them again, those chattering people in hair nets, and I hadn't even gotten to know their names. I said good-bye in my mind to the cafeteria, the patio, the holes in the camera matrix. I said so long to the grey painted over everything, the flat lighting, the sterile corners. Karen came in, all unkind angles and protruding bones. I excused myself from Margie, who waved me off, and stood next to Karen as she plopped her journal on the tray.

"Hey," I said. "I'm getting my recommendation in, like, twenty minutes, then I'm outtie."

"It was good to see you again," she said flatly.

"You should call me when you get home. I mean it."

"I don't think I can do an Ojai again." She poked through a basket of perfect yellow bananas as if unable to choose one, though they all looked the same to me.

"Yeah, me neither." I said it, but did I mean it?

Deacon had kept me away from the life for months, but I didn't know where he and I stood. He might be out of my world forever, and if that was the case, then what did I have left but more of what had gone before? I found I wasn't looking forward to anything. I was terrified of speaking to Deacon, of being in my big empty condo. I didn't care to see Earl or Charlie. Didn't want to delve into what had happened with Martin or Debbie. But mostly, I wasn't looking forward to partying. Didn't want coke, but knew I'd snort it when I got bored. Didn't want sex, but knew I'd need it when I got sad.

Karen got to the bottom of the basket. The banana at the end was black and soft. No one would want it. She picked it up and put it on her tray instead of all the firm, ripe ones.

I'd figure it all out once I was home. I might figure it out licking the base of some guy's cock or tied to the ceiling like an enraptured side of flesh, but I'd figure it out. I just had to go deeper. Harder. Full throttle into whatever tornado I'd walked into. Yet when I spoke, something completely different came out.

"Something has to change," I said. "I don't think I can live like that anymore."

"Yeah," Karen said pensively. "If I knew how to stop doing this, I would."

"It's a problem. Me, I mean. I have a problem." I said it with a little laugh, as if to disavow it even as I said it. I was taking a practice run at thinking I had something to fix. It was like an audition for recovery to see if I had the talent to pull off the role.

"Fiona," Margie said, putting her hand on my shoulder. "We're up."

I hugged Karen. "Good-bye. Eat something, would you? You're skin and bones."

"I will. Good luck out there."

Elliot and Frances entered through the glass doors, and I noticed that he was frowning. We walked in silence to the conference room. I said good-bye to the linoleum, the garden outside the window. Silently, as a prayer to people not present, I said good-bye to Jack who was completely unfuckable, Warren who was an act of violence waiting to happen, Mark who was one of a hundred or more.

I didn't know what waited for me outside. I didn't know if Deacon would take me back, didn't know if the media would crush me, but I was ready to be out of Westonwood—that was for damn sure.

Chapter 17

Mom didn't come back. It was just me and Margie with Elliot and Frances. The table shined in all its lacquer glory under the horizontal shadows of the window blinds. A black spider of a conference call unit sat in the middle of the table, ignored. I tried to make eye contact with Elliot, and he met my eyes once we sat. I saw no reassurances in the gaze, but he was never one to let a crack in his professional veneer show.

I tucked my hair behind my ears. Had I brushed it? I was about to go back into the world, and I'd hate to do it ungroomed, sloppy, with scraggly red hair and no makeup. I already felt as though I had one foot out the door.

"Ms. Drazen," Frances said to Margie, "can we get you anything?"

"Out of here?"

She smiled so disarmingly, Frances laughed, and the tension of the room broke a little.

"Well, thanks for coming." Frances looked as if she'd applied lipstick fifteen seconds before opening the glass doors. "This conversation is being recorded for the patient's protection."

I almost laughed out loud but choked it down.

Frances continued. "Doctor Chapman and I will be issuing our recommendations to the judge and district attorney for the City of Los

Angeles, in the case of Fiona Maura Drazen." Frances folded her hands in front of her and looked me in the eye. "After careful consideration by the administration of this hospital, and the bearing in mind the counsel of Dr. Chapman, we've decided to recommend you stay at Westonwood or another accredited facility for an additional fourteen to forty-five days of observation, pursuant to Section 5250 of the California Welfare and Institutions code."

I swallowed. "Excuse me?"

"What's this about?" Margie demanded. "She's functioning. She's capable. I've seen far sicker people released on their own recognizance."

"She's had three violent outbursts while under our care," Frances said.

I spun on Elliot. "You said the meds caused the outbursts."

"I said maybe," he said gently. "I'm sorry, but—"

Frances broke in, "And she still has no recall of the incident."

"There was no incident," Margie growled. "You can ask Deacon Bruce."

"The judge thinks there was," Frances said. "He's concerned about letting a woman with psychotic episodes back into society."

"We just accepted a plea deal."

"From the prosecutor. Judge trumps lawyer."

Margie was holding herself together admirably, but I could see her gears turning. I bet the two psychologists across the table could as well.

"Our recommendation is that she be kept here for her own safety," Elliot said softly. He closed his little folder and stood. "I'm in session in two minutes. Excuse me." He nodded to each of us and strode out.

I was left sitting in shock. What had just happened?

I had been so sure I was leaving. I'd said good-bye to the place, checked my room for personal items, looked at the cafeteria for the last time. Staying was worse than a defeat. It was a humiliation.

How was I letting that motherfucker walk out of there?

I spun out of my chair and dashed into the reception area. He was just beyond the glass doors.

"Elliot," I called.

He slowed down, as if deciding what to do.

I ran to catch up. "What happened? Come on, you know I'm not going to hurt anyone."

He shook his head. "It's for the best."

"I'll have you in session tomorrow, and I'm not saying a word until you tell me what happened."

"Fiona, I—"

"You can shove your little pen tip up your ass. I'm going to make your life miserable."

He smiled ruefully and looked at the floor. "I'm not your therapist anymore. I'm going back to Compton."

"Fuck you are."

"I'm sorry I can't be here. I think you'll be just fine. You're doing great."

"Save the platitudes for the ones who need them."

His neck tensed, and his eyes got hard. That was my gotcha moment, and I didn't want it. His voice went from heavy cream to wire brush, and the stroke of every syllable drew blood. "Once you get out there with your cute little plea deal, you'll get eaten alive. Maybe by the press. Maybe by that man you almost killed. Maybe he'll kill you this time instead of breaking your teeth. The judge on your case is not out to help you, trust me. You don't have the tools to handle life outside these doors. You'll go back to using, and I'm not willing to wonder if I could have done something else to help you. I'm just going to do it. This is the only way to protect you."

"It was your job to assess my sanity. Not protect me."

He held his hands out, his clipboard clutched in his fingers. "That's just tough, Fiona. This was the last real thing I did here, and I'm okay with it."

"Fuck you."

He nodded, making me feel like a tantrum-prone child. And now what? He was going to say good-bye and leave me? No. Not allowed.

"This is not done," I said.

"Good-bye, Fiona. Meeting you was something else."

I turned around and ran back down the hall before he could say a word. I didn't know what I was trying to stop. Some freight train of my thwarted expectations before it ran me over? Maybe the moment where I would wake up and realize I'd failed, and I was stuck here? So help me God, I couldn't be there, cut off from everything for another month. Something had to be done, and if no one would do it for me, I would do it myself. I slammed past the glass doors, out of breath.

Margie stood staring at her phone.

"You have to keep Doctor Chapman here," I said in a breath. "Make them. He can't walk away."

Margie heard me, I knew she did. I was right there, but she wasn't listening.

"I fucked up," she said.

"How? You made a deal, they can't—"

"Dad was right. I'm too inexperienced. I would have had my finger on the judge's pulse if I'd known better."

What she was saying hit me like a slap.

"No," I said.

"I'm sorry, Fiona. I tried, but you need a better lawyer. It's not fair to you."

"Not fair to me? I'm here now with nothing and no one… I don't have Elliot, and now you're leaving? What am I supposed to do? Margie, how am I supposed to make it? Don't leave me." My hands were flying. I was screaming.

Margie was trying to grab my hands and shush me at the same time. "Calm down."

"Stay, and I'll calm down. Stay with me."

"I can't. It's not the best—"

"Don't leave me! Don't leave me! Don't leave me!"

When I tried to hold her close, hands on me pulled and tugged. There was a floor under me, and shadows in the light, and voices in all kinds of timbres and shades of gentleness. There was a discomfort in my arm like a stiff finger pushing against me, and soon after that, the hands relaxed, and everything went grey.

▭

PART II

USE

Chapter 18

FIONA

I OFTEN DRIFTED off into a trance-like state that reminded me of the hypnosis sessions I used to have with Elliot. I fazed out in the evenings between dinner and lights out while I sat in front of the TV, watching the ocean waves on a loop, and I let my mind do whatever it wanted.

While I thought about nothing, in a cotton-candy medicated haze, the cardboard cone of my rage was hidden under the pink tufts of sugar. In the ten days since Elliot left, they'd changed my meds and I'd run the gamut from zoned out to acting out.

Too much slap, not enough tickle.

I missed Elliot and his cold professionalism, the little tics and movements he used to funnel his emotions, the promise of his naked body under his clothes. He'd been gone twelve hours before I started entertaining vivid sexual fantasies about him. I didn't need him for anything. In the heat of our non-relationship, I didn't need him to set me free or call me sane, so I didn't have to block out the thoughts. Since I'd rediscovered the feel of my fingers on my body, I'd entertained thoughts of him at night once, twice, three times after lights out, falling into a sleepless daze with my hands cupped over my cunt.

My favorite fantasy was so chaste it set my clit on fire.

I'm in a coffee shop on Charleville, the one where I could get a buttercup, which was a drip coffee with butter. I'm alone which, in and of itself, is a fantasy. There are no cameras or paparazzi anywhere. I sit at a table on the sidewalk and open a book. The sun shines. The breeze is light in my hair, and the mug is made of red porcelain.

He stands over me with his paper cup, casting a shadow on my book. "Fiona?"

I look up, and I put him together as I remember him: light brown hair, green/blue/grey eyes, narrow brows, long neck, and a smile that, for once, is genuine, unburdened by self-reproach or professional courtesy.

"Elliot, hi."

"How are you?"

"Great. Do you have time to sit?"

He always sits. Sometimes he's on his way somewhere and decides to take the time out, and sometimes he has nothing to do. But he always sits. I imagine our conversation. I have to make his life up, because I know so little about him. I tell him how well I am. How I'm cured. How I don't do drugs anymore and how sex is no longer a need. Sometimes I tell him I haven't had sex since I was released, and sometimes I tell him I have, just a couple of times.

When I claim chastity, that's when the fantasy is most vibrant. That's when he walks me to my car and his words of affection, of longing, of repressed desire pulse between my legs. The kiss I imagine, with his hands on my face and his dick pushing against me, makes me so wet I have to rub it off in my mental ward cot.

I imagine going down to Compton, to some rat-infested shelter or run-down church, and seeing him. Our hurt for each other is so strong that the magnetic pull makes our will to remain professional and proper impossible.

He says, "I always wanted you."

I replayed our short time together, looking for moments when that might have been true. As the days wore on, I imagined he has me on the bed. He takes my ankles and spreads my legs so far, and looks at my wet cunt for a second before kissing it. The look on his face is one of bliss, as if he'd been starving and imprisoned and I was a great meal of freedom. When he fucked me, he did it like in the movies, with his face close to mine, eyes half closed, breathing my name.

I knew it was fantasy and impossible. I didn't know the man at all, yet I did. He was normal, straight-laced, probably vanilla. He'd never be with a fuck-up sex addict, a druggie slave worthless whore camera-magnet like me. I'd never attract a man who was plain nice. I didn't have access to the ordinary world, yet I craved it. My darkest desires were for an inaccessible normality.

I hadn't wanted that until Elliot left. In the days following, as my fantasies became more outrageously mild, I thought of Deacon, my master, the one who had helped me function and who I had betrayed. Maybe one day I'd remember the sticky web of circumstances that put us both in the stables, but did it matter a fuck? In the end, did I stab him to be free of him?

And free to do what?

Fuck? Snort? Party?

Or free to be normal?

Chapter 19

ELLIOT

I DIDN'T LIKE RUSHING. If everything was done properly and in the right order, I never had to rush. Even the most tedious parts of the day could be managed effortlessly if they happened when they were supposed to.

On Tuesdays, I had therapy before work. As a therapist, I needed my own therapy sessions in order to maintain my sanity, though some weeks I had nothing to discuss and my sanity was only impaired by having to spend yet another fifty minutes in Lee's office, talking about nothing. Those sessions supposedly gave me an angle from which to see the seemingly unproductive sessions with my own patients, but I felt more and more like I was wasting my time.

I opened my car door. The bougainvillea that hung over the driveway needed a trim. I often did the trimming myself because I found it soothing, but since I took the job at Westonwood, I had stopped. Since the gardeners had been instructed to leave it alone, they did, and it exploded into a waterfall of purple blooms that dropped onto my windshield.

I'd gone back to work at the Alondra Avenue Family Clinic in

Compton. I'd left a chaplaincy there that had had a limited time frame. They'd asked me to stay on, but I went to Westonwood. When I left the enclave for the rich and troubled, I picked up some part-time work at Alondra while I sorted out my life. I didn't like the instability any more than I liked the upset schedule, but I needed the balance badly.

L.A. traffic was famously brutal, but it was easily managed if one took into consideration the season as it related to the LAUSD, the time of day, the weather, and were willing to change routes at a moment's notice. If I turned right on LaCienega at 7:01 a.m. on a normal Tuesday, I'd be on time. Turning at 7:02 made me upward of ten minutes late. I never figured out where the eight minutes went, but that extra sixty seconds seemed to increase the density of the traffic arteries by an order of magnitude.

So when I turned at 7:04, I assumed I'd have to apologize as soon as I walked into my session. That always led to an explanation of why I was late, and why it was important to be punctual, and back to how I felt about it, and so began the digging like kids in the yard, looking for treasure that wasn't there. But I'd forgotten that it was still Christmas break for the LAUSD, and the roads were clearish. I pulled into the alley behind Lee's office and took a deep breath. I'd made it, and I'd get to Alondra in time because the traffic was light. Being late for Lee was forgivable. Being late for my patients was egregious. They were people who had nothing reliable in their lives but me.

"Why do you worry about them?" asked Lee, her fingers laced together over her pregnant belly. She'd managed to get knocked up at forty-two, and I often found her in a state of bliss, sickness, or a meld of the two.

"Because I'm human. It's human to care."

"But it's not your job."

We'd had that discussion a hundred times. My job was to give patients a safe place to work on their problems. If I cared about them, I'd be emotionally shredded at the end of the week/month/year, and unable to work with the rest.

I didn't answer her. There was no point. I felt fidgety and caught myself rubbing my upper lip with my middle finger. I had nowhere to put the energy. I'd been that way since I left Westonwood.

"You were almost late this morning. I saw you pull in." Lee indicated the window beside her desk, looking onto the parking spaces. She didn't have any tics. World's perfect therapist, recommended by my mentor for her completely calm, organized, non-distracting demeanor.

"Jana caught me in the shower," I said, remembering the perfectly pleasant, if ill-timed lovemaking in the bathroom. "Set my morning back." She'd moved in six months before, after a whirlwind of dating, and had made little or no impression on the house except to be the prettiest thing that had ever stepped foot in the kitchen.

"Ah," she said. "Can I assume things are going well?"

"The usual. She wants me somewhere safe. She thinks I'm going to get jacked every day. She puts on a show of panic and worry. I soothe her. It works for a little while, et cetera et cetera…"

"And she wants you back at Westonwood."

"Yes."

"Did you tell her why you left?"

That was sticky, very sticky. Only Lee was qualified to unravel it, and she was the only person I'd trust with that level of complexity. I'd downloaded my desire to protect Fiona from her family and the media to her during the fist session after I left Westonwood, and she'd let me dance around it, waiting for me to describe my exact feelings in my own time.

"Jana wouldn't understand," I said.

"You should try."

"She's a delicate person. If I tell her about a patient's family pressuring me, she'll worry. If I tell her about the countertransference, it's worse."

"Countertransference happens. The thing with the girl's family, that's something she deserves to know, and it's well outside the privilege of the room."

"There's nothing to tell," I said. "That's what I told you—it was all inference. If I express inference, she's not going to have a place to put it, so it goes in the panic bucket. She can't deal with things that aren't facts."

"How are you going to live like that, Elliot?"

"You make my eyeballs ache, you know that?"

"You've said the same about Jana."

I sneered, knowing it was a sneer and she'd think it was funny. She was pointing out my transference, the redirection of feelings related to someone outside the room to the therapist. Transference was necessary. Countertransference, where the therapist placed unresolved feelings onto the patient, was trickier. Though it was normal, my countertransference with Fiona had to be dealt with. That was why we needed therapy for the therapy, to keep things in check.

"I didn't trust her father's motives," I said. "He comes in and tells me I should let her go. Tells me they'll take her in and watch her and thanks me very much for my time. The way he said it, it was off."

"So you think he should have asked you to keep her for more observation?"

"I think the fact that he even asked is a problem. If he'd asked me to feed her at noon, I would have fed her at eleven because I don't trust him."

"That's very reactionary," Lee said.

"You've never met the guy."

"And do you consider your decision meddling?"

"Anyone with a television knows what's going on. The media frenzy around her brother's accident and her stabbing her boyfriend; no sane person could survive it. She'd go back to using. Letting her out would have been setting her up for failure."

She leaned back in her chair. I didn't know if she needed the belly space or if she was taken aback by my tone.

"You believe that you made this decision based solely on the data?" she asked.

"Lee, what's the difference if it was the right decision?"

"You tell me."

I didn't, because I wasn't ready to say out loud that I had feelings for Fiona Drazen.

$$\text{————————————}$$

Chapter 20

$$\text{————————————}$$

FIONA

I DIDN'T REQUIRE black dark to sleep, which was good since I fucked anywhere, any time, and sometimes I needed to drop off afterward. Once I woke up on top of Owen Branch on the floor of Club Permission Granted at ten thirty in the morning. All the lights were on, and ladies in blue smocks were vacuuming to the Spanish music on the boombox. Owen wasn't even fully awake when he lit a doob and handed it to me. I went back to sleep for another half an hour.

But at Westonwood, I had a problem I'd never had before: Everything kept me up. I knew I couldn't blame it on the light coming through the door window, or the crickets, or the whooshing of the pipes whenever someone, somewhere flushed.

It was stabbing Deacon and the waterfall of guilt that followed. Everything I'd done in my young life. Everyone heartbreak. Every careless betrayal. Every time I hurt someone to fulfill some minor need or wisp of a desire. For ditching Owen the morning after the high school prom. For sucking his dick the next week because it happened to be there. For throwing his phone out my car window on the 101 when he told me he'd snuck a shot of my mouth on his cock because it was such a pretty sight. For pulling the car over and punching him in the face, then telling everyone what he'd done until no one would hang out with him any more.

People in my position—meaning people other people looked at—didn't like Sneaky Petes taping fuck sessions, even if they told me nicely what they did and only did it for themselves. No. Just no. That was why phones were surrendered at Deacon's place.

But still. I wasn't focused on my rightness. My rightness didn't hurt, and I was after full-bore self-immolation. So I did what I did every night at Westonwood: I chose a random incident from my life and turned it over in the dark. That night it was Owen. I didn't have to punch him in the face. He'd been a harmless surfer with a huge dick and a permanent boner. I didn't have to make sure none of my friends spoke to him again, or throw his phone out the window on the freeway. It was expensive to him, and I hadn't given a fuck.

Somewhere, a toilet flushed. The pipes whooshed.

It was morning.

▭

I DIDN'T TELL my new therapist shit. She was just a bitch behind a desk who pretended to support my "healing process." The fact that I'd never put my fist in her face was a testament to my healing process, but I walked out of there twisted in knots every time. I was sure she and the fistful of drugs they gave me were the source of my insomnia. I hadn't slept more than a couple of hours a night since Elliot left.

"You're not schizophrenic," my new doctor bitch said. "You don't suffer from narcissistic personality disorder. You have no history of compulsion."

Her office was a museum of Native American artifacts. Dream-catchers. Masks. Beaded wall hangings and handmade blankets in frames.

"You're saying there's nothing wrong with me." I wasn't even hopeful, just killing time. We'd had that conversation a hundred times already. I didn't know what she was waiting for me to realize, because I'd have the epiphany of the century if I knew.

"The whole idea of sex addiction is a way to impose cultural models to make normal people seem abnormal. Mostly, these normal people are women. If you're not upset with your behavior, then there's nothing to say what you're doing is wrong."

"Then you're going to let me go?"

"What I'm trying not to do it pathologize your sexuality, but your mind is still not clear. Your memory is garbled, and I suspect you went through more in those stables than you're ready to admit. You're still prone to violence, mostly when men are in the room. I'd like to get to the bottom of it."

Considering I usually lost my shit in the cafeteria at about three o'clock, she was right. It was a co-ed facility, so there were always men around. The only time men weren't around was in that room with her.

"Do I need to be here for you to do that?" I asked. "Because you know, we're supposed get me back to functioning in society. This isn't a whole thing where I'm walking out some healed person who can get a job and land a good husband, right?"

"You're here. This time is for you. Think about it. I could buy you enough time to really get to the bottom of your issues with Deacon and your father."

She presented it like a birthday cake. The luxury of the century. An indefinite amount of time at Westonwood Spa, with the mental equivalent of hot rocks and exfoliating rubs, with her inferences about my father, who I hadn't mentioned to her, and Deacon, who was none of her business.

"And you walk out with what?" I said.

"I don't understand your meaning." She tilted her head, her pin-straight Brazilian blowout falling perpendicular to the earth while her face rested at the angle of inquisitiveness.

"I mean, we find some deep trauma in like, what two, three months, and you? It's a lot of work for you."

"It's work I love. Helping you to heal yourself," she said.

"Don't you have some high-paying gig in Beverly Hills?"

"I have a private practice, yes. Where are you going with this, Fiona? Are you afraid I'll abandon you like your last therapist?"

She should have known better. I'd cut her off the last time she'd tried to come down on Elliot for leaving, because I figured out that when he'd admitted to leaving to protect me, he'd only admitted it to me. I wouldn't betray him, and more than that, I respected him. But there she was, with her patronizing little smile and her forearms on the desk, accusing Elliot of shit outside her sphere of fucking knowledge.

I hated her. Maybe I hated her because she wasn't Elliot. Or maybe I hated her because I didn't want to be there. Maybe I just hated her because she was hateful, and because she was trying to get me to hate men instead of her Brazilian blowout.

And fuck, I hated her Brazilian blowout.

Most of our sessions went like that. I just disagreed with whatever she said. She said the sky was up, and I insisted I walked on clouds. She told me I was sick, and I said I was fine. She'd tried to con me into agreeing that my father had molested me, that Deacon beat me in a way that was non-consensual, that in fucking whomever I wanted, I'd agreed to be degraded. She couldn't get that the fucking itself wasn't degrading. The intentional degradation was degrading. And hot.

I didn't understand her. Why did she seem to care so much? Why couldn't she just listen to my problems, decide whether or not I was sane enough to be questioned, keep my meds low so I didn't feel like throwing things, and let me go? Surely the hospital didn't need my family's money that badly.

"It's not about money," Karen said one day at lunch. She was on a feeding tube and rolled her IV around with her. Mostly she was too weak to even get up, but when she did, she managed to find me. "You're like this rare creature. Rich. Famous. Living in a fish bowl. How many of you are there in the world? And you're in their chair. They can latch on to you and use you."

"For what? It's all confidential, isn't it?"

"Sure. But you know, over drinks? Who knows what they say at parties to get another client. Or to their own therapists. There aren't any secrets. My last guy wrote a paper about anorexia and wealth, and there was a patient in the paper who sounded just like me. My lawyer couldn't do anything."

"Jesus."

"Yeah. I don't tell these fuckers anything anymore. I don't tell anyone anything. Not even my friends."

What had I told Elliot? Anything? Everything? Dr. Brazilian Blowout hadn't gotten much more than evasion, but Elliot had gotten more from me before he split. I trusted him, but should I? I missed my fish-bowl friends who understood what to say when. I trusted them because they lived a shade of my life.

"It's not all like Ojai," I said. "You've been hanging out with the wrong people. Chill with me when you're out. We'll lay back. It's all on the DL."

"Really?"

"Yes." I pushed my food around. What if Elliot told everyone about me? That I was a sex-addict celebutante who didn't know how or why she'd stabbed the only man who loved her?

I didn't care what people thought, but imagining Elliot at a party, casually talking about my problems without mentioning my name, people's eyes going wide as they judged me—the scene I created bothered me. Elliot casually discussing my problems hurt in a way I couldn't even pin down. It was *him,* how *he* felt.

Did he feel nothing?

Was I just a curiosity to him?

Did he leave because he couldn't stand me?

I couldn't tolerate the thought, and I couldn't banish it from my mind. It played on a loop, and with each successive telling, he was more and more dismissive and contemptuous. I gripped my fork so tightly, the edge indented the flesh of my fingers. I pulled it away and looked at the brown-and-purple ridge it created. I ran my thumb over the skin. It was both numb and oversensitive.

"Did you sleep last night?" Karen whispered.

"No. I can't."

"Are they giving you something for it?"

"It's not working. I need Halcion. That's the only one that works."

When someone put their hand on my shoulder, I jumped.

"Sorry," Frances said. "I didn't mean to frighten you."

I hadn't heard her come up behind me. "It's okay." I said it, but I didn't mean it. She dealt with people like me all day. She knew how to approach. But I was so tired I was docile.

"You have visitors."

I didn't know why I thought it might be Deacon. I still held some childish hope that he'd come get me. The thrill of the thought must have been all over my face.

"It's your sisters."

Chapter 21

FIONA

MY SISTERS.

I had six of them, and a brother. So though Frances had said it as if she was talking about a complete set, there was no way all of them had shown up at Westonwood all at once.

Margie got up as I walked out onto the patio, and she hugged me.

"I'm sorry, sweetheart," she said. "I'm sorry I left you." She pushed me away, holding my biceps. "You look good."

"Are you my lawyer again?"

"No. I just came to see you."

"I didn't like that other guy."

"He's very experienced," Theresa said from behind Margie. "He already got you a new judge."

"Jesus, Theresa. Don't sneak up on me like that." I hugged her, and when we separated, she got her hair back into place.

Some girls become stuck-up bitches early in life, and at eighteen, Theresa was just as stuck up as any of them. Always good, always correct. She sat up straight and chewed with her mouth closed, said please and thank you and dressed right for the occasion. It was an accident of her birth, that perfection. None of the rest of us were as pin straight as she was. She wore her little soup of redheaded genes like a tiara. I had no idea why she even showed up to see me. She hated me.

"So?" I said, throwing myself onto the garden bench and spreading my legs in an unladylike fashion. I wanted to throw my whore body in her face, just to make her uncomfortable. "How are you guys?"

"I'm fine," Theresa replied, pressing her knees together. "How are you?"

"Crazy. What do you want?"

"I came checking after you. It's a courtesy."

"Great, I'm having tea with Spence and Chip at three, then a little badminton. Shall you join for a swipe at the shuttlecock?" I tipped my head back toward the field where the croquet and badminton had been set up.

"Oh, Fiona." Margie swung a chair around.

"Small talk is a lubricant, not an insult," Theresa huffed.

"I've never needed lubricant unless I'm getting it in the ass."

I'd aimed to shock her, and I'd done it. Her face, a mask of perfection under her red ponytail, seemed to fall for a second. I thought I'd hit home until she laughed. Then Margie laughed. I felt a swell of pride in pleasing them, even though Theresa was younger and hateful, and I was mad at Margie. It was as if, in that laugh, they accepted me. They didn't, I knew that, but it was my moment.

"Okay, guys. I'm busy finding wholeness," I said. "Seriously. Why didn't you come with Mom and Dad?"

"They're busy," Margie cut in.

"Yeah, more like, Mom hates discomfort, and since she came around here last time asking if Dad ever touched me, I'm thinking I'm not a happy sight for her right now."

"What did you tell her?" Margie's voice was clipped.

I pressed my lips together then puckered them. "He never touched me."

"Is that what you told her, or is that just a fact?" Margie asked.

"Both."

She scanned my face, looking for any other tidbit, like an open pledge I'd betrayed or the slip of an unsavory truth.

"What do you want from me, Margaret?"

"The judge changed. Dad wants you out. Why, is a matter of speculation," she said.

"He wants to divert attention," Theresa said softly, into her hands. "Away from what's happening with Jonathan. I know him. I know how he thinks." She held up her hand, but she looked reluctant to open pledge. As second youngest, she rarely did. There was a tacit, unspoken courtesy to the elders that they opened it.

"I swear to god," I said, holding up my hand, "sixty percent of my brain capacity is taken up by what's said under pledge and who was under pledge when it was said. I'm not that bright, guys. Don't fill up the bucket, or it's gonna spill."

"Pledge open," Theresa said.

"Okay, go."

"Jonathan." All Margie said was our brother's name, and the beginning of that potentially long sentence ended in silence. The chatter of birds and insects in the garden seemed too loud to bear.

"I know there was something with his girlfriend..." Something about it nagged me, as if I'd met her or done something I should be ashamed of.

"Rachel. She's dead," Theresa said, closing her eyes as if gathering strength. Margie put her hand over Theresa's and let her finish. "Sheila had a party Christmas night. Rachel and I went two days before to help her set up. She knew the neighborhood. So, night of the party, Rachel shows after most of the family leaves. Jonathan gets drunk and starts acting like an ass. She takes off in his car and...." She cleared her throat before continuing. "They found the car, but not the body."

"I'm sorry," I said.

"Rachel was my friend. She had a tough home life, so she came back to the house with me a lot. Dad, he... Well, she started getting all gifts and wouldn't say from where, and this was a few years ago. So." She cleared her throat again, and her eyes darted over the garden.

"She and Dad, when she was fifteen," Margie cut in with her businesslike tone.

Theresa picked up the thread. "Jon didn't know until a few weeks ago."

"None of us did," Margie said.

"It's the creepiest thing ever," I said. "Seriously, I thought his thing with Mom was like true love that transcended age. I'm a rose-colored dumbfuck."

"You shouldn't use words like that."

"Fuck fuck fuck."

"Can you stop? This doesn't need to be harder." Theresa's face was tense, her fingers clenched into hooks.

Margie glanced at me, her look telling me to shut the fuck up. Delivering bad news was usually Margie's job, but Theresa seemed hell bent on saying hard things, and it appeared Margie was backing her up.

"Okay, go on," I said.

"They haven't told you because they didn't want to upset you."

"They don't want to upset themselves."

"Jon tried to commit suicide," Theresa said.

"What? When?"

"Little less than a week ago." Her voice dropped. "I found him. He took a handful of pills and gave himself a heart attack. It was awful. I mean, really awful. It's going to break Mom."

I looked at Margie. "He's okay?" My brother, the only boy and the youngest of eight, was the scion, the gem, and an arrogant ass I'd never want harmed.

"He's fine. They admitted him here last night. Supposedly Mom is coming this afternoon to tell you, but you know how that goes."

"Here? They admitted him *here*?"

Margie grabbed Theresa's hand, relieving her of the responsibility of speaking. "They don't send you home after a suicide attempt. They have to figure out if you're a risk to yourself. It's like babysitting, only really fucking expensive."

"You don't have to say that word," Theresa whispered. Theresa turned toward the patio.

In the direct light, I saw she had dark circles under her eyes, and renegade hairs had escaped her ponytail. She'd lost her friend, and her brother had almost died. She had a sister in an institution and a father who liked girls slightly younger than her. I realized she was as much of an addict as I was, and refinement was her drug of choice.

"Are you okay, Theresa? You look like hell," I said.

"She was my friend, but she was also a little in love with money, which is probably why she went from Dad to Jon… God, it's even hard to say that."

"Not easy to hear either."

"I think she was trying to blackmail Dad," Theresa said. "It's such a mess. I've never seen Dad like this. He's *afraid*. That's scarier than anything."

"He's not scared," Margie cut in. "He's playing at it. And yes, she was trying to blackmail Dad. I got that through my own channels."

"Why didn't he just pay it?"

"Maybe he did," Margie said. "But she kept coming after him."

"Then me," Theresa said. "She kept saying hateful things to me about Jonathan and Dad, like she was trying to get me to hate them. I was weird about her dating my brother, then I wasn't. Now I am again. But when you see Jonathan, can you tell him I'm sorry? We had this big fight just before. I called him names, which was… I don't know what came over me." Her hands sat palm up in her lap, and she stared at them. "We can't fight amongst ourselves. Reporters are asking questions. It's nuts out there. They're asking about Rachel, about you. They want to use us. Everyone has a camera, and I don't want us to be used any more."

"We're the world's circus," I said. "Third ring to the right. I don't know how to shake it."

"I'm going to." Theresa set her jaw, and a steel curtain dropped over her face. "I'm going to be normal. I'm going to work and have a job like anyone else. I'm going to have friends who like me for me. Not for money or fame or any of this."

"Good luck with that," I said, already shaking my head over her failure to achieve the dream of being no better than ordinary.

On the way out, with Theresa half a hall away, Margie took my hand. "Keep your shit together, and you can get out. Your mandated time is only a few more days, and your boyfriend's not pressing charges, so you can probably avoid a lot of questioning and ugliness if you stay low. But a little sisterly advice."

"As opposed to what you usually give?"

"Jonathan's going to need you. He's not himself. Be there for him. It really is a circus. They've been poking around Dad, which means there are going to be questions."

"I told Mom to talk to Carrie. I'm sorry, I just—"

"It's okay. Forget it."

"Carrie always knew Dad had a thing for… I can't even say it. I always thought she… I can't say that either." I couldn't say that Carrie had always maintained that Dad liked young girls, and that made me think she'd gotten some form of sexual attention none of the rest of us had. I had no proof, just a twist in the gut. Carrie had never said one way or the other.

"Carrie can take care of herself," Margie said. "If I were you, I'd stay in here as long as possible. As a matter of fact, I'd like to admit myself right now."

"If you were in here, I'd work like hell to get you out."

"You're implying… what?"

"You ditched me."

She put her hands on her hips. "For your own good."

"Isn't it about time other people stopped deciding what was for my own good? Maybe treat me like an adult who can make her own decisions? I have my own reason for wanting you to be my lawyer, and it has nothing to do with your experience. I don't want to explain myself to some strange, experienced person. I need someone to work with who I am. Do you get it?"

She didn't answer. She pecked me on the cheek and stalked off for the door. From Margie, that might as well have been a signature on the dotted line.

Chapter 22

FIONA

I'D LEFT my sisters with promises and comfort I was ill-equipped to give. Only someone as naïve as Theresa would tell a psycho like me a thing, and only a Drazen psycho would keep that fucking promise to death.

"They wanted to visit. What's the big deal, Deena?"

Brazilian Blowout's name was Deena. It made me want to kick a puppy.

"You look upset," she said.

"I'm not upset."

"You still have no recollection of what happened the night before you arrived here. Honestly, I find it hard to send you home before you remember."

"It's not a condition of my release. Not according to my lawyer."

"We have some latitude."

"You mean *you* have latitude. You know the violent outbursts were valid. This other bullshit is just bullshit."

"What exactly do you think is going on, Fiona?" She had her forearms on the edge of the desk, and her fucking blowout at a right angle to the earth, and a practiced, blank expression that created a vacuum that sucked the truth out of me.

"I think you're looking to make a career jump." Even as the voice in my head told me to stop, I kept on. "I think you're going to change the names to protect the guilty and write a paper about the famous, debased heiress with a father who married his wife real young. I think you put me back on Paxil, which Elliot took me off of, so I'd have less control over myself and I'd get snappy in the afternoons."

"There's no proof Paxil has that side effect." She sat back, crossing her wrists in her lap. "It's interesting you think Dr. Chapman had your best interests at heart though."

"I think you're vile." I was white hot, and nothing could stop me from burning that shit down. "I think you're a heartless cunt. I'm a *thing* to you. A new trinket on your shelf. You think I'm your fucking gravy train, and I think this hokey Indian crap is all for show unless sleeping with that blanket's going to give me smallpox."

"Let's talk about—"

"Fuck you."

"Your feelings are—"

"Fuck you."

"Fiona, this is—"

"Fuck you."

"Deacon contacted the hospital."

"Fuck you."

"He wanted to see you."

She'd done it. She'd stopped my torrent of hate with a sliver of hope. "This is a trick. I—"

"I told him that until you participated fully in your therapy, he would not be allowed in."

"What?"

"Tell me, Fiona, would you allow him here if you were on this side of the desk? Your last violent episode outside these walls involved him. You've blocked out the memory of it. Seeing him could open floodgates you're not prepared to—"

At the word floodgates, I was finished. Floodgates had opened all right. I remembered it very clearly. The pressure on my right foot as I stood, the pressure of the hard wooden desk on my left knee, the feeling of falling as I straightened my leg on her desk, my thrust forward as I made sure to get my arms out in time to latch my hands around her motherfucking lying throat.

I think I was screaming, which must have been what saved that bitch's life.

Chapter 23

ELLIOT

LIKE ANY SELF-RESPECTING monied hippie from San Francisco, Jana was
in therapy. And like any functioning neurotic, she didn't reveal the
depths of her neuroses until we were deeply involved.

My father said my time in seminary had made me too concerned, too
warm, too compassionate to see what was face value to everyone else,
but my father had never been known for his humanity, only his data
analysis and domineering attitude. The data told him Jana was beautiful,
and his dominance told him she was a handful.

In the sweet opening months of our relationship, while I was doing
good work in a chaplaincy at Alondra House in Compton, Jana was my
refuge. She didn't want to talk about my work, making my time with her
restful. We cooked together, played volleyball on the beach, and sat on
my porch and drank beer into the night, watching the West Hollywood
partiers traipse up and down the block.

But I couldn't keep work and life separated forever. A mother I'd
been treating at Alondra had been pimping out her son for drugs. He

was eight. I reported it, and the ensuing threats from her gang were pretty frightening. I understood fear as well as the next person. I understood that no one wanted to put someone they loved in the way of hurt, but I wouldn't let an eight-year-old have sex with men in exchange for his mother's drugs.

Sorry.

That had been six months ago, and though the boy had been taken to foster care, and the gang calmed, Jana still bled fear, and I spent most of my free time torn between a desire to soothe her and a compulsion to run away.

"Good morning," Jana said when I came downstairs. She was dressed in an embroidered jacket and suede skirt she and no one else could pull off. Her light brown hair was pulled back in the front and allowed to drape in the back. She was the assistant head of upper school at a swanky little private school, where self expression was the selling point and rigid academics were the reality.

"Hey," I said, refusing the coffee she handed me. "I'm running late."

The TV was on an entertainment news show. Another Drazen story about Fiona. The same clip we'd all seen a hundred times: her approaching a black Range Rover with her pierced nipples exposed by her unbuttoned shirt. Knowing the story behind the famous shot didn't make it any less compelling when she winked at the cameras before closing the door.

"Uhm," Jana said, snapping my attention from the TV. "I thought you left at eight thirty?"

"I have a working mother who needs to meet at eight, or she loses her job." I shrugged into my jacket. I don't know what satisfaction I got out of being sharp with her.

"Okay, I wanted to tell you we're looking for a school counselor," she said. "Psychological counselor, and I thought..."

I was intimidating her. I knew it from her expression and the way her sentence drifted off. I hated that. I hated thinking she didn't feel as though she could express herself freely because of my reaction. I put my arms around her. "You thought, 'Elliot doesn't have anything steady, so he might like it?'"

"Yeah. I have your resume. I can just shoot it to Mary."

I kissed her, her apple lip balm leaving residue on my mouth. "Sure. Send it over."

Chapter 24

FIONA

I WOULDN'T SAY I woke. I didn't actually wake up. I more or less flew over the clouds, dipped below, went back above them and in them. The swash of soft white light hit me in the face as I felt the movement of my body, but not a change in my visual field.

Only my pussy grounded me. Somehow, while my senses were dulled, the throb of arousal became a focal point around which everything else swirled. The physical affected the mental, and the pressure between my legs demanded action.

I opened my eyes. The room around my bed was white with microsuede walls. The floor was a warm linoleum without a seam or disturbance. The fiberglass ceiling had three disks of soft lighting, one with a plastic dome around it. A camera for sure. A sparkling clean toilet. The door was closed, sealed, locked, and there was no window in it.

Solitary.

I snaked my right hand under my waistband because I couldn't think until I rubbed out my exploding clit. Once past my Westonwood-approved undergarments, I felt a sting.

I was sore. Very sore. Red, raw, Sunday morning sore. I put the fingers of my left hand to my nose and smelled pussy. Whatever this stupid drug was, I'd been conscious enough to masturbate for however long I'd been in that room, and still I needed it.

I looked at the corners of the bed. Restraints were hanging from the corners, so they had chosen to keep my hands free. They let me beat myself raw. Maybe they even wanted it. Well, I wouldn't give them what they wanted.

I sat up and looked around, but there was nothing else to see. How long had I been in there? No way to know. I didn't have a watch. I would have had to be conscious to take a meal, and I was sure they weren't interested in starving me.

I looked at the camera, waving. "Hey! Hungry."

I wasn't really, but I wanted to get a reaction out of someone, somewhere. I slid off the cot and stepped forward, cringing. It became easy then to figure out how long I'd been in that room. Some time before I got really hungry, and some time after I rubbed my clit so sore I couldn't walk.

I peed in the little bowl and washed my hands in the little white sink. Were they watching? I was sure they were. Lucky for me I didn't care.

"Hey!" I shouted at the camera. "Was that fun? Watching me piss? It hurt too. You know, for once, I wish you'd have tied me down."

I paced the room, thinking that getting tied down had a purpose. This was punishment. I was being punished for trying to choke my therapist. God, I wanted Elliot. I threw myself on the cot, wanting him. All my sexual fantasies of him went out the window. I wanted to sit across his desk and talk, or lie on the couch and listen to him count backward.

Three.

Two.

One.

DEACON HAS TIED me and left me longer than usual.

It's an asymmetrical knotting, a demonstration for Martin. I'm in underpants and a tank top, not that both of them haven't seen and done plenty to my body before. Today is strictly clinical. Supposedly.

I face the ceiling. My right knee is tied bent and looped so my knee is connected to my neck. Left leg extended and connected to my left wrist. Right arm behind my back. Ropes around my jaw, holding my mouth open, and my head connected to the suspending rope.

The crotch of my panties has shifted, as they often do, so that air hits between my legs, and I feel the coolness of moisture drying. Deacon's voice becomes a hum. He shows Martin how to knot, his hands touching my skin where the rope dents it, demonstrating the right tightness and the way to handle a sub without hurting her. Martin's hands, careless and dangerous, fix the ropes at my inner thigh. His eyes are on me as if I'm some object, some fuckthing, the thought of it burning like a rage. He wants me today. I feel it in the way his fingers linger on me.

I can't talk or move, and I'm as swelled as I've ever been. I'm deep in subspace, surrendered to my arousal and my master as he uses me like a doll to teach Martin shibari.

Deacon, whose hands I know even if I can't see him, pulls on a rope, and I swing back and forth like a pendulum. I hear Martin leave as, in my mind, the color of my cunt streaks the air in an arc, the shape of heaven. When I wind down to a small slice of a circle, Deacon put his hands on my shoulders and stops me.

"He is not to touch you, ever," he says, running his hands down my prone body. "He has no control. I'm dropping him when I get back." He pulls the rope from my mouth, leaving me with a taste of hemp.

"Yes, Sir."

"You look beautiful."

"I feel… God, I feel everything."

"How are the ropes?"

"Fine, Sir."

He stands between my legs in a button shirt and jeans, looking at the angles of my body. "You're the most perfect model I've ever had." He puts his hands on my stomach and rests them on my breasts. He strokes the points of my nipples, ending in a pinch and a pull on the rings. "Every time I fuck you, I want to possess you. Your pleasure, your pain. Look." He yanks on the nipple rings, and I strain against my bonds.

"How sweet to control you with two pieces of metal and some rope. Do you want me to fuck you?"

"Please."

He slides his finger along my slit, the backs of his fingers on my clit. "Open your eyes." He puts two fingers in me, then three, and my eyes flutter open. His hands are instruments of desire. "Look at me."

I do. He's backlit against the window, and his gaze on me is like ten hands. He takes his fingers out of me and licks them then brushes his thumb over my lips.

"Who do you taste?" he whispers, but his voice has the command of a shout.

"I taste us."

He puts four cunt-soaked fingers down my throat, then slides them out and grabs my jaw, pressing my tongue down with his fingertips. He leans over and speaks in my ear, saying the words he always says before he fucks me, sending me to a place where I surrender all anxiety to him.

"Empty your heart, my kitten. Empty your mind. Open your eyes. Who do you see?" His fingers slide out of my mouth and rest on my throat.

"You," I croak.

"Are you empty?"

"I am."

"Release your body to me. I have you."

He pulls out his dick with his other hand and puts it right at my opening.

"I could watch you all day," he says as he slides in. I groan. "And I might."

He pulls his cock out and presses it against me. His grip on my jaw is tight and painful, and when he slaps my breast before yanking on the ring, I feel a surge between my legs. He slaps again, each one a sting of love.

I am outside myself, in pleasure and pain. He is gentle, for Deacon, even when he put his cock so deep in me it hurts. He doesn't move, using the gravity of the suspension to keep the pressure on. He yanks on a rope, then another, until I am upright. He puts his hand back on my mouth and shifts until the whole of my weight is on him. He's in so deep, not moving, not thrusting, just digging.

"I'm staying like this," he says. "Inside you, until I let you come." Drool drips between us, landing on his stomach. "You're a little whore, kitten, but you're my little whore. Do you understand? I own this mouth. I can fuck it with my hand until you drool. I own this ass, and I'll put a hook in it when I like. Your cunt is mine to fuck with anything I want."

I agree in spittle and grunts. I'm so close, but he's moving so little, it could take forever.

He pulls his hand from my mouth and draws it across my cheek, leaving a trail of drying spit. "You're my prized possession." He thrusts get longer and stronger. He puts his nose to mine as I shift further and further from conscious. "Say it."

"I'm yours." He knows something about the surrender of ownership, the delegation of will, turns me on, and the pressure of pleasure is near explosive.

"Again."

"I belong to you." I gasp between every word. He's so strong, so real, and I feel as if I'm made of foam. "May I come, Sir?"

"Say it."

"I would die without you, Deacon."

"Do you want to come?"

"I would die."

I feel him smile against my cheek, and I think of how we'd started and what we became. Back in that blank room, my fingers rolled over my sore, aching clit on the toilet of the solitary room in a mental hospital.

<hr>

Chapter 25

<hr>

FIONA

A MEAL with a little cup of meds came through the flap in the bottom of the door. It was the usual gourmet shit, eaten on the edge of my bed. I took my meds and slid the tray back out. I'd had two meals in that room, one with eggs and another with a sandwich. I'd masturbated twice more, but the last time, I couldn't come because of the pain.

I spent most of the time sitting on the edge of the bed, wondering when they'd let me out. I slept. I thought about my life, everything in it, and all the rotten things I'd done. I'd stolen Amanda's boyfriend in high school, luring him away with the promise and delivery of a blow job. I'd played it off, because who wanted a man who could be taken away so easily? And the time I fucked Kevin Hartneick and made him cry when I didn't want to anymore. Or inviting Gary Adelstein to join Evan Fronet and me in bed, even after Evan objected. Or my first anal, just before I turned eighteen, when Gary held me down over the kitchen table while he and Evan fucked my ass until I cried like a little bitch.

Afterward, I'd wept on Evan's shoulder, because it had been my fault, hadn't it? I'd hurt his feelings, and I'd wanted that threesome, right? That's what he said when he pushed my mouth onto his cock later that night—that we were even, and I'd gotten the threesome I wanted. If I'd just relaxed, it wouldn't have been painful, and they wouldn't have had to hold me down.

In the white room in Westonwood, there was nothing to distract me. I couldn't even fuck myself. All I could do was stare at that toilet and that little sink and think, *my fucking God, what have I done?* What have I done? What have I done?

When I'd had that hoof knife in my hand, it was the first time in years. I was cleaning Snowcone's sole. It was already pretty clean because Lindsey cared for my horse more than I did, but I got at the loose frog. My hands blistered, and I was crying.

In that room, with nothing but the toilet to tell, I rubbed my hands. There had been blisters. I saw the little rough brown spots where they'd been. I'd been holding that knife that day. Of all the shitty things I'd done, all the backstabbing, heartbreaking, coldhearted shit I'd done, the worst was hurting Deacon.

In that room that had been stripped of everything sensory, I smelled the stables, the manure and dander, the sharp sting of hay. I heard the scrape of the hooves as I cleaned them. Snowcone, so good, so warm, had taken a minute to remember me. I'd been afraid he'd kick me, so I sat where he couldn't reach. The fear was there, right in the rib that always hurt when I thought of how he'd kicked me last time.

I thought over and over about how I'd abandoned him. How intolerant and hateful I was to dump my responsibilities on Lindsay.

I remembered that night. The dark, the crickets, the fear, the anxiety, the self-loathing. I'd been dead sober. And sad because Deacon and I had broken up. The sharp pain in my wrist reminded me of the breakup, and I thought to myself that I deserved it. That pain was mine. I'd brought it on myself. I scraped too hard, thinking about it, and Snowcone let me know I'd ventured into unacceptable territory by shifting in a way that made me jump.

When I did, I noticed someone behind me, and I sat bolt upright.

It was the door of the white room opening, and Frances walking in.

I didn't remember how many days I'd been in there, if I'd been hopped up on meds or if it had been half a day without meds and just me and the boredom. But I felt changed by the white emptiness, sent through some kind of process that had changed me enough to remember what I'd chosen to forget.

Though I knew it was Frances, I was muddled, somehow still in the scene at the stables, and Frances became the person who'd surprised me. As if propelled to act out the memory, I stabbed her twice in the chest with the knife of my imagination.

Chapter 26

ELLIOT

JANA WAS CUTTING open a head of broccoli when I got home. I was nine minutes late, and I hadn't called. I only called if I was ten minutes late, and by the time I turned north on LaCienega, I knew I'd make it inside my no-call window.

And I didn't want to talk to anyone.

"Hi," I said, kissing the top of her head. "How was school?"

"Fine. And your day? How was it?"

"Fine," I said. Fine meant I'd only been slightly beaten down by the events at The Alondra Clinic, where my skills were useless against the constant barrage of suffering. Cushy Westonwood, where the psychic pain had a different cause and the same result, was a cakewalk. "How did the testing meeting go?"

"The fourth-grade teachers want more latitude." I flipped through the mail as she spoke. "The parents' association thinks it's a great idea. But when their kids' scores are low and they can't get into middle school, who gets in trouble?" She pointed at herself with the knife.

I still didn't want to talk to her or anyone, but it looked as though it would be an okay evening. "And Mary Queen of Scots? Did you talk to her?"

"No." She chopped broccoli with a slap. Mary was the head of school, and Jana wanted more control over admissions.

"You should talk to her."

"I did. Your Westonwood experience wasn't on your resume."

I hadn't meant that. I meant she should talk to her boss about what she wanted out of her job.

"You must have sent me the old one by accident," she said.

Freud would have said it was no accident. He would have said I'd known damn well the one piece of experience Mary wanted to see wasn't on the resume I told Jana to forward. What did that say about me?

"I thought you had an updated one, sorry."

"I had a thought," she said, sliding the knife over the cutting board. She glanced at me flirtatiously.

"Really?" I pushed her hair from her neck. She had a lovely neck.

"If you went back to St. Paul's, you could reorganize the discernment committee."

"No," I whispered. I didn't want a committee of good Episcopalian laypeople to decide my future. That last step needed to be mine and mine alone.

"If they approve you, you could get ordained. You could have something steady."

"That's not a reason to give your life to God."

She set down her knife, and I felt her jaw tighten against my lips.

"You complain about suffering and God, and then you go to Alondra where there's nothing but suffering," she said. "It's like you're sticking your face in it out of spite."

I pulled away. I wanted to talk about baseball, or the state of the garden, or traffic patterns at rush hour. The last thing I wanted was an exegesis on earthly suffering. "There's suffering everywhere." Fiona, my little countertransference case, flashed on the screen in my mind. Her suffering was nothing like mine, and of a different grade than any I'd seen.

Jana picked up her knife. After tapping it on the cutting board once, as if releasing her negative feelings, she smiled. "Do you want the spicy sauce with the chicken? Or the mustard?"

"Spicy is fine." I headed to the bedroom to change out of my work clothes.

Jana called to me as I walked. "You were late. I was worried."

I pretended not to hear her. I didn't know why I was so grouchy. Traffic. Low blood sugar. Overwhelmed. Late getting home. Jana's dresser drawer was half open, which made me nuts, and the light in the bathroom was on. Normally those things didn't bother me, but that evening, as I took my jacket off, I walked a razor's edge.

The phone rank. It was Frances's extension from Westonwood. She had no reason to call me. I'd taken an indefinite sabbatical, and the paperwork was all in order.

"Dr. Chapman?" she said.

"Hello, Dr. Ramone."

"I'm sorry to bother you."

"It's fine."

"Your patient, Fiona Drazen, says she remembers what happened the day she was brought in."

I wasn't supposed to be moved by curiosity or anything else. A therapist was simply a vessel for what the patient found important. Curiosity made the therapist's desires more important than the patient's, and that wasn't acceptable.

Except damn, I was curious.

"Really?" I said. "That's interesting."

"She'll only tell you though."

I sighed. I didn't mean for it to be audible, because though one might assume it was a sigh of resignation, it was a sigh of relief.

Chapter 27

FIONA

I DON'T KNOW how long I was in there, but I was peeled off Frances, given a shot of something, and left on the floor. That would've sucked shit out of a dead dog's ass if whatever was in that needle hadn't made me care about exactly nothing. I was high as a kite, living between sleep and wakefulness, completely aware yet unable to control my own thoughts or body. At least the pain of arousal was gone, like a candle snuffed with spit-wet fingers.

Over and over, I went back to the moment I'd attacked Deacon because I'd been frightened. I discovered details, scents, sounds, and I found peace in it. I'd done it as some sort of reaction to the night, not out of anger. Not in some Machiavellian vision of sharp premeditation. It was just some crazy shit where I was startled and stabbed him.

A little voice piped in through the scene. *Who does this? Have you ever heard of this happening before? Why would this make sense?*

But that voice didn't want me to be happy. That voice was my father with his critical disappointment and my sisters with their distaste.

No, fear made the most sense.

"Fiona."

I came around enough to feel the hard floor beneath me, my cheek on cold linoleum.

"Fiona."

That voice again. Soft putty. The thick fat at the top of the cream jar.

"Doctor," I said with a chapped voice.

He crouched beside me with his elbows on his knees, his wrists dangling. "I see your therapy is coming along."

"I've been proactive about my well-being." I don't know how I put the sentence together, but it slid out, and he smiled. "Are you back?"

"It's complicated."

"Be back."

"I'm not coming back unless you play ball."

I got up on an elbow, and the world swam until Elliot looked as if he was doing a sidestroke when he righted me.

"I'll play."

"You're going to need to rest."

"I remember it," I said. "What happened at the stables. I remember the whole thing."

"And? It makes you feel good or bad?"

Therapist to the core. Facts were fine, but feelings ruled.

"Good," I said. "Great even."

"Focus on that for now."

My brain was cloudy, but I was awake enough to be suspicious of what I had been asked to focus on.

———————————

Chapter 28

———————————

ELLIOT

 Deena said.

She sat at the round lunch table, a ball of white waxed paper and a half-eaten prosciutto and buratta sandwich in front of her. She'd picked off the arugula.

"You're not getting a response. I don't see the benefit of keeping you on it." I leaned my back on the counter and crossed my arms. The grey room, with its workers' comp poster and featureless cabinets, had been the scene of many a discussion about patients when I worked at Westonwood, and I fell right back into it.

"A real response takes time, not parlor tricks."

She was referring to hypnosis, which wasn't a trick. I didn't need to defend myself against her for another minute, but I had to get through her first. It begged the question of why I was doing it in the first place.

"How long do you think she's going to be here?" I said. "This isn't a long-term facility."

"What do you want out of this, Elliot? Don't you have souls to save?"

Frances burst in carrying a stack of folders. She attacked the refrigerator and grabbed a wrapped burrito from the freezer. "Dr. Chapman, thanks for coming."

"Frances," Deena said, wrapping up the remainder of her sandwich with a loud crackle. "Do you know—"

"I know everything. It's my job." She threw the burrito in the microwave and slammed the door. "What's not my job is getting attacked. So, first. The family wants her out. Why? I don't know. But the pressure's making it hard to run this hospital."

I didn't know why either. Frances set the timer with three loud beeps, and the machine hissed and creaked.

"They want her out to care for her," Deena said.

"Oh, please," I mumbled.

"First they want her in, then they want her out. I've got whiplash already." Frances was in rare form. The pressure was really getting to her. "I'd lock my kids in a box before I let them face that media circus."

"They're oddly unprotective," I said.

"She needs us to protect her," Deena said.

"Not our job," Frances cut in. "My first responsibility is to this facility. If you ask me, they don't want two kids in here at the same time. It looks bad. So that leads us to the second thing. The judge is irrelevant after thirty days. So as much as he wants her here in spite of everything— because he's in the media circus too, and he wants her off his docket— he's got less say once she can put sentences together and not choke random people. Like her therapist."

"Or her brother," I said.

The microwave beeped. Frances opened the door.

"She has a problem with men," Deena exclaimed as if she'd hit gold. "Having him here could unleash a torrent of old feelings."

"The only misandrist in the room is you, Deena," I said.

She stood like a shot, knocking over the chrome-and-plastic chair. "That is—"

"True," I said. "It's—"

Frances slammed the microwave door. "Enough. Just, enough. I have a budget to put together, and I have a major donor's kid in solitary, and I just got attacked by a hundred-ten-pound heiress, and I'm hungry. Dr.

Chapman, do you have room in your schedule to finish this? I know you left, but I'm on my knees."

"No, you're not."

"Don't split hairs."

"I want her off the Paxil."

"Frances," Deena said, "please, I can do this."

"Deal," she said to me before turning to Deena. "No, you can't. I'm sorry, but I need this to run smoothly."

"I'll do it," I said without thinking. At the very least, Jana would be happy about my impulsive decision.

"Thank you."

"Can I do the brother then?" Deena asked.

Frances and I spoke together. "No!"

Chapter 29

FIONA

JONATHAN WAS in the rec room playing ping pong with a wall. Between the reddish hair, his height, and his fluid motion, he was hard for me to miss. The ball hit his paddle with a *thup*, then the wall and the table with a *crackcrack*.

He was a grown man. He'd been the baby, the little boy king for as long as I'd known him. But seeing him there, knocking that ball back and forth, with his arms and shoulders broad and built, I realized how much time had gone by. I felt old.

"Hey," I said, sitting on the windowsill next to the table.

The table was bent in the middle like an L, and he was beating the ball against the other side. He moved fast and never even seemed close to missing.

"Hi," he said, eyes on the ball.

"How are you feeling?"

He didn't answer. *thup crackcrack*

"You look good," I said.

"You want something?"

thup crackcrack

"We're imprisoned together. I thought I'd say hello."

"Hello."

He looked like a man, but he was a boy.

thup crackcrack

"Who's your therapist?"

thup crackcrack

"Guy named Rogers."

thup crackcrack thup

"Don't tell him anything."

crackcrack He caught the ball midair. "What?"

"They're out to use us," I said.

"You're nuts, Fee." He knocked the ball against the table and started again. "Nuts, but I never had you for paranoid."

thup crackcrack

"And what happened with you?" I asked. "I mean, Jesus, Jonathan. Were you really trying to end it?"

thup crackcrack

"You muscling in on my therapist's territory?"

"I just don't understand."

thup crackcrack

"You're really bad at this," he said.

"I'm your sister. I want to know."

"It's none of your business."

thup crackcrack

"Was it Dad? Was it that he was with Rachel when she—"

He smacked the ball onto the horizontal surface, sending it flying to the ceiling. "Shut up!"

"Take it easy, Jon."

"Take it easy? Sure, I'll take advice from you. You're a fucking out-of-control druggie party girl doing God knows what. I don't even want to say more because you're my sister, but I read the papers, okay? You disappear for months, show up at Easter, and no one's seen you since. Even the fucking paparazzi can't find you. Then you're arrested, and shit explodes. Now you want to tell me to keep it under control? I don't even want to be seen with you."

"I know what I am, Jon. I know damn well what I am, and I know better than you who to be seen with when, which was why you didn't hear from me for months. Okay? And fuck you too."

"I asked them to keep you away from me," he said, pointing the ping-pong paddle at me. "You get on my last fucking nerve."

He was a boy in a man's body. I knew about plenty of his exploits. He was at least as out of control as I was. I tried to keep myself from reacting strongly, because I knew someone, somewhere was watching closely. I didn't have to break my gaze with my brother to know it. I took a deep breath. He was family, which made us especially prone to poking at our raw places.

"I just got out of solitary," I said, dropping my voice. "I was in for two days, and it felt like a week. Keep your shit together. In here, losing control has a price. They're paid good money, and they'll do what they want. They will drug you and lock you down. They will restrain you for as long as they want."

It paid to be an older sister, because in his face, I saw that something had gotten through. His arms were still taut and his chin still jutted out, but on some level, he'd accepted the gift I gave him.

"Promise me," I said, holding out my arms. "Promise you'll try to keep it together."

He put his paddle down and accepted my embrace. "I can't believe she's dead. It's my fault. What this family did to her was so wrong. I couldn't live with it. They euthanize animals, and that's what I am."

"Were you driving?"

"I was so drunk, I don't remember."

Then, as if blindsided with a pie to the face in front of a large studio audience, I laughed.

He pulled away. "What? I…"

I just kept laughing. I pointed at myself, then at him. "It's genetic," I squeaked then held out my hands. "Drazen Dementia."

It wasn't funny. Not really. It was very sad, but he got it. Though he didn't laugh as hard as I did, he chuckled and picked up his little white ball.

thup crackcrack

Chapter 30

FIONA

I COULDN'T BELIEVE I was sitting in front of Elliot again. After talking to Jonathan, I'd showered and eaten before my afternoon session, trying not to think my most sexual Elliot thoughts. He'd see them, or I'd slip, and I didn't want him to know.

Some of his things had been removed from the office, but the fixtures and furniture were the same. The lighting was still warm, and he looked exactly the same.

"You need a haircut," I said.

"I'll get right on that."

"I'm glad you're back."

"Well, I'm not fully back. I'm back for you, but I still have duties at my other job," he said.

"I feel special."

"You are special, but it's simply a matter of redressing a wrong. I shouldn't have left things unfinished with you. I should have known better."

"So why did you do it?"

He shifted his pen on his desk three quarters of an inch. "I had pressure in my personal life."

Two words in, I knew he'd prepared his answer very carefully.

"Really? Someone didn't like you working with the rich kids?"

"My girlfriend wants me here."

I tightened when he said he had a girlfriend. Men who dug ditches didn't work harder than I worked to hide the shot of adrenaline that went through my system.

"Okay?" I said. "So you should be here then."

"It would be inappropriate for me to get deeply into it, but I can't do things to please other people. Things came to a head at home just as my recommendation for you was due. The other job came up, I felt I was needed there, and I finished here. But I wasn't. I'm not finished with you at all."

He couldn't have meant it the way it sounded, with his eyes on me as they were. He couldn't have intended to send a stinging rush of fluid between my legs or to set my nipples on end. My throat closed. I had no words, and I always had words. No man in the history of my cunt had ever rendered me speechless.

"I'm told you're not sleeping," he said.

"It's not out of spite."

"Does this happen often? Insomnia?"

I shrugged, looking out the window. The sight of him distracted me. "Sometimes, when Deacon was away. Other times, when there was a lot going on. I get stressed, you know."

"You're on Ambien."

"It's not working. Halcion works."

"It's very habit forming," he said.

"So is talking to you." Talk about habits! Coming on to an attractive man just because I could, even with my little Velcro-closure shoes and V-neck scrubs with no tie at the waistband. I laughed softly in a little huff of breath. I was a mystery even to myself. I needed sleep, and I needed sex. "Deena said Deacon wanted to see me."

"Yes."

"Well?"

"Well, what?"

"Are you letting him come?" I asked.

"I'll meet with him first. Then if I feel that you aren't a danger to each other, and you still want to see him, you can see him."

"I want to see him."

"What do you think he'll say?"

He wanted to know how I felt about Deacon and where we were in our relationship. What he didn't know was that I was so happy about the visit that I didn't care what Deacon would say. I wanted to suck Elliot's cock for just allowing it.

"I think he'll say lots of things."

"Such as?"

I leaned forward, putting my elbows on the desk and the heels of my hands on my cheeks. "He'll tell me I look nice."

"What if he tells you what happened at the stables?"

"I know what happened. I was there scraping Snowcone's hoof. It was late. When he came in, the horse shifted. I had been afraid Snowcone was going to kick me, and I had an adrenaline rush. When I saw a man standing behind me, I went after him with the knife. I guess I freaked out. I mean, stabbing your Dom is not a small deal."

"And you came up with this when?"

"In solitary. I kind of tranced out and remembered."

"You used self hypnosis. That's good, mostly."

I didn't care about the conversation. My body felt aligned with his, poles of energy wanting to attract into a wider, stronger bolt of life. Maybe he felt it and maybe he denied it, but it was there. Sex was my superpower, and I knew when a man wanted me.

"Why mostly?" I ran my fingertip over his desk, considering the ridge between the blotter and the wood with a lazy intensity.

"Mostly, because your memory makes no sense. It has to jibe. I've been startled before, but that goes away in an instant."

"You think I made it up?"

"False memories under hypnosis are pretty common, and they're always in the subject's favor."

Wait, he was implying that the stabbing was premeditated? Was that it? Or was it that I was lying to myself? That the relief I felt was false and based on nothing? Bullshit. I knew that memory was right. *Knew.* The fucker… Was he trying to keep me here, or was he just trying to get some kind of upper hand?

I kept calm and sighed. I pushed a pen a couple of inches before popping it in his cup. He was right across the desk, and I wanted him to take me like his little vanilla whore.

"I think I know what Deacon's going to say," I said.

"Go on."

I leaned forward, my butt barely on the chair, and made my voice milkshake thick. "Kitten, you've been so bad. So very naughty. Do you think I won't punish you? My sweet little slut, you do these things so I'll hurt you. So I'm going to have to now. Let me tell you what we're going to do when you're back. You're going into my office. You're going to bend over the desk, pull your panties down halfway, and spread your legs. There will be a paddle on the desk. You will place it on your lower back. Then you're going to wait. When I come to you, I will take the paddle. You're getting a full twenty strokes on your bottom and the backs of your thighs with it, kitten. Call out the numbers as I do it. You are not to scream. You may spit, you may cry, but you may not shout. You may only thank me. When I've done twenty, you are to take your ass cheeks in your hands and spread yourself for me. Your fingers on your raw skin will burn, but I don't want to hear any complaints. No crying. No blubbering. You may beg me to fuck you. When I believe you mean it, I'll take you. I'll push your face to the desk when I'm fucking your cunt, then your tight little ass. I'll bury myself in you until your skin is too tight to take me, and I want nothing but gratitude when I come on your back, do you understand?"

I watched Elliot's face and saw nothing. Not a blip.

"You must think he's very angry at you."

"That's what he'll say if he's *not* angry. If he's pissed, well, he won't make promises. I know him." I waited for a response and thought I saw a flicker of emotion. I expected disgust, which was how most people reacted to a relationship like Deacon and I shared, but it wasn't that.

"Session over," he said. "See you in the morning."

Chapter 31

ELLIOT

I SLAMMED the door behind me and locked it, fumbling with my belt and zipper as if I was an adolescent twisting the last few moves of a Rubik's Cube.

My dick was swollen purple, the skin stretched over throbbing blood vessels. The pressure on my balls was enormous, as if a million troops stormed the gate. I stroked myself over the toilet three times then exploded, biting back a grunt as I unleashed a torrent onto the back of the lid. It was more than a release, the pleasure of it lasting beyond a simple discharge.

My mind wasn't my own. I let it make the pictures Fiona had called up, her pink ass under my hands, her cries, her legs restrained by her clothing, her body stiffening with a wet grunt when she came, crying my name then whispering it like a prayer.

God help me.

Chapter 32

FIONA

ONE OF THE rec rooms overlooked the front of the grounds. I knew he was coming. I knew Elliot would call right after the session, and Deacon wouldn't delay a second to see me. When I saw my master's black Range Rover come around the front drive and pass into the parking lot, I felt as if a hundred interlocking pieces had fallen into place.

I said it, I meant it, things happened as predicted. That was what it was to have Deacon in my life.

"Hey, someone here?" Karen was behind me, toting her IV tower. The sun blasting through the windows made her look hollow.

I wanted to hold her down and force-feed her a cupcake. "Deacon."

She stood next to me and peered out the window. We'd heard much about each other's lives in the past weeks. I'd have even have called her a friend at that point.

She leaned over beside me. "I can get you Halcion."

"How?" I whispered back.

"Warren's out for his sister's wedding. He's getting me something. I can put in an order for you."

I looked at her skull of a face, blue eyes bulging without flesh to hold them in. She'd been so pretty when I met her.

"What is he getting you?" I asked.

"Something I need and they won't give me."

"Please tell me it's not uppers."

"I have a mother already."

I dropped my voice to barely a whisper. "You don't need diet pills, Karen."

"Do you want the Halcion or not?"

Deacon gave the valet his keys and headed for the door. He buttoned his jacket and walked in that way only Deacon could, a mix of fierce intention and poise, a stew of dignity and ruthlessness.

"He's beautiful," she whispered.

"A thoroughbred."

As if his inner GPS had a little red dot homed in on my location, he looked up at me as he crossed the drive. I put my finger to the glass. He smiled and held up a finger, pressing it against an imaginary glass pane between us. He got closer to the building, and when I could only see the top of his head, he disappeared from sight.

I hadn't realized how anxious I'd been until I couldn't see him. Like the hum of a car engine that didn't bother you until it was gone, the thrum of my heart stopped and the pain disappeared. Karen put her arm around me because I'd put my hand to my mouth to hold back the tears.

"It's okay," she said, not even knowing why I was emotional.

"He's not mad," I said. "He still loves me, and he's not mad."

I would have said that nothing could disrupt his love for me. Not even a hoof knife twice in the chest. But seeing him smile and put up that finger, I realized I'd been crushed with worry. When that worry disappeared, the space it occupied was filled with joy. I hugged Karen, rattling her tubes, and she gave me a rare laugh.

"I'm just…" I started but couldn't finish. "I can actually breathe without pain. I have to get used to it." I threw myself onto the light grey couch.

Karen sat next to me carefully, so as not to disrupt her IV. "You're relieved."

"Yeah. I feel like everything's under control again."

"He did that with a look?"

"That's us."

"Maybe you'll sleep now."

"No. Just have Warren get the pills. I'll pay him when I get out."

Karen waved the idea away. "He doesn't want money. He has plenty. He'll ask for a favor or something. He just wants friends. He's lonely."

"Okay." I craned my neck to watch the valet drive Deacon's car into the lot.

"Aren't you going to run down and see him?" asked Karen.

"Elliot wanted to meet with him first. I guess to make sure he won't upset me. Which, I mean, I know he won't now. So they'll schedule a visiting time and, oh God, this is so great."

I leaned back on the couch, and Karen sat straight up. She looked tired and wrung out. Her battle with food wasn't going well. She said the only time she felt in control was when she wasn't eating. She was defined by her refusal, and when she accepted food, she felt indefinite, sloppy, out of control.

I knew plenty about her life. Before Amanda died, we'd had a lot in common, between the drugs and the sex. Food wasn't what should have made her feel out of control, but who was I to judge?

"I wish I had a Deacon," she said.

"One day, you might."

I felt like the queen of the ball.

Chapter 33

ELLIOT

I HAD to get to Alondra, but I had to meet Deacon. Frances had offered to take the meeting, but protocol be damned, I didn't trust her motives. Mostly though, after Fiona's monologue about pain and pleasure, I found myself driven by an unprofessional level of curiosity again.

He wasn't what I expected.

I'd expected a dirtbag in a wifebeater and camo. I expected a trashy goatee and a flashy car. Mostly, I expected to look at him and wonder how he could make a slave of a woman who could have any man she wanted.

But he wasn't any of those things. He was wealthy, obviously. His jacket fit as if it was custom made, and his hair fell in a conservative drape. His face hadn't been shaved in a day or so, but it was the style. He carried himself with assurance. I couldn't see the valet's position, as he was behind the hedge with someone else, but Deacon seemed to sense his presence. He didn't concern himself with the valet until he was close enough to hand over his keys. Deacon seemed at one with the space around him, at peace and in control.

I knew the patients looked out the east window to see who was visiting, and when he looked and held a finger to the upper floor, I knew he must have seen her. In that gesture, much of my curiosity was sated. Another tangle of emotions took its place.

"Mister Bruce," I introduced myself as he approached reception. "I'm Dr. Chapman."

"Nice to meet you."

We shook hands. He looked me in the eye. Two gentlemen trying to protect the same woman, probably from each other.

I led him to my office and showed him the chair in front of my desk. In a last millisecond decision, I didn't sit behind the desk but in the chair next to his.

"I notice an accent," I said.

"I'm Afrikaner. From the south." He said it with a thick Dutch accent. I could almost hear the k. "I grew up on a farm about two hundred clicks outside Queenstown."

"I've never been."

"To Queenstown?"

"To Africa."

He smirked, and I felt like an ignorant American.

"How long have you been in Los Angeles?" I asked.

"A few years. Business takes me back every few months, to the DRC mostly. Not home."

"May I ask your business?"

"I run a photography agency. Photojournalists working in risky assignments. We hire photographers, buy ransom insurance, track them down if they don't check in, liaison with embassies, negotiate terms of release, this sort of thing."

"Terms of release?"

"When they're kidnapped. The authorities are as useless there as anywhere else." He said it with cold aplomb, as if reminding me of something I had forgotten.

"Ah," I said. It wasn't a question, but an opening for more. It was a hole in which the other person was supposed to pour information, and it usually worked.

In the case of Deacon Bruce, something else happened. "How is she?"

"Without betraying a confidence, she's better. She came in confused. She's gotten her bearings, and she's managing. She's still struggling with her memory of what happened that night."

He nodded.

"I assume you remember?" I asked.

"I tripped and fell."

"You always so clumsy?"

"I get my coordination from my mother's side. Dutch, you know?" He smiled ruefully, and I knew I wouldn't get anywhere with him. "I'm concerned about Fiona. She's not violent. Fiesty, sure. And strong. Very strong. Almost impossibly so. It's not like her to snap. I want you to know, I want her out of here as much as she probably wants out, but I'm not going to push for it. If you think my visit will cause her stress before she's ready, you need to say so. I have no problem staying away until she's ready."

"I honestly don't know when she's going to be ready. And I'm going to be honest about something else."

"Please."

"I'm concerned that she attacked you because she was harboring some anger toward you. Apparently there was a violent incident?"

He smiled again and leaned back in his chair to one side, as if tucking himself in a corner to get comfortable. He was almost laughing.

The mockery burned me as much as the fact that I had to explain myself. "I'm not talking about anything associated with consensual—"

"This is something she told you?"

"I can't explain further. She came in here with a cracked molar and nerve damage to her wrist."

He pressed his lips together and nodded. Though I sensed a bit of guilt in the expression, it wasn't defensive. It was remorseful and sad.

"Fiona and I have certain rules, and the rules are there for her safety," he said. "Hurting her for breaking them defeats the purpose, don't you think?"

"So she did break some rule?"

"These rules aren't arbitrary."

"I understand."

"I'm sure you do."

From his tone, I could tell he was sure I didn't understand at all, and he was right. I didn't. Not one bit.

"Fiona needs to channel her energies," he said. "What we developed together does just that."

"What's in it for you?"

"Are you psychoanalyzing me, Doctor?"

"It's hard to resist."

He laughed. "All right," he said, sitting straight in his chair. "I'll give you a gift for your honesty. South African farms are far removed from each other, and when I was younger, we had so much privilege, it never occurred to us to protect them. Until, of course, the situation in my country changed. There were too many unemployed young men for the government to deal with, and these young men, they were angry. They were angry at families with money and land. So they gathered in groups and went into the farmhouses and took what they wanted. The farmers were armed usually. My father was, but he was a peaceful man. Of the seven men who came into our house, he shot only one in the leg. He paid for his kindness with his life. My brother was locked in the basement while my mother and sister were badly abused. Our workers… the people were beaten bloody. Two died. I'd grown up with these men. They were my friends."

"Were you there?"

"I was in Queenstown on business, and one of our foremen came in the morning to tell me. He was covered in blood. By the time I got there, it was too late." For a moment, he stared into the middle distance.

I didn't interrupt with any of the hundred questions stewing.

"What happened right after is irrelevant," he said. "But I am serious about protecting what's mine." He smiled, and his smile ended the discussion. He was very shrewd, very self aware.

Plying him further seemed like a waste of time. I was already missing a meeting at Alondra. More small talk would force me to miss an appointment with a patient.

But who was I kidding? Sure, I needed to get out of there, but I'd already assessed whether or not he was a threat to her. What was at the front of my mind, what made me react in ways I didn't understand, was that he loved her. I couldn't pretend to understand how their relationship worked, but when he said her name and asked about her, when he looked at me as if deciding who I was in her life… He cared about her more deeply than I understood.

"Let me talk to Fiona," I said, standing. "Then I'll get back to you."

"Thank you for your consideration."

When he stood, I saw him slow for a second as he shifted. He'd been stabbed in the chest almost two weeks before with a wide, thick blade, yet he'd shown no signs of injury until that moment. Even then, it was so slight I knew no one who wasn't trained to observe people would have noticed it.

"You'll be restricted to the grounds," I said. "And I'm sorry, but you'll have to be supervised."

"Of course. Wouldn't want her to crack another molar."

He didn't seem the type to joke over something so serious, but the fact that he had sent a chill up my spine.

Chapter 34

FIONA

I SKIPPED lunch to sit at the window. Karen went down to sit in front of a plate of food because she had to, but no such requirements were made of me. I could stare into the grey winter sky and wait.

Deacon was everything to me. What a sad turn of events that someone with a perfectly functioning brain, identified as gifted in third grade, should let her life revolve around a man for her sanity; an unreliable, overcommitted man at that. Worse than a doctor or a cop, there were times he couldn't be around, and I was ill-equipped to deal with them. But that was my fault, wasn't it? A strong woman would have been able to manage during his absences without fucking around, without pissing him off, without breaking every single rule.

But what other man would tolerate my needs? Who else would work with them instead of fighting them? What other person could help me function the way he did?

The goal, once I got out of there, was to either remove Deacon from my life or make sure he didn't leave Los Angeles all the time. Or something between those impossible poles.

I shifted in my chair. The pain in my right wrist ran to my inner elbow. I'd been leaning on it for too long. When Deacon had pinned it against the wall, it had hurt.

But the day he'd showed me how to hold my arms for a knotting, he said that it wouldn't hurt. I'd only realized later that I'd damaged it, so I had to be extra mindful of where the ropes fell before I went into subspace.

He'd knotted me, that time after he returned. The last time. A simple shrimp tie during play, and I'd cringed when he moved my arm.

That was off. If he'd damaged my arm when he pinned it, it wouldn't have hurt until later.

I rubbed my arm. It might never heal. He was very serious about the wrists. Would he have pinned me? Even in anger? And had he held my arm long enough to really injure it?

The soup of questions didn't confuse me, but as I dug into the memory of what happened, it became clear.

HIS BREATH FALLS on my cheek, and a pain in my arm runs from my wrist to the sensitive side of my bicep.

"You did not let someone else knot you," he says from deep in his throat. He's naked, stunning. He pins me to the wall, the friction making the open skin on my ass scream.

Regret. Pounds of it. Miles wide. Regret to the depth of my broken spirit.

"I'm sorry." I am. I'm devastated and ashamed.

"Why?"

My wrist hurts. He's pressing it so hard against the wall, as if I'd leave, as if I'd ever turn my back on him. Yet I want to get away, to run, to show him that I can abandon him the way he abandons me.

I wiggle, but he only presses harder and demands, "Why?"

"Get off me!"

"Tell me why!" His eyes are wider, his teeth flashing as if he wants to rip out my throat. "Why?"

"I need it!" The words come out before I think, and they're poison to him.

Before I expect it, he grabs my jaw, and I feel pain where his fingers press. He looks into me, cutting through me with his eyes, and I want to curl up into a blackened char of desiccation.

He lets me go, and I fall to the floor.

I ALMOST MISSED Deacon come out of the building. The valet handed him his keys, and he took them without moving his face from the window. He looked concerned. I didn't know if he could see me since I'd leaned back in the chair, thinking about the last time we'd been naked together.

He stood still, looking up at me. He wouldn't move out of the driveway until I acknowledged him. It was all over his face and posture. I leaned forward and put my finger to the glass. Seeing me, he smiled and put up a finger.

He needed me.

Chapter 35

ELLIOT

I USED to be happy at Alondra.

Maybe I was freakish to think of it that way. It was impossible to explain how working with such troubled people made me content, but the small victories looked so large. Then I went to Westonwood, and wound up feeling as though the small victories were the same no matter who the patients were. I felt as if the world was full of too much pain to soothe.

After I left Westonwood then went back, I didn't want to be anywhere, and I wanted to be everywhere. My discontent flourished in a garden of anguish and brokenness.

I'd left my chaplaincy at Alondra and put away the collar. I put off ordination over God's sadistic torture of his only son, and subsequent torture of millions of people, because what was the point of salvation if you still existed at the whims of God and man? What was the point of faith if you were still subject to suffering? I understood all the theologies, but I didn't see why I had to align myself with it. I understood the idea of God as compassionate observer, healer, and strength. Those were all nice ideas. But why choose to stand by them as partner? Why become a mouthpiece?

My mentor, and old horse who never wrote down a sermon in his life, told me I was scared to wear the collar, and though he said it kindly, as if it was totally normal, I'd stormed out of the office.

He was right of course. A step away from becoming a man of God, a commitment I'd always wanted to make, and I ran like a coward. I had no excuse besides fear and an unwillingness to conquer it.

I dried myself after my shower, putting my day together in my mind. Therapy, then a session at Alondra, paperwork, and a quick meeting at Westonwood to discuss scheduling. I couldn't do this for long. I couldn't hold down two jobs. The commute was deadening. Alondra had to go and Westonwood had to go, but I needed them. Everything I was doing, I was doing for the wrong reasons. I was proving to Jana I could do what I wanted by being at Alondra, and I was sating some indefinite hunger by being at Westonwood. I still didn't know what I wanted.

Jana came into the bathroom, her long hair tangled from sleep, her nipples poking through her cloud-and-kitten pajamas. "You done?"

"Just about."

"You going to that place today?"

"That place? Yes." I hung my towel and stood naked in front of her.

"My father is worried about the gangs again, since you're back at Alondra." She turned toward the mirror. "He wants to get us an alarm system."

"No." I moved her hair from her neck.

"He'll pay for it."

"I'm not living in a cage." I kissed the back of her neck.

She shrugged me off. "It's not a cage." She ran her fingers through her hair. "The triggers are so small. You can get one so the alarm just notifies the police. It doesn't even make a sound here."

Her wrist looked so delicate peeking from her pajama sleeves, so vulnerable, with a little gold chain around it. Nothing was more feminine than the wrist. Between her exposed throat and the bracelet, I was fully erect.

From behind her, I wrapped my fingers around her wrist and pulled her arm down. I whispered, "I don't want an alarm system."

I pushed my dick against her and pressed her wrist to her lower back. She tried to pull away, but I held firm. Her resistance sent a wave of pressure between my legs, and something else came to mind. Something that shouldn't have been there while I was trying to seduce Jana.

"I want it," she said.

Was she talking about the stupid alarm system? I didn't care. I had a head full of pink ass cheeks and paddles, of bound wrists and begging.

"You'll get it." I bent her over the vanity.

"Elliot, really…"

I held her wrist with one hand and yanked her pajama pants down with the other. Her ass—unblemished, round, perfectly soft in my hand —creased as I grabbed the flesh.

"Ouch. I have to go to work. What are you doing?"

She wriggled under me, and I held her down. "Something different. Tell me how you feel about it." I slapped her ass. "Later."

"Elliot!"

I slapped her ass again. The sound and the sight of pink finger-shaped marks on soft skin swelled my cock against her.

"I'm at Westonwood. You should be happy." I slapped her again.

She squealed. "What are you—?"

Slap.

"I'm getting ready to fuck you."

She looked around at me, as if checking to see if I was the man she lived with. I couldn't do this much longer or I would come all over her back. I put my dick against her. She was wet. Very wet. And she hadn't told me to stop.

I pushed inside her, and I twisted her arm behind her back, pressing her to the vanity, when I felt her shudder. Her mouth opened a little. Her cheeks flushed when I moved inside her. God, she'd never felt so tight. When I slapped her ass again, she clenched around me.

I leaned over her, letting her wrist go as I curved my body to hers. "You get tight when I spank you. Did you know that?"

I pulled her a little away from the sink and put my fingers on her clit. I'd never handled her so roughly, and I wanted more. I wanted to bite her shoulder. I wanted to pull out, pull her onto the bed, and drive her crazy for an hour. I wanted to tie her up and call in sick. I wanted control over her body as I've never wanted anything before.

But she wouldn't. Not this girl. No time. Got to get to work. Got to argue. Got to talk about fear.

I teased her clit. She stopped pulling away.

"I'm not getting an alarm system, and I'll work wherever I want," I said. "The next time you suggest anything, I'm tying you to the bed with your legs in the air, and I'm going to spank you and tease you with my tongue until you learn who's in control here. Do you understand?"

"No, I don't." The truth was in her moan, not her words.

"Let me be clear then." I buried myself in her, pulled out, and slammed back in.

She clenched and grunted, coming with a gasp and a long vowel, stiffening under me. I lost control of my own imagination which, for some reason, had fixated on Fiona in the afternoon light, moving her finger against my desk blotter. The sexless cut of her shirt made the knobs of her nipples even more prominent, lips over her teeth in a half smile.

I let myself want those nipples. I let myself want to fuck her mouth. I let myself picture her under me, her red hair splayed on the pillow and wrists tied above her.

I came so hard, I thought my body had expanded to the size of the room, pulsing against the walls, the towel rack, the ass pressed against me. I collapsed against Jana, my girlfriend of two years, and kissed the soft skin of her neck.

When she spoke, she did it softly. Not hurt or upset, just matter-of-fact. "Get off me."

JANA SHOWERED IMMEDIATELY AFTER. She stayed in long enough to make it impossible for me to see her before I left.

So I drove.

When I was ten, I'd woken from a nightmare and tiptoed into my parents' room. We'd just moved to Menlo Park from Fresno, and I was scared of everything. My mother, who seemed more and more withdrawn. My sister, who was growing breasts and curves, changing in ways that made me feel the loss of a friend and the fear of a new creature that I didn't understand. My father, however, was the same. Bigger than life, never arguing or raising his voice, he was a lion whose power was in his gait and mien. I looked just like him in the end, but I knew that power he had wasn't mine to wield.

On the night I dreamed of toilet bowls overflowing with reams of shit, I'd run to Mommy and Daddy's room. I saw them. Mother and Father on top of the sheets, him taking her from behind like an animal. The noises. God, the adult in me had to laugh. I'd been through that memory a hundred times, how he had his hands on her throat. The way he hit her bottom. My mother, groaning.

I'd run back to my room, as if the terror outside it was greater than the terror inside, and curled up, trying to pretend my erection didn't exist. Hadn't I sought God for the same reason I shut my eyes that night? To bathe my mind and soul in light and goodness?

Right in my bathroom, I'd just replayed the whole scene, lick for lick. Why? Because of Fiona Drazen and her coyly baited nuggets of dirty talk. I wanted to be angry at her for it, but I couldn't. I knew better. It wasn't her; it was me.

I wasn't sure I could continue to be Fiona's therapist, and I was positive I couldn't stop. She had abandonment issues, and my leaving the first time had sent her into a tailspin. Leaving again would only reinforce her idea that she was worthless.

Yet my sexual fantasies about her were affecting my life, and seeing her only reminded me that I wanted her. I kept thinking *just once* and *maybe after she gets out,* neither of which would help her.

I kept imagining her body twined with mine, her pink ass, her willing submission, her tiny breasts under my palms. I wanted to taste her. I thought about it whenever I got into my car. Whenever I stepped into the shower. She was like a ghost hanging over me.

"Countertransference isn't about the patient," Lee said.

"I can read a textbook any time."

"You're being hostile. You know as well as I do that you have to look at your own life and decide what needs aren't being addressed that you're imagining she can fill."

"I met her partner. He's an interesting guy. Grew up in South Africa. I think I've been out of the United States twice."

"You talk about him like he's competition. She's not a conquest. She's a patient."

My sessions with Lee had gone from chiding, pleasant, and slightly annoying to highly uncomfortable. I wanted to run away, but like any good therapist, I stood astride my discomfort and observed it.

"I want to just feel something without turning it over constantly," I said.

"That's not your job," she said. "I have to tell you, I'm getting concerned about you. This is dangerous territory. Wanting to explore feelings like this without scrutiny? Come on. What's going on with Jana?"

I didn't want to describe our post-shower fuck. It was too wrapped up in feelings and fantasies Lee would want to spend the next twenty minutes uncoiling. And it didn't matter. What mattered was *why* I was having those feelings and fantasies. What mattered was the situation before Fiona Drazen ever walked into my office.

"I think the worst thing I ever did was cave to what she wanted and work at Westonwood. I'm carrying around a ton of resentment. And the pressure hasn't stopped; she's just moved it to something else. I mean, you'd think we were compatible. I worry. I cope by being organized. She worries. She copes by being organized. But it's deadening. I find I'm the one who's trying to be unsystematic, and I'm not good at chaos."

"Then your problem is with your own life. Please, I'm begging you, don't jeopardize your career by confusing that with redirected feelings for a patient."

Chapter 36

FIONA

"YOU SEEM DIFFERENT," I said.

Elliot smirked from behind his desk. He did seem different. He sat a little straighter maybe, or was nervous, or more relaxed. I couldn't put my finger on it.

"I'm the same," he said. "Maybe you've changed."

I shrugged. "Sure, I guess that's why I'm here."

"You saw Deacon come in yesterday, I presume?"

"Yeah."

"Well?" He smiled. "You know what I'm going to ask."

"How I feel about it? Fine. Great. When can I see him?"

"First I want to talk about your injuries. Your tooth and wrist."

"I don't think that memory was real," I blurted. "You said that I could create false memories under hypnosis, and I think I did. You said that the made-up stuff always favors the person remembering, and I think that however I got hurt, I was doing something I wasn't supposed to do. Like, something really bad. So I made the other thing up."

"That just points to you being afraid of him."

I sank a little deeper into my chair. I was afraid of Deacon, in a way. I was terrified he'd leave me and I'd go crazy without him. And how did that jibe with my growing pipedream of being normal? I swallowed hard. I didn't want to even think about it, much less talk about it.

Elliot leaned forward. "Here's my problem. It's my job to make sure you're safe for as long as you're here. It's very difficult for me to let you see him if I believe he's hurt you, or that he will again. If I think he has some sort of unhealthy control over you, and if I think that'll affect your treatment, I can't allow it."

"What do I have to promise?"

"I'll take your firstborn."

A wisecrack was the last thing I'd expected, but it was exactly what I needed. I put my forehead to my knees and groaned. "Take it. I don't want kids anyway."

"It's a deal," he said.

My head shot up with surprise.

"Tomorrow morning."

"Oh my God," I said, "can I kiss you?"

"No." He stood.

I stood as well and looked down at my pale blue psycho suit. "Fuck."

"What?"

"Does he have to see me like this? I mean, it's bad enough I'm here, but I look like a janitor."

He looked at me, toes to crown, as if I was a real woman with curves under my clothes and a choice about what I wore, then took his eyes from me and looked at his hand on the doorknob. I pretended I'd imagined the sex in his gaze.

"All right," he said as he opened the door. "I'll see if we can arrange some normal clothes for you."

<hr>

Chapter 37

<hr>

ELLIOT

MY BELIEF that Deacon wouldn't hurt Fiona wasn't based on any kind of data, but on instinct. He might have an unhealthy control over her, but I didn't think he was an immediate threat. I feared that if I didn't allow him to see her, I was preventing it because I wanted her for myself. After my session with Lee, I could at least think the words.

I wanted her.

I couldn't do a damn thing about it, but I would call it what it was. I would look it in the face and say "no" with conscious intention. I would want her until she stopped being my patient, then I would forget her and deal with Jana as if I'd never met the beautiful, vibrant, decadent heiress.

"Hello?" Jana's voice came over the phone, crisp and taut.

It was dark as I pulled onto the freeway, making my choice to call her even more stupid. Maybe I felt a little suicidal. "I'm going to be late."

"How late?"

"I have to run an errand."

"Thanks for telling me. Um, can you come in tomorrow to meet Mary? They really need to hire someone."

The school counselor position. I'd never given her a new resume, but Jana must have smoothed it over.

"I'm working at Westonwood in the morning," I said.

"You aren't at Alondra until two. Maybe you could squeeze it in? Think how great it would be to work together. We could have lunch together every day in the break room. It would be like a vacation."

I changed lanes, giving myself a second to think, but I had no way around it. The school was the third option that solved everything. "Sure. Noon should work. Thanks."

"Okay, see you in a bit."

"Okay."

"I love you," she said.

"I love you too." I hung up.

▭

THERE WAS ONLY one Maundy Street in all of Los Angeles. It was a block long, at the crown of hills above Beechwood Canyon. I twisted up the treacherous slope, back and around, only seeing the headlights of oncoming traffic a second before the car got close enough to hit. To my right, the landscape got longer and longer, the city stretching beneath in a plaid of lights.

Maundy had three houses on it, all behind an iron gate. I stopped the car in front of the gate, my headlights illuminating the houses and trees. All were on the left, facing the view. The house closest was the smallest, and the lights were off. Number three. The house in the center had a few lights on. The back house had huge double doors and hooks in the front facade.

An intercom and keypad were set into the gate, but my lights had alerted the occupants of the middle house to my presence. A slim Asian woman in a mandarin collar walked down the hill. As she got closer, I realized she was barely a woman at all, just at the beginning stages of adulthood.

"Hi," I said. "You must be Debbie."

"Yes, Doctor Chapman?" She shifted the bag to her forearm and pushed numbers on her side of the gate. I heard a *clack*, and she slid the gate open.

"Nice to meet you," I said.

"How is she? Are you allowed to say?" Debbie asked.

"Better. Thanks for the clothes."

Smiling, Debbie handed me the bag. "I packed her something comfortable. If she doesn't like the shoes, she can complain later."

I was tempted to open the bag and see what shoes she was talking about, but I didn't want to walk away just yet. "Do you have a minute?"

She looked me up and down, as if assessing the danger I posed, then slid the gate all the way open. "Pull in. I'll be out in a second."

She went to the small house in the center. I went back to my car to drive through. When I was in, the gate closed automatically. I got out. The door to the little house was still closed, but it wasn't as small as I thought. Only the top was visible; the rest was built into the hill.

I approached the last building. The front windows were covered from the inside. The hooks I'd seen were lower than I expected. Hooks to hold plants were usually above the doorframe, but these were about seven feet off the ground, and more hoops than hooks. Beneath them were smaller U-shaped loops that looked more functional than decorative.

That was number one, Maundy. Of course I should have left it alone. I should have let Fiona's descriptions, which were heavy with her emotions, suffice as a matter of principle. But I couldn't stop myself from walking around the house.

The windows on the side were less carefully covered. Maundy was a private street, so I could understand why they weren't sealed all around. Had the street been subject to any kind of traffic, they would have had to brick up the windows.

A huge room with a floor-to-ceiling window overlooked the mountain, and along the wall I could see, wooden Xs were bolted to the tufted wall. There was a line of chairs that couldn't be called chairs. They were more cushions configured in a way I couldn't understand until I imagined human bodies on them, crouching, kneeling, legs up, spread, arms back or above the head, shackled down with another body. Then their function became clear. The tables for observers only highlighted the fact that the window looked over Los Angeles if anyone cared to watch.

Had that been safe for Fiona with her paparazzi-magnet lifestyle? Why had no pictures of her strapped to U-shaped mattresses and wooden Xs surfaced? Screaming, wet, come-dripping pink-slapped skin, begging for more more more?

"That big window facing the view is one-way," Debbie said from behind me. "You can see out, but no one can see in."

I jumped as if she'd caught me fucking.

"It's the first thing anyone asks," she continued. "You imagine you're seen, but you're safe. It's got to be safe, or it doesn't work."

"Good to know," I said.

"Obviously, the side windows are two-way, but the coverings are sealed on the inside when the house is in use." She smiled, hands folded in front of her. "Come on in." She stepped aside so I could take the stone path to the center house.

The center house was stunning, if understated. Two floors, a modest pool, large windows, and a balcony where I sat on a sofa spanning the length of it. The patio overlooked a terraced yard, the lights of the city, and the black ocean. On one of the terraces, in the dotted lamplight, a slim figure danced, flinging her long, straight hair. No, she wasn't dancing. She was doing some sort of martial art.

Behind me, an indoor light went on, illuminating the figure. I saw the bare chest and loose black pants. The dancer was a man, and he was working with a sword. He moved it with grace and beauty, like a gymnast with an apparatus. I couldn't see him well enough to tell more, but his practice was hypnotic.

Debbie brought out a tray of tea.

"You didn't have to," I said.

"I already had it steeping." She sat across from me on a wicker-and-metal chair and pressed her legs together while she poured.

"This is a fantastic view," I said.

"Yes. I take it for granted, but whenever someone new comes, I'm reminded."

"Do you live here alone?"

"With another student. Martin. The middle house is for functions only, and in the end house, the shibari master lives." She said "master" with a sort of reverence I admired.

"Deacon."

"Yes."

"And Fiona?"

"Yes and no. She's here when he's here. When he's not, she's not."

"May I ask why?"

"You may ask." She sipped her tea, giving away nothing, telling me I could ask, but I'd better be ready to hear something I didn't like.

"Is that Martin?" I asked, referring to the man below.

"No. Junto is mine. Martin was removed just before Christmas. He hasn't been back since."

"Martin was in Los Angeles the days before Fiona went to the stables?"

"Yes, why?"

I shook my head. I didn't know why that rankled, but it did. "I thought he was gone. I don't know why it's relevant. Probably isn't."

But it was, because Fiona had mentioned that time in session.

Even if I was so stoned I'd let them knot me, well, Debbie wouldn't have disobeyed, and Martin was in New York.

Fiona had a memory of being tied while Deacon was away, and had no idea who had done it. But from what I could see, if Martin had been in town, he was the knotter.

"I reported all this to the police," Debbie said. "I knew something was wrong that night. I could tell. Fiona ran out of the house with a bag. I stopped her and asked what was wrong. She was crying. She said she was going to Snowcone. When I saw Master Deacon later, I asked him what that meant. He went to get her." She stopped and looked at Junto, as if clicking pieces of the night in her mind. "Master Deacon told me I shouldn't feel responsible for what happened. But sometimes I do."

"Anyone would have done what you did."

"You care about her," Debbie said.

I almost choked on my tea. She watched me sidelong, her gaze suddenly pointed with intention. I felt as if I was being taken apart and scanned.

"She's my patient. So yes, I do care." I was sure she saw right through me. "What about you?"

"Fiona is one of the few friends I've made since I came here. She is very loyal, very strong. When I came, I had nothing. Deacon pulled me from hell because he recognized something in me. And Fiona was right there, making sure I had everything I needed. She introduced me to important people. They're a beautiful couple."

"What did he recognize?"

"I'm a female Dominant."

"Ah."

"And good with knots." She smiled into the rim of her cup, still dissecting me.

"I've been told you're very talented."

"I have skill with certain things. The most difficult knottings involve multiple strands. Anyone can tie two, but tying three, from crotch and over the shoulders, it's hard to get them to work in harmony. It's hard to make it strong so that each works equally. But I've been taught by the best." She put her cup down and changed the subject by changing her posture. "Do you run to get clothes for all your clients?"

"Not usually, but I wanted to see this place. Her life here is part of who she is, and I've had trouble imagining it. It's been a block for me. I can't understand the day-to-day."

"You're curious?"

"Not necessarily."

"I can get you an invitation to an event."

"No." I couldn't have been more definite about crossing that line. It would damage Fiona's trust in me completely.

"Really?" She obviously didn't believe me.

"Really. I'm just here to learn about Fiona."

She sighed. "Is it breaking a trust for me to tell you what everyone already knows? It's in the news every night. The public feeds off her like birds on suet. And she doesn't have the upbringing to stand up against it. No grounding."

"She's had a very traditional upbringing," I said. "Her folks are religious. She has seven siblings to lean on."

"She has a wire mother."

I sat back, considering my tea. The study she referred to involved removing newborn monkeys from their mothers and putting them in the arms of a chicken-wire figure that dispensed milk. "Are you referring to the Harry Harlow experiments?"

"I'm sure I don't remember the name of the doctor. But I saw a film of monkeys clutching a wire mother and biting each other. Almost all of them, in one way or another, was a sexual deviant. It was hard to watch."

"That study showed that a newborn without attachment to an adult has a higher chance of being impulsive and violent," I said. The experiments had been inhumane and horrifying. Human babies rarely faced that level of distance from all adult love. But the point had been made that a wire mother permanently damaged children. "And what's your theory on what this has to do with Fiona?" I hid the stress in my voice. I'd always seen Fiona as someone with solvable problems. Debbie apparently thought differently.

She folded her hands in her lap, calmly considering me. "The babies had no warm mother, but they were given every single other comfort they needed. Even more than they needed. What happens when the child of a wire mother is given every indulgence, and then has to deal with the slightest pain? Does the pain break them? Or are they already broken from the pleasure?"

I leaned toward the railing and looked over the city. The man with the sword had stopped his dance. He sat cross-legged, facing the same direction I was, with his hands out in supplication.

"When she looks out into the world, she sees only herself," Debbie continued. "She has a large family with wire parents. Those children are a brood of rich orphans. The fact that she can eke out as much humanity as she does is beautiful to me."

I felt the friction of my middle finger on my upper lip before I even realized I was rubbing it. I shifted my hand down. That habit triggered my mind's gears, no matter how much I didn't like it. Her parents still hadn't visited to tell her about her brother. They were leaving it to the children to sort out amongst themselves. Had it always been that way? Had something else broken her? Did there need to be more?

Everyone had a bucket that represented their capacity for pain. Some buckets were bigger than others, and everyone maintained the overflow differently. Did it matter that Fiona's bucket had been filled slowly, drip by drip, over years, if she hadn't been given the tools to manage the runoff?

"People are terribly complex in their simplicity." My general statement wouldn't betray any confidences, but it was possibly that simple. Or not. I had enough to chew on.

"I'm glad you came by." Debbie placed her cup carefully back on the tray. "It was nice to meet the man who is helping Fiona. She's a good person with a good heart."

I stood. "Nice to meet you as well."

We shook hands, and I left. I dropped the bag of clothes on the passenger seat, but I was halfway down the hill when I couldn't take it anymore. I had to know what she'd packed, what she expected Fiona to wear.

The zipper on the bag screeched when I opened it. The shoes were in a separate drawstring bag. They were white sneakers with Velcro, plain and simple. Was it wrong that I found them so sexual in their pure plainness? The lack of sensuality, the creases at the backs where they'd been smashed. The way the tongues were off kilter. The back heel of the left shoe was more worn than the right. She favored her left foot. It was the sexiest thing I'd ever seen.

I was having intimate feelings for a patient by way of a pair of running shoes.

I jammed them back in the bag without looking at the clothes and zipped it up, declaring to myself that I'd never look at them again. But it wasn't the sneakers that were the problem. It was me. I was the problem.

Chapter 38

JONATHAN SEEMED OBSESSED with physical activity. He wasn't at the ping-pong table when I went looking for him after dinner, but he was on the basketball court under the lights. His motions were much the same as they'd been with the paddle: dribble twice, then a *whoosh* into the net. He caught the ball and started over. The grounds were populated with all kinds of psychos huddling in little groups under the lights and in the dark corners of night. None went near Jonathan. He was a red menace all his own. Mister Joker. Mister Tons-of-Buds.

I leaned on the pole that held the hoop. "Making friends, I see."

"I have you, Fee." *Swoosh.* "I don't need friends." He smiled.

I hadn't expected any kind of cheer from him. "Who removed the stick from your ass?"

"Guy can't catch a break. What am I supposed to do? Have another heart attack?" He took his shot. "And how are you doing? Try to attack your therapist lately?"

"Not lately, fucktard."

He passed me the ball, hard. It took the wind out of me, but I caught it.

"Twenty-four hours of self-control," he said. "A personal best for you."

Jonathan was back. The guy who couldn't stand me, who ribbed, chided, and pushed my buttons until I either stormed off or slapped him.

"And you?" I said, passing it back as hard as I could.

He caught it without a problem and dribbled.

"You aren't some great example of self-control. If I want that, I'm looking at Theresa."

"She's gonna bust one day." *Swoosh.* "Leave a bunch of lace and pearls all over the place." He made an exploding gesture with his hands. "Boom."

I caught the ball on its way down. "She said she's sorry she got mad at you, by the way." I tossed it to him. "She called you names, apparently."

"I don't blame her. But yeah, she lost it. From now on, I'll be a model of having my shit together. Anything I can control, I will. Done. And sorry, Fee, but I'm staying away from you. You're a bad influence. Staying away from Dad too. He's worse. He makes me want to break his face." He took his shot and missed. Retrieving the ball, he said, "Control. Everything in my line of sight."

"You think it's so easy?"

"Yeah, I do. It's a choice. I can see crazy coming now. You. Then Rachel. Then me. I know the signs now. I got it." *Bang.* The ball went off the rim. "I'm watching Theresa next. Margie's on her way. We'll all be here at some point until we learn."

I caught his ball mid-bounce. "You're delusional."

"You know who my girlfriend was obsessed with before she died?"

"Jesus?" I took a shot and, *bang*, missed. I was never much of an athlete.

"You." He snapped the ball out of the air. "Talk about delusional. She thought you were the shit. Thought you had the life."

"Why?" That knowledge poked me in a weird place. I was many things, but admirable wasn't even on the list. Yet, a swell of unexplained intimacy throbbed around the admiration when I was sure I'd never met Rachel at all.

He bounced his ball but didn't take the shot. "She was a normal, regular girl. Bad family, but otherwise, she was real. The way we live was like a fairytale to her." He laughed and bounced the ball until it flew over his head. He caught it and dribbled again. "When she saw how you lived, the way you spend money, she admired it. I should have caught it then. I think what bothered me the most when I heard about her and Dad was that I hadn't seen it. How did that shit slip under my radar? I don't like being blind. I felt like I got it in the back of the head with a baseball bat. Then, the party, and I wake up, and she's gone." He took a shot. *Swoosh.* "She was real, and then… not."

"Because she wanted to be us."

"Crazy fucking world," he said, passing me the ball.

I stood in front of the net and tossed the ball up. By some miracle of chance and physics, it went *swoosh*.

"Nice shot." The male voice came from my left.

I turned to find Warren Chilton palming the ball I'd let fly.

"Drazen," he said, flipping Jonathan the ball.

"Hey," Jonathan said back.

I was sure he was trying to place Warren's face. Warren was about seven or eight years older, but there was a good chance they'd pulled smoke from the same bong, somewhere. Jonathan took his shot, missing because he seemed cautious in a way he hadn't before. He passed it back to Warren.

"Where have you been?" I asked, returning to the pole as Warren jumped for the hoop and missed. *Bang.*

"I had a dispensation to go to my sister's wedding. Got the ankle bracelet off with a blowtorch and bolted." He lifted his pant leg, revealing a red, raw burn wound.

"Wow, dude." Jonathan dribbled, staring at Warren's ankle. "Where'd you go?"

"Stole my dad's car and went up to Santa Barbara."

"Cool." He flicked the ball to Warren, who missed the net again. I couldn't believe Jonathan would be impressed with the high drama, but he was sixteen.

"Wasn't even a blip on TMZ. You guys are still eating up all the bandwidth."

Jonathan laughed as his rebounded Warren's miss. Warren fouled Jonathan and bounced into me, shoving a little baggie of blue oval pills into my hand. I tucked them into my waistband as he winked at me.

"What's on the news about us?" Jonathan said as he passed to Warren. "Anything that'll get me laid when I get out?"

I glanced around to see if anyone had seen me tuck away the baggie.

"Fiona," Frances called to me.

I turned. She was standing next to Elliot. They waved me over.

Shit.

Chapter 39

ELLIOT

I COULD SEE she was on her best behavior, hands in her lap, sentences short and spoken softly. Her effort to not come back at us appeared monumental, and I was proud of her for keeping it together in front of Frances and sympathetic to how hard it was to seem awake when saying "yes" and "no" when she wanted to say so much more.

"Do you understand the rules for tomorrow's visit?" Frances asked. She spoke to her peers with bite and wit, but she spoke to patients as if they were children.

"Yes," Fiona said, looking each of us in the eyes from across the conference room table, the same table we'd betrayed her at two weeks earlier. "One hour. Just talking. No going outside the garden area. You'll have a guy on us the whole time."

"Miss Drazen," Frances said, softening her voice slightly, "I hope you don't feel persecuted. We're trying to make sure this is a safe visit. This man is the reason you're here, for better or worse. There is violence in your past together, so we have to be careful for your good and the good of the other residents."

"I get it."

"It's only Doctor Chapman's word that makes this possible."

She glanced at me. "Thank you."

"My pleasure," I lied.

JANA WAS CLEANING up the dishes when I got home.

"Hi," I said.

"Hey." She was mad.

I was far later than I should have been, but I'd needed to update Frances on Deacon, and then she insisted on a conversation with Fiona. The explanation was on the tip of my tongue, but I bit it back. I counted the dishes. "Who was here?"

"I had Mary come to talk to you about the job. I figured I'd kill two birds with one stone. But you didn't show up, so…" She shrugged and picked up her wine glass.

"We're meeting tomorrow. You can't dump an interview on me twelve hours early."

"If you were serious in general, you would have been here, home with me. But now you look unreliable, and I'm embarrassed."

"That's unfair," I said.

"What were you doing?"

"Working."

"Is there someone else?"

"What?"

"Are. You. Fucking. Someone. Else?" She said every word slowly. She'd had a glass too many, making her words wet and thick with emotion.

I crossed the room in two steps and removed the glass from her hand before it reached her lips. I pushed her up against the refrigerator and held her by her sternum. With my other hand, I reached up her skirt.

"Why?" I asked with my lips against her cheek. "Have I come home with the smell of pussy on my face?" I pushed past the crotch of her panties and jammed two fingers inside her.

She gasped. It couldn't have felt good, and I didn't care.

"Lipstick on my collar? Have I called you another name?" I dug my hand against her, pressing her clit.

"What are you doing?" she squeaked.

"I'm taking you." I added a third finger. She was wet now. I slid them out and against her clit, then back inside. "I'm tired of this shit. There's too much talking and not enough screaming."

"God, what—"

"Say my name."

"Elliot," she moaned when I stroked her clit.

"Again."

"Elliot."

"When I say to get on your knees, get on your knees." I stroked her clit, gathering moisture around it gently. "I'm going to drag you to the bedroom by your hair and throw you on the bed. Get on your back and spread your legs." I put three fingers in her again, roughly, digging down to the knuckle. I had no idea what I was doing but telling a story of the next half an hour. "Then I'm going to bend your legs at the knees and kiss inside your thighs. My tongue will go from one knee to the other, stopping at your pussy for only a second. Then thigh to thigh. Then I'll land on your clit. I'll kiss it and lick it until you beg me to fuck you."

I had her. She was wild, with hooded eyes, and her hair was in front of her face. When she looked at me, I was sure that when I said *get on your knees*, she would. I was rock hard, waiting for it.

Instead she said, "Is this how you talk to her?"

I stepped back, pulling my wet fingers out of her. I'd intended to put them in my mouth in front of her, but now they felt sticky and dirty. "Forget it. Just forget it."

"I can't shake this feeling there's someone else." She adjusted her clothes.

"I'll be in the guest room." I wasn't supposed to stalk off into the other room and close the door. I was supposed to keep communication open, but I couldn't, because I didn't even know what I wanted from her. I didn't know what I felt. What could I expect when I came at her like that after an evening looking at a BDSM playroom?

I should have opened my heart to her. I could have told her that a new part of myself was opening up, even if I didn't understand it. But I didn't want her to know. I wanted to stew in my desires without volleying someone else's needs.

This was mine.

Chapter 40

FIONA

BY THE TIME I went for my nine o'clock session, I was jumping out of my skin. Deacon was coming at eleven. Two more hours. I'd already put on my jeans and blouse, laughing at the unsexy, dowdy shoes.

"Who picked these?" I asked Elliot. "You?"

"Debbie."

I laughed again. "She and I used to joke that these were the least sexual type of footwear in the world. She obviously thinks I need to tone it down a bit."

"Is there a way to be who you are without thinking sex is all you're meant for?"

I didn't even know if I could answer him, because his fingertips on the blotter were making me crazy. How lightly they touched it, as if enjoying the warmth of the leather. I tried not to stare, but I kept seeing his hand out of the corner of my eye and hearing the light rustle of his touch. I wanted to finger myself in lieu of trying to seduce him, because he was unseduceable. I was lower than a rat in a sewer to a guy like him.

"I'm not ashamed of what I am, so I never thought of needing 'more,' if you know what I mean," I said. "I would show up at Maundy and strip down to my underwear. Deacon would leave my stuff by the door. When I put my ankles in the leg spreaders, it was like my job. I did it, and when I got turned on, it was just me doing what I was meant to do. I walked to Deacon's room, and he'd be waiting. Except it's not like I could walk in the spreader, so I'd tip or do something wrong. That was also my job. To fuck up so he could tie me down with my legs open. To beg when he asked. To be a whore for him."

Elliot's finger stopped stroking the leather, and he swallowed. If he stood, I would have seen a rock-hard erection. That was also my job.

"You take a lot of pleasure in talking about sex," he said.

"I do."

"I need less of that."

"Why?"

"Because you're trying to arouse me, and I want to keep being your therapist."

"I'm not trying," I said.

"Please try *not* to then."

"I'm a fucker. It's what I do."

"You're not. You are not defined by sex."

"I'll define myself any way I want." My voice was shot through with defensiveness, and I hated it. He made me feel as if I'd wasted my precious time doing and learning things that were worthless. "I'll decide what about me is worthwhile. I'll decide what I talk about and what I do."

"You're not deciding. Your addiction is deciding."

He was so confident he was right, and I felt a swell of violence I had to quell. I was T-minus ninety minutes to seeing Deacon. I would not be baited by a sexually frustrated motherfucker who wanted to rip away who I was. My lip quivered with the effort, and my eyes filled with tears. I resisted the urge to tell him how grateful he'd be for my skills if I got my lips around his cock for five minutes.

"Do not tell me who I am," I whispered.

"I don't know who you are. But I know who you're not." He slapped a box of tissues in front of me. "You're not a mindless, heartless 'fucker.'

Maybe you should listen to the people around you talk about you. They don't think you're a bag of sex either."

I ripped a tissue out of the box as if it had personally offended me, which it did. Fucking tissue. I blew my nose in it. "I decide, okay? I decide what goes and what doesn't. How other people see that, I can't help it. People get hurt, you know, it happens, but I don't lie. Everyone's on board."

"Everyone? You just said people get hurt."

"Sometimes."

He moved his notebook out of the way and leaned on his desk as if I'd said something he wanted to latch on to. "Tell me the first time someone got hurt."

"The last time was Deacon—"

"Not the last time. The first time."

"The first time was my fault."

"Okay. Let's hear it."

I didn't want to tell that story. I didn't want to say what I'd done, how careless I'd been. But Elliot had come back for me, and I said I'd play ball. So I just had to spit it out, didn't I?

"Evan. I won't use his last name, because you know his father. I mean, not know know, but know."

"That's fine."

I cleared my throat. Could I just pretend he wasn't there while I told this story? Like maybe I was lying in bed, staring at the door to the bathroom as the sun came up. "So summer after high school graduation, I'm dating this guy Evan, who's going to Brown in August. We don't have a permanent thing, because he's leaving and I'm just going to UCLA. And so he's fine and all, but his best friend Gary is pretty hot, and he's staying in town. So I suggest to Evan that it would be fun for the three of us to get together more or less at the same time."

Why was I hemming and hawing? Why was I using soft words? That was bullshit. I held my chin up and rephrased the last part. "I told Evan I wanted a threesome with his buddy Gary. It hurt his feelings. He said no, because he liked me for a girlfriend. I hadn't told him I wasn't girlfriend material."

"And he broke up with you? How did that feel?"

Fucking feelings already? Jesus. "It felt nothing because he didn't break up with me. Not until later. Not until… He went to Brown anyway, so it didn't matter."

"So he stayed with you for the summer?"

"Why do you want so many details?"

He shrugged. "If you'd stop skipping things, I'd stop asking questions."

"What makes you think I'm skipping things?"

"It's my job."

Fine.

Fuck him.

"After Evan said no, Gary invited me to his place. Which was fine, because fuck it. If Evan was going to get his knickers in a bunch, fine. But Evan was there. And I think, *This is not a threesome. This is not them being cool with it.* Because there's no drinks and there's no drugs, and the music is off and all the lights are on. So I'm like, 'Hi, guys, what's up?' Evan makes a dumb comment like, 'my dick' or some dumb jock thing like that, and Gary…" I stop, because I feel my face crunching up.

Elliot lets me sniff and get it together.

"Gary pushes me. He puts my face on his kitchen table. He does it hard. So I'm like, 'Get off me.' But Evan, he comes around and yanks down my jeans. And then… I couldn't move, because Gary was holding me down. God, I can't tell you."

"You don't have to."

But I needed to. I needed to fucking finish it because I'd told my therapist I'd play ball. Just because I had fantasies of a normal life with that therapist didn't mean anything had changed for him. I was the one who had to just get through it and do what I said I'd do.

"I'd never had anal before. I didn't know you have to lube a lot and do prep and you have to be really turned on. Evan didn't either, because he just opened up my crack and spit, which is never enough… God, it hurt. It hurt my ass, and it hurt my insides. And he wouldn't stop. I kept saying, 'Stop, stop. You're hurting me.' Gary wouldn't let go, and Evan kept doing it. After he came, they switched places." I stopped. I wasn't crying because I'd shut off all my emotions. If I let them out, I wouldn't have been able to tell the story to the object of my silly, normal fantasies.

"I'm sorry that happened."

His face was ice cold, as if he didn't care. As if it was one of a hundred stories he'd heard about a girl getting ass-fucked twice with a mouthful of spit for lube. Just another patient with a stupid story. That was all I was.

"It was my fault," I said. "See, I did face consequences once."

"For what? For wanting to explore your sexuality? For wanting to move on from a relationship that wasn't going anywhere? No, Fiona. No."

"Well, fuck it. I said never again. From then on, I was crystal clear. I'm not anyone's girlfriend. I fuck around. Period."

"So you can never have non-consensual sex if you consent to everything?"

"If you want to put it that way," I said, crossing my arms. I had to hold back tears when he said it though.

"That's brought you to quite an impasse."

"It was working really well."

"Until it wasn't."

"Yeah." I sniffed. If he was trying to empty my head of snot and fluid, he was three quarters of the way to me opening the valves.

"I spoke to Debbie when I got your clothes," he said softly. "She talked about you as if you were a real person. One with honorable qualities."

"Debbie sees the good in everyone."

"She said you helped her acclimate when she got to Maundy."

I rubbed my nose. "She's very young, but she didn't need me. She's plenty mature. Martin would tell you what I am, and how good I am at it. But you wouldn't believe his opinion because you don't already agree with it. Right?"

He paused too long. I took that as a victory. I'd stumped him with his own relativism. I didn't stick my middle finger in his face and piss on his desk, but I felt that good… until he spoke.

"Martin wasn't in New York before Christmas. You said he was away when you were knotted by someone else, or something like that?"

I felt myself blink. Felt a skip in my brain. He was right of course.

Martin hadn't been in New York. I knew that. So why did I feel as if a mental drain was clogged?

I felt a shot of pain in my tooth. I put my hands over my mouth, because neurons that hadn't fired since the stables connected again, and I was afraid that memory would fly out of my head.

"Martin. He knotted me while Deacon was away. Oh my God, that's worse than fucking him. That's why he was so mad." The words spilled out of me with the memory.

Hanging, the sway of the ropes in a deep fog, and the ceilings, a pale blue instead of Deacon's wood beams. I wanted it so bad, but his hands were wrong. They pulled at odd angles, unsupportive when I needed it, and my stomach roiled with alcohol and drugs. The colors blurred, and the rough hemp ran on my raw skin as everything under me fell away before the lightning bolt crack of the floor.

"Martin was sloppy, and he dropped me. I fell on my face, and my wrist was tied all wrong. I didn't feel it because I was fucked up on something." I pressed my fingertips to my cheek, where the damaged molar was. "Deacon really didn't hit me. I thought he might not have, but I didn't know what to believe anymore. But it was that dumb shit."

"The dumb shit who knows what you should be valued for? *That* dumb shit?"

I didn't say anything for a minute, maybe two. It took me that long to shake the surprise.

As if he could tell when I was ready to hear it, Elliot said, "I told you the memories you called up under hypnosis would be colored. What was important were the feelings you unearthed. You weren't afraid of Deacon when you remembered him hitting you, and that's important. But you colored the event to absolve yourself of guilt for breaking the rules with Martin."

"What about the stables?" I said. "What did I change there?"

"You're going to have to ask Deacon."

I nodded and folded up my tissue.

"We have two minutes," Elliot said. "I'm taking those to give you a task. When you talk to yourself about yourself, I want you to try something new. I want you to use different words."

"Like?"

"Like loyal. Strong. Trustworthy. Spirited. Brave. Selfless. Use those words, Fiona. Stop lying to yourself about who you are."

Chapter 41

ELLIOT

I DIDN'T KNOW when my emotions flipped during the session. If I
hazarded a guess, it was when I gave Fiona that box of tissues. I defined
her not just to her but to myself, and speaking those words, I saw past all
of her bullshit and my own arousal. In asking her to define herself, I'd
done the same in my own mind, and I knew how deep my trouble cut.

Then when she told me she'd been raped by her boyfriend and his
friend, my detachment went to hell. I'd heard a hundred more violent
stories, yet I wanted to find those two men and eviscerate them for
hurting her. I hoped for Fiona's sake that I'd kept my shit together.

I heard her brother one rec room over, banging on a ping-pong ball.
But in this room, it was quiet. Patients read and chattered softly. This
room had a window overlooking the drive. It was my turn to watch and
ask myself how I felt when the black Range Rover rolled past the gate.

I felt insignificant. I felt lost in a whirlwind. When Deacon Bruce
handed the valet the keys and I stood in that fucking window like a
stalker, I felt like a pebble in a shoe, waiting to get shaken out and
discarded. When he looked up for Fiona and saw only me, I felt as if my

heart was being squeezed. He saw me and waved. He knew what I was doing. He knew he had what I wanted, but he wasn't worried. I was the also-ran, the second place, the beta in a pack of wolves. I waved back as if accepting my position.

How did I feel?

I felt as though I was going to be late. I felt the weight of my responsibilities to other people shedding from me. I walked to my office which overlooked the garden, and on the way, I pulled my phone out of my pocket. I barely paused as I called Jana.

"Hey, are you—"

"No. I'm going to be late." I spoke quietly and tersely.

"How late?"

I'd used the wrong word. I'd shuffled and shimmied when I should have just stated the facts. "I'm not going."

"Should we reschedule?"

"Cancel it. And I'm not discussing it further. I'm sorry. I don't know what I'm going to do, but I'm not working at Carlton Prep."

"Elliot, we agreed."

"You agreed. I have to go." I hung up and pocketed my phone.

There would be painful repercussions to just about every decision I'd made in the past thirty minutes, but they were the best decisions I'd made in the past two years.

—————————————

Chapter 42

—————————————

FIONA

IN THE END, I wore the psycho suit with the sneakers. On the one hand, I was sick of their damn indoor/outdoor Velcro slippers. On the other, I didn't want to be different. I didn't want to hide what I was from Deacon. I was troubled, and he knew it. I knew it. Jeans and a blouse wouldn't change that. So I wore the sneakers remembering the laces under the Velcro, like a bit of adulthood hidden under the child-safe fastening. I never bothered to unlace and retighten them. I'd rather jam the back of the shoe down and pivot my foot as if I was doing the twist.

And I wore the panties, because I was sick of the gross, disposable mental-ward underwear that rode up my ass.

I sat in the lobby, running my fingers over the damask. Peeked out the glass doors. Then stood and looked at the three-foot-high fresh flower arrangement. Then sat in front of the wood-burning modernist fireplace. Then peeked out the glass doors.

He wasn't late, ever. Not that he fussed about it. He owned a watch as black as his car and as big as a dinner plate, but he always seemed to know what time it was without looking.

I, on the other hand, looked at the wall clocks as if they ran backward when my back was turned.

He was coming.

I knew that he hadn't hit me. That I'd let Martin knot me, which was forbidden because it was dangerous and just another instance of infidelity. I knew nothing about the stables except that I'd been startled when someone came in, and Deacon knew everything. Only he knew the level of my betrayal, and only he could forgive me.

Behind me, a closet door slammed. Mark, the pierced orderly, came out.

I'd slammed a door that night. I jumped when I heard a car door slam outside.

Deacon. He was here.

I'd slammed the door on the way out when I'd gone to the stables. I left in a rage, warring with my shame and self-loathing.

It was him, the man walking toward me in a black wool jacket and flat-front trousers. Him, with the blazing blue eyes that had seen so much and the hands that could grasp, inflict, caress all at the same time.

He'd left me for letting Martin knot me. No, he hadn't hit me or broken my tooth, that I'd done to myself, but he'd kicked me out.

▭

"EMPTY YOUR HEART, my kitten. Empty your mind. Open your eyes. Who do you see?"

Deacon yanks my hair back until I'm looking at him. I feel at home and excited. He's back. He was gone, and he's back.

"You," I croak.

"Are you empty?" He pulls my arm back and stops.

"Yes," I say.

But the fluidity of the moment is gone when Deacon rubs a sore spot on my wrist with his thumb. He's behind me, on his knees, his throbbing cock at my crack. I don't want him to rub my wrist. I want him to fuck me.

"What's this?" he asks.

I thought the bruises were gone, but Deacon has an eagle eye. No detail has ever slipped by him, and no lie has ever gone undetected.

"A bruise." I intercept the next question because he already knows the answer. "From rope."

He leans back, and I know it's over. He's not fucking me. He'll forgive me, but he won't fuck me.

"Who?" he asks it as if it's relevant.

It's not. Someone else knotted me. We reserved that for each other. I stand, because I can't admit this while in a submissive posture. I have to hold up my head. Have to.

"Martin. He wanted to work on that last asymmetrical pose."

"Was Debbie there?"

"No."

"And?" He's standing now, hard as a rock. Terrifying.

"And what?"

He won't ask me if I fucked him, because that's secondary. He's just going to stand still with a look of shock, and then he's going to step forward in a way that makes me step back, once, twice, until the wall prevents me from going farther. His breath falls on my cheek, and a pain in my arm runs from my wrist to the sensitive side of my bicep.

"You did not," he says from deep in his throat. He's naked, stunning. He pins me to the wall, the friction making the open skin on my ass scream.

Regret. Pounds of it. Miles wide. Regret to the depth of my broken spirit.

"I'm sorry." Am I? Or am I just saying that?

"Why?"

My wrist hurts. He's pressing it so hard against the wall, as if I'd leave, as if I'd ever turn my back on him. Yet I want to get away, to run, to show him I can abandon him the way he abandons me.

I wiggle, but he only presses harder and demands, "Why?"

"Get off me!"

"Tell me why!" His eyes are wider, his teeth flashing as if he wants to rip out my throat. "Why?"

"I need it!"

He breathes once, heavily, as if filling his lungs to say something he doesn't want to say. He reaches for me, and I think he might say it's all right. He brushes his fingertip across my bottom lip, and I'm about to burst with gratitude. His face is soft and loving, and he's mine as much as I am his.

"I'm sorry," he whispers. "You have to go. I can't trust you."

I'm still in shock when the door slams behind him.

I WATCHED him sign himself in with my hand over my mouth. He was there, breathing the same air as me. He'd come. Maybe he hadn't come on a white horse to catch me as I jumped from a tower. Maybe we weren't going to ride off into the sunset, but he'd come for me.

He'd come for me.

I kept repeating those words, awash in gratitude to him, to Westonwood, to Elliot, to the people who built his car and pumped his gas.

He came through the glass door. It whooshed and breathed when it closed, and he stopped when he saw me. I was a wreck, and I knew it. But I wasn't worried about how I looked. Nothing could be further from my mind. It was never about that between us, because he saw *me*.

I didn't have a word or a gesture to express how I felt. I kept my hand over my mouth so I didn't spit when I cried. He took four steps, big ones, across the length of the hallway and wrapped his arms around me, lifting me off the floor. He smelled of hickory and leather, adventure and brokenness. He smelled of pleasure and pain given without regret, and when he held me tight, I felt both.

"Fiona," he said as if expressing longing and hope.

"I'm sorry," I said through my tears. "I'm so sorry."

Chapter 43

ELLIOT

I CLOSED my office door and went to the window. I waited like a spider waiting for the web to vibrate, arms stretched, owning my vulnerability to her, the fact that I wanted her and someone else had her.

It wasn't long before they came out and sat on a bench. When he put his hand over hers, I felt how Fiona felt. Worthless, consumable, a cold faraway planet circling a brilliant sun. That was my pain. Mine. No excuses. I would steep it in boiling water until it bled out of the bag and colored me the dark, opaque crimson of shame.

Chapter 44

FIONA

I PULLED Deacon outside like a kid showing off her dollhouse.

"And we have one guy here I went to school with. He knows every flower and all its medicinal properties. I mean, he's nuts, but right? You can't help it." I walked backward to the patio.

"You're not nuts, kitten. Haven't I told you that?"

"God, it's so nice to see you."

"Nice?"

It was session time, so the rec room was empty. I was a fucklot happy about that, because I didn't want anyone to see us. What we had wasn't public. It wasn't meant to be shared by sight or smell. The next hour was ours. Fuck all of them. I wanted every curious eye the fuck off me.

He put his arm around me, and we walked out into the yard. I pulled him to a bench halfway between the building and the treeline. He didn't take his eyes from me. We were like a long-separated couple who couldn't imagine being in each other's presence again. He sat next to me and twisted to face me, bending one arm over the back of the bench and putting his other hand over mine.

"You look beautiful," he said, and he never, ever lied.

"You too. Like no one ever stabbed you."

"It wasn't that bad. A flesh wound. Two Band-Aids and mercurochrome. Kiss it and make it better. Nothing."

"You were in the hospital."

"A luxury hotel."

"The knife missed your heart by how much?"

He shrugged. "It missed."

"I don't need you to forgive me," I blurted. "Even if you did, I'd never forgive myself. For everything. For letting Martin work with me, for trying to kill you. Everything."

His hands were so tender on mine, I felt as if they'd break the bones.

"You don't remember anything?" he asked.

"I've just started to remember that night at Maundy, when you threw me out." I choked a little on the last part. "I'm not saying I blame you."

"How are you?" It wasn't a polite question or small talk. He wanted a real answer.

"I don't know. I keep looking for an answer from other people, like they're going to tell me how I am. I feel myself wanting you to tell me if I'm okay. I didn't realize that was what I expected from you, and you know, you can't tell me. No one can, but… this is crazy."

"I'm ready."

"I don't know how to talk to myself, so I'll listen."

He laughed, not with humor but recognition. "You are more brutal on yourself than anyone else." He put his fingers on my lips.

I tasted him, and the desire to open my mouth and take him down to the knuckles was overwhelming.

"I think we hurt each other," he said. "I asked you for monogamy for the wrong reasons, and that's what started the whole thing."

"If it's what you want, it's not wrong. I can try again."

He shook his head. "I thought you wanted it. But I don't need you to be exclusive. I don't get jealous of other men as long as I know them and know you're protected. I thought it would make you happy. I thought you'd be safer if you were completely mine. But it doesn't. It makes you trapped. It makes you do stupid things. I'll never ask that of you again."

"I can."

"Well, then do it. Just do it, if that's what you want. I haven't touched another woman since you, and I won't. None of them are interesting to me. But that's my choice. It has to be your choice too. I can't impose it on you, and I can't punish you for who you are."

He couldn't punish me for who I was. A whore. A fucker. A sex bag with no goals, no worries, nothing inside her. But he didn't mean that. I knew he meant I was some sort of life-giving spirit-goddess above the care of mundane things like fidelity, but he was cutting me.

"You mean that?" I said. "You mean you could just let me swell and fuck when you're not around, and it'd be okay with you?"

"I'm probably the only man in the world who doesn't get jealous at that thought, but you have to be you. I take you that way or nothing. You know what you are to me. You're my reason to feel good. Even after everything, when I think of you, I'm happy. That's all I want, to feel that freedom. I'm not interested in the baggage that comes with enforced exclusivity. Kids, marriage, the myth of the happy home. None of it is for us."

He'd said it before, and I'd embraced it then.

"I want to ask you something," I said, casting my eyes down.

"Yes?" He raised an eyebrow. He knew what I was going to ask; I'd bet the entirety of my trust fund on that.

"Can you tell me what happened? How I stabbed you? I can't get my head around it."

He looked away. In profile, he looked thoughtful, statuesque, with a bump on his nose where it had been broken and his chin at a right angle to his neck. "There's no point, me narrating a story, is there? You need to remember."

"I can't."

He leaned in. "You can." His voice got low, turning breaths into words.

When he spoke like that, I could understand him no matter how loud the music was. I shook my head with a sting in my sinuses, tears borne of shame.

"I can help you."

"By telling me. Please."

"No, I can help you remember. Do you want that?"

I nodded. Fuck, he was so close, breathing on me, his stubble so near I had to twitch to feel it. "Yes."

"We need to be alone," he said.

"What do you have in mind?"

He raised an eyebrow. He had no intention of telling me. God, I loved him. The power he carried in his bones, as if everything in his reach would be all right. No wonder I fell apart when he went away.

"Okay," I said. I didn't mention that being alone was against the rules or that breaking them could keep me incarcerated longer than either of us wanted. "Wait here."

He leaned back, and I got up. I glanced at Mark on the way to the bathroom, jerking my head toward the inside. Like a good little monkey, he followed me, catching me outside the door to the ladies'.

"What?" he asked. "You doing all right?"

"I need to be left alone by the fence."

"With the guy?"

"With the guy."

He crossed his arms. "I could get fired for that."

"I'll make it worth the risk."

"You ain't that good, baby."

I should have put a little more effort into our bathroom encounter. That would have made for an easier negotiation. "Five grand when I get out."

"Ten."

"Seven. No more bullshit. You're not the only orderly in here."

He considered that for a second, probably spending the money in his mind.

"And I gotta have the guy at the monitors turn the camera. He could get fired too."

"Five for him."

We were taking too long. I already knew I was being watched, and talking to Mark outside the bathroom would be noticed anyway.

"You gave pretty good head," he said.

"Jesus, you're a pig."

He seemed to like that. I should have called him a gentleman.

"My cock needs sucking, dollface. I'm on night shift, and it gets a little boring watching you whack jobs beat off."

"Fine. Just take care of it." I pushed my way into the bathroom before he could demand my ass as well.

Karen was coming out of a stall. "That Deacon? The guy on the bench I saw you with?" Her breath smelled of puke. Her voice and gait were weak and drowsy.

"Yeah."

"Wow. He's like… I don't know the word. Powerful, maybe? Jesus. And those eyes."

"Yeah. He's great on the inside too." I didn't have to pee, so I just straightened my hair in the mirror. I needed a minute for Mark to do his thing.

"Good for you," she said, going for the door. "You could use a break."

"Thanks." She was about to open the door when I said, "Can you keep away from the holes by the creek?"

"Sure. Everyone's in session, more or less. You should be fine."

I held the door open for her, because she was having trouble with the weight of it. Mark was across the room, moving a tray of medication. He saw me and winked. A little nod of his chin told me what I needed to know.

I went outside. Deacon was waiting for me, a beautiful streak smeared on a miserable landscape. I held my hand out for him.

"All taken care of," I said.

"You have real skill."

I pulled him into the garden. "You have no idea."

"Don't I?"

He did actually, but I didn't want to tell him I'd just spent twelve grand and promised a distasteful blowjob in exchange for thirty minutes of privacy with him. I would have spent more. I would have tacked on more money and let that pathetic fucker come in my ass a hundred times just to be with Deacon.

"Here we are," I said when we got to the chain link. A new hole had been opened. "Not glamorous, but it's what I got."

He pulled the hole wide. "Go on."

I slipped through, and he followed, getting his wide shoulders through the narrow opening without mussing a stitch of his clothing or mellowing his intensity. I felt as if we'd crossed some sort of threshold together. He stood straight above me, and I knew there would be no more talking. No more promises. No more sweet words. Not until we'd slipped back to the other side of the gate.

My heart pounded. "Master, may I speak?"

"Go ahead."

"We need to stay on the other side of this tree if we're going to be out of the camera's range." I kept my eyes on his shoes. I was trying not to smile with joy and excitement. "If that's what you want."

"Take your shoes off," was all he said.

I slipped them off and handed them over.

"Good girl," he said. "Now go to the other side of the tree. Pull your pants down to mid thigh, spread those pretty legs, and wait for me."

Breathless with anticipation, I walked my socks to the other side of the tree. With my back to the trunk, I hooked my fingers under my elastic waistbands and pulled my pants and pretty cotton underwear halfway between my crotch and my knee. The forest air hit my ass and my wet cunt like a slap. I put my hands at my sides and stretched my legs as far apart as the clothing would allow.

Deacon was there. I tingled all over with that thought.

But he didn't come around the tree right away. He spoke from the other side. "Pull your shirt up so I can see your tits. Hold it there."

He knew my tits weren't big enough to hold up the shirt, so I was left with my hands on the hem, showing myself to no one but the Deacon-to-come, the specter of a promise soon to be fulfilled. My nipples stood erect, and my pussy seemed made of pulsing blood.

Deacon came around the tree soon after. A shoelace was draped over his arm. He had a sneaker in his hands. The Velcro was pulled back to reveal the lace underneath. He yanked it out hole by hole. *Whup. Snap. Whup. Snap.* The laces were quite long. I could have hanged myself with them easily.

"Debbie told me you were babbling about taking care of something that night. She described a leather bag you were carrying that she'd never seen before, but I knew was your horse grooming kit."

"I don't—"

He slapped me across the tits. The sting was delicious.

"Let me finish." He grabbed my jaw tightly. "I'll ask a question when I want one answered."

"Yes, Sir," I whispered.

"She said you told her you were going to be a grown-up for once. So I went to get you. I was angry." *Whup. Snap. Whup. Snap.* "I didn't want to be manipulated, and Fiona, make no mistake, you can be manipulative." *Whup. Snap.* The last bit of shoelace was free. He dropped the shoe and ran the laces through his fingers. "But Debbie was worried which, from her, I take seriously."

He looped the laces, knotting them in a way I couldn't detect, and stepped toward me until I felt his jacket on my skin.

"Put your hands on the branch above you. Grab it."

I did, letting my shirt drop. The branch was just above my reach, making me stand on my tiptoes to grasp the rough winter bark. He twisted the laces around my wrists then around the branch, securing me.

"And I found you there," he said, letting the ends of the shoelace drop around my shoulder. "Alone, or so I thought."

I knew better than to speak though I wanted his brutal touch on me again. He wrapped the last of the lace under my tits, squeezing them every time I moved. I felt him behind me, doing the last knot. He yanked on the lace as if he was running out of length, then made it and pushed me. I swung. God, it was blissful. I closed my eyes and went outside myself to a place where I was no one, nothing.

"Look at me."

I did. He was backlit against the speckled canopy of leaves, and his gaze on me was like a caress in hard metal and soft flesh.

He leaned over whispered, saying the words he always said before he fucked me, sending me to a place where I surrender all anxiety to him.

"Empty your heart, my kitten. Empty your mind. Open your eyes. Who do you see?" He took my nipple in his fingers and twisted it.

"You," I gasped.

"Are you empty?"

"I am."

"Release your body to me. I have you. Even in the stables, I had you." He placed my right leg over his hip and said, "Remember."

━━━

I SMELL hay and shaved bone. I'm cramped between the horse and the back wall. There's no thrush on Snowcone's frog, and that kind of pisses me off. He's been taken care of like a favorite child, even with me gone. He kicked me two years ago, and I'd walked out, blaming the horse for what the rider should have known.

Here I am again, showing up like I belong here, and he looks at me as if he knows good god damn well I abandoned him for doing what horses do. I hate myself. Disappointment. Deserter. I've been abandoned for being who I am, and I'd done the same to this poor baby.

It's night, which is a stupid time to show up hoping my key still works, but where else was I going to go? Who else would bear me? I had to see if Snowy would take me back. I had to see if even an animal would have me. And I want to do something for him, to repay him for the unrestrained nuzzle. I want to groom and love him. A brush would be fine, but any hand can brush. I want to go an extra mile.

But his hooves are near perfect. He's old, and richly indulged, and unloved.

I need to stop crying. I can't see the frog and the knife isn't pointy, but the edge is sharp, and I don't want to hurt the horse.

I needed to stop crying. Deacon was whispering to me, 'remember, remember, remember.' His cock's at my opening, and I was sure I would come when he entered me.

"Fiona? Fiona Drazen?"

Her voice surprises both me and Snowcone. I leap up with my knife, and the horse shifts and clops.

"Who are you?" I ask.

She's in her late teens, and she has long blond hair and muddy eyes. Jeans, zip-front cardigan; she's average in dress, but she has an intensity that makes me wary.

"My name is Rachel Demarest. I want to talk to you."

"About what?"

She steps forward. "I'm a friend of your family. Maybe Jonathan talked about me?"

"No."

"Well, we're dating so…" She twists the ends of her hair. "Theresa? Did she mention—?"

"What's your name again?"

"Rachel. Jeeze, I feel so stupid. I mean, look at the time. You've never even heard of me. You must think I'm some sort of stalker."

"You looking for a picture or something?" Maybe if I snap a picture with her, she'll go away and I can go on swimming in my own shit.

"No. I'm just… How can I say? Um, I just… I was meeting Theresa at your sister's. Sheila, I mean. She's having this Christmas party, and we're helping set up. It's right by the water." She waves vaguely west, to the shore edge of Rancho Palos Verdes. "So Theresa mentioned that you had a horse in these stables, which are, like, just over the hill, and I've been thinking of riding again so… God, this sounds just awful."

"How is Theresa?"

She shrugs. "You know, perfect."

Her eyes don't roll, but her tone matches a snarky eye roll, and I feel a little more comfortable with her. Theresa makes me want to roll my eyes too.

"This is a beautiful horse." She approaches Snowcone with her hand out and strokes his neck. "He's a hotblood?"

Deacon's cock slid in and out of me while I was tied to a tree, his voice in my ear. He told me over and over that it was all right, that he had me. I felt his arms around my waist, his hips holding me up, the swelling heat between my legs.

"Arabian."

He was so good. So perfect. He took everything away.

"Gorgeous."

"My brother's girlfriend, huh? Sorry. I haven't talked to the little fucker in a long time."

"I'll tell the fucker you said hello."

I laughed a little, letting go of a slice of my sadness and loneliness. Maybe I needed to spend more time with friends. Maybe that was the way to forget about Deacon.

"I think you're amazing," she whispers so softly I don't know if she's talking to me or the horse. "You're so composed. So confident. Even when they come after you the way they do."

"I don't feel so confident." I sit and get back to Snowcone's hoof.

He huffs and fidgets more than he did before. He doesn't like two people handling him. Was he always that way? I don't even know.

"Hey, Rachel, could you—"

"I thought I could be someone like you."

"Just take a step back while I finish up, okay? He's skittish."

She does, and Snowcone calms a little. I'm in control. I have this. As empty as I feel, I take this as a good sign.

"I wanted to go to an Ivy," she says. "I have the grades. Did you know they give a ton of financial aid?"

"Really?" I let his leg down.

"But I can't get any. My parents make too much, but not enough to actually pay the tuition. Isn't that funny? And here's my boyfriend, who could pay with his pocket change."

I don't have an answer for her. I already feel like shit. I put the knife on top of the kit while I put away the stool. I slip past her, my back grazing Snowcone's side in the tight stall. In that second, from the way she looks at me, I know I could have her right there. Why not? What does anything matter anymore? All this pain could go away for a second, cocooned in a silky knot of sex.

"Master." He fucked me full, pushing himself against my clit. I was a white swirl of pleasure. "I'm going to come."

"Have you remembered?"

"No, but—"

"Then you may not."

I kiss her, because she's there and I'm an addict. Addicts don't give a shit. Addicts are only concerned with pausing their own pain. I put my tongue in her mouth and grab her hair, yanking it. She kisses me back, groaning and pushing her luscious tits on me. I put my hand up her shirt, under her bra, and run a thumb over her nipple. She gasps. Snowcone shuffles.

"Are we going to fuck or what?" I say.

"I've never—"

"Gotten your clit sucked by a woman? Oh, honey, you've never been licked and fingered until a woman's done it." I bend my knee between her legs, pressing against her cunt.

She grinds against me. "Jonathan… Don't you care about him?"

So close to her face, I see a flash of something in her eyes. Something less than innocent. Something more experienced than she's letting on. I pretend I didn't see that. I can't think about her motives, because I have a need and she's going to satisfy it.

"He'll get over it," I say.

"Remember, kitten. I have you." He was so tender.

I was crying and close. I cried for the careless bitch I was and the fact that I didn't feel changed at all. Who deserved me? Not even my family deserved such a reckless whore.

"I'm sorry," I said, more to everyone I'd ever fucked over than to Deacon.

"You're forgiven."

I yank her pants down and get my finger on her pussy. She's soaking wet, a slippery mass of flesh I know how to navigate. When I touch her clit, she squeaks. I'm in control; I have this bitch. I can make her cluck like a god damn chicken or come like a queen.

I take her hand and put it flat against my belly then push down. "Come on, touch it. It feels just like yours."

She bites her lip and timidly touches my clit.

"That's right," I say.

She runs circles around the hood, making me groan. I hook my fingers in her hole and press the heel of my hand to her clit, sliding it back and forth. She looks at me with her mouth open, eyes hooded.

"Don't come," Deacon said.

"Don't come," I say.

"I don't think I can stop."

"I can't stop it."

"Stay with me, Fiona."

"Stay with me, Rachel."

"I—"

"I—"

"I have you."

"I have you."

"Fiona?" It's Deacon's voice, and then it all happens very fast.

Rachel screams in surprise. Enormous pressure on my back as Snowcone bucks. Deacon's voice. Rachel letting out a war cry as she pushes me away. The horse slams me back toward her. Deacon grabs the bridle. Rachel has the knife, and I hear her scream, "I hate you! I hate all of you!" She thrusts for my face, and I can't move. The horse and wall are in my way. I move. She misses, but I'm cornered. Deacon shouts something I can't hear over Snowcone's bucking and neighing.

The horse moves.

I fall.

She's on top of me.

"He'll kill you. Your brother. Your cunt's all over my hands."

The horse's feet clop around me. They could crush my head. But Rachel is so mad, and she doesn't know.

"You're all going to pay." She's laughing. Crying.

Where's Deacon?

Snowy's losing it.

It's loud.

The paddock shakes when Snowcone rears.

The hoof knife falls toward my face, handle first.

I roll, missing getting my head crushed by an inch.

Rachel is sucked away, backward, clawing for my face. She grabs the knife.

I get my feet under me. Snowcone bucks his rear to the right, into Rachel's knife hand. It drops. I grab it, and I'm confused. Because Rachel is fighting him, and I'm still heavy between my legs. She's calling him a lowlife pervert. That's Deacon she's talking to. He's trying to wrestle her away without hurting her, but we're in this tiny space with a bucking horse. My sexual arousal changes to unmitigated fire when she hits him in the face.

He hurt me. He left me broken and adrift, but he's mine. She can't do that. She can't hit him, because when she does that, sh'se threatening me, my life, my love, my world.

And I have a knife. It's for scraping not stabbing, but the handle is hard in my hand, and she has to get the fuck away from him. She's a wildcat. He's trying to grab her wrists.

"Fiona!" he calls.

I don't know if it's to help him or to get back, but I'm mid swing. I realize why he called my name, but it's too late. Snowcone bucks again, making everything nuts. Rachel is pushed away, and the knife finds its way into Deacon's chest. I yank it out in a reflex. There's no blood. Not yet. He just looks like a stricken man with a ripped shirt.

He's not mine. He's not my world. He just cut me loose to drift into an endless void.

I'm a rush of hormones and endorphins, a slave to my anger and pain. "Fuck you!" I punch his chest. But there's a knife in my hand.

He deflects. The wound is shallow, but it's the one made with intention. I scream.

Though Snowcone seems to calm despite everything, and Deacon at first seems bemused and stunned, Rachel is still pure adrenaline. She pushes me down to get out of the claustrophobic paddock.

Then the blood appears. Deacon's mouth and eyes are open, and they're filled with me. The knife falls. A door slams. Everything goes black.

I felt as though I was going to die. Not die.

Cease.

As if my existence was about to be snuffed into a tiny dot as big as the universe and black as the sun. Though I usually dove into the obliteration, I didn't this time. I feared this orgasm as I'd feared no other, until I heard his voice.

"Come, darling. I have you."

Chapter 45

FIONA

HE'D UNTIED me and put my shoes back on, kneeling before me as I sat on a tree trunk. It seemed as though hours had passed, but it had only been twenty minutes, plus five for him to take me down and another five for me to tell him my memory.

"I'm sorry, again. I'm sorry," I said.

"You didn't mean it. It was an accident."

"The second one. I meant that one."

"Barely a scratch."

"Deacon—"

He put his fingers on my lips. I needed him to make me suffer, and not within the boundaries of funishment. I needed to writhe from his anger. I needed to feel as though I was dying. That was only fair.

"When I negotiate with the men holding my people, I have to see past their anger," he said. "I have to see their suffering. If I can't see the human inside them who saw their fathers killed or maimed, or if I can't speak to their slow starvation, I can't get to them. I stay on the outside. In order for me to find them, I need to be inside." He put his hand on his heart. "When you took that second stab, I was inside you."

"But those guys, when you negotiate with them, and you find them—"

"They aren't my reason for living." He stood and held his hand out to me. "Once my guys are safe, those men are tools for a message."

I took his hand, and he pulled me up. "So you're not going to have me dragged into the square?"

"Never. Martin, on the other hand..." He didn't finish, just put his arm around me, and we walked to the fence. "Your father. She was trying to blackmail him?"

"That's what Theresa and Margie said."

"I think she needed one of you to speak against your father. She needed you to break apart to do that."

"We'd never," I said.

"Not her, not this time. But you're only human. All eight of you. One day, you're going to fall apart. But not because of me. So I didn't tell anyone about that girl until I had the whole story."

"I think Jonathan would break if he knew."

"I won't tell."

"I know how you feel about the cops anyway. But she's dead now. It won't help anything."

We walked to the fence, and he pulled it open a little for me. I crawled through as a different person, a cleansed one. I was a woman who, if not sinless, had had her gravest sins washed clean.

The garden was quiet. No one had found us. Mark had kept up his end of the deal. Deacon and I walked back to the garden, then to the front lobby. His time was up.

"Deacon, I have something to say."

"Say it."

"I love you," I said.

"I know."

"I don't know if this is what I want. What we have. I don't know. I don't want to lose you, but I can't string you along if I don't know."

He touched my chin with his thumb. "What we have is exactly what you need. Nothing else will work for you. We fix each other's brokenness."

"I don't want to be broken."

He shook his head. "You don't get to choose that. You can choose to let me protect you, and I will Fiona. If you stay with me, I'll stand between you and anything that comes at you. I'll be your guardian and avenging angel."

When he left and I watched him roll away in his black car from the upstairs window, wondereing if I could make it without him. He didn't fix me. He didn't make me whole. He took my broken pieces and gave the cracks between them a purpose. Who was I without that? I shuddered with fear at the thought. I'd be adrift without him, a dinghy in an ocean, but until I faced that lonely expanse, I'd never find land.

Chapter 46

FIONA

THE LIGHTS WENT OUT.

My arms ached from being tied, and the abrasions from the shoelaces throbbed a little. I didn't want to touch myself. My clit had rolled over and gone to sleep finally.

I'd left the bathroom door open a crack. I thought I should close it or the whoosh of the pipes would keep me up. I'd forgotten to take the Halcion. I thought I should get up and take it. I was meeting with Elliot in the morning to talk about whether or not I was ready to be released, and I wanted to be rested. I closed my eyes and thought about the stables, about Jonathan's girlfriend, about kissing and fingering a woman I'd never met knowing that she belonged to him.

That was the old me.

The new me wouldn't do stuff like that anymore.

Someone somewhere flushed a toilet. The pipes whooshed. I considered getting up and closing the bathroom door, but I was asleep before I could.

―――――――――――

Chapter 47

―――――――――――

ELLIOT

SHE LOOKED RESTED. Her eyes were lit with awareness, and her face was alert and reactive. That was the effect Deacon had on her. Much as I wanted to hate him for touching her the way he did or get angry that he had what I wanted, the change in her demeanor could not be ignored.

"I saw you go into the trees," I said. "You were supposed to stay in sight."

She swallowed hard. "Why didn't you ring an alarm or something?"

"It would achieve nothing."

"But isn't that what it's always been?" she said. "People keeping me from the consequences of my actions?"

"Do you want to know the consequences of your actions yesterday?"

"I'd have to stay."

"No. You'd get kicked out."

She laughed to herself and shifted in her seat.

I continued, "It was clear to me, after I met Deacon, that he wouldn't hurt you. I didn't think he'd put himself in a position again where you could hurt him."

Which was partly dishonest. I knew no one was going to get hurt. But I was jealous. Seething. If I'd sent someone after them, it would have been nothing but a reaction to my jealousy. I couldn't let that happen. I was still her therapist.

"Thank you," she said.

"You didn't hurt him, and he didn't hurt you. So keeping you here to keep you away from Deacon isn't enough reason. You're sane and stable enough to face questioning. I don't think we can hold you anymore." I should have been relieved or at least happy, but I was confused.

"When am I going?"

"I have to do some paperwork, but probably in a day."

I gauged her reaction, and it was surprise, not fear. That was good.

"Are you okay?" I asked.

"I think so."

"You look a little shell-shocked."

"I'm scared to go out there. I'm scared of the cameras, and my family, and honestly, I'm scared of myself. I don't know what I'll do, but I have to decide whether to go back to Maundy or not. Right now, I think no. I have to get control of my life, and Deacon was a crutch. When he was gone, then this place became a crutch. I get, right now, why people want to stay in here."

"You should probably continue some sort of therapy," I said.

"Yeah. But I don't live in Compton."

"I can't be your therapist anymore."

"Why not?" She sat straighter, and her voice went up an octave. She was hurt.

I hadn't intended to hurt her. "Because I don't have a private practice."

Because I can't look at you.

Because all I want to do is touch you.

Because I want to hunt and kill everyone who ever hurt you.

Because healing you is personal to me.

Because I'm going to fall in love with you.

"I don't want to talk to anyone else," she said.

"I'll recommend someone you'd like." I stood, buttoning my jacket.

"Give yourself some time after you leave before you decide how to proceed with therapy. But not too much."

"Sure," she said, standing.

We went to the door together, and I put my hand on the knob. We did that every time, but this was the last time, and I was slow to open the door. She came close to me.

"Fiona." I said her name as if I was entering another place, another state where words were warmer, and the things I felt didn't have to be locked away.

"Yeah?"

I had to press my lips between my teeth before I said something stupid. I released them when something sane was ready to come out. "I liked working with you."

"You know how I feel," she said.

In her voice… did I hear that same warm place? If I did, was it even valid? "I guess I do, I just…" *Shut up.*

Her hand flicked to the ends of her red hair. As it fell back down, a reflex came straight from my lizard brain.

I caught it.

What the fuck are you doing?

Her fingers rested on mine, and with my thumb…

Don't.

…I brushed the tops of them.

You're breaking a sacred trust.

I looked from the hands to her face. Her eyes flicked back and forth, her lips parted. She was motionless as I leaned closer, like a ship keening on the sea. If I kissed her now…

Your career is over.

She'd open her mouth, and our tongues would touch. I'd taste her. I'd feel her warmth. I wanted to. I wanted her more than I wanted my career. My nose ran astride hers, and I tasted her breath. She was there for it. She wanted me to.

She's probably going back to Deacon.

I closed my mouth and tilted my head to put my lips, and the kiss, out of reach. "I'm sorry." I dropped her hand.

"It's okay."

"No, it's not."

"The other day, when you told me all the words to use to describe myself, you forgot one."

"Really? What?"

"Irresistible."

Chapter 48

FIONA

I RAN AS FAST as I could in those stupid shoes. I was getting out, and even as scared as I was, my joy at my freedom wasn't easily contained.

And there was Elliot. It had been a moment. His thumb on my fingers. His mouth so close to mine at twitch would have brought our lips together.

He wouldn't have me. He wouldn't come near me again, not if his life depended on it. I knew that. But I also knew that a normal man with normal desires who wanted a normal life could, in the short run at least, find someone like me attractive. And in that, a crack opened, and a stream of possibilities poured in.

I barely stopped in front of Karen's room. Discovering she wasn't there, I checked the upstairs rec room. Jonathan was playing ping pong with Warren as if it was a full-contact, high-stakes sport.

"Jon! I'm out tomorrow!"

"Thank god," he said with a *thup crack thup.* "I'm sick of looking at you."

I was about to go down to the cafeteria when I saw the ambulance outside. "What happened? There are paramedics in the driveway?"

Warren didn't lose a beat. "Karen had a heart attack."

Jonathan caught the ball midair. "What? How?"

Warren shrugged, but I knew god damn well what had happened. She'd taken Warren Pharma's uppers to kill her appetite, and her heart gave out. I stared Warren down, and he smirked and shrugged. Jonathan joined me at the window.

"Shit," he mumbled.

I ran downstairs. A crowd stood outside the cafeteria doors, but having clubbed my whole life, they were a permeable barrier, as long as I didn't care who I pissed off.

Mark stopped me. "Hold on. If you're not an EMT, you're on this side of the line."

Past him, six paramedics lifted Karen onto a gurney.

I pushed Mark out of the way and ran to her. "Karen!"

I didn't know if she'd heard me. Tubes were sticking out of her face and arm, and her head was held still by a white contraption. Hands grabbed me. I shook them off until I got to her, and she saw me. Her eyes were half-closed but alert.

"We're friends outside this place. You got it?"

She blinked. She'd heard me. Mark came behind me and wrestled my arms behind my back.

"Okay, okay!" I shouted. "We're good. I'm going."

I stood with my hands up, perfectly still, and Mark stepped back to let me pass.

Chapter 49

ELLIOT

HOME. The house I'd bought in a flurry of financial optimism during an economic downturn. The last bit of luck I'd ever had.

The lights were off, but Jana was home. Her car was in the drive, and I saw the dim flickering of the fireplace through the front curtains. I'd almost kissed Fiona Drazen in my office. So much went through my head, the churning excuses, the feeling of autonomy, the crushing guilt.

I dropped my bag at the door and walked into the living room. Jana stood in front of the fireplace, her short silk nightgown falling over her breasts like light pink syrup over a vanilla sundae. Her hands were at her sides, fingertips tight against each other. Her big toes lay right over left.

"Hi," she said.

"Hi."

"How was your day?"

"Fine. Yours?"

"I'm sorry," she blurted. "For accusing you. But you've been distant, and that was where my mind went."

I stepped close to her, raising my hand over her breast without touching it. If I lowered my hand, I'd feel the nub of her erect nipple under the silk. I'd draw my hand down the fabric until I got to the hem, then I'd reach under and find out what was happening beneath that nightgown.

"I'm sorry too," I said. "I've been distant. You're right."

I didn't lower my hand. If I admitted I had another woman on my mind, the fact that I'd never actually laid a hand on her would be utterly irrelevant. I'd cheated emotionally. If I told Jana that, how deeply would it hurt her, standing there in her pink silk nightgown before a roaring fire?

If I touched that tit, I would fuck her and fuck her hard. I would think of Fiona, and that wasn't right. She'd put on that nightgown for a difficult evening. I couldn't take her with a clean conscience, and I couldn't refuse without leaving her.

I put my hand in my pocket.

She swallowed. "There's someone else."

"No, but..."

"But what?"

"But there may as well be."

Was that cruel? Was there an easy way to do this? Was there ever a good time to tell someone that your heart had been looking for someplace to land for a long time, and the fact that it had landed with someone inaccessible didn't mend the unhappiness?

"What does that mean?" Her lower lip quivered.

I wanted to take it back, fuck her senseless, and break up with her later during a convenient little fight that I'd engineer. But that was the coward's way out, wasn't it? "I'm sorry."

"You want me to leave?"

"You're a beautiful woman. You're smart and caring, and... It's not you, it's—"

The slap on my cheek rang my bell. Of all her fine qualities, I hadn't counted a left hook among them.

"You are a fucking prick," she said, finger pointed. "You're a drifter. You haven't been able to hold down a job since you walked away from your discernment committee. You don't talk about it. You don't talk about anything. You only start all this weird fucking dirty talk. You spank my ass in the bathroom and expect me to what, enjoy that? And now you have the nerve to tell me how 'beautiful' I am? And that's what? Prelude to a break up?"

I noticed that her nipples were no longer making peaks through the fabric of the nightgown. We were doing it, right here, right now, breaking up. It was the right thing, the only thing, and it felt like hell. "I'm sorry."

"Well, guess what? Maybe I'm not interested in a guy who'll bring gang bangers to the house. Maybe I'm not about to let my kids hear you tell me what you're going to do to my pussy by the refrigerator. You've changed, Elliot. I don't know if this is a phase or what, but you've changed."

"And you haven't." I tried to stop myself but couldn't. "You're still a sheltered, scared child."

"You're just pissed off you couldn't fix me. This is not my failure. It's yours."

Everything we needed to say to each other had just been said, but it would go on all night. The beginning parts had gone down easier with a dose of uncontrolled rage.

She stormed into the bedroom, slamming the door. I looked at the ceiling, my hands still in my pockets. She was right about everything, and I was too. None of the obstacles between us were insurmountable. We could work on all of it, stay together, and be happy-ish. But I wasn't willing to climb that mountain. It seemed a long, hard slog for a peak overlooking a view I didn't care to see.

I poked at the fire, moving a log so it would go out sooner rather than later. I didn't feel good about what I was about to do, but it was honest. I stood, replaced the poker, and went into the bedroom to do what I should have done months ago.

Chapter 50

FIONA

I WALKED BACK from breakfast drowsy with contentment after a night of non-Halcion-aided sleep. I was leaving. A few hours more, and I was free. Free to deal with my family's shit. My father and his proclivities. My mother and her constant terrors. My brother's dead girlfriend. The media.

Deacon.

I was done at Maundy. It had been a chapter of my life, and it was time to move along and control myself, my desires, my dreams. My plan was to focus on riding. I'd maybe train another horse, maybe do some coaching. I couldn't do that with Deacon allowing me a life driven by my cunt. When that thing was at the wheel, every other life's desire went dark.

"Hey," Mark called. He was in his street clothes, torn black jeans and a black sleeveless Metallica tee. "You owe me. I got ten minutes."

"You know I can't get money from here."

"I ain't talking about the money."

I rolled my eyes. "Fine. Let's get this over with."

As I kneeled on the bathroom floor and took his cock down my throat while he called me names, I was kind of relieved. Once I got out of Westonwood, I wouldn't make deals like that anymore. Blowjobs weren't currency. I could say no like a normal person and find some other way to pay for what I needed.

Mark wouldn't appreciate the fact that he would be the last stranger who grabbed my hair to hold my head still so he could come on my face. That was all right. He didn't need to know. I needed to know. I had control over my shit.

I wiped his jizz off my eyelid and looked in the mirror at the queen of her domain, master of her universe.

Chapter 51

FIONA

THE GROUNDS never seemed so huge as when I was looking for my brother and couldn't find him.

"Warren," I said, approaching a small group of guys, "have you seen Jonathan?"

He looked me up and down, as if assessing more than a lost sibling. "I think he went past the gate for a smoke. Come on, I need to catch up with him too."

I followed him past the treeline.

"So," he said, "I hear you're getting out today?"

"Yeah, I just have to run upstairs and change. I wanted to catch him before second sessions."

"He's around somewhere." He peeled the chain link back for me.

"Hey," I said from the other side, "can you kind of look out for him? Make sure he doesn't lose his temper over stupid shit?"

He slid through. "Sure. He's all right, that kid."

"Yeah, he is." I walked on, scanning for the kid Warren spoke about as if he wasn't close by. "I don't see him." I skirted the edge of the creek. "Maybe he's back in his room?"

"Jonny?" Warren barked, getting ahead of me. "How's the Halcion panning out?" he called back to me.

"Great." I followed him. "Thanks for it."

"Good." He put his arm around me. "You know, you owe me for that shit."

"How much do you need?"

"I have money." He looked at my lips and down my shirt, flicking his tongue over his top lip.

Shit. "Warren, I'm not interested in that kind of trade. Can you think of something else?"

"Sure." He wove his fingers in my hair.

I dropped my arm from his waist and leaned away.

He balled his hand into a fist, grabbing my hair, and pulled me to my knees. "I can think of something else, but it's not what I *want*, okay?"

"Ow! Warren! Stop!"

He threw me onto the ground, and my cheek slapped onto a layer of wet leaves and rock. I tried to scramble up, but he used my forward motion to get my pants down, sliding them to my calves. I screamed, but it came out as a grunt since the wind was still knocked out of me. He threw his weight on top of me and clamped his hand over my mouth.

"Scream." He was breathless himself, holding my mouth with one hand and wiggling his dick out with the other. "Maybe your brother will come. He'll walk away when he sees his whore sister getting it up the ass. Then how's that release gonna work out? You caught here doing what you do?"

I shook my head. I felt the skin of his cock against my butt cheek. "No," I said into his hand.

"I don't hear that. Not from you. You had it in your ass so much in Ojai I can't believe you ever sat again. I'm moving my hand. You scream, and I'll tell them you wanted it. Ain't nothing to me if I have to stay."

My fingertips gripped the soft earth. My ass was already sweaty from being pressed against him.

"I'm moving my hand," he said.

I groaned, not agreeing to anything. He slipped it away.

"Please don't," I said.

"There's some shit Daddy can't pay for." He put his dick between my ass cheeks. I tried to get away, but he yanked my hair back. "Stay still and take it, you little whore."

With that, he jammed himself forward, missing my ass. Undaunted, he adjusted and pushed himself inside. My face contorted. Tears fell. My breath went out of me.

"Oh, you're so fucking tight for a slut."

"Warren, it hurts. Please. Lube me or something. God, fuck."

He pulled out and pummeled me again. "I like it dry."

He hitched my hips up. I was crying as he bore into me.

"I hate you," I growled through my tears. "I'm going to get you for this, you fuck." My face was inches from the ground, so close my breath bounced back into my face.

A caterpillar crawled from under a leaf, his body curling around the edge, changing its shape with as his teeth ate it slowly.

"How much Halcion you got in your blood?" He pounded relentlessly, shredding my ass. "That's mine. I paid for this fuck, little slut. Yeah, take it all the way. You love it in the ass like this. All whores want a dick in their ass. Say it."

"No!" Fuck him. He wasn't getting consent. Not for anything. Not for one stroke.

He put his hands around my throat. "Am I not fucking you hard enough?"

He tightened his grip, and the edges of my vision darkened as he beat my asshole with his cock. I only saw, in a pinpoint of light, the little caterpillar eat his way across a leaf. I waited in the center of my pain for that caterpillar to grow his wings and fly away.

Chapter 52

ELLIOT

RIGHT ABOUT LUNCHTIME, I thought about Fiona. I thought about where she was in her day, when she was being released, how she was getting home, where home was, and who was taking her. I thought about her over my sandwich, and pushed it away not because I felt full but too dissatisfied to eat.

Our final good-bye gnawed at me. After I'd told Lee about my eternal night with Jana, as we negotiated the emotional parts of our breakup, I mentioned the almost kiss with Fiona.

"You're kidding," she said, her face white.

"Almost, but we didn't."

"*We* didn't? No, no, you do not put it on the patient when you—"

"She's a grown woman."

"—clearly crossed a line—"

"Nothing happened."

"—taking advantage of her—"

"Come on, Lee. She's gone. It's over. I'll never see her again."

She slammed her hands on the desk. "Do not absolve yourself of responsibility. I am stunned, stunned at what's gone on."

"You're losing your professional countenance."

"I'm livid for her. The fact that you can sit there and make lame, embarrassing excuses for totally inappropriate behavior sickens me. I know I'm your therapist. I'm supposed to sit here and ask you how you feel about what did or didn't happen, but I don't care how you feel." Her face was beet red, fists clenched, her unborn baby getting cortisol by the quart. "I'm enraged for the entire psychiatric community."

"Then fuck the psychiatric community entirely."

I'd walked out in a tight ball of anger, unable to see a past opening my car door, getting in it, and turning left out of the lot. Right. Right. Left. Straight. Around the corner to Alondra, where I sat with my sandwich, wondering what Fiona was doing in her last hour before release.

I couldn't see her. Lee had been right, if unprofessional in her delivery. The therapist and patient had a relationship based on the therapist's power. By using that power inappropriately, I'd broken a wall that had been erected for a reason. A good reason.

I crunched up my paper wrapping and told myself I wouldn't see Fiona again. I exited the lunch room to get to the paperwork I needed to finish before I went home to my empty house.

Minutes later, with the paperwork undone on my desk, I got in my car. Naturally I was going home. I was too distracted to fill in little boxes and put together sentences coherent enough for insurance companies and government agencies. As a matter of fact, I thought, as I turned south on the 110 instead of north, I didn't think I could ever do that work again.

As I went west off the exit, deep into Rancho Palos Verdes with its exclusive horse-and-pony enclaves, lawyers' mansions, actors' estates, winding roads around nature preserves, and of course, facilities for the mental health of the very monied, I thought I could do better than that paperwork. So much better.

As long as I kept my hands off the patients.

Chapter 53

FIONA

I COULDN'T CRY.

If I cried, I wouldn't stop. They'd see me and ask me what was wrong, and then everything was a crapshoot.

If I cried and managed to stop, I'd have puffy eyes, and they'd ask me what was wrong. Then I wouldn't know what came next.

So I didn't. I put my head down and walked to my room smiling at everyone I knew. I didn't slow down. I acted as though I had to pee. As though I'd be back in a minute to say good-bye. My ass felt as though I was in the middle of taking a crap, and fuck if I didn't feel blood dripping down my leg.

But fuck it. Maybe I was rushing because I had my period.

Right?

I got into my room and snapped the bathroom door closed behind me. *Do not motherfucking cry, or you're not getting out of here.*

I had to breathe. Just breathe.

Warren had pulled out of my ass and slapped my butt cheek. He'd said, "Thanks, Fiona," as if I'd only told him "no" a hundred times to fulfill his little rape fantasy.

"Fuck off, Warren."

"Aw, come on." He'd tucked his dick back into his pants. "You're being a poor sport."

I'd been kneeling at that point, my pants still around my ankles, and the front of my shirt was covered in leaves and dirt. When I'd looked at him, I thought about what I would do to him when we were both out. I smiled.

The color drained from his face.

As I got in the shower I held that in my memory, nothing else. Cleaning myself. Soap. Washcloth. Drained face. Wiping, scrubbing.

Don't think about it.

My busted ass, the pain inside and out. The pressure marks on my neck. I could think about all that. I could feel all of it.

But my vulnerability? My mortality? My pathetic, helpless whimpers? I wouldn't think about those until I walked out the door.

I got dressed, wincing as I lifted a leg into my pants. No. No wincing. No pain. No outward manifestation of what just happened.

I didn't know what I planned to do about Warren, but I was in control of that. I wouldn't let the emotions of the moment dictate my plan.

"Hey," Jonathan called as I walked down the hall.

"I was looking for you," I said.

"Warren told me."

I swallowed. I was edgy, raw, and a touch away from breaking down, but if I told Jonathan, he'd beat the shit out of the motherfucking psycho-rapist. Then Jon would be stuck in Westonwood, and Warren would get pity. That wouldn't do at all.

"Good," I said. "Margie's picking me up. Wanna come say hi?"

"Nah. I gotta run." He looked me up and down. "You all right?"

"I'm fine."

"You sure? I saw Warren come out of the trees right before you."

"I have to go." When I went to hug him, he grabbed my jaw. I pushed him away. "What's your deal?"

"There are red marks on your neck."

"It's nothing. God, it was grungy behind my ears. I probably just scrubbed too hard."

He didn't believe me. It was all over his face. He held up his hand. "I'm opening pledge."

"No, you don't." I slapped down his hand. If he asked me one more time, I would tell him about not just Warren but Rachel, and we would both go into a tailspin. No, just no. I needed to stay together for five fucking minutes. I didn't want to collapse.

"I don't like that guy," he growled. "He keeps bringing up Dad like it's a joke."

"Ignore him."

"I'm going to punch him."

"Don't, Jon. You were right." I took him by the shoulders. He was so tall, so much a man with his shaved whiskers and lines of rage. "Bite it back. Don't do anything that puts you in a situation where you're not in control. Do you hear me?"

In his green eyes, something flickered, a recognition of the truth, an openness to me I'd never had from him before.

"Are you hearing me?" I said.

"I'm not going to make it."

"You are. You have to. Lock it down. Think. Plan. Will you? Will you be everything I fail at being?"

"You're crazy, you know that?" The crack in his voice belied his words.

I hugged him so hard I thought we'd never separate.

I SAT at the conference table as if my ass didn't hurt. I concentrated on each breath and just getting the fuck out of there. Margie looked over the papers. Deeming them acceptable, she passed them to me to sign.

"This one verifies you have no complaints against Westonwood you'd like to file," she said.

I signed it.

"This one," Marge said, "is a non-disclosure agreement. You won't disclose their treatment methods or names of any of the patients you met in here."

I signed.

Frances passed her new papers. Margie looked them over, sometimes said this or that, and passed them to me, pointing to the little highlighted ticks indicating where I should scrawl my name. I smiled through the whole thing, even though it was killing me.

"I'll bring the car around," Margie said when it was done.

I counted six couches in the lobby, but I didn't sit on any of them. I had no idea what I would do after Margie pulled around, but I would be out. I would keep everything under control.

Frances hustled through the glass doors. "Fiona."

"Yes?"

She handed me a clipboard. "I forgot this release."

"Oh, okay." I looked for my place to sign, but everything looked hazy.

"Are you all right?" she asked, pointing at the line at the bottom.

"Excited to get going." I signed.

"Have a good trip home, Fiona."

"Thanks."

She was gone in a moment. I glanced at the door. Elliot, a silhouette in the afternoon backlight, opened it and stepped into the building. My heart stopped.

I could have him. With a little effort on my part, and a lot of patience, I could be that perfect, monogamous, plain Jane. I could change my life completely. I pressed my lips together when he stepped toward me. I could be his.

But I couldn't.

How could I do that to him? I was a whore. I was the girl who gave up her ass for a few pills. Even though I knew in my mind it hadn't been my fault and Warren was a piece of shit, another part of me begged to differ. I was a worthless piece of fuckmeat, and even if I kept a lid on my desires for the rest of my life, the fact that my heart was made of cunt wouldn't change.

"Hi," I said.

"Hi," he said. "I was just around, and do you need a lift home?"

He hadn't shaved, and he looked somehow wild and out of sorts. He was so good, so real, a chance at a different life than I'd been prepared for.

"I'm good. But thanks." I couldn't stand there another second. I walked to the door, steeling myself against looking back at him.

As I approached the doors, I felt him behind me. His hand went over mine as it gripped the bar. Margie's BMW was coming around the corner of the drive. I had to just make that difference in distance.

"Fiona, listen," he whispered.

"I can't, Elliot. I can't. I'll destroy you. It's not right." I pushed the door open.

Margie pulled up as if she'd timed it so I wouldn't have to wait more than a second. As I stepped across the concrete toward her, I saw something twenty feet to the right that wasn't visible from the door. A black Range Rover, and a man in a charcoal jacket standing next to it.

Deacon.

It all became clear to me then. I had everything in the world I needed right with him, and he'd come for me as promised, as he always did. He protected me, loved me, worked with who I was instead of trying to transform me into something I'd never be.

I waved at Margie and walked past her. I knew Elliot was behind me, and I knew he saw me approach the Range Rover.

"Master," I said, casting my eyes down.

"My girl."

"May I come with you?"

"There are going to be rules. Do you understand?"

"Yes, Sir."

"And consequences. This can't happen again."

"I understand."

He took me by the chin. "Look at me, kitten."

I did and felt safe. Deacon wouldn't let anything happen to me.

"Who do you see?" he asked.

"My master."

"I have you, darling." He gripped my chin tightly. "I have you."

As I got into the car, I saw Elliot in front of the building with his hands in his pockets. He and Deacon exchanged a stare as my master crossed in front of the car. I closed my eyes and leaned my head back.

I was free, and enslaved, and in control.

I had this.

PART III

BREAK

Chapter 54

FIONA

THREE WORDS TO describe the feeling of driving with Deacon, trying to sit as if my ass hadn't just been ripped open. Vulnerable. Insecure. Guilty.

The paparazzi had been waiting outside the gates like fucking fuckers. Leeches. Slurping sucking animals who fucked you even when you said no. Who thought they were doing you a favor or at the very least thought they weren't hurting you when they were. They were.

Deacon hadn't said anything. He turned his face—blue eyes deadly, cheekbones of a god—toward one on the passenger side and stared down the man with the lens until he backed away from the car.

They knew who he was. A photojournalist. No more, no less. So they didn't know shit, but when he looked at people that way, they had to know he was a force of nature.

I put my fingertips on my cheek, slid them over to cover my mouth. My hand shook. How long had I been shaking? I hadn't even felt it. What parts of me were kinetic? I put my hand between my legs and hoped he didn't notice.

"I moved us out of Maundy," he said. "To the place in Laurel Canyon."

"What did you do with my stuff?"

"Your stuff is safe in your room."

I didn't actually care.

Who was I?

What was I supposed to do?

This wasn't new.

My ass hurt.

I was going to get Warren for this.

I'd said no.

One syllable and the same word in a dozen languages.

En-oh.

Deacon glanced at me. He was a dangerous man. If I told him about Warren, what would happen?

The easiest thing in the world. Like blowing up a building to take it down.

But they never talked about the mess it took months to clean up.

I'd said no. Clearly. And there I was with a ripped asshole while Warren was behind an electrified fence in a luxury institution.

The sun caught Deacon's eyes when he looked at me.

Never seen blue like that on a face. Not before him or since. Never seen a nose that had been broken so many times look so seamless. Nothing like it. And the look on his perfect face? Fuck him too. He couldn't tolerate lying, and I had to decide right then if I was going to do the intolerable.

Only Elliot had done things to me no man had before. He'd given me permission to choose to do things differently. He'd opened me the same way Deacon's look had, and Warren had walked right into the wound and ripped out my guts.

Deacon pulled up the private road off Laurel Canyon. I wanted to go home, and I didn't really have one anymore.

Why was I letting all these men do this to me? I was in the middle of nowhere, and I couldn't even get out of the car and get home. The door, the seats, the ceiling, and dashboard were leather-padded.

I laughed to myself.
Oh, God of irony, thou art great.

Chapter 55

FIONA

ONCE WE DROVE through the gate of the Laurel Canyon house, Deacon took my face and pulled me toward him. He kissed me in the way only Deacon did, owning me, sending a message that my mouth was his. I gave in to it, letting his tongue flick against mine, letting his lips guide mine in a dance of ownership. Even his hand was part of the kiss, pressing my jaw open. I breathed him in.

"Welcome back," he said.

Sex was never the point with Deacon. Sex was optional. Getting off didn't always mean unloading his balls on or in me, though when he did, I was in ecstasy. Getting off meant dominating me. And when I met him, it took me a while to understand that. Because I'm hot and horny, and he's a man. A man I wanted a lot.

But I'd forgotten a lot of things in Westonwood. And when I stepped onto the leaf-padded drive, I knew I'd changed.

And my insides hurt.

And I didn't know what to feel.

I was so confused. That caterpillar. Eating that leaf. And the pain. The same pain I'd felt a hundred times, but this time, I'd said no. I didn't ask for it. And that confused me and pissed me off, and I couldn't show it because Deacon's reaction wasn't something I could control.

The house was a classic, part of another small compound in the mountains. There would be coyotes, and he'd shoot them. There would be hippies and stoners, and he'd tolerate them.

Something about all of it made me sad. I should have felt relieved and safe, but all I felt was fucking sad. Not passive sad. Sad like I wanted to break something.

The house was furnished in hand-wrought chairs and wool rugs. I'd seen the place when he bought it, but I'd spent no time there.

"Where did you put me?" I asked before I could scream.

"Tell me what's wrong first."

We were headed into a conflict. We solved those by talking or by knotting. By me transferring my power to him. He'd ripped my memory from me in Westonwood without telling me what he was doing. Fucked me sane for half a minute. He'd do it again, and I wasn't sure if I could stand it. If he opened me, I didn't know if I'd be able to give myself time to think before he started making plans for Warren's destruction.

"I'm tired," I said. My guts were bubbling tar, foul and hot. Uncontainable. I wanted to destroy Warren. I wanted to do it myself, and I wanted Deacon to back the fuck up.

"You can tell me in bed." He took me by the shoulders. "Speak."

"It's stressful, that's all. Everything. What I did to you. And now I'm out, and I feel fucked up about it."

And now you're a liar.

Use different words to describe yourself.

He didn't believe me.

We went into the house. He took off my jacket. I didn't have a thing to say. The house had windows like most houses had walls. He leaned on a chair and folded his arms. He had a leather band on his wrist, and a silver bracelet with a feather engraved on it. His hair was perfectly mussed, and his hands had built fences and dug ditches. They'd pulled triggers and tied ropes.

"Deacon, I…" Words failed me. They got in their own way.

He picked me up and carried me. I put my head on his shoulder.

"I'm sorry," I said.

"I know."

He laid me on his bed. It was still daytime, but I was stone-dead tired, lost at sea in the white foam of his duvet.

"Do you think our limits move? Did you ever think you would have let anyone hurt you like that before?" The words slipped out like escapees. I hadn't thought about them for a second, and there I was, watching them run into the field without looking back.

"Why do you ask?" he asked without reproach.

He was a picture in a magazine. Lit for his angles, the ruddiness of his skin, the light beard, the way his hair draped in a sideways S. Flawless and secure. A wish blown off a dry dandelion.

He brought his hand up and drew his thumb along my lips. Suddenly I wanted to open up to him. I wanted to be broken all over again. Now. Right there. I didn't want to wait until I'd put Warren in a box or wait until my ass healed. I wanted to crack like an egg for him.

And yet, I didn't want that at all. My intentions stabbed each other in the back.

"I don't know." Trying not to cry was the most obvious sign something was wrong, and I didn't want him to know. Not yet. So I didn't cry. I just knew my limits had shifted from a foggy line miles and miles away to a cinderblock wall I'd just been smashed against.

Chapter 56

FIONA - Two years earlier

I LEANED over Amanda and called into the little security mic on the driver's side. "Fiona Drazen."

The gate to Maundy Street clicked and opened slowly, and the driveway lights flicked on. Amanda and I were sober. The handsome older guy in the leather jacket had specifically requested sobriety and more. We weren't permitted to even bring stuff with us.

"This better be good," Amanda said, turning her Mercedes into the gate. "Or I'm going to Phoebe's."

"There're a hundred paps outside that place. The rest are always pointing and looking away like they don't care. I'm sick of it already."

"You love it."

"You can take the car if you want to bolt," I replied, checking my face in the visor mirror.

"So you're staying the night? Jesus. You haven't even seen his dick."

"He's unbelievably sexy. I cannot deal with how wet I am right now."

She parked beside a Bentley, one of six or seven cars parked along the private street and hardly the most expensive. "Is this number two?"

I pointed at the steel number 2 bolted onto the front of the house. "I don't hear any music." I opened the car door.

"Maybe it's some old fart party."

We walked up to the door and rang the bell. A woman opened it almost immediately. She was in her mid-twenties, wearing a long silk dress that looked as if it were made of motor oil. Her figure was a perfect hourglass shape, and her posture made her seem taller than she actually was. Raven hair draped her shoulders, and her eyes were a clear blue that just looked clear in the night lights.

"Are you Miss Drazen?" Her voice was silky and lower than I'd thought it would be.

"Yes." We shook hands.

"And this must be Miss Westin."

"Hey," Amanda said, taking the woman's hand.

"I'm Tiffany. Come on in."

I glanced at Amanda. She touched her curls. She was so vain. She'd probably leave because Tiffany had better hair.

We followed Tiffany down the long, carpeted hallway. Her shoes were wicked high, explaining the height but not the posture, because they looked like they hurt to wear.

"Did Master Deacon explain what kind of party this is?"

"It's a kinky BDSM party," Amanda piped in. "Which is cool. I've been to those before. It's not a big deal."

I wished she'd shut up.

"It's a big deal to us," Tiffany said, stopping at a little wooden table in front of an interior door. "So we do ask that you sign non-disclosure agreements and liability waivers before entering."

She picked up two leather folders from the table and handed us each one. I opened mine and sifted through the paperwork. Amanda stood there with her folder unopened.

"It looks standard," I said.

My friend looked a little stricken. "Wait, what if something happens? We can't tell anyone?"

Amanda, at her core, was a worrier. The weight of every single thing that could happen kept her from doing much of anything, except when she drank or snorted or shot up. Then she didn't worry, and that was how she liked it. So taking her to a new place sober was already tricky.

"You don't have to participate your first time," Tiffany said. "As a matter of fact, we'd prefer you didn't."

"So then you don't need me to sign this." She handed back the folder.

"Amanda, stop being weird."

"I have a bad feeling."

Tiffany took the folder. "It's important that you be honest with yourself about your limits."

Limits. I knew mine. I had none.

"I'm honest about my limits." I signed the paper and snapped the folder closed. I handed it to Tiffany then turned to Amanda. "I'll find my way home."

Chapter 57

FIONA

THE ROOM WAS FLOODED in sunlight, and still I slept. Deacon left and came back a few times. He crawled into bed with me and held me, stroked my hair while a headache raged through me. He gave me water, fed me. He took calls, and I heard him speaking Afrikaans in the other room, using a voice that had brought me to my knees a hundred times. I didn't realize how fucked up I was, how exhausted from Westonwood even before the events of the last day. But I wouldn't have slept for twenty-four solid hours if I wasn't.

In that haze of sleep, with all my filters down, I heard Elliot's buttercream voice.

Count backward.

Use different words to describe yourself.

Fiona, listen.

In my half-lucid state, I played the scene at the front door of Westonwood differently. I stopped. I listened to him. He said different things every time I rewound it and started again, but it always ended with him asking me to come home with him.

Fiona, listen.

When the fantasy ended well, I did go home with him, and I listened, and I slept until I woke biting back my scream, fogginess gone, too lucid, thoughts like broken glass.

I was alone in my new room, staring out the window at the little stables. I felt as if I were still in Westonwood, in a room someone else had made up for me. A box. A hole. The windows were open to the sounds of the wilderness, but I still felt imprisoned. The rustle of the leaves, the scamper of little night animals, the crickets. The dirt in my fingers. The twisting in my gut. Taking it like a whore, as I'd done a million times already except for the en-oh.

I couldn't sleep.

I didn't feel safe.

Warren was locked up, and I wasn't thinking about him. Or it. Or anything. I was trying to fucking sleep at two in the motherfucking morning.

I got up and walked down the hall. The light under Willem's door was on. I passed it and knocked lightly on Debbie's door.

She didn't answer. I walked in and snapped the door closed.

She turned in the bed. "Fiona?"

"Yes." I crawled into her bed and put my arms around her.

"You smell like soap."

I'd scrubbed myself red, drawing blood from my butt cheeks and twisting to scour the places on my back where he'd held me down. But I didn't mention it, because I was asleep before I was tempted to explain.

▭

I WOKE from bed at dinnertime.

Woke being a word meaning, "bolted up straight."

From bed meaning, "Debbie's bed in a strange room Deacon owned."

Dinnertime meaning, "I was hungry, it was dark, and I didn't have a watch."

Outside, I saw the stables. They were the size of a school gym. The smell of horses had been painted over in studio white. The lights were on inside, and Deacon stood atop a ladder, stretching his mighty form to do something to the ceiling. He was shirtless, and from across the yard, his abs were tight enough to kiss.

I heard voices in another room.

A robe and slippers had been laid out for me. I put them on and followed the voices to the kitchen. I'd hoped to see Debbie, but from half a hallway away, I discovered Margie reading a file of some sort on the counter.

"Welcome back." She didn't look up from the file.

"Who were you talking to?" I asked.

"I'm really not sure." She closed the folder and turned to me.

I didn't realize my arms were folded across my chest until she looked at them, and as if her eyes were hands, she made them uncross.

"Come here," she said.

Belying her request, she came to me, three steps, *one two three*, and put her arms around me. Again, I had to fight the urge to cry.

"We all want to see you," she said into my ear.

"Not yet." I pulled away a little. "Just, can it wait?"

"I talked to Jonathan. He said you were acting strange when you left. And you looked beat up. Is there something you want to tell me?"

"Yes."

Don't cry.

You wanted it, whore.

Use different words.

"Okay?" Margie said.

The words were on my lips. *He pushed me down and raped me. He hurt me.* I was still hurt there. I could prove it. They could take pictures and do the kit. Though I'd washed away most of the evidence, I could talk about it. Then everyone would know, and they'd gossip, and it would be in all the papers, and the stink it created would be forgotten and…

"You want to tell me what?"

"Jonathan needs to worry about his own fucked-up ass."

She let me go. "Ain't that the truth." She snapped open her briefcase. "Do you want to talk business? Or Mom's spiraling nerves?"

"Business please."

"I'm glad you're back."

"That's not business."

"It is. But so is this. You're an outpatient, and you have to be under observation. Five sessions, just to make sure you're recovering. I got you the therapist you liked."

I almost breathed his first name, but stopped it in the tangle of longing and regret. "Doctor Chapman?"

I think I squeaked. I didn't want to see him because I wanted to see him so badly my ribs felt like jelly.

"Yeah. That's the one." She put the file in her case.

I felt pulled to the sky with joy and the earth with dread until the middle of me thinned and disappeared like taffy pulled to its breaking point.

"And your friend?" Margie added. "I think her name was Karen Hinnley?"

"Yes?"

"She's fine. Released this morning. Her lawyer called me and said she was asking for you. You all right?" Margie asked, snapping her briefcase shut.

"Hungry. I've been asleep for, like, thirty hours."

She slid her case off the counter and kissed my cheek tenderly. "Are you all right here? Do you want to come back with me?"

"I'm fine."

"Will you call me if you need anything?"

"No."

"Say yes."

"Yes. I promise. I'll call you if I need anything. Like a latte or a foot rub."

"Good girl." She started out the door but turned. "You can change, sister. Don't let anyone tell you that you can't."

"What if I told you I don't want to?"

"You're a shitty liar."

She walked out before I could prove what an excellent liar I was.

Chapter 58

FIONA

DEACON HAD LEFT my pager on the nightstand. It was his way of
reaching me no matter what. My lifeline. My umbilical cord. I wrapped
my fingers around it and checked it.

—I'M IN THE STABLES—

Out the door, to the left, in the stables. It would take me moments to
get across that strip of yard. And then what?

I regretted getting into his car for the first time since I'd chosen it over
Margie's. I'd needed to feel his protection—from myself and the world—
at that moment, but I hadn't intended to go with him. I hadn't intended
anything but to leave Westonwood, go to my place in Malibu, and not
think about anything for a day or a year. I didn't delude myself into
thinking that had been a good plan, but it was something. I felt derailed
in that strange white house, with a man I'd tried to kill and no purpose
at all except to hide what had happened in the hours before he picked
me up.

And Elliot. I had to hide Elliot. He was mine. The memory of his fingers as they aligned the pen with the edge of his blotter, the lips that shaped his voice, they were mine. If I gave them life, my memories would be dismissed as a schoolgirl crush on a man who had helped me.

Now Margie, with the best of intentions, had requested him as my outpatient therapist. I was surprised he'd agreed. I knew he wanted me, and I knew the better part of himself would want to stay away from me.

Did he have a death wish for his career? Did he know how much I wanted to see him? How I looked forward to that first session?

I took a deep breath. I couldn't let Deacon see how excited I was about another man. He tolerated a lot of shit, but something about Elliot wouldn't sit well with him. And Elliot and I weren't going to happen. He was too good to be with me. He wouldn't let his dick lead him around. Not for long.

And I needed Deacon. I'd spin into crazy without him.

Shit.

I didn't know what I wanted. What a fuckup I was. What a royal fucking fuckup.

"Use different words to describe yourself."

"Excuse me?"

I didn't realize I'd spoken aloud until Deacon answered from the doorway.

"Oh, nothing. Hi," I said.

"Come with me." He held out his hand.

I did what I always did when he told me to do something. I followed instructions. I took his hand, and he led me outside. Crickets scraped their night song, and leaves and needles rustled in the shadows.

Deacon put his hand on the back of my neck and guided me toward the light of the bigger stables. "Maundy was going to have too many memories, so I thought we should start fresh."

He opened the side door, and light poured out.

The building had been converted into the party room, and a smaller extension into Deacon's private studio. It looked empty, without a table or a shelf, but the white cabinets built into two of the walls were obvious to me because I knew what was behind them.

"Have you used it yet?" I asked, looking at the thick hooks bolted to the crossbeams.

"I was waiting for you."

"I'm here."

"You're different," he said.

"That good or bad?"

He looked out the window, moonlight full on his face, glorious golden arms bent over his chest. He wasn't much of a talker, but he spoke with his lips and his hands.

"Get into position," he said. "I haven't changed that much."

Thank God. At least I knew what that was. I knew where it fit into the scheme of our relationship. I turned away from him and laid my arms together so that the tender insides of my forearms were pressed together.

A cabinet opened behind me, and he began.

Chapter 59

DEACON

I DIDN'T THINK this way until I walked out of Westonwood the first time, after you remembered what happened when you stabbed me. Before that, all I was worried about was whether or not you were sick. Or lonely. You don't like being alone, and I knew they had you in solitary for at least part of that stint.

I should have been relieved that you remembered.

But I wasn't.

There are things I've known about you from the minute we met. And I tried to power through. I regret that. There are horses you can train. Wild horses. The stallions you think will never have a rider. I've had two of those, and they'll only let me ride them, but they're not broken. They're not docile. Not really. Each and every one will turn on me if they can. Once you're wild, you're always wild.

You have no idea why you stabbed me, but I'm going to tell you.

You hate me. I'm an easy guy to hate. You're not alone. I get off on your pain. I get off on dominating you. You're small, and I'm in charge.

Your goal is to please me, and that makes me feel good. I loved you because you hurt worse than any of the others. And now I know why.

Don't resist the ropes. They get tighter when you do. You know that. And don't argue when you model. I'm telling you this when you're knotted for a reason. Look at you, trying to shake your head. You'll rip your hair out to deny it. Stop it and listen.

Everything I've done to you goes against your nature. You don't fight it because you truly hate yourself. I can't cure that. Not with love or domination. So when you broke, you didn't really break. Not the way a real sub does. You got confirmation that you were right. I don't do that. I don't play with confusion. But I did, and it ends now. There are new rules. I'll take you and do what I want to you because you like it, but we have a new understanding, you and I.

You're not submissive, Fiona.

Chapter 60

FIONA

I AM SO.

What the fuck are you talking about? We've been doing this for how long? You've been beating me raw, watching your friends fuck me, tying me into uncomfortable positions and showing me off. What the hell is that if not submissive?

But I couldn't argue outside my head. I couldn't talk because he had a bit gag around my head, and my head pointing down at exactly the right angle to let my drool form a neat little puddle.

What the fuck was this?

Deacon, you get in front of me where I can see you.

You let me talk.

You son of a bitch.

I hate you.

He pushed me, and I swung, splayed like Peter Pan. I'd been glad he tied me with my clothes on so I could somehow hide what Warren had done to me, but now I didn't want to be tied at all. I wanted to run away. Somewhere.

"I love you, Kitten," he said. "And I'm sorry I tied you up to say this. But I need you to hear it, and I need your defenses down."

I screamed in my throat, but I couldn't move. This was such a shitty thing. The shittiest of shitty things. And again, in every way, I'd consented to it. I'd asked for this shit. Begged even. I couldn't be mad at him even though I was. He really thought he was doing what was best for me. And fuck him.

He kneeled in front of me so I could see him.

I said something through the gag that I hoped sounded like, "Fuck you." He pulled it down.

"Is this your shitty way of dumping me?" I spit out.

"See? Not submissive." He held up his finger. "You *enjoy* being sexually dominated. You only *require* someone else's control outside play, in the world. And this, I missed because I wanted you."

He didn't look half as upset as I felt. He looked like he always looked, as if he'd figured it all out and was just laying out the obvious.

"Get away from me," I said through my teeth.

"You're still mine." He was gentle enough to soothe, and firm enough to assure me.

"I don't know what that means right now."

"This is not my shitty way of dumping you. It's a way of redefining what we are."

"You need a sub."

He tsked and shook his head slightly. "I need to dominate, and I need you. But you don't *need* to submit sexually. Do you understand the difference?"

"I understand," I started as if I was agreeing, then I flipped it, "that the world is full of people telling me what I need and what I don't. You know what I need? I need someone else to get me down. I have to pee."

I didn't have to pee, but I wanted to be down, away, out of this room, and away from him and his fucking definitions. I already found Laurel Canyon oppressive, and the ropes around my body only reminded me of Westonwood strait jackets.

"Debbie can get you down," he said, standing. He kissed me on the mouth and strode out the door, his ass a perfect oval, stirring desire through my anger and confusion.

He closed the door behind him. Ten seconds later, it opened, and Debbie came in. She wore black jeans and a red shirt with three buttons undone. She was younger than me, but decades beyond me.

I must have been crying, because she took a red silk kerchief out of her pocket and wiped my cheeks.

"He hasn't been himself," she said.

She put her arms around me and held me as the ropes loosened and I fell. Debbie was my friend and more. She was a rock, a counselor. She put things in perspective even if I never listened to her. So I let her hold me, and she did it with affection and sincerity.

"I don't know what to do," I said.

"I have every confidence you'll figure it out. Be patient with yourself."

"Your hair smells nice."

"Willem is here," Debbie said.

"Ugh."

"He was a great help while Deacon was laid up."

Before I could articulate why I had to grunt at the sound of his name, Willem appeared. Deacon's younger brother was a solid muscular mass of what Dad would call distemper. I'd just call him a cranky asshole.

And as he stood in the doorway with his arms folded and a sour face from here to the LA River, my opinion wasn't changed. His hair was shorter than it had to be, as if he'd wanted to chop it off as an act of defiance. His eyes were as blue as Deacon's, but colder, sharper, scarier to everyone but the few of us who thought he needed an attitude adjustment.

"Hello, Willem."

His feet, in worn cowboy boots, were set far apart, knees locked, jeans rubbed-in with South African farm dirt. He got laid a lot because of his looks, but it was always a short-term thing.

"He might forgive you, but I don't," Willem said.

"Thanks for bringing that up. You can go home now."

Rather than go home, he strode in, heels clopping on the hardwood. His hair was lighter than Deacon's and his beard was a short growth of copper. "You bring shame on this family. You're dangerous. You can't control yourself. You're a child. A goddamn child."

Even without having been knotted ten minutes earlier, and even without Deacon having said terrible things to me and walking out, his words would have hurt me. I could tolerate being called a whore and a party animal. I didn't mind if someone called me stupid, but his thinking of me as a child hurt. Hurt bad.

"You're a bore, Willem. No wonder you can't keep a woman."

"That's enough," Debbie said in her Dominant voice. Willem wouldn't recognize the tone, but I did. "Will, Mary set out lunch for you. You should eat it."

I saw his conflicting emotions. He was compelled to obey, but he had more to say. He turned his body halfway to the door and looked at me as if he didn't want to lose so definitively.

"I don't deserve his forgiveness," I said. "I'll be around later if you want to yell at me more."

He huffed and walked out. We watched him go. Once he was out, Debbie and I cleaned up the ropes together.

I caught myself doing something weird. Something that tied together two parts of a disconnected story. I was walking the Laurel Canyon property, trying to do it straight so I didn't look like a rape victim, and as I looped the ropes into tight spirals, I had a fantasy.

In the fantasy, I told Elliot what Warren had done.

I told him straight and strong. I told him about my pain, physical and emotional. About where denying consent had gotten me. I told him I didn't feel like it was my fault. That I'd been clear. That I felt all right with myself about it. Fiona didn't blame Fiona. I blamed Warren and wanted to put my fist in his ass.

I fantasized that he understood. That he didn't get mad. He didn't try to wreak vengeance. He didn't act like a therapist, and he didn't act like a man on a mission. He took me in his arms and told me it was all right. That my reaction was normal. That my body would heal some day, but it would take time and I could be okay with that.

He kissed me in that fantasy, as he'd kissed me in so many. But I'd just been knotted, and my emotions were open and raw, and the effect of my imagination was sharp and strong. The hair on the back of my neck stood on end, and I froze, because I could taste him. My lips shaped themselves against his, and his want was real and deep, man to woman.

"Fiona?" Debbie said.

An idea was fixing in my brain, slowly with every fantasy, that it could happen. That he'd allow it. That I'd accept it. That I could be the adult Elliot had faith existed and not the fuckup Deacon accepted.

Debbie caught the ropes as they dropped from my hands. "What happened to you?"

I shook off the crust of Elliot, but not the core.

"I'm fine," I said, convincing myself I could muddle through. "Just fine. I have a shoot tomorrow with Irving Wittenstein. Can you imagine? It was scheduled six months ago, and I'm back just in time. It's crazy how things get back to normal. The machine keeps turning no matter what."

I smiled. She looked at me long and hard. She didn't believe me, and as much as I wasn't supposed to care what she thought, I realized I did care a great deal.

Chapter 61

FIONA - Two years earlier

NUMBER TWO MAUNDY stank of sex, and though there was low ambient music, I heard the cries and moans of people in pleasure and pain. Thwacks. Pops. The whoosh of a whip in the air and the hick of it meeting flesh. I'd done it all before, but there was something new about that night. I crossed my legs under the table and fidgeted with my soda, clicking the ice around until the edges were gone.

My friend Ahmed and I had gone to the Dome in New York a few times. We'd rented a couch and a Mistress had led a girl to me on a leash. She'd knelt before me, and I opened my legs to her. I called her a good little bitch when she licked my cunt, and I came good and hard. But I'd felt like a visitor even after the Mistress kissed me on the mouth.

I didn't feel like an observer on Maundy. I wasn't looking in the window. I wasn't an honored guest but a piece in a puzzle. I only had to be snapped into place.

In front of me, across a narrow marble strip, crouched a naked woman on all fours. Her hair was tied in a neat bun, and her back was planar under the weight of a man's feet as he reclined on the grey couch.

She didn't move, even when the sole of one shoe pushed on her, leveraging against her as if she were a coffee table.

He put his iced drink between her shoulder blades. No coaster. She winced from the cold but didn't even look as he turned to the second woman kneeling before him. She wore garters and had pink hair and tattoos.

He put his finger down Pink Hair's throat. She took it. All the way down. He thrust his finger into her repeatedly, fucking her mouth with his hand. He wore a suit, but he wasn't Deacon.

Master Deacon Tiffany had called him. Suited him. I wasn't surprised.

I sat alone, riveted by the coffee-table woman. Tiffany had walked away seconds ago, after walking me through and seating me. I'd seen all the trappings before: the straps in the walls, the hooks in the ceilings, the wooden Xs between the windows that overlooked Los Angeles.

"What do you see?"

I spun around to see Deacon standing by my side. I'd only seen him sitting in the front seat of his car. He was gorgeous when he stood. Tall. Straight. Shoulders in a dark suit tapering to a slim waist. Shirt open a few buttons. Tooled leather belt with a buckle shaped into two twisted feathers.

"A lot."

"May I sit?"

"It's your party."

He sat. To my left, someone came with a grunt and a cry. I couldn't even look, he was so gorgeous. So self-assured. He had confidence where most men had no more than their cocks.

"I don't usually come downstairs, but Tiffany said you were here. She said you came with a friend."

"She left."

He nodded. The light from the little table lamp brought out the hard precision of his face. The short beard, the scar on his cheek, the one on his beautiful upper lip. His tongue flicked out, licking his lip so quickly I barely remembered it happening. "What do you do, Miss Drazen?"

"Like, for a living?"

"If you want to call it that."

I shrugged. "I'm seen. I get paid to wear things people want me to wear. Or get photographed. Otherwise I have plenty to live off."

"Who photographs you?"

"I have something with Irving Wittenstein on Wednesday."

"Impressive."

"Not really. I just go and smile. Look defiant. La-di-da."

"You make people think of you for a living. You remind them you exist."

I hadn't ever thought of it like that, but something about it made me bristle. "I don't care what they think."

"I'm sure you don't."

He didn't believe me. I could see it on his superior grin. He'd believe it soon enough.

"What do you do?" I asked. "Just the club?"

"I'm a photographer." He'd only lied a little. He didn't know me well enough to tell me what he really did.

We smiled at each other then. Stupid thing. To find a connection between his job and mine. I met Hollywood people all the time and had more in common with them than I had with him, but I felt something click nonetheless.

"You're watching this scene play out," he said, pointing across the marble path.

Another man had joined the scene, kneeling in front of the coffee-table woman and unzipping his pants. He was in his twenties, handsome, tattooed—what hipsters tried to be when hipsters tried to be rough.

"Yes." I didn't have more words, because the rough man put his cock in her mouth and pumped, looking elsewhere, and she couldn't rock with him. Couldn't spill the cold drink. I was a throbbing gushing mess, watching him fuck her face. My clit was a hard nodule, and I pressed my thighs together because it felt good.

"What about it appeals to you? Or disgusts you? What intrigues you?"

"That's a personal question."

"It is, but you've got your legs crossed for a reason. I bet if I put my hands between them, like this"—he slipped his hand over my knee to uncross my legs and drew his palm up the inside of my thigh—"you'd open your legs."

Under the table, my knees parted for him. He went under my skirt. I was on fire, and I was a whore, generally, so letting a strange man finger me was just another Tuesday.

Except it wasn't, because no one had ever touched me like they owned me. No trepidation. No questions. No fumbling. Just his thumb along the line of my underwear.

"This scene," he said. "He's fucking her face, and it's doing something to you. When I touch you, you're going to be wet, and your clit is going to be hard. Your lips will be swollen, and you're going to come in only a few strokes."

He had a point. No reason to be coy. Fuck it anyway. I was above people's judgments.

I ripped my eyes from the scene and put my elbows on the table. I wasn't ashamed of feeling the way I did, and I wanted to be utterly clear with him about that. "Make me come, then."

"What turns you on, Kitten? What about the coffee table?"

"He's using her. I see the scene, and I'm turned on. She's not even a whore. She's insignificant. Nothing. Unworthy of anyone even looking at her. Not even worth degrading… and I want it. I want it now."

"It takes time to get there, Miss Drazen." He spoke as if his hands weren't teasing my skin.

"Time is one thing I have plenty of," I said. "And money."

He pressed his lips together and looked me up and down. "I don't need money." He seemed genuinely interested and detached at the same time.

His thumb brushed my clit.

"Oh—"

"Shh. Look at me. Act as if nothing is happening under the table." He put his fingers on the walls of my opening. "Do you imagine you're her, or the man with his dick in her mouth?"

I obeyed him, trying to look as if this was dinner conversation, but there was no tablecloth. Anyone who looked could see his hand under my skirt. "I am her."

His finger brushed my clit.

"Watch her."

I turned from him as he stroked the length of my wetness so gently. The rugged man pumped the naked woman's mouth as if she were a hole in the wall.

"She's not even moving," Deacon said. "Not even sucking his cock. She's a receptacle. She has no will of her own but to please him."

He pulled out and shot streams all over her. She left her mouth open, but it was obvious he wasn't interested in keeping it neat. He came in her mouth, on her cheeks, her eyes. He left her with her mouth open, come dripping off her face, not wiping it away or looking at her as he tucked himself back in. It was so dirty and degrading, especially when he stood and zipped his fly as if she wasn't even there. She couldn't wipe it away. She just dribbled like an object.

The man in the suit dropped a wadded up napkin on her back. It was that act and the Master's fingers on my clit that brought me to orgasm.

"Look at me," Deacon growled.

My face contorted and my muscles tightened, yet I stayed still as his fingers stroked my clit, and I came and came. Eye to eye. He was so powerful, and I was under him. I'd known him a few minutes, and already I was a servant in his kingdom.

Chapter 62

FIONA

I CHECKED MY WATCH. I could make it to my appointment with Elliot before Irving. Just get it done with. He was across town from the photographer's studio, but I could do it. Just take the 10 to Robertson. Go north.

Deacon had made sure my Bentley was waiting for me at Laurel Canyon. Complete tune-up. Full tank of gas, new wiper blades.

North to Wilshire.

Over to Westwood.

Wait. Right or left?

You'd think I hadn't lived here my whole life.

I should have used a driver. I wasn't functioning right. I was disoriented in my own head, never mind the west side.

I found Elliot's office just north of Santa Monica. A pleasant non-descript building with industrial carpet and hardy plants in pots. The whole building buzzed with therapists and clinical social workers in private pods like a hive of encouragement.

I checked my watch outside his door. I had plenty of time to get to

Irving, but I was as eager to skip my appointment as I was to make it, and a shoot with Irving was the perfect excuse.

Elliot opened the door clothed in professionalism.

What a handsome little fucker. He looked at me from toes to eyes, and I turned to liquid. Not fire. Just a melted mass of tears and emotions. A sort of surrender I hadn't experienced.

I wanted to run toward him and away from him at the same time.

Chapter 63

ELLIOT

I TOOK outpatients once a week in an office in Century City. It was small, and clean, and on the impersonal side. My office in Westonwood had more of my touches, but I was there twice a week, and the patients there would be put off by a standard, sterile therapy room.

I rearranged my desk, dusted a shelf that was already clean, and considered meeting her out on the patio. I hadn't wanted to be her outpatient administrator, but once her sister/lawyer requested it, saying no wouldn't have looked any better than saying yes. I still held out hope that this would all go away. She'd walk in and seeing her out in the real world would kill my feelings.

"I don't think that's in the cards," I said to the brass cross on the back of the door.

My mother had given it to me when I'd taken my First Communion. The dying Jesus was symbolized by a flat, stylized shroud. No tortured three-dimensional body like a Catholic crucifix. Just a symbol of death and resurrection. I'd prayed to it a hundred times. It never answered, but it wasn't supposed to. The conversation was with myself.

"I think I should just sign off on her. Just say she's fine and let her go. I don't… I don't understand what's happening to me. I love Jana. She's good for me. A hundred times over, she made sense. And thank you. Thank you for her. But I'm throwing her back in your face. You set me up, and I reject you. Or not."

Tell me something.

Tell me how I'm supposed to discern what to do?

She's going to walk in here in a few minutes, and I'm going to what? Tell her how I feel? Lee is right. That's a massive breach of trust. I don't know if I can even sit through the five sessions with her. Five sessions. That's all I have to last. The length of her outpatient probation. Then I cut her out of my heart. I have to do that. I have to guide her through the transition and move on. I need your help, God. Jesus. Holy Spirit, listen. Just give me the strength. Back me up here. Do what you're supposed to do.

I wasn't entitled to pray for God to do his job, because it wasn't his job to make things easy for me. But I needed help, and when the little light went on telling me that there was a patient in the waiting room, my heart jumped.

Maybe I'll open the door and I won't care.

Maybe I just needed to leave Jana to change.

Maybe she'll be just another patient.

I opened the door.

Her feet were pressed together, and her bag was in front of her. I was a dead man. She didn't look particularly beautiful. She hadn't made herself up. Hadn't dressed to the nines, or any other number, but something about the color of her skin and the way the sun through the window hit the ends of her hair just clicked with my desire.

"Come in." I stood to the side and let her in.

"No couch," she said, surveying the room. "How are you going to hypnotize me?"

"I'll get one in if we need it."

She sat. I sat. My desk faced the wall, so I turned the chair around. There was nothing between us. I could smell her perfume.

Her foot pointed and straightened. Her naked flexing ankle. My lips around the bone, popping off, letting the tongue linger.

"How are you doing?" I asked.

She pressed her lips together as if she was keeping them from saying what was on her mind.

"You can tell me."

This was a breach. Posing as a therapist so she could tell me what was wrong when I would use all that to bring her closer to me.

She looked down.

Her recalcitrance wound me tightly around the spool of concern. When she pinched the bridge of her nose, I had to grip the arms of the chair to keep from kneeling before her.

"It's nothing," she said.

Needless to say, my glands fired. Nothing didn't mean nothing. Nothing meant "I'm not telling you," and knowing there was something wrong that she wouldn't share, that I couldn't help her with, or protect her from, made my skin prickle with angry heat.

"Fiona." I growled it in the most untherapeutic way imaginable.

Shit. I'd crossed the line.

"I can't do this," she said, standing.

"Wait—"

She headed for the door, and I got between her and it. Her chest heaved, and her eyes looked panicked.

"You have to know," I said with my hands up, "I'd never do anything to hurt you."

"I know."

Do not fuck this up by thinking with your dick. She needs you.

"I'm here for you. Not the other way around. If you want to talk, this is the place to do it."

She crossed her arms and took a second to realign her jaw. As strong as she tried to look, she was falling apart at the seams.

"You want to talk about something?" she said.

"Yes."

"You want to talk about something really painful and hard?"

My hands landed on her shoulders as if they had a will of their own. God damn my porous boundaries. "Talk to me."

"I want to tell you things I won't tell anyone, but I can't. You'll just make me relive it, and you'll want to tell people who will only make it worse. But you have this way… you open me up. You crack me open and pour me out, and all you do is look at me. So you need to stop looking at me because it just makes me love you more."

Her eyes went wide with shock, as if she'd just been slapped or surprised by what she'd said. I took my hands off her shoulders, because I didn't want her to feel pressured, but she took it as a sign to leave.

I let her go, because that was the professional thing to do, and as I stood there looking at the seam between the door and jamb, my father's voice broke the fog of my disbelief.

Go get her, you stupid shit.

Chapter 64

ELLIOT BURST out of the building just as I was opening the car door.

"Wait!" he called.

I didn't. Because fuck everyone. And my brain. Fuck my brain and my stupid mouth. I must have been out of my motherfucking mind.

I didn't love him. I loved Deacon, who was perfect for me, even if I wasn't submissive according to him, and who I still wasn't sure about, love or no love. All these men. All of them could go fuck themselves.

I peeled out of the parking lot, leaving that fucker in the rearview. He'd almost gotten to me. Almost made me tell him about Warren. Well, I wasn't ready. That shit at the creek did not happen, and I was not recounting it for him, and I didn't love him so fuck my stupid brain.

Use different words.

Confused brain.

Truthful brain.

Lying, stupid brain fuck the holes in my brain.

Of course, there was an accident on the 10. The 10 was an accident factory.

"Late!" I said to the dashboard. "That's a word I'd use to describe myself. Late."

I wasn't late. Not yet. But I needed to call myself terrible things.

"Late," I said, speeding across Santa Monica Boulevard. "Of course there's traffic, and I'm late."

I focused on getting downtown without killing myself or anyone else. My hands loosened, my breathing slowed, and I got there in one piece. I checked myself in the rearview. I couldn't even see myself. I looked like a Fiona Drazen mask.

Fuck it. I took a deep breath and got out of the car.

Irving Wittenstein was the best celebrity photographer in Hollywood. He had been when we met, the Wednesday after Deacon put his fingers up my skirt, and when I got out of Westonwood, he was still the best. Worthy of keeping a six-month-old appointment at the worst time in my life.

He had a studio in the guts of downtown between a garment factory and a Mexican food warehouse.

"Hey," I said when he opened the door.

He kissed both of my cheeks. "Welcome back."

He was a clean-cut guy with a serious face and an arm that had lost the battle with polio when he was a child. But he managed to come off as handsome and competent, and when he'd taken my picture the first time, I looked at the results and felt as though the camera saw my insides.

Which, at the time, had seemed like a good thing. Back when I was young and stupid, or just stupid. Before Westonwood, and days before Deacon got me under control.

Before Warren.

Which I realized I was trying not to think about. I told myself I was all right with it, but if I was all right with it, I wouldn't be thinking about it all the goddamned time.

"You look rested," Irving said at his door. "Your team's here."

My team. Right. I had a hair stylist. A makeup stylist. A makeup applicator. A clothing stylist. A nail person. Each of them had an assistant.

Look casual.

I smiled and put my hand on his lame arm. "Wanna do something real?"

"For *Vanity Fair*? Not likely."

I didn't think I was sabotaging the shoot. I thought of it as bringing it to the next level. No more same old, same old. I walked into the green room and was immediately attacked by giggles and kisses. Someone put a drink in my hand. I heard the words "blow" and "flake" in the form of a question.

"Stop!" I said, throwing up my hands. I put down the drink.

They had huge kohl-lined eyes and open red lips.

"I'm doing this different. You'll get paid. But get out." I pointed toward the door.

"Come back for the next shoot."

They hustled out until it was just me, Irving, and Piper Lundgren, the *Vanity Fair* editor. With a crop of bright white hair and a soft blue jacket by a Japanese designer, she looked like an ad for New York City.

Once the last of them went, Piper slow-clapped. "Stunning performance."

I kissed her cheek then the other.

"So wearing Photoshop then?" she asked.

"Oh, shut up." I powdered my nose. I'd do foundation, mascara, lipstick. No more than that. "Let's make history again."

"You getting naked again?" she asked, brow raised.

I hadn't known what I wanted out of the first shoot, but I hadn't thought about making history or anything else.

The last cover I'd done for *Vanity Fair* had excited and scared the shit out of me. I'd been naked but for shoes and a copy of *First Touch* covering what couldn't be printed. The book itself was about a woman understanding her need to be dominated and degraded, a journey I was about to begin during that first shoot, and a journey that was about to end during the second.

That first shoot had taken on a life of its own, and when I wiggled into the silken drapey thing I was supposed to wear and the air-light fabric touched my skin, I shivered.

Deacon had been at the first shoot.

A man I barely knew.

He'd shown up because he knew Irving, and I'd asked him to stay. Irving had it under control, but Deacon distracted me with the burn of his gaze.

"If you're going to undress me with your eyes," I'd said to him in a room full of people, "why not just ask me to get undressed?"

The room went silent. Someone turned off the music. Piper bit the end of her pencil and looked at Deacon as if she wanted to jump his bones, but he kept his focus on me.

With half a smile, he said, "Take off your clothes."

It wasn't salacious. It wasn't "Show me your tits," which I'd done a hundred times, even sober. It was uttered in a normal tone, and it was an order.

I unbuttoned my shirt, and the reaction from the stylists and friends was hooting and howling with a side of clapping. Piper looked unsure. Deacon's eyes didn't move off me.

"Out!" Irving shouted, waving his good arm with the camera at the end.

I kept unbuttoning, because outside Deacon and me, no one was in that room. And Irving, doing his fucking job like a fucking badass, took those pictures. I'd been cut open, turned on, high on little black pills and the man with the blue eyes.

Deacon had been the one to pick up *First Touch* off a bench and hand it to me to cover myself. I got on my knees and opened my mouth. Spreading my knees on the floor and putting the book between my legs. Forearm over my little breasts.

The book was a reflection of how I felt, and how I wanted to feel. How I looked. Like a degraded slut with a ton of money.

The cover had been famous, and if the paparazzi couldn't get enough of me before, the nude added to their hunger.

I hadn't intended to go on without makeup when I got the booking for the second shoot. Piper flipped open her phone, and Irving relieved her of it. He was great. After Westonwood, he was the only one I trusted to photograph me.

I shouldn't have trusted anyone.

I should have stayed home, wherever that was. Crawled into my dusty condo on Venice Beach and stretched out in the middle of the floor.

Let the sun set on me and kept all my shit in the dark. Because the dark was where it all belonged. Deacon. Warren. Elliot. Debbie. Even Willem, who annoyed the holy fuck out of me.

But the lights, and the heat, and feeling all those people looking at me…

"You all right, Fiona?" Irving said, camera down. He changed the roll of film. "I was going to do some large format stuff, but if you don't feel it…"

"We can't reschedule," Piper said.

"I feel it," I said. "I'm fine."

Because fuck Piper Lundgren from *Vanity Fair*. I could turn this shit on and off in a heartbeat. This was my job, motherfucker. This was all I had to do. Party, be seen partying, get photographed between parties.

"I'm putting a strobe in and using slower film," he said, snapping the large format cartridge into the camera. "So no quick moves." He put the camera on a tripod.

"Okay." I nodded more to myself than him.

"Fiona?"

"Irving?"

"Are you all right?"

"Do you want me to repeat my safe word? Or are you just going to believe me?"

Party.

Be seen partying.

Get photographed between parties.

I looked at the camera and jutted my hip to the right.

"Open up, Fiona," Irving said.

The flash went off, and I was exposed. Bare. Skin and mask ripped away. All defenses burned to the ground. It wasn't the flash. It was the flash and time. The lens found the cracks. It was him telling me to open up the millisecond before I couldn't shore myself up, and the flash going off, and Piper with her bitten pencil, and the four-thousand-dollar dress, and Deacon's voice when he said he wasn't going to break me, and that god-fucking caterpillar in my face as I was a little shit-eating whore with an asshole surrounded by sentient skin, and I choked.

I just choked.

I choked on spit and bile, and both came out in a sob. A part of me was thinking, looking at myself, observing the meltdown with crystal clarity, and saying, "Oh well, I guess we're doing this now, are we?"

And I did it. I dropped to my knees and wailed. Every ounce of pain came though my face. My narcissism and self-loathing. My moral emptiness and emotional fullness. I wasn't prepared for pain. Wasn't raised for it. And it hurt. Everything hurt. I felt so alone, so abandoned, so worthless, and at the same time so cherished and prized, burdened with a responsibility to strangers I couldn't shoulder. Not through what I'd done. Not through hurting Deacon. Not through this grinding foul hate I couldn't ignore.

I didn't know what I was saying as I twisted my body on itself and wept. Large-format abandoned, the camera clicked even when I got back up on my knees and looked into my cupped hands, where I'd caught a line of spit. I thought how much they looked like leaves, and how the streak of mascara across my palm looked like a caterpillar. And I got mad.

I'd gotten away with everything in my life. I'd banged up cars, spent money, done more drugs than a body should be able to do. And Warren was from my tribe. He'd walk away. I knew it was the truth. The only one who could punish him for what he'd done was me.

I looked at the ceiling and cried out, because I was joyful in my rage. My face was smeared with kohl. A red gash of lipstick lacerated across my cheek. The dress had shifted, exposing a breast.

They'd ask me later if I'd been aware of the camera. And I was. Of course I was. I was born to be aware of the camera. But I was also born to be honest before it.

I was born to party.

To be seen partying.

To be photographed between parties.

And there was my power.

This life was my life. Fuck anyone who tried to take it away.

Chapter 65

FIONA

I LEFT THE STUDIO DRAINED. Nice and empty. I was going to spend the night filling myself up with something fun, something positive for a change. I was done with this weepy shit. My life. My choices. My control.

As if he'd heard my determination, Deacon was leaning on my car when I got out of Irving's.

When he saw me, he opened the passenger side for me. He'd taken the fucking liberty of putting Wagner in the stereo.

I approached him, eyes locked on his, his face peaceful and powerful, as if I was just a section in an orchestra he conducted.

"I don't do this old world shit," I said.

"You fuck to it all the time."

I swallowed. I'd done lots of things to classical music, mostly staying still while being manhandled, and they all flashed through my head. "Who said anything about fucking?"

See, that was a denial. I was telling him I didn't want to fuck him, even though I did. And that meant I was looking for a sweet beating or a knotting or something else. But I wasn't looking for anything I would have looked for before. I didn't know what I wanted besides swift, sharp change.

He saw that. In the way he looked down, and the way his sculpted hand moved a lock of my hair away from my eyes, he saw everything. "What's going on with you, Kitten?"

"You're the one who jacked my car."

"Get in then." He stepped aside, and I got in the passenger seat. He slapped the door closed and walked around the front. Jeans. Boots. Jacket. Six-three in a full suit of badass.

"Where are we going?" I asked.

"Where were you headed?"

I had been headed somewhere he wouldn't want to go. Somewhere he wouldn't be welcome, where he'd see things he didn't want to see.

"Is this what you meant by 'not submissive?' You my chauffeur now?"

"I'm whatever you need."

"Let's hit the 405." I snapped the lap belt closed. "Really open this bitch up."

"I can't get arrested."

"I know."

Deacon was on a watch list. He could move in and out of the country, but if he was arrested, the domino effect from the investigation would put him in jail, or worse, get him extradited to Sudan. He'd never elaborated on why that was bad or what he'd been caught doing in Sudan, but I had enough of an imagination to make me not ask.

"I'm moving out," I said. "I'm going back to my place in Malibu."

I saw him mostly in silhouette against the painted sunset and grey geometry of the city. He looked like he wasn't going to answer, but I knew better. He didn't speak for the sake of speaking or answer because I'd asked a question. He was a Dominant, a Master, and he knew his words had power.

"I need to know you're all right, and when you're not living under my roof, anything can happen. That's very uncomfortable for me."

Saying it was uncomfortable for him as well, that I knew. He didn't enjoy expressing his feelings as much as he enjoyed acting on them.

"I'm sorry," I said. "I don't know if I can be that for you anymore. You said so yourself."

"You'll always be mine, whether you're submissive or not. You can just make it easy or hard."

"I don't want it to be hard for you, but something changed. I don't know what changed. Believe me, I'd love to have things stay the way they were. I never felt so safe as with you on Maundy. But it's not the same. And I don't mean the location is different. I mean… something happened in Westonwood."

I froze. I meant something psychological. I meant a change in my own chemistry. But to my ears, it sounded like I was segueing into Warren.

"With the doctor?"

"No!" The denial came too hard and too fast. "Yes, but no."

We hit the 405, and I thought for the first time that maybe he shouldn't open this bitch up. Maybe he should drive straight and clean and well under the speed limit.

"Yes, but no? What does that mean?"

"Are you jealous?" It was a ridiculous question. Deacon wasn't jealous. He just didn't have that gene.

"Just tell me," he growled. "I want to know."

Yet he'd avoided my question.

"Yes, he changed me, because he asked questions and told me things and saw me in a way I've never been seen before. But to the heart of what you want to know, no, I didn't fuck him."

The acceleration of the car was so smooth and powerful, it reminded me of a horse moving fluidly from walk to canter to gallop. And Deacon, whose grace always reminded me of a stallion, was wound tight.

"I don't care if you fuck him!"

I'd never heard him raise his voice. Ever. I didn't know if I looked as deer-in-headlights as I felt.

The car sped into the eighties. The freeway was empty for a change. The *whup* of the tires under me was soothing. I paced my breathing with the seams in the road.

"Deacon. I was joking. Slow down!"

"You let him in!" His hair whipped over his forehead, and mine swirled over my face.

"He was my therapist."

"He loves you. From the minute I saw his face, I knew it. But you... I didn't think you'd let it happen."

"Nothing happened! Would you stop it?"

I didn't even know what I was denying or why. I was only defending my position, which was stupid. I knew damn well I felt something for Elliot. My mouth had betrayed me in that session; it hadn't lied.

"You're mine," he said, finger jabbing in my direction. "Nothing you do will change that. Nothing he does or feels will ever change that. He's temporary. He's a fucking leaf falling off the tree and dying. But we, you and I, we are the forest."

He was taking control of the situation and, apparently, the laws of physics as cars rushed to get out of his lane. More importantly, he was taking control of me by trapping me in a car.

"Slow down, or I'm bailing!"

He acted as though he didn't even hear me. "No. You're coming back. I'm shackling you to the wall until you understand that this is not a game. We're not teenagers. There is no puppy love, Fiona. Not for the broken."

"You know what? Fuck you!" The car was going about ninety when I opened the door.

He swerved, getting the inertia of the door to slap it closed. "Don't do that again!"

I popped my seat belt, reaching my foot over to his side. He tried to push me away, but I got it down on the brake. The car didn't know whether to stop or go.

Horns. Smoke. Swerving. Torque.

Deacon got his foot off the gas and pulled over, landing on the shoulder with a lurch. He turned on me.

He was mad. So mad he probably couldn't do more than shackle me. He'd never beat me when he was mad.

Maybe. Because I'd never seen him that angry before.

I wasn't ready to find out what he was going to do.

I snapped up my bag and crawled over the door, jumping to the asphalt.

"Fiona!"

I barely heard him as I ran into traffic. All the noises were loud. The screeching. The horns. The rap music coming from the white Honda that brushed against me. Even the movement of air around me was ear-squeezing. Deacon's voice existed in an indistinct middle ground. Only my breath was low enough to pay attention to.

Because fuck this.

I found the broken white lines between lanes. They were the only shapes that were solid in the indefinite blurs of cars.

These perceptions didn't even have a foothold in my mind. I didn't even think of them. I was in a now that was so short, I stopped wanting anything but to live. To get across, to get away.

Cars just stopped, once they could, and the air became thick with smoke and the smell of rubber.

"Fiona!" Deacon was getting closer, holding his hand up to a car on the fucking 405 and stopping it with his fucking will to make it stop for him, then loping toward me like he was just crossing La Brea with the light.

That was Deacon. And that power over people and physics was the biggest reason I'd given him control of my life. It turned me on.

It *had* turned me on.

A yellow Mazda lurched to a stop in front of me. A cab. The driver looked terrified, his brown eyes open to the size of doorknobs.

"Fiona!"

I'd somehow crossed three lanes of traffic, and Deacon was heading across lane number two.

I pointed at the guy driving the cab. "Can you take me to Holmby Hills?"

He didn't answer. I reached for the back door, and it was unlocked.

"Hundred dollar tip if you get me out of here."

He took off. I straightened myself as the knot of cars I'd tied up dissipated. Out the window, I saw a lady hold up a camera, taking a picture. And next to me sat a girl of about twenty, wearing makeup and a sparkly dress, two swaths of lipstick parted in surprise.

"Sorry," I said, "he can drop you off first. And I'll pay your fare."

She lifted a camera and snapped a picture.

Chapter 66

FIONA

DAISY ASKED me to autograph the back of a receipt she found in the bottom of her bag. I did it, leaving her a little note about how cool she was to share a cab with me.

"What's it like? To be you?" she asked as she folded up her precious paper.

"Pretty cool. I guess. I don't have anything to compare it to. You know, I got problems. Money's just not one of them."

"Yeah, you just got out of the"—she stopped herself and, whatever she was thinking, chose another word—"institution. Was it bad?"

"When they put you in isolation. That was bad. But otherwise, I guess it was all right."

I could have told her plenty about the drugs and the shitty woman psychiatrist whose name I forgot. I could have told her about being tied down or about the cameras everywhere. But I didn't know her, and all that seemed way too personal.

A voicemail came in from Karen. I listened to it while Daisy told me about her life.

Me and Arrow are going to Baby's if you want to join. You should. We've been locked up too long.

"I like being by myself," Daisy said. Behind her, box stores turned into cityscape as we zipped along the 405. "My mom is always on me to get another job. She has diabetes, so she can't work, and I have to drive her to dialysis clinic three times a week." I must have made a face or put on an expression that asked the question in my head, because she rolled her eyes. "Right, I'm in the back of a cab because I missed a payment and blah blah. I hate banks."

She made a little nervous laugh I hadn't heard until then, but once I noticed it, I realized she'd been tittering the whole time.

"So I take the bus, but if I make enough in tips, I pick up a cab home because the bus at night isn't really cool."

I almost told her I'd never actually ridden a bus, but I caught the words before they left my mouth.

"So you're headed home?" I asked.

"Yeah. Carthay Circle. I think wherever you're going is closer, so if you want to get dropped first…"

"It's Saturday." I said it as if every assumption should be obvious. The rest of the world partied harder on Saturday. Every day was more or less the same to me, but she must have adhered to the rules of normal people.

"Yeah?" she said.

"Aren't you going out?"

"No." She didn't look happy about it. She looked kind of down and lonely.

"I have an idea." I leaned over the front seat. The driver made eye contact with me in the rearview. "What's your name?"

"Basham."

"Basham, can you get off on Sunset? We're going to Holmby Hills."

Chapter 67

FIONA

SOME THINGS NEVER CHANGED. Parties always had the same ingredients: People. A pool. Music. Drinks. Drugs. Maybe some food. A few dozen people in white shirts picking up empties. Big Samoan guys frowning in the corners. Because you could get wild in the house, but you couldn't destroy the house. That cost money.

I lost track of Daisy sometime around my fourth Mojito High, which looked just like a mojito, but had pot leaves instead of mint leaves. I saw her by the pool with a drink, talking to Ivan.

My pager buzzed.

—WHERE ARE YOU?—

Deacon. Again. It was the seventh page like that. Just a question he felt entitled to ask.

Fuck his entitlement. Fuck his rules and his control.

"Fiona!" Jack called. "You have got to try this." He was still a nerd but a useful one, so the former Carlton Prep kids let him hang around their parties.

He crouched by a small mid-century table littered with sticks and flowers. A pile of what looked like mud sat in a saucer. Onna Michaels sat across from him, pinching her lower lip.

"My chin tingles," she said after Jack and I hugged.

"Give it a minute to travel down," he said, knee bumping like a jackhammer.

"What is it?" I said.

"*Catha edulis* hybrid with *ricinus comunis* I was working on before I got stashed in the pokey. Concentrated it down in rubbing alcohol. Delivery method needs a little work. You tuck it between your cheek and gum. Calling it TarBaby." He pinched the mud, extracting a bit and bouncing his hand above the pile to loosen some black, fibrous strands. He held it up to me.

"Dude," I said, "I'm not your guinea pig. I gotta see what it does first."

"Gets you fucked up." He tucked the pinch into the front bottom fold of his mouth.

"Oh, man," Onna said. Her eyes rolled up, flicking and blinking to white. "Ah, that's good."

Gerald, another Carlton nerd who grew up muscular and fuckable, stuck his finger against his lower gum and said around it, "You found the key to the kingdom, Jack."

"Yeah," Onna groaned.

"When did you get out?" I asked.

"Week slash ten days," Jack answered. "Something like that. I'm thinking of going back in. There's a real market for this shit in the bunkhouse."

"Really?"

"Yeah. Chilton deals, but delivery is always a problem. He's paid off just about everyone who matters, but that front door's the toughest. He promised cash up front. He lets inmates pay him in trade. Girls and boys. He doesn't even care."

"He's sick."

Jack raised his eyebrow. "You some kinda homophobe?"

"You invent a new drug to sell to mental patients who pay in sex, and you're offended that I'm homophobic? Seriously? Warren's a sick fuck. Period."

But the argument was over. Jack's lips had gone slack and his eyes were half closed, revealing only white. He scratched his chin. Onna was welting her face and close to drawing blood.

Everyone in Westonwood would be walking around looking like they'd stuck their face in a shredder.

Yeah. The delivery system needed work.

I went out to the pool and nearly crashed into Karen.

I hadn't even seen her until then. Either she was too skinny or she had been busy in one of the bedrooms. But I squeezed her so tightly I could practically touch my opposite shoulders.

"How are you?" I asked, too excited for an answer. "You look great!"

She didn't. She looked like a fork. I was projecting my joy onto her.

"Staying at their place." She rolled her eyes. I knew she meant her parents. "Her and Dad can't decide where to take me. Dad thinks south of France and I'll eat because 'French food.' Mom says Aspen, because she wants to ski with her little drunk friends. They don't even ask me where I want to go."

"Where do you want to go?"

"I don't know."

"Figure it out, and we'll go together."

She smiled. "Yeah. I like that."

I kissed her cheek and we walked deeper out back.

Baby and Arrow were at a bank of couches with a bunch of other actors and industry douches. I found a spot and wedged myself in, joining the conversation about how long a guy's goatee should be.

I took a hit from the crystal bong going around. It was filled with straight Tennessee moonshine acquired from a busboy at Victoria's dad's restaurant. He supposedly had a still in his driveway. The shit tasted like tomato juice and rubbing alcohol, so we'd put it in the bong and smoked ecstasy-laced hash through it. The high was like a knife made of ice. It stabbed me in the spine and melted like cold water in my gut.

From the poolside couch, I entered another plane.

There was me.

And the Everything.

And the Everything pressed against me, hugging me.

I was safe in the Everything. Bound to it. When I shifted my body, it followed, molding to my movements, my dancing, my laughter, absorbing sound like a vacuum—a clear jelly mass nothing could penetrate. Not Arrow, who was kissing me with lips a million women died for. Not Derek, whose hands pressed my belly to him when we danced.

The Everything said it was okay to let them inside. I wasn't aroused. Not physically. I was just encased in joy and well-being and fucking was going to happen. Arrow, who had smoked from the same bong, carried me to a couch, legs wrapped around his hips. I was just starting to feel my feet. The Everything had released them first.

"Where's the bong?" I said.

Derek swirled the resin-brown moonshine. Arrow pulled a baggie from his pocket and tossed it to Derek. The music had started to cut through the gel of my awareness. I hated this song.

"What's in this?" Derek asked.

"It's vanilla. All I got." He looked down at me. His dick wasn't out yet, but it was on its way. "You in, Fee-Fie-Fo-Fum?"

"Let me get another hit."

"This stuff smells like asshole," Derek said, warming the bowl.

His voice grated on me, and the light from his Bic was too high and bright.

"See what Baby's got," Arrow said.

Baby Chilton turned around in her seat. Her turquoise hair was crimped, and her sunglasses were still on her head even though it was after midnight. She wasn't wearing a shirt, and her tits hung like silicone volleyballs in plastic bags. She'd had them done so many times, the guys said they could bite her nipples as hard as they wanted. She couldn't feel them anymore.

"I'm out," she said, turning to face us. "Holy shit! Fiona! When did you get here?"

She leaned over to hug me and landed on me before I could get up. She showered me with kisses, so I gave her a little tongue and a cheer went up. She got off me, and we sat.

Daisy stood nearby.

"You all right there, Daisy?" I asked, yanking my underwear from around my ankle. I thought I was supposed to be fucking someone, but I forgot to want it any more.

"Yeah!" she said enthusiastically. Good. Her drink was full, and she was smiling. That was all I needed to see.

"Give the new girl a hit," I said after I took mine.

Derek handed Daisy the bong. "Bowl's ash. Pack it or drink it."

"Shut the fuck up, Derek. You pack it." Fuck him. "She doesn't have shit. Your parents coproduce money-spitting Oscar bait every two years."

"I'm tapped, Fee-Fie." He put his hand on my knee. "You got some nuthouse shit you wanna share?"

"Can't smoke what I got."

"Oh my God!" Baby exclaimed. "I forgot to ask. Did you see my brother in there?"

Warren.

Her brother.

The hit I'd just taken went sour. My mouth tasted like the bottom of a foot. I wanted to go home.

"Yeah," I said.

"How was he?"

"Asshole as ever."

She snorted and lit a cigarette. A flake of ash fell on her left tit. She saw it and brushed it away. "They're talking about letting him out. Finally."

I had my phone out while she was talking about Warren getting out and the sick party that would commence. I didn't know what to do with myself. Sure, there would be a party and I'd be invited, but that wasn't the point. I didn't have to go. I could avoid him. It wasn't that hard.

Especially if I lived with Deacon.

My hands shook. I felt trapped in a matchbox. I held the phone to my face but didn't even know who to call for a rescue. My brain was stone soup. I knew there was an order to how to use the phone. This, then that, then the other, but I felt desperate and couldn't find the right little grey buttons.

Breathe breathe

Home button > green call button > code > contacts > Elliot Chapman

Now what?

I couldn't just casually ask if Warren was getting out without raising a flag. And hadn't I just told Elliot I loved him? Where was that fucking bong?

I stared at the phone. It was one in the morning. He'd be asleep. I didn't know where he lived. Lucky him.

I navigated to his number and hit SEND.

I wasn't even sorry in a way that necessitated an apology. I was saying I was sorry to myself.

Red button. Call ended.

"Drink it or pack it," Derek said from my right as Daisy still held the bong. He was so handsome, and his real-life persona was exactly the same as his reality-TV persona. Arrogant Hollywood douchebag. That was his brand.

I'd forgotten that I was about to fuck Arrow. I glanced at Arrow, who was chatting up Winny Sanchez. His hand was halfway up her skirt. We both forgot. That's how meaningful it all was.

Elliot called back. His name flashed on the screen with two options over the buttons.

Answer.

Ignore.

He'd answered. He'd gotten out of bed or rolled over and answered and missed the call and called back or whatever. He probably had crud in his eyes and hair all over the place. I wanted to stroke it back into place.

The song changed to one I liked, and I answered the phone.

"You called?" he said. "Is everything okay?"

"What are you wearing?" I purred or slurred. Maybe both.

He didn't say anything right away. I didn't like the silence. It was like having him watch what I was doing and shake his head with disapproval.

"We need to talk." His voice was clearer.

"We are talking."

"In person at a decent hour."

Fuck him for being right. And fuck him for being ethical, and for making me ashamed of wanting to know, ashamed of my high, of my hundred-dollar panties bunched on the floor, of the taste of Baby's mouth on me. What was I doing? Where was I? Why was I even here? And suddenly I was gripped with fear.

"Don't give me to another therapist."

"What?"

I glanced at my surroundings. Jesus. Where was I? Purgatory. Derek looked at Daisy expectantly. She swirled the hash-and-ecstasy-laced moonshine in the tube.

"Don't drink it, Daisy," I said. "You'll puke your guts up."

"But you'll be so fucking high you won't care," Karen said.

"Fiona? Where are you?" Was Elliot still on the phone? Had he heard me?

It was the third time he'd asked me that. Deacon, who was an early-to-bed-early-to-rise type when he wasn't hosting a party, was either awake, or hosting, or had these pages on a schedule, because his message came right after Elliot's question.

—WHERE ARE YOU?—

"I'm at a party in Holmby Hills," I said. "I can't find my underwear, and I'm so high. So. Fucking. High. Wanna come? I'll give you the address and you can—"

"Get a cab if you need one. Call me when you're sober."

He hung up.

—WHERE ARE YOU?—

—Fucking sucking snorting. Thanks for asking—

"Fuck you both," I said to the pager. I launched it into the pool. It dropped with a *plunk,* the cone of water collapsing into itself in slow motion.

Daisy still stood on the other side of the table, tilting the bong to her face.

"Give me that," I said, holding my hand out for it.

"Let her finish." Karen lit a cigarette.

Maybe it was because the famous-for-being-anorexic Karen Hinnley was defending her, but Daisy beamed a little and quickly, as if she wanted to do it without thinking about it, took a swig of the resin-saturated bong moonshine. Everyone groaned.

Bong water was bad. Bong moonshine was worse. Bong moonshine with the pure chemical happiness of Jump was more disgusting than I could imagine, and probably had never been tried before. Baby gave Daisy a bottle of water as she coughed. Everyone laughed. Even Daisy. Even me.

"You are about to get so fucked up," Derek said as he took the bong and gave it to me. "I salute you."

I put the bong on the table. "Who's got flake?"

Baby replied, "I got a couple lines' worth."

I held out my hand. Baby put a folded-up hundred dollar bill in my hand. I opened the bill, exposing the lovely white flake.

"What are you doing?" Baby asked.

"Can you get your dick out, sweetheart?" I said to Derek.

Collective laughter.

"Sure." Derek took out his cock. "You want it hard, you gotta work for it."

I rolled my eyes. "Stand up, stud."

I took it in my mouth. The taste of skin and sweat got rid of the sourness on my tongue, and I worked it until I thought he could maintain it. Some of my friends watched. Most had seen and done it all before, and it was boring.

"Man, you are good," he said as I stroked his cock with my hand.

Daisy stood watching, swaying a little.

"Too bad I'm not going to finish you."

"Ball-breaker."

"Stay still." I picked up the powder and tapped it onto his erection.

"Hey!" Baby cried.

I'd just dumped all her stash on Derek's dick, and I was going to snort it for spite. Because the last time I'd done that, I'd met Deacon. As I looked at the mess of powder on a douchebag dick, I wondered…was I crying out for Deacon again? Was I trying to recreate the circumstances before he got my life under control?

My mouth already tasted like malice. Fuck this.

"All yours," I said to Baby.

"What do I get?" Derek cried.

"If you're nice, she'll let you come in her mouth."

Baby leaned down and snorted the coke off Derek's dick, licking off the last flake.

I wanted my pager back. My blood felt like gravel in my veins. I could call him. Them. Both of them.

Baby had left Derek hanging, and everyone thought that was pretty funny. I snapped up the panties and wiggled them back under my skirt.

Daisy laughed then puked. Karen got her Pradas out of the way just in time. I was going to have to get Daisy home. She'd have stories to tell, but I thought she might not. She seemed like a nice person. A person who leaves her boobs in her bra. Who didn't suck a dick in front of everyone for fun.

I looked at my phone. My messages to Deacon and my call to Elliot would give exactly the right impression and they'd be rightfully disgusted with me. They wouldn't know all the things I *didn't* do in Holmby Hills that night.

I'd felt this before.

This hateful unworthiness. My reaction to it was so ingrained I could predict it. The shame made me angry. The shame drew me into it and made me proud of what I'd done. I'd stand by it and deny it even existed. I stepped outside myself and saw myself the way others saw me, which wasn't new. But this time I didn't see the disdain and the worship. Nor did I internalize the thread of envy. I saw myself through Deacon and Elliot's eyes as if they were one man.

Surrounded by the music and the drugs, the stink of moonshine THC, the beautiful night, and the worthless humans around me, I sank into disgrace. I didn't run. I didn't cover it. Deacon would come for me. Elliot wouldn't.

"Fuck this," I whispered, pocketing the phone.

Next to me, Daisy was on her knees in front of reality star and winner of the genetic lottery, Derek Douchebag, and his cock was in her mouth.

She was so fucking stoned she couldn't even keep her mouth open wide, and everyone found this funny.

"Derek, for Chrissakes," I said.

"What?"

"You got ten girls and a few guys you can stick it in. Leave her alone."

"Unless I can stick it in you, just shut the fuck up, Fee-fie Nuthouse."

I pushed him, hard.

He grabbed my wrist and bent it back. "Don't you fucking get judgy on me, you slut."

The bong stood like a twelve-inch clear phallus on the table, and there was nothing I could do but grab it and swing. It landed on Derek's head with a *thunk,* breaking in a wash of blood and brown-stained moonshine. He screamed and let go, dick suddenly flaccid. Everyone jumped back but Daisy, who didn't seem to know what had happened.

"You fucking crazy bitch!" Derek screamed. "You Drazen freak! You're all freaks! Crazy fucking freaks!"

God, Daisy had puke down her shirt.

I turned to Baby. "Sorry."

"Yeah. The Samoans'll take you out. Ping me next week if you want to hang."

I hoisted Daisy up from under her arms. She was no help at all, and I was halfway to hell myself. Derek was still screaming. Arrow gave him his shirt to soak up the blood.

Two gigantic men picked up Daisy and me, threw us over their shoulders, and put us in one of the party's hired cabs.

Chapter 68

FIONA

THE PENTHOUSE SUITE of the Markham was dusty and unused. Total waste of a view and a pool. Mid-century Danish craftsmen had lovingly wrought chairs that hadn't felt the weight of an ass in months. It was all waste.

There were no paparazzi outside. I hadn't lived there in months. Likely they were outside Maundy. And certainly, they hadn't gotten wind of the night's drama, but they rarely did. Not the real shit. The real shit was like the mafia. No one talked.

That didn't change the facts.

It was my fault.

Nothing had happened that I couldn't have predicted.

From pissing off Deacon and Elliot, to acting like a fucking fool, to breaking Derek's face… even to Daisy, who wasn't prepared for a party without boundaries.

I'd wanted to hit bottom.

That was the plan.

Hit bottom and get seen doing it.

But Daisy threw me. And Derek Doucherson, who was just doing what Derek Doucherson did. I hadn't needed to open up his face.

"You don't hit bottom alone, do you?" I asked the elevator doors but made the statement to myself. *You don't do it alone.*

I owned the floor, so the elevator opened up onto a foyer and a door. Outside the door stood Debbie in a black suit. She stood so straight, she could have been a doll.

"Hey," I said.

"Hello, Fiona."

I punched my code into the door, and it clicked open. "Deacon send you?" I was way too sober for this conversation.

"Yes and no."

Her face told me nothing. She was implacable. She had to be. She'd grown up in a North Korean concentration camp where letting the wrong people know what you were thinking could get someone killed.

"You know who else has that thing you have?" I said as I opened the door.

"To which thing do you refer?"

She stepped in, and I closed the door behind her, letting the moonlight pattern the room in distorted rectangles.

"The thing where you make it so no one knows what you're thinking."

"Ah. Who else?"

"My sister. Theresa. It's like talking to a mask."

She stepped forward into the dark room until her face hit the light from outside. She looked different in that light. Sad, broken, held together with spit and chewing gum, every crack leading to the center of the earth. "Is this better?"

"No. Yes. But no."

"Do you know that you're loved?"

I turned on the lights. "Sure."

I knew it. I knew it like I knew how to hold my wrists when I was getting knotted. It was a fact, not a feeling. Not something that made me a better person. Actually, it made me feel worse for everyone else's wasted love.

"Want something to drink?" I asked.

"Water, please."

My kitchen had been used four times, so I had to look in all the cabinets for the glasses. I didn't have to search for the Advil for more than a second. I poured us water from the filtered tap I'd forgotten was there and gave her the glass from across the kitchen bar. She sat on a stool. I drank all the water and popped four Advil.

I didn't think ahead. I swam in the wake of any number of narcotics. My mind felt as if it was made of puzzle pieces that were in the right places but hadn't quite snapped together yet. I could make sense of my thoughts but not the space in between them.

Part of me wanted another line or another pull off a laced bowl. I'd always been impatient with the time between the high and the not-high. Can't sleep. Can't eat. Can't feel. Can't think. Might as well take another hit/snort/drink/whatever.

"Why didn't he come himself?" I asked.

"There's a crisis. In Eretria, I believe. One of his photographers was drugged and is travelling with a group of ENA soldiers."

"Jesus. Those are problems." I put my glass in the sink. "Let me ask you something. How do you even deal with someone like me? You've been through so much, and you're so together. I've never had a real problem in my life."

She nodded, eyes on me. "If you shoot a man's chest and he's wearing a bullet-proof vest, he'll walk away unharmed. If you stab him, he'll be able to defend himself. But if you punch a naked chest, especially if that person is weak and vulnerable, the heart could stop. If you stab or shoot that chest, they are dead."

"Am I the naked chest?"

"All I can say is I have a vest on. What you feel pity about, my childhood, is what protects me. You were given nothing. You were free from want. From even the slightest anxiety. Now you have nothing to protect you. Every slap feels like a bullet wound. You tolerate more pain in your life right now than I do."

I couldn't help but look at her lips when she spoke, because I couldn't look her in the eye. She was validating my pain. She was giving me permission to hurt. Of all people, she was probably the one I needed it most from.

I got out two short glasses so I didn't have to face her.

Behind me, she continued. "In the camp, they took away my humanity from the day I got there. They made me an animal. So as an adult, every day, I have to choose to be human."

I opened another cabinet and grabbed the first bottle I saw, slapping it next to my glass. I pulled out the cork. I didn't even know what the liquid was except brown.

Debbie put her hand over her glass. "It was easy for me. The choice wasn't really a choice. It was life or death. For you, the privileged, you cannot believe you've ever done anything to deserve to be a part of this world. You're told you're royalty, but you don't feel it. You can't. Because you haven't chosen to be human."

She took her hand away, and I poured a finger of whatever-it-was into the glass.

"There was a girl with me tonight. Just a regular girl." I swirled the drink but didn't drink it. "I thought I'd show her a little fun. I'd take her out to a party and get her drunk on free booze and send her home in a cab. I thought I was doing her a favor."

I let my eyes linger on the amber liquid for a long time. Debbie didn't say a word, just gave me time and space to think.

"I think if I hadn't pulled her out of there, she would have died of an overdose with movie star jizz all over her." I tapped the edge of the glass on the marble counter.

"You took her to your Camp 22," Debbie said.

"I won't belittle what you went through."

"You're not. I made the comparison."

"I don't know what happened to me tonight. It wasn't fun."

"You don't have to go back to it."

"I can't stop alone. Not when I'm like…" Shit, I was crying. The thought of giving it all up by myself was painful. "Everything hurts, and nothing bothers me. I feel all backward. I get bored for five minutes, and I just want to go get fucked or fucked up." I rubbed my tears with the backs of my hand. "Then I run back to Deacon because he gets it all under control."

"You say you can't do it alone."

I sighed and looked at the whiskey. I didn't even like whiskey. "The last day, before I got out, I kind of felt good, because of all the work my therapist had done."

"The man I gave the shoes to?"

"Yeah."

"He's in love with you."

I sniffed a little laugh. "Yeah. He told me to get a cab. That was… wow."

"I bet it wasn't easy for him," she said.

I knocked back the whiskey and cringed. Breathed out hard. Corked the bottle. "I want to be worthy of Elliot because he has faith in me. And I want to be worthy of Deacon because of all the work he put into…" I stopped because I hadn't had the words until a few minutes ago. Everything clicked into place that night. "All the times he tried to get me to choose to be human."

"It gets easier."

"Yeah." I put the whiskey back in the cabinet. That little shot had done nothing for me. I had the tolerance of a hard-core drinker.

"I didn't come to save you," she said.

"No?"

"No." She drank the whiskey gently and quickly. Not a drop was left on her lipstick. "Deacon sent me to show you something specific, but I came to show you how to choose."

She stood and moved to the center of the room. I was on the other side of the counter without a clue as to what she wanted. She looked down and unbuttoned the loops of her tunic. She let the tunic fall down her arms, holding it by her fingertips for a split second before letting it drop to the floor.

Her hands stayed at her sides. Eyes downcast. I understood right away what she needed. We'd known Debbie the Domme, and she was utterly and completely a Dominant, but she'd only ever topped men.

I felt it. Everything Deacon had told me about. The arousing power. The anticipation of a slice of the world that was in my control. The throb of a need to bring a person to the edge for my pleasure.

"Debbie, I can't."

"I think you can."

Could I? I'd never considered it.

I'd had sex with women before, but the only time I'd Dominated one —not just topped, but Dominated—was at the Dome. Before Deacon, back when I did shit because no one was there to stop me, and even then, I wasn't in control.

I touched Debbie's nipple. Light brown on Asian-cast skin, it hardened immediately, and I rolled it under my thumb. I felt her breathe, watched her chest heave a little.

I untied her loose silk pants. They dropped below her navel. Under those silken dresses, she had a beautiful body, feminine and strong, with a long waist and narrow hips. With a flick of my fingers, her pants fell.

I thought to ask her if she was sure, but that would defeat the purpose of her request. I took her jaw in my hand and pulled her face up to look at me. She was so beautiful, and suddenly, the thought of having her was more than a lark. It was all I could think about. I kissed her, and it was lovely. The way she reacted to how I moved, submitted her lips to mine, let my tongue invade her mouth. She tasted like oranges. I'd kissed women before, but not like this. Not with purpose.

I took my mouth from hers and put her hands in mine. "Deacon told me he thought I wasn't submissive."

She surprised me by dropping her gaze, and I knew right then that I'd had no idea who she was. "He told you because I told him."

"I don't know what I'm doing."

"Yes, you do, and you don't need him."

I took a step back. Her words were so hard, so definite, and so correct.

Could I do this? Could I spend an hour dominating this woman? I didn't want to hurt her. She was precious to me.

Maybe that would be what made it work. At least for the next hour. As long as I didn't have to think past that, I could play this game.

"Take off my clothes," I said.

Looking downward, she unbuttoned my blouse. Her fingers on the placket were graceful and fine, and I didn't know if I'd ever been more aroused.

"We haven't set any boundaries," I said.

"I know."

I had to sound sure of myself. "Do you want a safe word?"

"My safe word is Pyongyang."

"All right." I hoped I'd remember it. At least for the next hour.

She slipped off my shirt, and I let her service me. Not helping, not hindering as she got on her knees and gently pulled down my skirt, then my panties. I stroked her hair when she ran her hands over my legs. I needed her comfort just then, but I was hesitating. That wasn't going to work.

"Stand up."

She did. We stood across from each other, naked but for shoes.

I reached for her breasts and ran the backs of my hands over them. So hard. Maybe as hard as my own. I pinched one nipple, twisting it. Her lips parted, but she stayed silent.

I walked around her, running my hands over her body. She was lovely. I just wanted to enjoy her without responsibility, but that wasn't why she was here. She'd come here to submit to me. I had a job.

"Back on your knees, beautiful," I said when I was in front of her again.

She dropped. I put my fingers in her hair, and she kissed my belly. *Fuck.* I could practically feel her lips on my clit even though she was nowhere near it.

Then I realized how close she was to seeing where I had been hurt. I didn't want her to see that. She'd know. Anyone who'd spent years as a Dominant would know. I scanned the room quickly. Her clothes were in a pile, including a red scarf. I stretched, grabbed it by the corner, and unwound it from the jacket

"Look at me." I had to suppress the need to say please. I didn't know where I'd gotten the compulsion to be courteous.

She looked up at me with her almond eyes, and I covered them with the scarf, knotting it behind her head.

I stepped back, halfway across the room, and sat on the floor. I bent my knees and spread my legs. "Crawl to me."

She did, putting her head down, letting her breasts swing. God, the things I wanted to do to those tits.

"Eat my pussy. Just your mouth. Lick it up."

She didn't hesitate but turned her head and kissed my swollen clit, then she drew her tongue along it.

"Suck on it."

She flicked her tongue over it then took it between her lips and sucked. I threw my head back. She licked again then sucked. My ass came off the floor. I was full, and ready, but more. I wanted more. More control.

I pushed her face away. "On your back."

She rolled over, and I crouched over her, knees on either side of her head. She looked at me in complete supplication, and I felt exactly right.

"Take my face," she said. "It's yours."

She opened her mouth, and I lowered myself onto it. "Take it. Eat it."

I rubbed myself on her face as she tried to grapple for control enough to make me come, sucking and licking whatever I let near her, pulling away then making her drown in me, until I shifted back and put my clit in her mouth.

"Suck it hard."

I landed on my hands as she pulled on my clit with her mouth, yanking a powerful orgasm out of me. I stiffened, clenched, rubbed myself on her face, and let go.

I crouched over her, panting.

God, how did Deacon do this?

He got the fuck up and made sure I got what I needed.

I stood, wobbly-legged, and moved the scarf off her eyes. "Bedroom's that way. Crawl in and get up on the bed. You're getting rewarded for that. Because it was awesome."

She smiled, face slick and shiny from my cunt. She twisted onto her hands and knees and crawled to the bedroom, head down, toes dragging in the high heels, ass swaying. I walked behind her, feeling a peace I barely understood. She knew how to do this. She was going to do exactly what I asked. Everything was under my control.

When she got up on the bed, she crouched on hands and knees, and I pulled her up to kneeling and kissed her.

"Are you all right with this so far?" I asked.

"Yes."

"I don't have any equipment or anything." I was expressing insecurity, and in the middle of the sentence, I realized what a complete buzzkill that would be for her. "So lean back and touch the headboard," I recovered. "Don't let it go."

I pushed her legs up and apart, letting my fingers drift down her belly into her wetness.

"I always loved your cunt," I said, putting two fingers into her. "It tasted like oranges." I put my fingers in my mouth and sucked on them. "Still does."

I reinserted them, then pulled them out with a swipe and a circle on her clit. Her eyes dropped, and her mouth opened.

"Here. Taste." I put my wet fingers in her mouth.

She sucked on them. I dug them into her throat. Three fingers. I wanted to enter her through my hand. To own her inside and out.

I knew what he felt, all those times, and I knew why it was nourishing for this little bit of the world to be mine.

I shifted over her and put my leg against her cunt until I felt its wetness. She curled herself around my leg, and we moved together. She sucked on my fingers and I pushed against her in ever-increasing rhythms. She looked at me, face scrunched, waiting.

I moved harder and faster against her. How much longer could I make her wait? She wouldn't come without me saying it was all right.

I wanted her to have the best orgasm of her life, so I made her wait as long as I could.

"Come," I said.

And she did, fingertips on the headboard, body arching forward then back. I'd never heard Debbie cry out in pleasure, and I'd seen her come plenty of times. But she cried out for me.

I felt like the queen of the universe, and for a moment, no more, I felt worthy.

I kissed her mouth when it was done and held her tightly.

"Deacon sent you to show me what it was like to dominate someone," I said.

"Yes."

"Should it feel like playacting?"

She sighed. "No."

"You knew I wasn't a Domme when you came here."

"Yes. But you know Deacon. You can't reason with him."

"So basically I'm just a horny perv?"

She laughed. "Yes. And you can do anything and go anywhere you want. That comes from me, not the Master."

I rolled onto my back and looked at the ceiling. "Isn't it funny… technically I could always do whatever I wanted, but I think now I really can. And it's scary."

"Freedom can be frightening," she whispered, half asleep. "You're only free to choose how you're going to not be free."

Had I been scared that whole time? Had I held myself back from doing things because I was afraid? I tried to put myself in the shoes of my younger self. Back in Carlton Prep, when they'd tried to place me in college and they suggested business, I thought they were saying something for the sake of saying it, and I'd felt the walls closing in. Once I chose something, I'd be trapped in it.

Was I trapped with Deacon? Was his freedom a lie?

I could live without him. In the vulnerable place between wakefulness and sleep, between the submissive I thought I was and the Domme I'd just tried to be, I saw the truth. I didn't need him. But did I want him?

I was almost asleep when a voicemail came in.

Elliot.

This is the deal. You show up at my office at eight sharp or I'll get you reassigned. There is no negotiation.

Relief filled the place where the last of the tension had been, as if a drain had opened in the bottom of me and the ugliness fell out. I only had to wait three hours to apologize.

Chapter 69

FIONA

"THIS IS THE DEAL. You show up at my office at eight sharp or I'll get you reassigned. There is no negotiation." I hung up before I could soften it or backpedal.

That was risky. She was as likely to make sure she never saw me again as she was to make an effort to ensure I stayed in her life. But I didn't have any other cards to play. Threatening to put her back into Westonwood might give her exactly what she had been trying to get, if even subconsciously.

The clock said 7:58. Her call had come in seven hours ago.

I'd made the task of getting to the session on time almost impossible for my own sake as well as hers. I couldn't live with her troubles and addictions. She'd ruin me. Calling her in at eight o'clock was self-preservation at its finest. She'd miss the appointment, I'd recuse myself from her care, and that would be it. I'd find a life somewhere in the rubble.

The little light behind my desk flashed.

Someone was in the waiting room.

Did I have another appointment?

I opened the door. She stood there, sunglasses on, smelling of soap, fingers twitching.

"Fiona." I didn't have anything more to say. I was overwhelmed with relief that she hadn't let me push her away. I'd never wanted so badly for a plan to fail.

"Apologetic. Ashamed. Scared. Tired as hell," she said.

"Excuse me?"

"I'm using different words to describe myself."

Chapter 70

FIONA

I UNLOADED everything about the party, all its debasement and debauchery. I didn't sugarcoat it. I was honest. I'd never been so honest in my life. I didn't hold back a thing.

"My call," I said. "It was… I'm sorry. I wanted to hurt you, and yes, I got high and stupid, and I lost interest in the whole thing. I think it was because you weren't coming for me. It pissed me off, but it made me look at myself. And I was glad you weren't coming."

"So you went home?"

"Yes."

"What did Deacon do?"

"What did he do? Well, let's see. Apparently he was on his way to Eretria, so he sent a mutual friend to fuck me?"

He raised an eyebrow.

"And I'm going to tell you what happened, but first I have to talk about the stupid thing I said to you yesterday and it was… did I say stupid?"

"What did you say?"

"I said I loved you. I think I meant it." Fuck this. I wasn't a high school kid with a crush. I was Fiona Fucking Drazen. "Actually, I know I meant it."

He leaned forward, just a foot or so closer, and I felt the space between us contract and pull at me, as if I could lean forward another inch and close the gap.

"Transference," he said. "It's when the therapist fills a gap in your life that you recognize because of the therapy."

I pressed my lips together and broke his gaze before it broke me. "Maybe. Sure. I was missing a therapist in my life and there you were."

I sniffed. Stupid snot was gathering in my sinuses, and I had to sniff to get rid of it. I cleared my throat. Looked at my hands, then at him. I felt like an ass.

"I shouldn't joke," I said.

He smiled. "Countertransference is when the patient fills a place for the therapist."

Breathe. Breathe. You have to function. Breathe.

"That sounds like normal people," I said. "You know, with needs. They meet each other and they fill needs."

"When you left Westonwood, I saw you by the door. I asked you to wait."

"Yes."

"You didn't."

"No."

"Why?" He asked it as if he already knew the answer.

"I told you right there. I'll destroy you. Men like you… you're nice. I'd eat you up and spit you out. I'd fuck you and leave you and—look, this isn't my ego talking. Nice guys don't last in my world. Nice guys with boundaries and common sense? I'm not paying for your therapy bills."

He laughed. I laughed.

Then he rubbed his eyes. "You knew how I felt. So you may feel vulnerable about what you said yesterday, but I opened that door. And the professional man in me regrets that."

"What about the unprofessional man?"

It took him a long time to answer. Two hours. Two minutes. Time folded in on itself. Could have been no time at all. But I saw every single thought cross his mind. A war raged behind his eyes.

"I promised myself before you got here that I wouldn't do this."

I leaned forward, putting up my hand. "Don't. You're right. Don't do this. I'm not worth it."

He looked me dead in the face, his hair a little askew, an expression so certain that he could have told me black was white and I would have believed him.

"But you are. You're worth all of it."

I sat back in my chair. "What do you want?"

"This session is supposed to be about you."

"That's the stupidest thing you've ever said."

"We're even then. In saying stupid things that are true."

"No. We're not."

Another two hours passed while he looked at me, and I fell into him. Maybe my feelings were transference, like he'd said, and maybe I was filling some gap in his life, but that didn't make it a lie.

Maybe it did, and I just didn't care.

As if we were pulled on the same string, he stood at the exact time I stood. He put his hand on my neck. I didn't realize I was cold until I felt the warmth of it. I leaned into his touch because it was so gentle, so firm, and I let him pull us closer.

"This is wrong," he said softly, as if giving it a name, accepting that name, and continuing.

I knew what he was doing, and I let him. Let his lips brush mine. Tasted the lemon water on his breath. Moved into the softness of his mouth, the wetness of his tongue as it entered me. His groan rumbled into my throat. I let him push our bodies together because I'd craved him from the minute I saw him. He understood me and he still wanted me, not in spite of my failings, but because of them.

I pushed my hips against him. He was hard. Very hard. Ready for it, and Fiona Drazen never turned down a hard cock. He pushed me against the wall, moving his mouth along my neck, his lips fire to the kindling of my skin.

I pushed him away, and we stood inches from each other, panting as if we'd run miles. I wasn't ready. I wanted more from him, but I couldn't expect anything yet. Not unless I wanted to ruin him.

"I can't," I said.

He smiled. "No. You can't." He kissed my cheek, lingering there, and I knew with a little prodding, I would have been on my back. Instead he whispered in my ear. "Not today." He ran his finger along my jaw and down my throat, leaving a path of tingling skin. "There's no looking back for me. So when I finally do what I've wanted to since I met you, that's it. No more fucking around."

I nodded and kissed him again. I didn't feel whole because of him. I felt whole because I'd chosen him.

Chapter 71

FIONA

WHEN I WAS A GIRL, I had one place where I felt at home. Where I didn't feel eyes on me or pressure to be anything. I had to be perfect, but dressage had a set of rules for perfection I could follow easily and be done with when I got off the horse.

I got on the 110, down to Rancho Palos Verdes, where Snowcone lived. The smell of hay and horseshit was like home to me, and all the world slipped away.

"Hey!" I said when I saw Lindy arranging tack in front of the stables.

"Fiona!" She approached with a hug. "It's so good to see you. You look great." Lindy had Ivory Girl skin and straight brown hair she kept cut to the top of her shoulders. She hadn't aged past thirty-five.

"Thanks."

"I have the last of Snowcone's things all put together." She started walking inside, boots landing in a pile of mustard-colored horseshit. A true horse person, she didn't even notice.

"Excuse me?" I said.

"I love that horse, but she's yours, and you taking her is—"

"Taking her?"

"Did you guys get your signals crossed? Your boyfriend came and got her an hour ago. I went to see the Laurel Canyon space yesterday, and it's perfect."

"Yes," I said. "Yes, of course it is. Thank you, Lindy. Thank you for everything."

Chapter 72

FIONA

I HAD to remind myself why I was irritated with Deacon because I'd already forgiven him for taking Snowcone. I had nothing to offer my horse but neglect.

But that wasn't the point. What the fuck was Deacon doing in Los Angeles? He couldn't leave me alone for a minute. Who even knew what kind of clusterfuck he'd turned his back on in favor of watching me? Probably twenty journalists being held in a closet and his team was supposed to rescue them, but no. Fiona was on a bender. So he stayed to bring her horse to his stables.

Deacon was walking Snowcone around the pen. He was most comfortable in jeans and boots with a heavy button-down shirt. His forearms were wiry and taut, and his jeans hugged his hips as if they were made for him. Both he and Snowcone were well-muscled machines, and I sighed.

"Hey," I said, falling into step with them. "I thought you had something to do over there." I jerked my head in the way I did when I meant *Africa*.

"It can wait." He was full of shit.

"You couldn't have gone there and back."

"I didn't go. I got off the plane before it took off."

God. Fuck him.

"I'm mad at you."

"Why?"

"I never agreed to let Snowcone move here. This pisses me off."

"You don't sound mad," he said.

"I am."

"You're not. You're relieved. You have an excuse to stay."

He was so sure of himself. So measured. There wasn't a woman in the world who wouldn't fuck him, so why should I be any different?

"Does everything always make sense to you? Like, you want to keep me here, so you find a way to do it and that's that? I mean, I don't even know what I want, so you just think, 'oh, let me want something for her'? Is that what goes on in your mind? Is that your power trip?"

"Stop pretending you don't want to stay with me."

"I don't know what I want."

He stopped, yanking Snowcone back. "You want to be here, and you need to be here. When you leave, you party. When you party—"

"I stabbed you to get away from you!"

"You didn't stab me. The drugs did."

I pushed him. He didn't budge, but I pushed him again. I wanted to wake him up, to show him what he wasn't looking at. "You trapped me. You trap me with shit like this." I pointed at my horse.

"By being perfect for you?"

"By letting me run around like a whore."

"That's not what it was, and you know it."

"By being perfect for all of my worst impulses."

"They're a part of you. What do you think you're going to do now? Settle down in a ranch house in the Valley with a disgraced therapist? Have two kids and take Valium and fuck the pool boy behind his back?" His face jutted forward and his arm was thrown back, pointing at an imaginary house in a real suburb. "You're better than that."

"I'm not. I'm not even good enough for him." I swallowed, because I hadn't meant to say that. Not "for him," but my emotions had swarmed until there was no stopping the words.

"Really?" he said. "Did you fuck him yet?"

"It's not your business."

"You're right." In a flash, he had me by the back of my hair. He yanked it until I was looking into his piercing blue eyes. "It doesn't matter. It. Does. Not. You're mine. Your home is with me. And you can stab me another hundred times, and I'll bring you back. Because there is not another man on this earth who understands you the way I do and no woman who understands me."

"Let me go."

"Never." He twisted my body under him. His teeth were clamped shut, making his jaw stronger, tighter, more square. He was beautiful when in power and anger.

"I forgot…"

He dragged me to my knees. "Forgot what? This? How much you need this?"

"My safe word," I said. "I forgot it."

His reaction was immediate, and he let me go. I was still on my knees, hands in the dried leaves and needles.

"What's he going to do when you need to be broken?"

"Nothing." I got up, shaking from nerves. "He's not you. No one is."

"Do you love him?"

I didn't answer right away. I just stared at the face of the man I'd loved first, and would always love. I was hurting him. Every day I stayed with him, I cracked his armor, and if I left, I'd tear the armor away. It wasn't fair. He was too strong, too confident to let me do this to him. I didn't want to answer. I wasn't ready to own how it would affect him.

"Do. You. Love. Him?"

"No," I whispered.

He surprised me by smiling. "No, of course you don't. You can't."

He laid his hands on my crossed arms. Bone and sinew, with a squared joint at the base of the thumb. The hands of a man. Hands that bruised and tied, fingers that disappeared into my body. I couldn't deny them. My arms dropped to my side. I practically groaned when my throbbing pussy woke up. Elliot had left me unsatisfied, and here was Deacon, ready to take me.

"I don't want to be saved," I said. "Not anymore."

"You never needed to be saved. You only ever needed to be broken." He touched my lips with the pad of his second finger. "Remember this. Remember that you are not an average woman. You don't have average needs."

He leaned in until I could smell his rough scent, his dominance, and I went liquid.

"Open your mouth," he whispered.

I parted my lips. He put in two fingers, pushing to the back of my throat. I was mush. Oatmeal. The thought of his ministrations left me powerless.

"Anyone can fuck you," he said, fucking my mouth with his fingers. "I'm the only one who can break you."

I groaned against his fingers.

"Pull your pants down," he commanded.

I unbuttoned them and yanked them to mid-thigh. Cool air hit my ass, and I had a moment of worry that was chased away when Deacon spoke again.

"Pull your shirt up." He jammed his fingers down my throat, and I took them, choking as I pulled my shirt over my tits.

He grabbed a pierced nipple and pinched, pulled, twisted all at the same time, using the silver ring as leverage. The pain went right between my legs. He slid his wet fingers out of my mouth and put them between my legs, roughly running past my clit and hooking them into my cunt. I squealed. The pleasure was like a gunshot.

"You want me to fuck you, Kitten?"

"No," I gasped, every breath a lie.

"What does your wet little cunt want?"

"Break me."

He twisted my clit, and I screamed in pleasure and pain. I was close. So close, and when he rubbed my clit again, I came, standing in the middle of the yard.

"Get on your knees," he said.

I fell as if pushed by invisible hands, knees landing on the soft earth.

"Crawl to the stables."

Pants at mid-thigh, shirt hoisted under my arms, I crawled, eyes on the leaf-strewn ground, ass out in the air, a man behind me.

The last time I'd been like this—

I'd said no.

The last time I'd been on my hands and knees in a little forest, I was being ass-raped by a psychopath. But I didn't have to think about that. This would be different because I was with Deacon. I felt a pressure on my back. He pushed me with his foot. It was humiliating, but I was safe, and I was aroused with a heavy tingling below the waist.

In a way, I was also bored. I wanted to walk because it was more efficient, and I wanted to talk through my annoyance with him. I wanted to just fuck. Just get on with it.

The stinging pain on my ass was a surprise.

"Crawl, Kitten." He thwacked my ass with the belt again. "To the door."

I was lost in the act. My pussy was heavy with wetness and lust. Giving up all pretenses of control, I was exploding with desire.

As I crested the doorway to the stables, the leaves and dirt turned to wood planks.

"Stop," Deacon said.

I did. He walked around me, and I could see his muddy boots and the cuffs of his jeans. He swung the end of the belt in my sightline.

He crouched. "Look at me." His face was perfectly calm and in charge. His voice was even and sure. "I'm not threatened by any man. Not when it comes to you."

"Yes, Master."

He looped the belt around my neck tenderly, threading the end through the buckle. He reminded me of the safe sign we always used when I was gagged. "Snap your fingers to safe out."

And with one motion so swift and sure, he yanked it closed until I couldn't breathe. He pulled me up to kneeling, unbuttoning his jeans and releasing his beautiful cock.

He let me breathe. "Your face is mine to fuck. Open your mouth."

He tightened his grip on the buckle at the back of my neck and thrust his cock down my throat. It tasted of sweat and skin. I kept my mouth open while he thrust into it, using the belt as leverage, pulling my head where he wanted it. Keeping it still when he wanted to push his cock down my throat in repeated bursts. The world went black, and he loosened the belt, moved his dick, let me breathe, and started again.

I wasn't even there. God, I did need this. I needed to not have a will, not exist outside his pleasure.

He came down my throat, sticky and hot. I breathed through my nose and took all of it, because it was mine.

When he was done, he let the belt go, and I dropped down on all fours. My pants were still around my thighs.

"I thought I wasn't submissive." I said it coyly, trying to be gentle. It was a lousy time to try to prove a Dom wrong, but I couldn't help it.

"I smell the drugs on you. I only know one way to get the message across."

My scalp tightened as he took me by the hair and dragged me, dropping me on the carpet near a wooden X set into the wall. Each end had adjustable cuffs, and I went liquid as he dragged my wrist to an ankle cuff and pulled it closed. He stood over me, belt still looped in one hand, looking down at his property. I hated myself for disappointing him, and at the same time, I felt safe in his care.

"Don't cross your legs, and don't come," he said. "You sit there with your legs spread, and I'll let you come after I break you."

He walked out and closed the door.

Chapter 73

THERE WAS a reason I didn't fuck you for months when we met. I needed you to get control of yourself before I could control you. Otherwise there would be a lot of wasted effort. And you didn't seem submissive to me. The perfect body type for knotting, and from working dressage, you knew how to control your legs and arms, but you didn't seem truly submissive.

So I watched. I had control of you for that length of time.

The way you set your mind to it. The way you got on your knees for me. Fiona Drazen. We got all that coy sexiness stripped off you, and you were bare to me. Because of your public persona, you were more naked than anyone I'd seen before.

You blinded me like a bright light in the night.

I told you I was going to break you, and the night I did, I made the biggest mistake of my life.

Chapter 74

FIONA - TWO YEARS EARLIER

"BREAKING A SUBMISSIVE ISN'T AN ACT. It isn't a result. Breaking is a process."

I looked at the floor. I was on my knees before him, hands behind me. I'd just seen my friend Earl at an afternoon birthday party that had seemed innocent enough. He offered me flake and cock. I had to run out like a schoolgirl to avoid snorting a line off his dick, but I couldn't stop thinking about it. Couldn't breathe from wanting it. Everywhere, the temptation to do things that would risk breaking what I was building with Deacon. I wanted it too badly. To be pushed off some kind of edge into controlled freefall.

"I still want it," I said.

"It's not something you want. It's something that happens when you're ready."

I didn't say anything. He put his fingers under my chin and forced me to look up at him.

"What's on your mind, Kitten?"

"Make me ready. Please."

From his face, I knew he would. I'd won. Whatever that meant.

Chapter 75

FIONA

I'D GOTTEN my back to the wall and my pants back up most of the way.
Deacon had locked the cuff with a key and left me alone. He wasn't
finished with me, but he had left me nonetheless. I was overcome with
sadness. The bottom dropped out of me, a black feeling made worse
from the dopamine rushing out of my brain.

He had to go. I couldn't deal with this all the time. This was the last
fuck. He was out. Gone. Done.

I wanted him, and he gave me what no one else could, but he had to
get out of my life.

Goddamn. After everything, I still wanted him to come back and
fuck me.

My phone buzzed. I wiggled and got it out of my pocket with my
free hand.

Elliot.

"What happened the day you left Westonwood?" His words were
clipped, but the tones were a balm on my wounds. Any urgency
surrounding Deacon went away in the smoothness of his voice.

"You stopped me at the door and chickened out."

"I had sessions after I saw you yesterday. Warren Chilton implied something in his group session that I need to confirm before—"

My blood curdled, and I cut him off before it went solid in my veins. "What kind of something?"

I heard a *tap tap* from his side. Pen on the desk? Finger on the counter?

"That he took something you didn't want to give."

I couldn't answer through my shock. He'd taken something I wasn't willing to give. What a nice way to say rape.

Elliot continued before I could answer. "And he smiles like a cat whenever he mentions you. And he mentions you too often."

I was tempted to deflect, just tell him Warren had gotten me sleeping pills and be done with it, but I didn't want to open that bag of shit until I could get a handle on the outcome.

"Maybe he wants to fuck me." I stretched out, wrist still bound to the bottom of the X. I was talking about Warren, but blocking him out with thoughts of my therapist made me purr.

"I don't doubt that, but there's something more to it."

He hadn't gotten the message, and that annoyed me.

"Isn't there some kind of rule about not talking about your patients?"

"I break rules with you. I'd break more. I'd break all of them."

"Doctor," I said, "you're not yourself."

"He's an antisocial psychopath who's fixated on someone I care about."

"Someone you want. It's different. You *want* me."

I heard him breathing. I'd downgraded our whole relationship after Deacon's exquisite humiliations, which was wrong. The light over Los Angeles was getting flat and grey in the late afternoon. Maybe Elliot and I were the only two souls awake in the world.

I waited for him to answer. Make up some lie about loving me or some bullshit.

"I want you," he said. "And I'm concerned."

"You want me?"

"You know that I do."

"What do you want?" I asked.

"You. The you you hide from everyone. You're under my skin. I can't live with myself until I make your world right and share it with you."

I lowered my voice so he'd get it. "That's not what I meant. What do you want *to do* to me?"

Another pause. This one shorter.

"You want to do this?" he challenged me.

"Yes."

"I want to fuck you." He roared a little. Like a lion prince who could grow to be the king of the jungle.

"How?" I clicked the speakerphone on and put the phone down. "Tell me. I'm all alone here."

"How?" His voice had changed, as if he'd made a decision to engage in this game. "By bending you backward on the kitchen table. By holding you down by the throat and pulling off your underwear. Spreading your legs so far apart. Then eating your pussy. It tastes like honey."

I throbbed. His tongue on me, sweet flicking softness on my cunt. I put my fingers under the crotch of my underwear. I was soaked. Slick.

"God, yes. I want that."

A laugh of relief escaped his throat. He'd taken a risk by engaging in this conversation, I knew that.

"I don't let you come. But you get close. I can feel you tighten on my tongue."

"Fuck me," I said.

"Are you touching yourself?"

"Yes. Don't stop."

"I pull your knees toward the table. I can see your cunt. It's beautiful. I slide my dick along it. You're so wet for it."

I heard him swallow. "Fuck me, Elliot. Just fuck me."

"You're so tight. And you look at me. You feel so good."

"I'm going to come."

"Yes."

I tightened around my fingers, pulling against the cuff that held my wrist. It was a good one. A warm wave over my body. Just as I heard him groan, the phone fell, skidding away when my foot lost leverage and kicked from under me.

I stayed sprawled there, breathing hard, looking at the ceiling as it turned dark grey.

"Fiona?" Elliot called from the phone.

I twisted to get it but couldn't reach. "Yeah."

"Where are you?"

"I'm at Deacon's. I can't reach the phone."

"What do you mean you can't reach the phone?" he asked.

"He cuffed me to the wall."

"What?"

"Take it easy. This is not a big deal," I said.

"What do you mean it's not a big deal?"

"It's the kink, Doctor E. Like phone sex. Stop being a prude."

"I'm coming for you." Somewhere in his world, a door slammed. Keys jingled.

"You don't even know where I am," I protested.

"You underestimate me, and you underestimate what I'm willing to do for you."

"I don't even know what that means."

"He couldn't just take you past the gate without saying where he was taking you. You're still an outpatient."

"Please don't come here," I said. "It's not going to be okay."

"It is going to be okay. It's going to be better than okay. I'm giving you permission to make it okay. And me, I can't live like this anymore. I can't settle anymore. I spent my entire life holding back. That's why I almost entered the priesthood. And I love God. I do. My faith is real, but my vocation wasn't. I used it so I'd have rules to follow to keep me in line."

"You see what happens when there are no rules, Elliot. You end up like me. I'm not what you want to be."

"I don't want Yesterday Fiona. I want Today Fiona. Tomorrow Fiona. We can break the right rules together. I got through that session yesterday with you, and I beat off like an adolescent. And when I went over to Westonwood and heard what they were saying—I want to kill him."

"You're crazy."

"I am."

I didn't answer but closed my eyes. I was used to being wanted by friends and strangers. Deacon protected me from those who wanted me by letting my world revolve around his, deflecting their desires and putting them under our control.

But Elliot was different. We'd met without Deacon's protection. He'd spoken to me in a way no one else had. I believed him. He may have been misguided or wrong, but he meant what he said.

"I don't know how I feel," I finally said. I'd committed myself to putting Warren down, and that goal precluded me from getting closer to Elliot, phone sex notwithstanding.

"I'll be there in fifteen minutes."

Deacon's voice cut through the room. "You're going to get an eyeful, doctor."

He entered in trousers and a button-up shirt, carrying a wooden paddle over his shoulder.

Without missing a beat, Elliot answered, "Let her go."

"See you later." Deacon scooped up the phone and hung up, then he slipped it in his pocket. "Well, Kitten. How was your afternoon?"

Deacon was in fine form, dropping the paddle to his side and tapping his knee. It had three large holes in it to cut air resistance.

"Fine, Master."

He tucked the paddle under his arm and unlocked me. I could smell his soap. He'd showered for me.

"You touched yourself," he said as he turned the key. He didn't say how he knew—he just did.

"I'm sorry. I wasn't supposed to."

"You never have. I'll restrain both hands next time."

I was on the floor, and he stood above me. I was afraid, and it was the fear and the anticipation of pain that turned me on. I was wet all over again. Yet it seemed too soon for the paddle. The paddle was the end of the line for me, and he was starting with it.

"Put your back to me. Hands over your head."

I did it, holding two thoughts in my head at the same time: that I was worthy of Elliot and that I was a piece of meat for Deacon to use.

"Master?" It felt weird, slipping back into that role. Part of me wanted to curse him and tell him to fuck off, which was how I knew he was right. In his eyes, I needed to be broken again.

"Yes?" He pulled my pants down just below my ass.

I was going to ask him his intentions, but that would have been out of line. I'd forgotten that in the space of an afternoon. "Where do you want me?"

He pointed the paddle at a white painted picnic bench. "Knees straight. Hands on the seat."

I did as he said, putting my ass in the air, and I wondered, despite all agreements to the contrary, could I just get up and walk away? As long as my mouth was free and I could utter my safe word, would he still do this?

"What did the doctor want?" he asked.

He pressed the wood to my ass. *Tap tap tap*, warming me up.

"To fuck me."

"Did you let him?"

"Over the phone."

The paddle landed on the backs of my thighs, and I bit back a scream.

"I could tell you'd climaxed as soon as I walked in. Thank you for being honest. But you didn't ask me first."

He hit me again. So soon after the previous smack, with no break between, no chance to breathe, my skin was on fire. I locked my jaw closed and grunted.

"You're out of control," he said, paddling me a third time.

My knees bent under me, and tears flowed. "Yes, sir," I grunted.

"We're getting it back. You and me. Count to twenty."

"It's too many!"

"Twenty-five then. And keep it quiet. Willem's here."

The paddle landed with an explosion of pain. My knees buckled, and I counted.

Chapter 76

FIONA - TWO YEARS EARLIER

ONCE I'D DECIDED to let him break me, it didn't get any easier. I didn't understand the concept. Didn't internalize it because I wanted it.

Number Two Maundy was packed to capacity. It was the heyday before the accident that killed Amanda. Before Deacon left that time, when he was still as committed to getting me under control as I was.

I was naked, face down, swinging three feet above the floor, legs spread below me, hands twisted behind me. My ass was up, and my ponytail was knotted behind my head, forcing my face up. I saw myself in the mirror, little tits making wide Vs under me. Some of the guests watched, some didn't. Some were in their own humiliations. But I was in the center of the room, drooling around a ball gag, taking the paddle, and crying. The bottom of my face shone with snot and spit, and Deacon had rolled up his shirtsleeves.

"One last, Kitten."

I barely heard him. The last *thwack* was all I heard as my vision broke into fragments from the pain. When I came back, I saw him. Mister

Rugged, from my first trip to Maundy, was rolling whiskey around the bottom of his glass.

Deacon came in front of me and faced me. I was at crotch level, and he bent to look me in the eye.

"Not broken," he said. "What do I have to do?"

The question was rhetorical. He'd told me exactly what he was going to do, and I'd agreed to it. He said I was safe, that he'd be close by. I wasn't even scared.

He popped off the ball gag.

"Break me," I begged. "Please."

"I can't, it seems. It takes a village."

He clapped twice. They were taking me. They were all taking me. I looked over at Deacon, who had stepped back and crossed his arms. He was there, watching.

Mister Rugged stepped up first. He shook hands with Deacon, and they spoke a few words in a language I didn't know. Then he looked at me.

Behind me, someone cupped my burning and wounded ass.

"Defiant one, you are," Rugged said.

He slapped me, open-handed. I was stunned, even past the scalding pain behind me. I twisted in my restraints, but I was fastened tight by Deacon's knots, and the more I moved, the more my hair felt as if it would get ripped from my head.

"Oh, this?" He slapped me again. "This bothers you?"

It did. He put his fingers down my throat and slapped my cheek with his other hand. No, I did not like this. The cock sliding into my lubed asshole? I could take that any time, but when Rugged slapped my left cheek, a piece of my heart broke off.

"He's too nice to you," he said, jerking his head toward Deacon, who must have moved behind me. "You're just a little fucktoy, and he treats you like a woman."

He removed his hand from my mouth. I choked and gurgled out a glob of spit. He slapped each cheek. Palm. Backhand. Like it was nothing.

I wanted to say my safe word. I didn't think I could stand him doing it again. I was humiliated, but not as a sex object. I could take sexual disgrace and eat it for lunch. But now I was degraded as a person. A human. His slaps weren't sexual or personal. They were detached, public, shameful. My nudity and my position were stripped of their power to seduce. And that was where I lost myself. I broke like a handful of spaghetti, right in the middle, pieces flying away.

He put his dick in my mouth and I took it down my throat, while someone I couldn't see fucked my ass as if I wasn't even there.

And in a sense, I wasn't.

I'd gotten myself in too deep on Maundy. I'd asked to be broken. Begged. Maybe it was the novelty of the idea, or maybe it was a real kink. But I dropped out of those ropes changed.

I was bone-tired. Cold. Aching everywhere. Sticky with the juice of half a dozen men. When Deacon tried to touch me, I thought I'd be physically ill.

"Get away from me."

Someone scooped me up and took me to the Care Room. I didn't want to be there. It was too generic a space. Like a hotel room for anyone stuck in subspace. I hated it suddenly, and wanted to be in a personal space that wasn't accessible to any sub who needed aftercare.

But I was too wrecked to protest. I was laid on the clean white sheets in the windowless room. I shivered. I didn't know I could be so cold. Candles were lit.

Soothing music came on, and a lovely female voice said, "Welcome to the world of the broken." Debbie covered me with a down blanket. "You were always lovely. But right now, you are most beautiful."

She sat by me and stroked my hair. I felt isolated, alone, floating in the stars, miles above the movements of the human race.

Chapter 77

FIONA

I WASN'T BROKEN during the paddling in Laurel Canyon. My ass hurt, and I was annoyed. I was waiting for Elliot to show up and make a scene. Then I would have to act quickly to defuse it.

"Twenty-five!" I said through gritted teeth, more relieved that we'd get to do something else than that I'd reached the end to the pain.

He tossed the paddle aside and pushed me down, pushing my face into the bench.

"Remember how I broke you last time?"

I couldn't answer from the pressure on my jaw.

"Desexualizing you." He put his other hand on the open wounds on my ass, digging in his fingers. "Same thing rarely works twice."

He pulled back, getting both hands on my bottom, and pulled the cheeks apart. I didn't know what he intended, and I never found out. Because he got a look at what was going on back there, and the cruelty dropped off him.

"What the—?"

"Wait, I—"

"Who did this to you? The fucking doctor?"

"No!"

He yanked up my underpants. Angry. Tender. All the things at once.

"This"—he indicated my body as one violated unit—"I've seen everything. This was not consensual. Fiona. Kitten. What happened? What did he do to you, and why are you protecting him?"

Deacon was always in control, but standing over me as I adjusted my pants, he exhibited a level of confusion and pain I'd never seen before. It was like the earth shifting beneath me. If he didn't know what to do, then every action I'd considered taking must be wrong.

Right before my eyes, all the confusion congealed into rage, and I feared for my friend, my plan, and my Master.

"Leave him alone." I could have denied further. I could have told him it was Warren, but I did a calculation faster than I ever had, and I made a choice to build a wall around Elliot. "I will rain hell on you, Deacon. I love you, and I will ruin you."

"Are you threatening me?"

Again, the confusion. Recognizing it for the second time, I knew what his confusion turned into when it transmuted into a solid emotion.

I said nothing. I held my hands at my sides, paddled ass waiting for the aftercare that wasn't coming. Wanting to let him hold me and care for me, to kneel before him because it would make everything all right. I wouldn't have to take responsibility for a damn thing. It would just work itself out in the form of violence.

A knock at the door, and a voice through it. Willem. "There's a guy at the gate."

He barely had the sentence out before I ran past Deacon, opened the door, and blew past Willem, past Debbie gathering fallen oranges in the yard, through the front house, to the driveway, which I took in loping strides, barefoot on sharp stones, and opened the pedestrian gate.

Elliot waited in his car.

I yanked on the door handle. "Unlock it!"

Clack.

I threw myself into the passenger side. "Get me out of here."

"What—?"

"Go!"

He backed out of the drive, little car spitting pebbles, and got on Mulholland. I turned my body around to see if anyone was following.

"Are you okay?" he asked.

"I'm fine." The coast looked clear for the moment.

"What happened?"

"Deacon thinks you raped me."

"*What?*" He skidded onto the shoulder.

"Keep driving!"

He pulled back onto the road. I twisted again, looking for the private road to spit out a black Range Rover.

"You told him I raped you?"

"Of course not. He saw…" I sank in my seat.

"What's happening?

"Just drive. Please."

"Where are we going?"

"You tell me."

"Fine," he said, as if making the decision was more of a relief than a burden.

He took a left, then a right, then a series of turns I'd never remember, heading deep into the basin. We didn't talk. There was too much for me to know where to start, where to end, what to tell him, and what to hide.

Chapter 78

FIONA

ELLIOT PULLED up to a meter on Wilshire, set the wheel to its straight
position, and put the car in park. He tapped the gearshift and said,
"You're squirming in your seat."

"I got twenty-five with a paddle."

He looked at me.

"That turns you on," I said. It wasn't a question.

"My dick is the last thing on my mind."

"But it reacted."

He stepped out of the car without confirming, and walked around to
my side. He opened my door. After I got out and he closed it, he guided
me into a little coffee house.

He whispered as I passed, "Everything about you makes my
body react."

I smiled at him. "I'll have a buttercup. No sugar."

I sat at one of the lacquered teak presswood tables under the
hardware store buckets hanging from the ceiling. A bonsai tree sat in the

center of each table and along the bar, and the Korean love ballads were loud enough to shield our words.

He put my cup in front of me and sat. I stirred the fat into marbling spirals in the black sludge.

"Thank you," I said.

"Do you want to tell me about Warren?"

I nodded, biting my upper lip. My eyes filled up. I hadn't told a soul, and admitting it made it real. I didn't look at him. I said the words to the swirling pat of butter in my espresso.

"By the creek. He hurt me badly enough for Deacon to see two days later. I said 'no.' I said, 'lube me up,' something, you know? Just… it was bad enough sitting still for it. Having to because no one would believe he raped me. But it hurt. Having him call me a whore who liked it. Because I had. I'd liked it like that often enough.

"It was so bad. It hurt inside. In my guts. I felt like I was getting ripped up. And he just… he felt like having anal and I was there. It wasn't that he liked that it hurt me. He just didn't care. I was invisible. I died. I feel like I died."

Elliot put his hands over my arms and tightened them around me. He didn't say a word.

The weight of it was too much. The flat grey mass of sadness broke me again. I should have broken that day behind the fence. I should have gone into subspace and had aftercare and walked out a shiny strong new woman. But I'd been holding myself together, and in that coffee shop in Koreatown, I was falling apart, leaking all the garbage and reeking toxins that I'd carried. My humiliation and pain spilled onto the cracked sidewalk with the rest of the trash no one picked up.

But it wasn't done. Maybe the valve on the bucket had been loosened. Maybe the pressure was relieved enough to continue with my head on straight.

I pulled away a little.

"You have to know it wasn't your fault," he said.

I nodded, but I didn't believe him. A part of me would always wonder how much my history had played into Warren's decision, and how much I should have expected from a guy who sold amphetamines to an anorexic. I always said I was smarter than that. Better equipped than the girls who woke up on the beach with their panties missing and blood under their fingernails. Sharper than the ones who had to abort fetuses with mystery fathers.

Maybe not.

"What do you want to do?" he asked.

His fingertips brushing my palm was sexual but comforting. He wanted me. You didn't need to be a rocket scientist to figure that out. But he wouldn't try to fuck me. Not while I was talking about rape. Not as long as the pall of inappropriateness hung over us.

"Nothing," I said.

"Nothing? You're going to let him get away with it?"

"I never said that."

"You need to tell someone."

"Who? His father owns the mayor's office. His mother? In Carlton, he cornered Robbie Sanchez in the bathroom and fistfucked him in front of the entire lacrosse team. Literally fistfucked him. Warren's mother decided he was pushed to do it, and guess what happened?"

"Robbie got suspended."

I put my finger on the tip of my nose.

"You're not a Sanchez," he said, running his thumb along my arm. "You're a Drazen."

"I'd rather take care of this myself."

"How?"

"I'm still deciding. But I'm pretty sure I'll run over anyone who gets in my way."

He nodded, as if accepting not only that I wasn't making an empty threat but that the threat could be directed at him. "I won't get in your way."

"You might."

He tilted his face toward me. "No. I don't think I would. I know what it meant for you to tell him no."

There was something strong and sure about him. Something overtly understated. I could love him, maybe. But not for long. I'd ruin him just for the challenge, even if it broke my heart.

He took my hand and squeezed it. His hand was dry and strong without hurting mine. The touch was tender without seduction.

"Again, it wasn't your fault," he said.

"How do you even know that?"

"Because there's no shame in you. If you wanted to do it, you'd just say so and tell everyone to fuck off."

I spit out a laugh that turned into a quick inhale and a sob. I pulled my hand away and covered my face. I didn't want him, or anyone, to see me cry. I wanted to be the one in control for a fucking change.

"I want to die," I said between my hands. "Like, really die."

"I won't let that happen."

I took my hands away from my face. "Elliot, come on."

"What?"

"You're not the type to be able to stop anything from happening to me or anyone else."

"The type?" He tapped the end of his spoon on the napkin, carving a stack of fading taupe frowns.

"Sweet guy. Sensitive. Measured."

He smiled at me. "Of course. I get it. A nice, measured guy can't protect you."

"A God-fearing, rule-following guy. And maybe that's the point. If I wanted someone to protect me, Deacon would do it."

"But you didn't tell him."

"I can't protect him. See, he gets a lot of things about the world and how it works. He's seen a lot of scary shit and… you know… done scary shit too. But he doesn't understand my world. Not even a little."

"You shouldn't handle this on your own."

"There's nothing to handle," I lied. I'd led him too close to my center and wanted to throw him. "I just have to deal and move on."

"A minute ago you wanted to die."

"I'm not known for being consistent."

He leaned against the wall, put his ankle on his knee, and tapped the table. "When we met, I wanted to make you better. I want to make everyone better, but you? I wanted to reach inside you and heal whatever it was. Now I think it's all flipped around. I want to wipe the evil off the face of the earth so it's safe for you. But I'm not the guy who's going to decapitate Warren Chilton. Because I know how his world works." He jabbed the table as if his point was there, and he turned his upper body to face me. "I know his status, and I know he's going to do it again. So he's not getting away with it. I promise you, because you have this face on like it's fine, but a minute ago, all your hurt spilled out. This fuck isn't getting away with shit. His life's going to be a living hell inside that place. Isolation's going to be a cakewalk."

"I don't want you to get involved."

His phone rang, and he pulled it out. He looked at the screen, smiled, and showed me the readout.

FIONA

"Too late, princess."

Shit, Deacon had my phone. I grabbed for Elliot's, but he pulled it away.

"Hello?" he said as if he didn't know who it was. "Yes, this is Doctor Chapman. We've met."

"Jesus, Elliot, come on."

I grabbed for the phone, but he turned away. Was he enjoying this?

"She's here. She looks beautiful, by the way."

"Do not bait him!"

He glanced at me then put his hand over the phone. "Why not? Are you afraid of him?"

"For your sake, I am."

He shook his head and put the phone back to his ear. "She's fine. You don't have to worry." Pause. "What's that supposed to mean?" He leaned back in his chair again.

Fucking men. You'd think they'd both pissed on me like a hydrant.

"I would never take what wasn't freely given. I think you know that." Elliot just smiled as if Deacon had said something particularly amusing. "I'll take that into consideration." He handed me the phone. "He wants to talk to you."

I took the phone. "Deacon."

"Come back. Come back now." He used his cold, Dominant voice, and it went right to my very soul.

"I can't."

"Kitten, you are in no place to get your life under control, and that man you're with is not qualified to keep you safe."

"Safe from what?"

"Yourself."

Fuckhim- Fuckhim - Fuckhim - Fuckhim

I hit the red button to cut him off and plopped the phone in front of Elliot.

"You all right?" he asked.

"I left my car at Laurel Canyon."

"I can get it for you."

"No. I want to go to my condo in Malibu. Can you take me?"

"Sure."

Chapter 79

FIONA

HE TOOK the 101 and dropped down through the mountains, over Las Virgenes because PCH was always a disaster. He didn't even tell me he was going around the civilian route. He just knew the best way to get to my place the way he knew how to get to me.

Estates hid behind hedges, and Bentleys stopped at lights, next to circa 1977 Chevys. Elliot had one hand on the wheel, fingers articulated and active when he turned it.

I didn't know what I wanted from the man. Maybe I wanted to destroy him. If that was the case, I'd certainly set on the right path.

"I don't want to freak you out," he said, "but I want to tell you something. Or some *things* before I even get you to your place."

"I'm a captive audience. But Doctor Chapman?"

"Elliot. Please."

"Whatever you say, it won't change anything."

Undaunted, he continued. "The first thing is, I'm as confused as you imagine I am. I shouldn't be doing this. You're considered my patient for at least two years after our last session. I shouldn't even let you in my car, much less track you down in Laurel Canyon. Much less call you. I'm risking everything. My license. My reputation. My jobs. And I know I'm going to walk away with nothing. I'm fully aware that either you're going to hurt me or I'm going to have to start my life over from scratch as a short-order cook or something. There really is no other way around it. I accept that. I'm a martyr for you right now."

A big package wrapped up in a bow. Ten tons. No sound from inside. My name written in fancy script on the tag. That was his life, and he'd just handed it to me. It wasn't even my birthday or Christmas or anything.

I didn't know if I wanted it or not. It was just a heavy box. But I couldn't give it back, couldn't thank him for it, and I wasn't ready to open it. Not yet. Its presence in my life was too overwhelming.

"Have you thought about why?" I asked. "Because there's no reason you should feel this way. I couldn't be more wrong for you."

He stopped at a light and looked at me. "Do you play chess?"

"I used to play with my sister. She creamed me."

The light changed, and he pulled forward. "The biggest learning curve in chess is the opening. Your first few moves. Your initial choices decide the game. With every move, nearly infinite options turn into fewer and fewer options until you're cornered. Or your opponent is cornered. You go from infinite possibilities to despair in fifty moves as a result of the first five.

"Life isn't like a game. Of course you go from board to board your whole life. You start over, make moves, options get limited, et cetera. I don't want to make big analogies that don't work. But I want to say, I was at my endgame until you walked into my office."

He stopped. I looked out my window.

"Am I talking too much?" he asked.

Was he? I'd gotten lost in the sound of his voice. I heard the words, I listened, but something in the way he put his syllables together clicked for me. I could listen to him all day.

"We're not on the clock," I said. "It's your turn to talk."

He paused as if considering the next part of his speech. "I was cornered. I had nowhere to go. And when you came in, I didn't understand it, but you felt like a way out. An open window. When you came in, the traffic cleared and I had an open road in front of me. Why? I don't know. Maybe because you were an escape hatch, or maybe because we're doomed. But you feel like a puzzle piece, and when you talk or move, there's something about it that clicks in place with me. I can only feel it, and no piece of paper or degree or job or anything is going to turn me back.

"The game changed when I met you. God help me, I am not going back to checkmate. I'm playing this board. I'm making my opening moves. I have never felt so awake, so alive, and yes, I'm going to call it like I see it. I'm not making you any promises. I'm not pretending this makes sense. But I feel closer to God when I'm with you, and that has meaning to me."

Inside the hum of his voice, breathing the comfort of it, I felt the weight of my responsibility to him.

I waited until he had to stop at a light before I answered. "I'm very hard to love, Elliot. I don't want to hurt you."

He took my hand and squeezed it. "I'll let you do it, but I'm not going to make it easy."

"I'm not sure where I am with Deacon."

He looked me in the eye and squeezed my hand harder. "He's in your past. You get a new board too."

Did I? Would I ever get a fresh start? I hadn't considered that I would ever deserve one, but there I was, with the light green and the ocean open wide before me.

Chapter 80

FIONA

IT WAS night when Elliot pulled up to the Markham.

"Thank you," I said.

"What are we going to do about Warren?" Elliot asked. "He's getting out next week."

"Once he does, I lose control of the situation, don't I?"

He tapped the steering wheel. "No. I do."

"I'm not dragging you into this." I turned in the passenger seat so I could see him. "The reason I didn't tell Deacon was because he'd hurt himself trying to kill Warren. I don't want that for you."

"And I don't want you going after him."

His eyes lost their color in the shadows, but his jaw became more defined. Straighter, stronger. I touched the line of it, down his neck, flattening his collar. He took me by the back of the neck and pulled me toward him. Our lips crashed together, tongues twisting, groaning, bodies finding each other. He put his hand between my legs and pressed my pussy through my jeans. I was damp through the fabric. He curled his fingers along the seam, and I threw my head back and moaned.

"Fiona," he said, his voice husky, "I want to see you come." He pinched the front of my jeans under the fly, pressing my clit.

I wanted him to make me come. I wanted him inside me. He pulled me to him until his lips were at my ear.

"Leave him," he whispered.

I knew that if I said I would, he'd take me right in the car, and I'd bring him upstairs and we'd fuck all night.

And would I leave Deacon?

Maybe. Maybe not.

"Not yet," I said, backing away.

"When?"

I kissed him on hard on the lips and got out of the car.

Chapter 81

FIONA

YOU TOLD me you could see the connections between people. Just like an observational thing. The time you did my aftercare. Remember, Debbie?

Yes. I remember it.

Have you seen a connection with Deacon and me?

⬚

I WENT into my bedroom and strode right to the closet. It had double racks of clothes and two rooms with windows. I'd had it lined in camphor, and the sharp scent woke my sinuses. I opened a floor cabinet and spun the dial of the safe. *Whush.* It opened, and there sat some jewelry, a black card, and a few envelopes of cash. I also had pills, mostly tranks, and a few vials of flake for emergencies. Was I going somewhere?

I needed money and my car. Right. The black card was right in front of me, and the keys to the car were with the valet downstairs. Which car? Did it matter?

It did. I didn't want to go back to Laurel Canyon. I wanted my freedom. I wanted to get control of my life without Deacon's little rituals and rules. That was fake. It had all been fake. He'd put me in a straitjacket then complimented himself for keeping me still. Now I had to crawl into the straitjacket myself. I had to cruise downhill at my own speed, and with my own purpose. I had to be better, stronger, more regulated than even Deacon could make me.

I took the card, slapped the safe closed, then the cabinet, and walked to the outer room, where I caught a view of myself in one of the closet mirrors.

Who the hell was I kidding?

I peeled off my clothes as if they burned me, tossing them aside to look at myself naked.

Did he own this?

He'd laid claim to me a hundred times, and I'd relished it. Now suddenly, I didn't need that anymore? Only if he was right and I wasn't truly submissive. And if that were true, who was this woman?

My A-plus tits perked up from the cold. I rubbed them, and the pink nubs got rock hard.

Was I a freak?

With everything going on my life, all I could think about was sex.

Elliot's kiss had warmed me up, and pushing him away had turned me on, the disappointment sending my libido into a rage. And Deacon's paddling had left its wounds on my ass, which I saw when I sat on the carpet and spread my legs in front of the mirror. I saw the raw redness on the backs of my legs when I bent my knees, and I rubbed my hands along the wounds to make them hurt.

I made it last, stroking myself slowly, then quickly, watching myself in the mirror in a haze of pleasure. I wanted to see how long I could hold it back. How long I could delay my gratification.

And I imagined my safest place. Deacon knotting me up until I couldn't move, and Elliot taking me in his arms and putting his cock in me.

"Don't come. Don't—"

I pressed down harder, rubbing faster, gathering juice from my cunt to make my clit all the more slippery.

I felt the door opening behind me, and my eyes flew open. Behind me, in the mirror, stood Deacon.

I bit back shock and fear. Pushed away annoyance.

He didn't say a word as we stared at each other in the mirror. I didn't move my hand away from between my legs. He didn't break our gaze while he undid his belt and took out his dick. I still had the taste of it on my tongue.

"Who did it to you?" he asked.

"Did what?"

"Who raped you?"

Telling him was as good as killing Warren. Not a bad idea, on the whole, but it wasn't what I wanted for Deacon. I loved him. I wanted him to be safe from his own impulses, because he'd made me safe from mine.

"It wasn't rape."

"Put your hands on the mirror," he said as he kneeled behind me.

I swallowed. "Don't."

"Don't what? Take what belongs to me?" He lifted my hand and put it on the mirror.

"Not my ass. You don't have to reclaim it. Please. It wasn't Elliot."

His mouth tightened. "I didn't come for that." He pressed my lower back down and lifted my ass, running his fingers along the welts he'd made. "But your tone tells me more than your words."

He took a bottle of lotion from his pocket, and I almost wept. He'd paddled me, and we hadn't had any aftercare. No cuddling. No cathartic tears. No salve on my physical or emotional wounds.

He popped the top and squeezed a lump of lotion into his palm. It was my favorite. Vanilla-scented. I let my head fall into a relaxed position as the cool cream soothed my bottom.

"You're not submissive," he said.

I raised my head and watched him in the mirror as he carefully tended my bottom.

"I still mean it. When you're strong and safe, overall, you can be whatever you want. You're so complex. Deep and wide. I know there's no one like you, but you remind me of that constantly. You're not submissive unless you're weak from drugs, or needs, or a hurt you won't tell me about. Then you need it."

Gently, he pulled me up and gathered me in his arms.

This was wrong. I should not be accepting succor from Deacon after kissing Elliot. I was never so dishonest in my life as when I leaned into his chest and let him stroke my hair.

"You need a sub," I said.

"I do."

"I don't know what I need."

"You need to submit when you feel weak and not when you feel strong."

Was he right? Did my bad days just require a good paddling? Was he some kind of medicine for what ailed me? If he was right, then I couldn't leave him. I was done. Put a fork in me. I'd always be sick.

Given the choice between being a true submissive and someone who used submission to regulate herself, I wished for the real thing or nothing.

"You've done so much for me," I said. "I want you to know I'm grateful. But I'm confused right now."

"No." He was firm and Dominant again, as if I'd pulled a switch. "Someone's getting to you. I saw you in the car. He had his hands on what's mine." He turned my face to the mirror. "Look at yourself. This is mine. No one takes your ass without me there."

He pulled my legs apart, and the very act of showing him my cunt made me wet for him. My back arched for him. I ached for him to subjugate me. Was he right? Was that desire a key to my weakness when it should have been the key to my strength?

"You're my property until I release you."

"Yes." I agreed through all my questions. Habit. Need. Desire. The drug of Deacon Bruce.

He put his cock on my seam, sliding it from clit to bruised asshole. Every sensation went through my body, electric pleasure to sharp pain. He slid into me. First stroke down to the balls, pressing me down by the sternum. I stretched my arms over my head. I was still well-trained.

He put his thumb between my legs with his other hand. "No one hurts you unless I say." He ran circles around my clit. "No one. You're my property. When they hurt you, they offend me. And when you lie to me, Kitten…" He slammed his cock into me. "It offends me."

I was so caught up in pleasure I couldn't even speak. I came around him, sucking him into me. His hand moved constantly, and the orgasm went on forever, breaking me apart with pleasure. He came in me at the end of it, pushing me down on him.

He flipped me onto my stomach and put all his weight between my shoulder blades. I was pinned.

"Who took you?" He slid his free hand between my ass cheeks.

"No one."

He found my asshole, and with a finger wet from my cunt, he pressed forward, sliding the finger inside my ass.

I loved ass play, but this hurt in a way I hadn't experienced. The shredding was more emotional than physical. I smelled wet leaves and soil. Heard the dribbling of the creek behind Warren's delighted voice.

Oh, you're so fucking tight for a slut.

I like it dry.

I'm going to get you for this.

Deacon's breath on me, so close, watching my face as he slid in a second finger.

"This hurts you," he growled, taking his fingers out. "It shouldn't hurt. Who did it?"

"Take me, Master," I said with my face smushed into the carpet. "Fuck me in the ass."

I dared him to do it when he knew it wasn't what I wanted, because these were our roles. He did what he wanted to my body to exhibit his dominance. Usually, that worked out just fine for me, because it pushed my limits. But in my walk-in closet that day, it was I who pushed boundaries, and Deacon, like the Dominant he was, would not be pushed.

He got up on his knees. I leaned on my elbow, crying, face knotted in tight red tension. I swallowed a mess of tears and gunk, wiping my cheeks with my wrist.

He looked helpless, on his knees with his dick out. Abandoned by his most valuable skill, the ability to get what he wanted.

"Who are you protecting?" he demanded.

"You."

His face fell before the last vowel left my lips. I'd just turned his whole world upside down with a thoughtless and honest word. I would have been gentler if I'd realized what it would do to him, but after the orgasm and the emotional violence of it, I didn't have the brain power to lie.

"Me?" He asked it as if I'd shocked him so badly he had to repeat it to understand it.

"You."

I didn't know how to make him believe it. I didn't know how to make myself believe it either. But the words hung there, suspended between us, and to leave them unsaid was to lie about what we were.

"I don't think this is the right thing for me anymore," I finished. "I'm using you, and it's not right for either of us."

I couldn't look at him while the world slipped through his fingers. I got up and ran to the bathroom, locked the door, and turned on the shower.

Jesus Christ. What had I done? I looked at the shower knob too long, wondering what was next. Where I would go? Who would love me the way I needed to be loved? Would I spend the rest of my life in a state of free fall, doing everything I could to find out where the bottom was?

"I hear you on the other side of the door," I said. "I need you to just go. I'm not playing."

I got in the shower. By the time I'd scrubbed myself raw, he was gone. My apartment felt as big and lonely as five thousand square feet could, and I longed for company away from Deacon, away from Elliot, away from parties and drugs. Just company.

I scrolled through my phone and found Karen's number.

Chapter 82

FIONA

KAREN'S POOL was inside a heated glass building. The roof retracted in the spring and fall, but in the summer, they just used the outdoor pool on the other side of the house. Her parents were gone. Her brothers were in school. The house was empty, as always. Her bikini was hooked around her hip bones, and she wore a huge T-shirt to cover imaginary fat. She smoothed it out so it didn't touch her skin. I wore a bikini top and shorts to cover the pink paddle marks.

"I used to want to be a fashion designer," she said. "I thought it would be so cool, you know. The runway shows. Getting girls all dressed up all the time. The parties."

"You could still do that."

"I'm too tired. I hear they actually work really hard." She bit her lip. "What do you want to do when you grow up?"

I was twenty-three years old, and I'd always wanted exactly what I had. Always been perfectly happy to be Fiona Drazen.

I said what I always said as if by rote. It all felt cold and hard in my mouth. "I want to be the girl all the paps want to shoot. The girl all the guys want to fuck. The girl who does what she wants. That's what everyone wants to be."

And it wasn't any more true by the pool than it had been in the weeks before Deacon showed me that what I wanted and needed were the same thing. Boundaries. Control. Rules. I'd been so happy to give myself to him, but I hadn't thought about what to do without him.

"You were always so happy with who you were," she said. "I hated you."

I laughed. "Sorry."

"Nah. It was me being jealous. Now I'm too tired to try to be you."

"Doesn't the IV drip help with that?" I popped my sunglasses to the top of my head.

"No," she said. "And I hate it. Even the stuff in the tube makes me feel full, and then it's like I can feel the fat getting on me."

It was no use telling her that she needed fat on her. I'd tried that. At the core of her being, she didn't believe it.

She laid back. "My nurse got me to take a bite of banana yesterday. I could feel it going down my throat. In my stomach. I felt dirty. It was like I was being invaded. No one gets it. I feel good when I'm hungry. I feel, I don't know, pure. Clean. It's the best feeling in the world. I'm not giving that up for a bite of banana."

"I guess I don't have to ask if you spit or swallow," I joked.

"Don't even get me started. Westonwood put me off men forever."

I froze, a million questions on my lips, but I knew asking any of them would only clam her up.

A few seconds later, after she put her head back and her face to the cold, glass-blocked sun, she spoke again. "Fucking Warren. I told him I wasn't taking his dick in my mouth. I said, specifically, no mouth. That stays clean. So what did he do? Fucker. I hate him."

"Shoulda bit it off." I said it as if it was nothing, but my heart was racing and my skin crawled.

"He got his buddy, what's his name… with the tattoos and the piercings he takes out? The orderly?"

"Mark."

"He held me down and pinched my nose. And Warren put his thing, like, way down. God, it was disgusting. I gagged, but I was empty. I had nothing to puke. He just kept putting it in me. His balls were on my lip. His literal gross balls. Ugh. And then when he came… I breathed and I said, 'Come on my face,' because I didn't want that shit inside me. But he shoved it back in and came down my throat. He held my mouth shut and made me swallow. And when Mark fucked me, he made him put me on my back so I couldn't puke it up."

She shook her head, and from under her sunglasses, a tear rolled along the side of her head.

"Karen, that's terrible."

"Whatever."

"Did you tell anyone?"

"Why? So he could tell them I got diet pills from him? I mean, seriously. It's not like I didn't fuck him willingly in Ojai, like, how many times? And his dad and my dad are, like, best friends from Overland. What's he going to do? Stop making Chilton movies? I don't think so. Whatever. I washed my mouth out with rubbing alcohol. It didn't kill me. I just won't go back there."

I didn't want to show her how upset I was, but my heart was racing. She weighed eighty pounds. Her voice was soft and raspy. I could rape her if I wanted. It was like torturing a small child.

"I'm going to pee," I said, standing. "You want something from inside? A tissue or something?"

"Sure."

I sat on the toilet in the pool house and buried my head in my hands, because I knew two things for certain: Karen was going back to Westonwood, and Warren was assaulting someone else every day.

The question was, what was I going to do about it?

I couldn't think straight. My body was crying out for sex. I wanted to get high, just a little high, so I could collect my thoughts. A line of flake would be fine. Just a line though. I couldn't get so fucked up I wouldn't be able to think.

But I knew there was no such thing as one line. I was a fuckup. I wasn't stupid.

If I went back to Deacon, I'd be in control. His control. So I'd be trapped.

Debbie. But she was inexorably tied with Deacon, and that meant she wasn't safe. She'd do whatever she thought was best for me.

Elliot.

Sure. He'd refer me to the proper authorities. That strategy was a loser from the gate. And he wouldn't fuck me, which chapped my hide.

It wasn't that hard. I had to figure it out. Maybe if I cleared my head, I'd wake up with a plan to get Elliot to… I didn't know. Get Deacon into Westonwood to remove Warren's asshole?

Even as I snapped tissues out of the dispenser, I knew I was lying to myself. I knew the old head-clearing methods didn't work. I knew I'd wake up useless. I'd go back to the old ways. Elliot would notice and then….

And then. Right.

Karen was dry-eyed when she took the tissues and left a dense pack of sand in my soul. I felt as if I'd abandoned the world to Warren Chilton, yet a heaviness filled me. Things had to be done. I didn't know what. I didn't know how. But a Fiona with an emotionless voice told me that this couldn't continue. She surprised me with her gravitas and her dominance over the constant questions that circled my thoughts.

You will make this stop.

And there it was. For what it was worth, it brought a peace to my heart.

"I'm hungry," I said. "I think everyone's going to The Thing later. Wanna come? They have water."

She shrugged, not getting my joke. "Sure."

"I have someone to meet now. See you there later."

Chapter 83

FIONA

BEHIND THE WESTONWOOD CAMPUS, on the shoulder of a two-lane blacktop with the electrified fence fifty feet away through trees and brush, I decided to let it go. My hands clenched the bottom of the steering wheel and my jaw hurt from my teeth grinding, but I could let it go.

I got out of the car.

I didn't know what I expected to see, or what I wanted, but I walked through the trees to the fence. Yellow-and-black signs warned against contact, and along the length of the chain link, over fallen needles and broken sandy earth, I came to the creek, and the tree, and the place where he'd raped me.

If I was giving up on going back, I was giving up on ever mentioning what had happened. No one would believe me. I was a whore. I spread myself open for anyone who could handle me.

I touched the chain link.

The shock was mild. Barely even painful.

Really? I'd thought I would get thrown back ten feet.

I curled my fingers around the diamond-twisted wires and looked in. The bones of my hand rattled and itched. My elbows tingled. I took my hand away. That hurt.

Under that tree, where Deacon had given me back my memory and Warren had taken what he wanted, the creek gurgled and the leaves rustled in the breeze. The tree didn't give a shit. It would go on as if nothing had ever happened.

Margie's car came up the twisted forest road, just below the legal speed limit. I was already leaning on my car. I'd been early. My sister was on time.

My ass would stop hurting. My ego would heal. I was back in the safety of the world.

Could I let it go?

Warren didn't have to be a problem if I didn't want him to be.

I let go of the fence.

"Bitch," I said, pointing at the spot, "I am not a tree."

I'd told Margie what had happened with Warren. It was less painful in the second telling, and the listener didn't want to fuck me, which was also nice. Of course she wanted to "do something," so I told her I was going to the scene of the crime if she wanted to join me for a little fun.

Margie stopped right behind my car. She seemed to take forever to get out. Me, I just turned off the ignition and got out of the car. She seemed to have a list of tasks. Roll up windows. Turn off radio. Dick with some settings I couldn't see. Put up visor. Slide folder under seat. Place keys in bag. Pick up bag. Get out.

"Where's the body?" She tried to hug me, but I turned away.

"He's not dead," I said. "He's still behind a bunch of walls."

"Sister," she said, "I thought you had him killed or something when you told me to meet you here. After that story."

"I don't know what I want out of you, exactly. I wanted to show you the place because… I don't know why. You'd know I was telling the truth if you saw it, which is ridic. It's just a patch of nothing land."

"You thought I wouldn't believe you?"

"You wouldn't believe I said no."

She leaned next to me, arms crossed, Hermes bag hanging. "I believe you. More than believe you. I'm angry and hurt for you. I have a plan for how to bring charges without—"

"No!"

"What do you mean 'no'? I can protect you."

"God, you're as bad as Elliot. Think about it. Charlie Chilton's oldest child. More money than the government, and more power too. Do you think he's going to Soledad? No. They'll cop a plea to a psych ward, and here he stays."

"They'll only cop a plea if the prosecution offers. If we don't offer it, he goes to trial."

"And?"

"And we nail him."

"You're such an optimist," I mumbled.

She shook her head and stared at the fenced-in area behind the facility. "Did you tell your therapist?"

"Yes." I didn't elaborate.

"He has to report it."

"Isn't there some kind of privilege?"

"Not when the law's broken." She pushed off the car and faced me. "I can't let this sit. It's rotting my stomach. Since you told me, all I can think about is helping you. I have a corporate client messaging me right now about three million in a Burmese account he can't access because of a subpoena, and I don't even care. All I care about is making this right for you."

"Okay, wait—"

"We may have different idea about right—"

"No, no, no. Stop." I had my hands up, and she clapped her mouth shut. "I'm the only one who can make this right for me."

"You're not an island."

"Yes, I am. We all are. We have to manage our own shit. We can't put it on other people."

"Okay then. You're an island in an archipelago. I'm the island right next to you, and I'm here for you. I'm going to pressure you to go through all the legal channels available to you."

I shook my head. "I wanted to meet you so you'd talk me into that. Didn't work, you know. I still feel like it's pointless."

"I'm your lifeline to reality. Don't hold on to this forever."

"I'll think about it, okay?"

My sister nodded and held me as a mother should. If she didn't talk me into it on that day, she would soon enough. Unless Elliot had told already.

Chapter 84

FIONA

"WE CAN'T GO BACK to this," Elliot said, leaning back in his chair.

His office at Alondra was the exact opposite of his office at Westonwood. Here in Compton, he had a plastic office chair with worn grey fabric on the back, a desk with enough folders to hold back a tsunami, and white horizontal blinds with a dusting of black soot. The window overlooked a parking lot.

"Back?" I said from the chair across from him. "I don't want to go back. I want to go forward. I don't have anyone else. And I trust you."

He pivoted his pen half a quarter inch from the top, then spun it ninety degrees. "I can't go back to sitting on this side of a desk from you anymore. I have to listen and be objective, and I'm not objective anymore." He fussed with the pen again.

"I'm really trying to keep my shit together," I said with a cracked voice.

"Me too." He rocked back in his chair, moved his pen over, then snapped it up and thrust it into a cup. "I want to hear it. I want you to talk to me. But I'm not safe anymore. I want to tell you that up-front. I can't look at you from a distance."

"I'm just going through the day, and I either feel nothing or I want to break stuff. And honestly, I prefer the feeling of wanting to break stuff. So, safe. Not safe. Whatever."

His face was so tender, so compassionate and real, that I wanted to fall into its warmth. He looked at his watch. "Let's go for a walk."

⸺

MY SHOES COST something like twelve hundred dollars. I could have thrown them in the trash and forgotten what they looked like before I even got home. The couple two benches down didn't seem to mind the fast food garbage everywhere, or the graffiti, or the patches of brown grass. If the lingering background scent of urine bothered them, I'd never know. I'd stopped smelling it when he brushed his fingers along the back of my neck.

"Once it's out, they're going to talk about my past. And I want you to know I'll never apologize for it. Never. I lived the way I wanted. I may or may not change that. It's my choice."

He smiled and looked down as if trying to hide it. I ignored the smirk. I wasn't done.

"And you're going to hear about it. You're going to know. Men and women are going to come out of the woodwork, and guess what? I'm not denying one goddamn orgy."

A laugh shot out of him as if it wouldn't be contained.

"What?"

"I love how you are." He put his hand over mine. "And I'm not being sarcastic. I love how you're not ashamed of what you chose."

"Well, yeah, I have plenty of shame. About things I lied about, and when I hurt people. I'm not happy about that stuff. But, all right, moving on."

"Moving on," he said into my cheek. "What do you want to do?"

His lips pressed on my skin. I leaned into him.

"I want you to do whatever you'd do if a patient told you she was raped by the creek."

"Administrator, then law enforcement."

"My sister Margie's going to the cops. She's a lawyer."

"I think this is the right thing. Are you ready though?"

"No. But let's do it anyway. I mean, it's a waste of time in a way. But since he's getting out, I think the world needs to know. I think Westonwood made him bold. If I don't say something, he's going to get out and use Los Angeles as a bigger hunting ground."

"Jail is a tough hunting ground."

"He's not going to jail. The most that'll happen? I'll be the least popular girl at all the parties, but hopefully it'll keep people from being alone in a room with him."

"I think it'll go better than you think."

I didn't have such high hopes. .

"I left Deacon."

"I figured."

"How do you figure?" Maybe I was defensive. I had the right to be. Since when was I so predictable?

And was he assuming I'd left for him? Because I hadn't, and I was about to run to my own defense when he leaned back, spread his legs and arms over the bench, and took in the view of the Compton park. He bounced one foot a couple of times.

"We break down and rebuild ourselves every seven to ten years. He built the last Fiona. But now you're rebuilding yourself, and he's just going to try to stop you." He turned back to me, and his smirk made me want to slap him and kiss him, in that order. "You didn't invent this."

"Why are you sitting here with me if I'm so predictable?"

"You walked into my office and demanded to see me."

"Fine. My bad." I got up and walked. I didn't know what direction I was walking in, but I'd figure it out.

Of course he came after me.

Of course he grabbed my arm and pulled me to him.

It wasn't like he was inventing this either.

"If you hadn't come, I would have found you."

"Then what? I'm not your project. I'm a girl you want to fuck. So instead of just saying to yourself, 'I want to fuck her,' you made up this line of bullshit about saving me from Deacon, from myself, from everything. What are you going to lose to make excuses for your dick? Huh? You already lost the girlfriend. You're this close to losing your job. All that for a fuck? Yeah, I get why you have to make up big reasons about rebuilding yourself. I get it. But let's do this instead." I stepped toward him until my chest was an inch from his and I had to tilt my head back to face him. "Let's just fuck. You don't have to save me. You don't have to pretend you love me. You. Just. Fuck."

"Fiona…" His voice was low and soft.

"Scared?"

"Come on."

"Afraid you might not measure up?"

He smiled. "I measure up."

"Then what are you scared of?"

"Nothing, just—"

"*Bok bok bok.*"

"You daring me?"

"I'm daring you to let me blow your mind. Nothing more. Nothing less. I'm daring you to stop trying to save me. Just take what you want without all the baggage."

"What's in it for you?" he asked.

"Getting you off my back."

"Really?"

"Really."

He stepped away and looked off into the smoggy horizon, a little smile on his face. I had my reasons for wanting to sleep with him, not the least of which was the fact that I liked him. A lot. I liked the way he spoke and the things he said. I liked his openness and vulnerability. He had beautiful hands, and deep inside him was a sexuality I wanted to experience.

But, yeah, the reasons.

"Let's do it," I said. "It'll be fun."

"Fun?"

"Yeah. Not too many men can resist a night with me."

"I'm not too many men. I'm one man. And when I have you, Fiona, I'll be sacrificing my career. So when I finally take you to bed, I won't be changing my life for a little pussy. I'm changing it for a woman."

"If you wait, doctor, I might not be around when you're ready."

"You'll wait."

He was right. I would. I'd changed in Westonwood. Partly it was Elliot. Partly it was Warren. And partly, well, who knew? But I was going to wait because I had the feeling he'd be worth it.

Chapter 85

FIONA

THE THING EXISTED for people exactly like me and was closed to gapers and hangers-on. No reservations required, but it was still the hardest meal to get in Los Angeles, unless you were me.

The second-floor dining room was accessed through the restaurant kitchen and up a narrow flight of stairs, where a man waited. His name was Diego, and he was a star. If he knew your face, you were in. If he didn't, you could go eat downstairs or go home. Not his problem.

Once you got through the door, the space opened up like a whore's legs. Two floors and fifteen thousand square feet. Windows that let the street see that something was happening up there, even if it was inaccessible.

The rectangular tables were set in a herringbone up and down the huge space, and everything was glow-in-the-dark white. Literally. The lights were shut for ten minutes every hour, and the tables, plates, and wall designs became visible in glowing green.

One dish was served to everyone. The Thing wasn't about the food.

I waved to Baby and Mindy in the back and made my way across the floor. Karen leaned on me. Arrow waved. I could tell from across the room he was jacked.

"Hey!" Baby cried, kissing my cheek. I could smell her makeup. "We were just talking about your brother."

"Jonathan?"

A plate with food appeared in front of me. Karen waved hers away.

"The one and only," Baby said, shifting the hump of beef stew around his enormous plate. "He's making my brother nuts. Won't take pills. Wants booze, the one thing Warren can't get in."

"You guys!" Mindy laughed. "You all are so crazy!" Her pupils were vinyl records with blue pencil around them.

"Jonathan's fucking with him," I said. "He's not a user."

"Oh, he uses," Baby said. "Uses that dick. It's famous."

"And the hands," Mindy added. "I had bruises for a week." She bit her lower lip.

By the look on her face, I was forced to imagine things I didn't want to imagine. She was twenty-six, and my brother was not in her fucking age group. But that didn't matter. Not a bit. Maybe in a different universe her comment would have stirred some emotion in me, but in mine, I was supposed to chuckle and blow it off. The conversation continued around other matters of no importance, and I seethed. I was sober. That was the problem. And the glass of wine I sat sipping did nothing to bring me to the plane of jacked-up silliness these people took so seriously. I was an outsider.

"That's my brother, bitch," I said too late and too loud. "He's six-fucking-teen."

The table dropped into silence.

"Go do a line, Fiona," Baby said. "You're being a drag."

Had she fucked my brother? And why did I care? He was a big boy. I knew he was sexually active with Rachel at the very least. He could decide what to do with his dick, though I didn't want to picture it, ever. Period. But for some reason, the thought of Baby fucking him was about to put me over the edge, even without imagining the act itself. Something about it being Baby Chilton.

The lights dropped, and the room exploded in glowing green shapes.

The dim echo of conversation went on, and I bit my lip before I could speak.

Why aren't you letting yourself think the obvious?

Is it because you love your brother?

Why isn't that comfortable for you?

Elliot's voice warmed me. Calmed me. With the lights out, I was back in his office under hypnosis.

Use different words to describe yourself.

Loyal.

Protective.

Capable of love.

I was uncomfortable. Emotionally out of sorts. A line of flake would have fixed that nicely, but I wanted to sit inside the discomfort and understand it. More proof I was crazy. But the ten minutes of dark was the perfect time to stare inward and observe the tangle, and the titter of my friends' voices was the perfect sound to back up against. I was another stroke in a larger painting, and even my discomfort over my brother's initiation into my sick life seemed like the right pigment.

Which didn't mean I was letting Jonathan make my mistakes. Once he was out—

The lights went on, and though nothing significant had changed for anyone else, two things had changed for me.

One, a tiny shift in my perception of myself and my ability to change the lives of people I loved.

Two, Deacon stood across from me.

Baby was looking at him like she wanted to eat him alive.

"Fiona," he said as if stating a fact.

I crossed my arms. I wasn't doing anything I should be ashamed of, and not because he hadn't given me permission to snort shit or whatever, but because I didn't want to. Because I'd come to The Thing looking for food and companionship.

"Deacon." I stood.

"Oh hey," purred Mindy. "I remember you! I—"

"I'm bringing you back to Laurel Canyon." His eyes never left mine.

For a second, I thought that was what I wanted. To be lost in the sharp calm of his world, where everything could be predicted and what was unplanned had a response.

I opened my mouth to tell him I wasn't doing anything wrong. I was clean. I was just eating and having a glass of wine. I wasn't even driving home. But I snapped my jaw shut.

You are a grown woman.

And he was just another drug.

Chapter 86

____

FIONA

WHY DO you want to know?

I've been with Deacon a long time, and you never said anything about that. Was it because there was a connection with us? You and me?

I can't see my own connections.

So?

So.

Debbie, are you going to answer my question?

WE HAD to cross a fake cobblestone lane to get to the parking lot. I'd taken a cab. Deacon drove. So we had to exit and cross, and I didn't even know if I wanted to go with him.

The paps waited outside in a pack. I'd be in the news with Deacon's hand on my back. They didn't faze him, no matter what they said. One time, early in our relationship, a pap had tried to get a rise out of him by calling me Deacon's Famous Little Fucktoy.

I thought he'd fly off the handle, but he didn't. He stared at the man, and the pap never came around again. After that, they didn't say much to me when he was around, unless they were new. Another stare, and it was done.

We walked into the lot.

A valet approached, and Deacon waved him off. "I'll get it myself."

We took the stairs, as always. No elevator. No one handles the car but him.

So many little things.

Like the way he walked a little bit behind me. The way he opened a door slowly and didn't go through right away, or the way he checked right then left before he let me walk through it first. The casual spot check of the car. The way he unlocked it from as far away as possible then locked it again so if it exploded, we were half a garage away.

I stopped and pressed my fingers to my eyelids. "I can't do this." My voice echoed in the empty concrete space.

"Then *what?*" he shouted.

He never shouted.

"I'm just using you. Don't you see that?"

"What do you want?" His jaw tightened. He pointed the key at me as if he were going to unlock me remotely with a light-flashing beep.

"I want to be normal."

"Jesus Christ. You might as well want to be taller. Normal wasn't the hand you were dealt. You and I, we're not normal. That's not a choice we have."

"I know. I…"

I stopped myself. Did I want to do this? Out here in the parking lot, with the sound of tires screeching around turns somewhere in the depths, did I want to do this? I'd done an incomplete job in my penthouse if he thought he could just show up.

"You were supposed to be away," I said. "On the continent. Why did you stay?"

"Africa's just one fucking crisis after another. But you? You're broken, and if I'm not here to fix it, I'm responsible for what happens."

"Okay, listen to me. You aren't responsible for my shit. You know who's responsible for that? Me. All me. I've been putting myself in stupid situations. I've been fucking crazy. And it's my fault. Not yours.

Everything that happens is my fault." I took a deep breath. "That's not true. Not everything is my fault, but the stuff I choose? That's mine. Yes, I put myself in a ton of shit this week, and yes, I got out of all of it. I think I was testing myself. But also…" I swallowed. My spit tasted like metal.

"Also?"

He brushed my forearm, his fingers landing in the curve of my palm. It was so easy to fall into him and just submit myself. I pulled my hand away.

"Don't. I can't use you anymore. And I can't treat you like a barometer. Or whatever. I don't even know what a barometer does. But if it's something a grown woman looks at to decide if she's doing right or wrong, then I can't use you for that."

"This is what it is. And if it works? What's the problem?"

"It doesn't work. I didn't tell you who hurt me in Westonwood because you'd freak out and kill someone."

He raised his finger. "I knew it—"

"You don't know anything."

"I saw what he did."

"I'm the only one who can make it right. I'm the only one who can stop it from happening to someone else. I just…" As if the underground parking lot had cracked open and sunlight shone through, I knew the problem. "I was scared. I thought if I brought it up, I'd be asking the universe for it to happen again."

He put his hands on my jaw and moved his face close to mine. I didn't feel safe or enclosed, but I didn't feel endangered. I felt a responsibility to him, as a man, as a lover, as a friend who cared about me.

"What happened?" he said in a low voice, not his Dominant tone, but something just as serious.

"Right before I left, I went to the creek with him to talk about the sleeping pills he got me. He raped me. It hurt. I told him to stop. But I had to get out of there, so I didn't tell anyone."

"You sat next to me in my car right after he did that?"

I nodded, looking down. "I wasn't trying to shut you out."

"Who was it?"

"Doesn't matter." I looked into his eyes. "I'm going to take care of it."

"I can't tell you what it does to me that someone hurt you. You're mine. I chose you. To not go there and kill him right now… where I'm from, I'd tie him to the back of my Jeep and drag him through the street until he didn't have a bone left that wasn't broken."

"To send a message."

"To make you feel safe. I have no tools here. Anyone can take what's mine, and I can't do anything."

"I have tools. But I can't drag him around the street. This isn't Africa."

"Let me help you then."

I pressed my lips together. "This is going public. You can help me by not getting mad about it. You should probably go back to Johannesburg, because your privacy is probably going to be not-so-private anymore."

He leaned on one foot, the picture of male perfection. His presence in the ugly parking lot made it more beautiful, yet he looked at a complete loss. "I don't know what I care about besides you."

I took a deep breath, because I had to expand my chest to fit a new love for him. I'd never known why he needed me, and with those words, I understood it all. By sheltering the unprotectable, controlling the out-of-control, he gave himself a task so impossible, he'd never run out of shit to keep him from his own problems.

I loved him more than ever.

I took his cheeks in my hands.

"I'm going home, Master."

———————————

Chapter 87

———————————

FIONA

I DREAMED dreams of a narrow wall reaching to the sky. I walked on the top, toe to heel. Then with wider strides, and wider, until I was running, fearlessly, recklessly, Los Angeles beneath me at cruising altitude. The wall ended, and I walked on the sky. Then I feared, and fell, and woke to another day.

I had a voice mail from Elliot when I got out of the shower.

I want you to know. I told the admins. They're investigating. You're going to be fine, no matter what. And I'm here for you, no matter what.

My lungs got too small for breaths. I nearly choked on my own spit. People were going to know. They'd talk about how I'd said no. They'd come and ask me about it. I sat on the bathroom floor, wet and naked, staring at his message.

The phone rang.

"Fiona?" Elliot asked. "Are you all right?"

"Yes."

"Your sister already told law enforcement. They came right after. They want to do an examination."

I didn't answer.

"Fiona?"

"I'm not a victim."

"You don't have to use that word."

"They will."

"You're not alone. I'm here. If you can't lean on me, I talked to your sister. She'll be there for you every step—"

I hung up. Half a second later, the screen lit up with Margie's name. It was all over.

Chapter 88

FIONA

THE RAPE KIT was as bad as I thought it would be, and it was probably
for nothing, because it had been days since the assault. But the woman
from LAPD insisted it could only help. After the first two hours, the
speculum, the swabs, the photographs of my ass, we hadn't even started.

"There's no point," Margie said from behind me. I was in stirrups,
and the young tech was coming at me with tape. "We have to skip
combing for hair. She's showered."

"We can skip anything you want."

"No," I said. "If we're doing it, we're doing it."

Margie squeezed my hand through the exam.

Afterward, we sat at a desk and I described everything in brutal,
painful detail to a female detective in a button down shirt. She seemed
more angry about it than I did, and I appreciated that. Margie was the
most irritated. I felt her anger at the process. It radiated through her tan
suit in the form of a calm, dead heat.

"It's okay," I said in the cafeteria when the detective had been called
away. Margie needed more comfort than I did.

My phone rang. Elliot again. I shut it. He wanted to be there, and I didn't want him anywhere near me. Not for this.

"Daddy's going to find out," she said.

"He's not going to believe me."

A shadow passed over us, and I looked up to find out who had blocked the light.

"Speak of the devil," Margie said.

"And he shall appear, Margaret."

Our father wore a perfect suit and held his hands in front of him as if he didn't want to appear too threatening. It didn't work. The full head of sandy-red hair came to a point at the center, reminding me that maybe I shouldn't speak of him if I didn't want him to show up.

"Where's Mom?" I asked.

"Ibiza. I told her to stay. I have this." He turned his sharp eyes to Margie. "Will you excuse us?"

"She's going to tell me everything anyway. So no."

Margie, of all of us, was the least afraid of Declan Drazen.

He swung a chair around and sat with us. He stared at me as if I had a really good book stuck to my face.

"What?" I asked.

"You're telling the truth?"

"Dad," Margie protested.

He ignored her.

"Of course I'm telling the truth."

"May I be frank and less than politically correct?" he asked.

"No," Margie said, but she was ignored again.

"Go the fuck ahead. I don't care."

"Your reputation precedes you. It's an ugly thing to say, but how you act affects how people treat you. You don't have to like it. It's the world."

"Really?" Margie looked ready to jump out of her skin. "Are you fucking with her?"

I pointed at him and spoke firmly. "I said no. No is no, regardless of how many guys fucked me this year or this week." I spat it out, hoping to upset him. I failed.

"I know. And for that, I'm going to destroy him and the family that created him. That kid's always been trouble, and they allowed it. I can't abide anyone knowing they took what wasn't theirs. That they took it *from us*. But that's why I need to make sure you're telling the truth and this isn't some game."

"You're sick if you think I'd play a game like this."

"Maybe. I'm guilty of plenty. Your mother too. The number one mistake we made was raising you the same way Warren was raised, and we're setting it right."

"You going to unraise her, Dad?" Margie's arms were crossed so tight, it looked as if she had one sleeve around both forearms.

"It's time you took some responsibility." He sat up straight. "I warned you this could happen if you slipped again, and you did. In Holmby Hills. We heard all about it. You can keep your non-liquid assets, but the trust is revocable. We're exercising our right to remove you until further notice. I'm sorry, Fiona. It's for the best."

"Miss Drazen?" The detective came back and leaned over the table. "Do you want to finish?"

I stood. "Yes. I'll finish." I turned to Dad. "You can take the money. I get your logic. It's stupid and too late, but I get it. Now fuck off. And thank Mom for coming by."

I threw up a middle finger and followed the detective to the back without seeing how Dad reacted.

Chapter 89

FIONA

"HOW DID IT GO?" Elliot asked from his doorway. Pajama bottoms. No shirt. Beautiful. He was better toned than I ever expected from a psychologist trained for the priesthood. And with his hair mussed from sleep and the scruff on his chin, I found myself attracted to him as if I hadn't been before. And I had been, but I'd been attracted to him as a person. I wanted to fuck him because of who he was, but standing in the doorway, I wanted him because he was physically beautiful in his bafflement.

"Terrible. Yesterday was the worst day of my life. I should have just hired someone to murder him."

Elliot didn't have blood in his revenge fantasies. He dreamed of justice and goodness. I wished I could be like him. I admired his squeaky-clean soul. His commitment to *rightness*. And there I was at five in the morning, like a devil on his shoulder.

"But it's kind of a relief. Like a weight's off."

"Come in," he said, stepping out of the way. "You can tell me all about how you'd murder him."

The house was dark. He'd gone to the door without turning on a light, and I wanted to see it. All of it. Would the house be as warm as his office? Would the rug and chair be inviting? Would the light ask gentle questions?

"Can I make you tea or something?" he asked.

"Do you have coffee?"

"No."

"Tea is fine." I could see the kitchen from where I stood. "I'll make it."

"Sit. I have it. Just give me a minute to clear the crap out of my eyes."

He padded down a short hall and into the bedroom. A soft light came from it. I wanted to see inside.

What the hell was wrong with me?

Was I nervous? I didn't get nervous. Not around men. Not around anyone I wanted to fuck. I was in charge.

I clicked a switch over the toaster. Cold light flooded the surfaces: the granite countertop, the tiles, the grain in the wood cabinets. I snapped the teapot off the stove and filled it. I didn't even like tea. Fuck this.

I put the teapot on the burner. *Click click click.* The stove wouldn't light.

Fuck this again. I'd waited all night, staring at the ceiling, debating whether to come see him or not, only to stand here unable to light the fucking stove.

The room light went from cold blue fluorescent to warm and dim with a click. With a *whoosh*, the burner flamed blue.

Elliot leaned in the doorway, hair straightened, T-shirt covering the body I'd just admired.

"Thanks," I said, taking my eyes off him. I should have just grabbed his dick. Nothing like a straight line between two points. But I didn't know what would go over with this guy, if anything. I was probably going to chase him all over LA and wind up turned away. "I like the incandescent light too."

"We have something in common. We need to write that down."

I wished the water to boil, which never worked. It just did its thing, and Elliot just waited. Goddamn him and his patience.

"I have a fantasy," I said.

"I'd love to hear it."

"As my therapist? Or my friend?"

"As your… I don't know what we are." He smiled as if it was funny. As if he was the relaxed one in the room. I was the wreck, and he was just fine with uncertainty.

My little dreams of revenge had never left my lips, and on the tip of my tongue, each one was, by varying degrees, embarrassing, shameful, painful, and very likely to make him hate me.

"I imagine I have a broom handle," I said, watching that stupid, inefficient teapot do nothing, "and I put a nail in it. I bend the head toward me, so it goes in his ass smooth and rips him up when I pull it out."

He didn't seem shocked or put off, so I continued.

"The rest involve his balls. And one where I give him a boner and tie off his dick until his erection turns purple. Then I just, you know, leave it for days."

"Making your dreams come true is going to require a whole serial killer setup."

I laughed and he smiled, looking at me with those grey-green eyes. I was smaller, more vulnerable, and somehow safer in that little joke, because it was said without passion or judgment.

"I thought you'd think I was sick," I said.

The teapot hissed but didn't boil.

He stepped into the kitchen and leaned on the counter. "There's this drug. It's called Nortyl. It's used for bipolar patients to manage manic episodes, and only under strict supervision. It brings them back down to earth. Helps. Really helps. But if the dose is too strong, it creates a feeling of utter despair. The psychic pain can be unbearable. They'll be terrified, but only have the feeling of terror, because there's nothing to be afraid of. No object. Just the feeling. The patient won't die from an overdose, but they will commit suicide if you don't catch them in time. I had one girl get her hands on a bunch and try to OD on it. We had to tie her down. She banged her head on the back of the chair until we tied that down too. She compared the feeling to her soul being ripped to shreds. She used words like desolation. Misery. Grief so deep she was in hell. Just the feeling, no reason for it." He took two cups and teabags from the cabinet as if he needed to keep his body moving. "When you told me what he did to you, I wondered, really wondered… could I arrange sixty milligrams? Maybe fifty would do it, but seventy would be optimum. God, a hundred milligrams would rip a person apart emotionally. And he's in a mental ward already, so he'd be tied down. Wouldn't even hurt him really. Not physically." He turned each cup a quarter turn until both handles faced him, and he stared into the empty cups as if an answer sat at the bottom of them. "For the last few days, doing it seemed not just possible, but sane."

The teapot whistled.

"I'm not the man I thought I was." He leaned over and shut off the burner. "I see him talking to your brother, and I can see he's fine. He doesn't even think about it. I start considering the Nortyl." He poured the water.

"I thought you were going to tell me to forgive him," I said.

He handed me the mug. It was warm against my palm.

"I ain't Jesus. I'm just a man."

"This whole thing got out of my hands yesterday."

"It's about the system, not you anymore."

I held the cup to my chin and looked over the edge at him. "I had no idea until yesterday, when I told the story the hundredth time. He thinks he's God, making trades and changing the rules."

"God doesn't make trades. He giveth and he taketh away. Period."

I nodded. Sure. It wasn't like I knew shit about theology. He took the cup from me and put his next to mine on the counter.

Then he kissed me.

He'd kissed me before. This was different. This was an invasion. His mouth, his tongue, the taste of toothpaste and tea. I put my hips on his, pushing against his erection, clutching him. He pulled back, lips popping when we separated.

"Yes," I said. "Yes."

He took a breath through his teeth. "I'm not a casual fuck."

"Neither am I. Not with you."

He put his hand between my legs, four fingers curling into me, the texture of my clothes a hot friction. I gasped.

"Are you wet?"

"Yes."

There was a moment as he looked at me when he had a second thought. It was all over his face. The ethics. The impropriety. The risk to his heart. I saw all of it come, and I watched all of it drop off him.

"Show me," he said.

I stuck my hand down my pants and touched myself. My clit was swollen with the possibility of him. Finally. I threw my head back it was so sensitive.

"Now, Fiona. Now."

I took my hand out and put my finger to his lips. He took it in his mouth and sucked off my juice.

"God forgive me," he said and dropped to his knees. "You taste like heaven."

He slipped my pants down and put his lips between my legs. He opened them and draped one knee over his shoulder. He kissed my clit, groaning.

This was it. All those weeks of talking across a desk. Watching his hands fidget, his lips move, the color of his eyes—the greyish-green the ocean actually was, not the way it was imagined. His voice behind me in the depths of hypnosis, and now his tongue flicking the wet skin between my legs. Those hands not fidgeting but moving up my body and grabbing my nipples, unafraid of the pain in the twist.

"Yes. Hurt them. Yes."

His stubble dug into the sensitive skin of my inner thigh when he opened his mouth to put his tongue inside me. I tugged his hair, and he slowed his mouth then stopped, leaving only the painful tug on my nipples.

"Do you want to come?"

"Yes."

"Beg for it." He ran the very tip of his tongue along the edge of my clit. He was going to drive me insane.

"Please, Elliot."

He pulled away. Paused. Set his jaw.

"Turn around. Hands on the counter." He raised an eyebrow, and a little smile played over his lips.

It was my turn to pause. Elliot wasn't Deacon. He meant it, but playfully. I put my chest to the counter.

I had no idea what to expect when he drew his hand down my back and over my ass. It went away then came down hard with a *smack*. I gasped with surprise. I couldn't see him, but he might have gasped as well.

"This is for being a tease." He slapped me twice more. Hard enough to sting. Hard enough to make my skin feel alive. "No. It's not. It's just because I want to."

He spanked me again, laying them quickly over each cheek, then he slid his fingers between, feeling how wet I was. I made a sharp vowel sound, and he was a little more articulate.

"Wow."

I shot out a laugh, and so did he.

"First time?" I asked over my shoulder.

"Not the last."

I sucked air through my teeth, breathing in the promise of it, and he leaned down to look me in the eye, then hit me again.

I groaned and whispered, "Harder."

He grabbed a handful of hair on the back of my head and tightened his fist while pressing me down until I couldn't move. The rain of open-handed blows stung, and I tried to wiggle away, but he held me still, moving unexpectedly to the backs of my thighs.

Two fingers, right inside, down to the webs of his hands.

I didn't have to be silent. What a relief to just say it.

"Fuck me," I growled. "Please. God. Just fuck me."

"Not yet."

He leaned down and put his tongue to the sore part of my ass, raising the sting in loops, then compressing the flesh and biting it.

"First, you come for me."

He bit the sore spot where my butt met my thigh, a new sort of pain awakening me. He opened the skin of my thighs, exposing my cunt to his tongue. He was rough with his fingers and gentle with his mouth, sucking on my clit while his fingers moved inside me.

"Elliot," I squeaked. "Please. Let me. I want to come so hard for you."

He reduced the pressure just a touch but kept moving consistently, so when I did shudder for him, tightening my muscles around his fingers and exploding in his mouth, the orgasm lasted until I felt boneless. My orgasm was defiance and surrender. Fuck him. Fuck the world for saying I couldn't have him. He owned me with his gentleness and roughness. This fucking fuck. I was his.

He pulled me onto the floor and got on top of me, wedging himself between my legs. I reached for his pants, but he slapped my hand away and got out his own damn dick.

"I haven't fucked anyone in my life as hard as I'm going to fuck you right now."

"I love it when you—"

I never finished the thought because he put his cock in me, sliding in against the slickness of my juice and his spit, and my words turned into a single groaning sound.

He fucked me as hard as he'd promised, but slower than I'd expected, letting each thrust explode into pleasure, fade, then rise again. I put my hands on his face, because I couldn't believe how beautiful he was, but he ripped them away and pinned them over my head. His thrusts picked up speed, driving deep, his body pressing against me with each stroke.

"I'm… God…" I gasped. "Again, I'm going to come again."

"Yes. You are. With. Me."

"Say when. Tell—"

"Now. Now, Fiona."

I saw the first seconds of his orgasm. His face went red, stiffening and slackening at the same time. I'd done that. I'd brought him there. He was mine. And with that thought, I said his name and exploded around him.

We slowed our rhythm, kissing the remnants of our pleasure away.

―――――――――――――――――

Chapter 90

―――――――――――――――――

ELLIOT

FREUD DEFINED three strata of the unconscious. They battle constantly.
The animal instinct that wants to hurt, to fuck, to eat and shit. The higher
self that want to love, to keep peace, to do right, to live in society. And
the director that manages the two actors, letting the animal out when
food was necessary and the conscience out when cooperation was
necessary.

Mostly, the referee shuts the two factions backstage so the subject can
function.

But the battle rages where it can't be seen, and when the ego is
weakened, the victor steps out from behind the curtain and pulls levers
and switches.

I brought her back to my bedroom and took her again and again. She
became vulnerable before me, opening herself and letting me own her
until I lost myself and became a beast.

Without her armor, she was more beautiful than I'd imagined
possible. In her sleep, lids fluttering, lashes glowing copper in the
morning light, I loved her. I just did. When she cringed in her sleep and

whispered, "No, stop. It hurts. No," and her eyes squeezed tight against a remembered pain, a need to jump from the bed and take action cut through me.

For too long a war had been raging behind the scenes. A war between a physical need for her and an intellectual need to detach myself from her. Fucking her tore the curtain down, ripped it to shreds, and burned the theater to cinders.

The director was gutted.

In the wreckage stood an animal.

I was willing to do whatever it took to keep her from that pain again. He'd marked her with it, and I wanted to take that away.

When she flipped onto her stomach, I drew my hand over her back and down her ass, feeling the depth of the seam between.

She sighed and opened her eyes. "Good morning again."

I got on top of her, hard again, and kissed her shoulders and the back of her neck. "Good morning." I put my hands under her waist and pulled up her hips. "On your knees, please."

She stuck out her ass. I pushed down between her shoulder blades, pinning her to the bed. The way she transferred all the power to me and let me do whatever I wanted stirred the animal part of me. I wanted to consume her and care for her in one bite.

I stuck my fingers in her. "How often do you wake up wet?"

"Whenever you tell me to get on my knees."

I spread her knees, drawing my fingers along her seam. She groaned, and I pressed my other hand down on her.

"Open yourself for me."

She reached behind and pulled her thighs apart, pinkies separating the soft flesh of her ass cheeks.

I put my dick to her opening and slid inside her. I could have narrated how tight she was. How wet. What a perfect fit her cunt was. But I had other plans.

"Touch yourself. Make yourself come."

She twisted her arm between her legs and moved her finger over her clit. I felt her warming and tensing. I'd never met such a sexually responsive woman. I could fuck her forever. I could fuck her and say filthy things I could never say to anyone else. She was free. Unrepressed. An open door.

She started gasping, clenching and releasing, as I fucked her.

"Come. Show me how you come."

I pressed open her cheeks and watched her ass clench when she came as she was told.

"Fiona," I said, losing my own control, "I'm taking you back. I'm marking you where you're hurt. It's mine." My balls ached, and the pressure became too much.

I pulled out of her. One hand on her ass cheek, exposing her, and the other on my dick, I came where he'd hurt her. I didn't enter it, she wasn't ready for that, but I shot myself on her ass, coating it until it was salved with me.

When I was empty, I kissed her lower back and pressed my thumb to her asshole, entering it slowly and my juices letting it slide in.

"Oh, Elliot." She gasped in pleasure.

"This is mine," I said. "No one can hurt you again."

Chapter 91

FIONA

IT WASN'T until the late morning that I started to see his room in the sunlight. I noticed things he wouldn't have chosen. A picture frame with flowers. Curtains in a modern pattern. Too many Q-tips in the bathroom and, behind the towels, tampons. He'd had a girlfriend. She must be gone or on vacation. Who was she? Did he love her? Was I just a fling?

I couldn't believe I cared. I was literally seething with jealousy.

The feeling was new. It was a sticky, putrid ochre bubbling inside me, and it felt valid and important. It puffed out its diarrhea-yellow chest and pounded its ribcage and demanded to be heard because it was its own justification.

He's mine.

He marked me.

There is no one else.

He was in the small backyard, talking on the phone. Two cups in front of him. He'd made me tea. Did he make her tea?

Maybe if I'd had more experience with jealousy, I wouldn't have taken it so seriously. But I had no calluses, no scars, no pattern recognition. Just asking him what was happening with the woman who lived there wasn't even on the table.

I was about to go outside and spew at him when my phone rang. I woke from emotional suffocation.

The number was unknown. That usually meant a reporter or a random fan who got my forwarding information. I usually sent those to voice mail, but I needed to stall going outside in this mood.

"Hello?" I sounded impatient. I knew that.

Elliot sat outside, still on the phone, leaning back. Now that I knew the body under the clothes, I was rabidly aroused.

"Fi!"

"Jonathan?"

"I miss you in here." His vowels were thick and heavy.

"How did you get a phone?"

"You can get shit when you need it hey what's with Chilton he keeps saying something about paying him for something the same way you paid and I didn't know how much?"

There was no punctuation or pause in his sentence.

"You're drunk."

That alone was weird. Jonathan could pack it away without blinking an eye. If anything, whiskey made him sharper and more awake. I'd had to throw his keys in the pool twice because he swore he was alert enough to drive.

"I had a little I think I have a cold so it's worse."

"You let Warren get you whiskey? What the fuck is wrong with you? All you had to do was stay straight for a month."

"Pot kettle something something can you get me some money to pay him?"

"No. Jonathan. Stay away from him. Don't be alone with him. Do you understand? And he spiked that shit. Don't drink any more. Not a drop."

"Fuck you. You have no business—"

There was a scuffle on the other side. A rustle of clothes and some laughter.

Another voice came on. "Who is this?"

"Warren, you fuck."

"Fiona! Nice to—"

"You leave him alone, you hear me?" I turned away from Elliot and faced the corner. I couldn't get distracted. I couldn't take an ounce more input, or my panic and rage were going to set something on fire.

"Aw, why does it have to be like that?" said the little fucker.

"How much? How much do you want for the booze or whatever. Cash, okay?"

"Money' for the poor, Fiona. Come on. It's not that big a deal. You're okay, right? I hear you've been out with everyone a few times already."

The insinuation in his voice made me sick.

"Stay. Away. From. Him."

"He won't remember a thing."

"You fuck. I will murder you."

"Shoulda kept a dick in your mouth, sweetheart, instead of talking. See, I'm already incarcerated, and they're keeping me away from the girls now."

"Warren!"

But he wasn't there. It was just me and my shaking hands. My breath hitched in a sound that had no vowels.

"Your tea's cold." Elliot was at the door.

When I looked at him, my face must have betrayed the tangle of emotions. He came in and put his hands on my wrists, pulling them up so he could see my hands. When he saw the phone, he let them go.

"Who called?"

"My brother. You have to get Warren out."

"Out? Not after yesterday."

"*Now,*" I said.

"Why?"

"Warren spiked the shit he got Jonathan, and if not today, tomorrow he's going to pay the same way I did."

"I'll have the orderlies watch him."

"He's paying off half the orderlies!" I shouted. "The place is fucked."

Elliot breathed deeply and looked into my face, studying it for the truth behind the emotions. "And Jonathan's drunk?"

"Three sheets at eleven in the morning."

He put up a finger. "Good. Don't worry. I can get you through today."

"How?"

"Do you trust me?"

"I trust you to do what's right. But it might not be the right thing."

"It's the right thing."

"What are you going to do?"

He snapped his keys off the counter. "Abuse my power."

Chapter 92

FIONA

I SPED NORTH, shutting out everything but the route back to Malibu until my phone rang and my defenses crashed. I pulled off the exit and picked up the phone as I pulled into a gas station parking lot. It was Margie returning my call.

"Jonathan," I said. "You have to get Warren out or Jonathan or something."

I explained my call with our brother. I could hear her breathing when I was done, but she didn't speak for too long.

"What?" I asked. "Just say it."

"He's denying everything," she said. "He says it was—"

"Consensual. We knew he'd say that. That's why we got the rape kit." More silence.

"What?"

"I just got out of the hearing. Westonwood fought it. They have a pack of lawyers. They make fifteen hundred an hour, these guys."

My heart sank. In the dead center of her silence were my worst fears. "Can we get Daddy's lawyers back?"

I heard a sniff from the other side. Jesus Christ, was she crying? Over this?

"Stop crying, Margie. This isn't over."

"It is. It's all over. The system is fucked. You can't win by doing things the right way in this world. No. There is no right and wrong. There's only what you get away with and what you don't."

"Okay, you know what? Thanks for the little pep talk. I'll be sure to slit my wrists after supper, but right now, Jonathan Drazen and Warren Chilton are trapped in a small box together, and one's a predator."

Another sniff. I waited. The morning fog blurred the horizon, and I counted cars going up PCH.

"I'll figure it out," she said.

"I will too. Don't forget to call."

"I love you," she said. "And I'm sorry."

My phone buzzed with another call. I looked at the screen. Elliot.

"I love you too."

I switched calls. "Elliot?"

"I have Jonathan in disciplinary isolation," he said softly.

"Is he safe?"

"I'm staying around to make sure. Chilton's in the rec room. Doesn't seem bothered."

"He's crazy."

"We have actual names for what he is. But crazy will do. Your brother can't get out of here any time soon. So the only way to separate them is to approve Warren's release next week. Is that what you want?"

Across from me was a hardware store parking lot with men sitting out front and waiting for a job, a convenience store, a garbage-strewn curb. None of it had anything to do with me. None of it had the answer. What did I want? I wanted to toss Warren to these men and tell them all what he did.

But I couldn't do that.

Warren would get out and go after Karen for fun. Then once Jonathan was released, he'd buddy up to him and make nice until my dumbass brother didn't know what hit him.

"Yes," I said. "That's what I want."

"There's a chance he'll be required to stay if the grand jury gets to it in time."

"They won't. Can you keep Jonathan in isolation for a whole week?"

"No. Forty-eight to seventy-two hours, max."

I slid down my seat. Huffed a breath.

"Where will you be later?" he asked.

I wanted him. His arms around me, his voice in my ear. With everything going on, his attention would soothe the memory of the police station. He could make it all go away for a few hours.

Just like a drug.

"Is it okay if I take some time?" I said. "I need a day to absorb everything. I feel overwhelmed."

He didn't answer right away.

"Of course it's fine."

We hung up. He'd paused before answering. Not too long, but long enough to make me wonder what it was about. Was he wondering whether or not to trust me? Did he want to mention that he expected me to be faithful, even when he wasn't around? Or was that just in my head?

I could obsess all day. Instead, I went home. I had to arrange getting Snowcone back to the stables, sell a car, take care of the practicalities of my life. Elliot could trust me. I just had to prove it.

Chapter 93

FIONA

I HADN'T UNPACKED my things in Laurel Canyon in the first place. The biggest problem I had was finding where Deacon had put everything.

"What are you looking for?" Debbie asked.

"I don't know. I feel like I had more than this." I indicated the two small duffels on the bed.

"You didn't."

"How can that be?"

Debbie shrugged. "On Maundy, you wore what you were told, and when you wore something else, you got it from your own house."

The place with the walk-in closets so big they needed windows. The one with a room just for shoes. Right.

"About the other night," I said, and she stood up straighter. "Thank you. I know what you were trying to do. Give me back the control I gave up a long time ago."

She put her hands on my face and her nose to mine. She smelled of tea and citrus, and I had to resist the urge to kiss her.

"Did it work?" she asked.

"Yeah. Mostly. Maybe?" I shrugged and dug around for an honest answer. "I can't tell, actually. One night of topping you was great, but the jury's still out on life-changing."

She kissed me quickly then stepped back. I was grateful. It was hard to think with her standing so close.

"You were a child too long," she said.

"I don't know what I want to be when I grow up."

"Just be a grown-up."

Yeah. It wasn't that easy, but why should it be?

I grabbed one duffel and started for the other, but Debbie took it.

"You never answered me," I said. "About the connection between Deacon and me. If you saw it or not."

She handed me the bag. "With you and him, I couldn't figure it out. There's a linking, but it's not complete. Not one hundred percent. You'll always be connected to him. Maybe not in a way either of you likes or understands, but there is a small space you fill for each other."

"I feel like you fill a space too."

"With you and me, it's just human. You gave me something I needed. Thank you."

I dropped the bags and hugged her. She wrapped her arms around me.

"Will I see you again?" I asked.

"Yes. I promise. Yes."

I went to the door. I didn't think I was going to get out clean. Nothing could be easy, especially the hard things.

Deacon stood by my car, looking as though he was going to get in and drive it away without me. It was perfect for him. Proportioned for a man with broad shoulders and a crooked nose. He opened the trunk.

"You're letting me go?" I asked.

"You'll be back."

I almost said no. Never. Returning to him would be like taking a step backward, but what would be the point of saying that? To hurt him? He looked fine. He looked like nothing touched him, but it was an act. His shell was hard and as strong as stone, but I'd always known the way in.

I dropped my bags in the trunk and kissed his cheek, letting his smell of earth and leather fill me for the last time. He let me hold him, but he was guarded.

When I drove through the gate and saw him in the rearview, I knew I hadn't seen the last of him. Elliot called, but I didn't pick up. It would have been disrespectful to what had just happened. What I had just *done*.

I drove up the 405 to the 101 to the 110 to the 105 back up the 405… the Meditation Loop around Los Angeles.

I pulled off the freeway and into a spot when my phone rang. It was Elliot.

"Jonathan was almost out of isolation," he said.

"How? What the hell do you have to do in that place to get stuck in isolation?"

"Attack your therapist."

I put my head on the wheel and closed my eyes. "What if I just signed myself in?"

"I won't admit you. Not so you can do the job I should be doing."

"We don't have time to wait to see if you can do your job."

"I checked his room and Warren's room for more alcohol, and there isn't any."

"Bullshit. Did you check him for Rohypnol?"

"We would have found it."

I looked out the window but couldn't see a thing past the glass. It was all colors and edges, movement and stillness. Nothing meant anything.

"He knows," I said. "And if you pay too much attention to him, you're going to expose yourself. You'll be a disgraced therapist."

I used Deacon's words because they were right. He was going to lose his work and feel more shame than he could bear, both for his affair with me and for manipulating Westonwood's system. That would be my fault. I'd dragged him into this, and he'd already done too much, told me too much, broken who-even-knew-how-many codes and ethics.

"Do you like your work?" I asked.

"Yes, I do. But I like you better."

"Do you believe in responsibility? Like, to heaven. Not the law or the rules. But that God or whatever knows what's your fault and what you should have done to make it right, and if you don't, you've done wrong?

Even if something wasn't directly your fault, but you caused it with some stupid decisions and you let bad shit happen when you could have stopped it? That kind of responsibility."

"I think that's a hamster on a wheel."

"I want to start over. I want a clean slate. I can't bear it. Everything that makes me happy hurts someone."

There was a long silence. A truck went by so fast my car lifted a little on its struts and dropped, as if it wanted to get ripped into the draft but was too heavy.

"It's not your fault, Fiona."

"Not yet it's not."

I heard a beep on his side.

"I have to go. When am I seeing you tonight?"

"I'll call you," I said.

Chapter 94

FIONA

CRAZY FIONA. I'd always been Crazy Fiona. It was easy. I just did what I wanted when I wanted. I loved my life, even the parts I hated. I saw myself through other people's eyes and knew only their need to be entertained.

I'd had a job to do, and I did it.

I still wanted flake. I still wanted sex. I still wanted to live in a lens.

But I didn't want to want to.

I wanted to feel the all-over everything of a really clean high and the freedom of a new dick, but I had a voice in my head telling me to just go one more day without them. I'd done good work. Don't throw it all away.

And the other voice in my head said, "It's for a good cause. You can do what you want one more time. Just one more time… to save Jonathan."

Fucking voice.

I DIDN'T KNOW how to walk that razor, and once the flake started flowing, I had no way to keep my balance. It would go however it would go.

Elliot came to my place after his day at Alondra. I peeled off his clothes, and he watched as I removed mine. Every time we fucked, he got a little bossier, a little more dominating, a little rougher. He'd never be Deacon. But if I wanted Deacon, I'd be with him.

The sun had set completely when he wrapped himself around me.

"I need to get back in," I said. "Before Warren figures out a way to get to Jonathan."

"We're watching him. Don't you trust me?"

"I trust you, but I don't trust the world. Can you take me in? Commit me? Just say the therapy is going bad?"

"You'd have to be a danger to yourself or others."

"Tell them I'm a danger to myself."

"But you're not. You're a danger to me."

I rolled on top of him. "I admire your faith. I admire how you want to do things the right way."

"You say it like you can't do the same."

It hadn't occurred to me that I was incapable, only that I was outside those rules. For better or worse, what had bound other people had never bound me.

"I know you won't save me from myself," I said. "If I'm doing something stupid, I have to just do it and face the consequences. But this is different. This is my brother, and you know as well as I do that he's in no position to deal with this himself. And I've got nothing on Warren. No proof he intends to do anything, and what are you going to do with a psycho's fucking intentions anyway? So we can muck around with the authorities all we want, and what happened to me is going to happen to my brother. I won't have that on my head. He was brought up the same way I was, and I know what it's like. He needs time to grow up, and Warren's going to take it away from him."

He kissed me. "I admire your nobility and your loyalty. It's beautiful. It makes me crazy about you. But it makes me afraid for you too. If you go back in, you're separated from me. I don't want that ever again. I want us going forward, not back."

I kissed him. He bit my bottom lip, gently keeping me from moving away.

He was right. My thinking was too literal and limited. Maybe there was another way to do this.

____

Chapter 95

____

FIONA

I'D DONE THE UNTHINKABLE. I'd spoken to outsiders about what happened between the privileged. We were the mafia. We were the law. We did not break the silence about what we did to each other.

"Is Baby here?" I asked Jack.

His chin was scratched raw under his lip and his hair had a bald patch. He kept playing with the area around it. "I don't know where she's at."

"What about Karen?"

"Nah, man."

"What's wrong with you?" I slapped his hand away from the bald patch by his ear. A hair was trapped between two fingers.

"They won't even talk to you if you find them."

We were on a Hollywood rooftop with a pool and pod chairs, twelve stories up. The roof was surrounded by three-foot-high stone walls that made you feel like you were about to fall onto Sunset.

I wore a bikini like all the other girls. Below us, the lights of a movie premier cast shafts into the sky. The music was low, the paparazzi waited in a pack on the sidewalk, and limos lined up around the block.

"Jackey!" Baby came between us, putting her arms around Jack. Her pink bag was open like a mouth spitting hundreds. Her chin was striped with pink scratch marks. "Do you have any more tar?"

"A little."

"Hey," I said, "I was looking for you."

She ignored me and whispered in Jack's ear. He swallowed. She moved her hand between his legs, and his eyes fluttered closed. Derek pulled me to the dance floor before I had to witness whatever it was Baby would have been happy for me to witness.

I turned. "Don't leave before I talk to you," I said to Baby.

She didn't even look at me when she held up her middle finger.

I called Karen while I gyrated against Derek. No answer.

Derek pulled up my bikini top while we danced, running his thumbs across my nipples. I pulled it back down. Derek's hands on me snapped me into a clarity where Elliot saw me with another man. I felt what he would have felt. I thought what he would have thought. The pain was palpable.

I wasn't there to hurt Elliot. I was there to talk to Baby. I needed to feel her out, see if she thought Daddy Chilton would cut a deal before his son turned into a PR nightmare.

"Have you seen Karen?" I asked Derek.

He put his arms around me and swayed his hips. "Nope." He untied the back of my bikini top.

"Jesus." I pulled away, feeling for the strings. "Quit it." I tied the top back together.

"Is this what it is now?" he asked in my ear. "You're a prude *and* a rat?"

Funny how not doing a bunch of drugs or fucking anyone who asked was considered weird. Or how telling the cops you were raped made you an outsider. But who could blame him? We had procedures in our world, and I wasn't following them.

"I'm both and more, asshole." I noticed a little mark on his chin, and I poked it. "What's this? Is this Jack's shit?"

"You should try it. Might make you normal again."

I nodded. It was probably fantastic. A high like no other. I turned and faced the pool, dropping my phone onto my little red chamois. Derek grabbed me from behind and I kicked him back. My foot landed near my phone and skidded, knocking it into the pool.

Crap.

The phone went vertical and accelerated to the bottom, landing soundlessly. I dove in. The water was bath warm, and the underwater lights made the black, and now useless, device easy to find. I scooped it up and swam for the surface.

When my head popped up from the surface and I felt the cold air on my face, saw the stars above, heard the sounds of the fans and people downstairs, I felt a gratitude and happiness for my simple existence on the earth. It was like being high, but not like that at all.

"Did you hear about Karen?" someone said next to me.

I snapped out of my reverie. It was Arrow.

"Hear what?" I asked, flipping my phone open. Yeah. Useless.

"Her parents found coke in her sheets and committed her."

"She's in Westonwood?" I waded to the edge and tossed my phone onto the tiles.

"Guess so."

"Huh." I lifted myself out of the water and pivoted until I was sitting on the edge. Karen was inside. She needed it, and I was glad she was getting help, but I wished it was anywhere but Westonwood.

"Hey, Fee," Arrow said from the pool. "You look good."

"Really?"

He'd taken me by surprise, sincerity all over his face.

"Yeah. Kind of, you know. Together." He nodded, eyes narrowed as if seeing something for the first time. "Kinda cool."

"Thanks, Arrow. You're all right."

He winked at me and leaned back into the water, swimming away from my all-rightness.

I got out of the pool and snapped up my chamois, leaving a path of water drops and wet footprints through the bar.

The locker rooms were paneled in dark teak and floored in warm matte marble. Orchids marked the empty spaces between the sinks, and

the lockers weren't even locked for the private party. I flipped
mine open.

I had to tell Elliot that Warren was after Karen, but my phone was
useless. I tapped the back, pushed the green button, shook it for
whatever that was worth. The black screen just mocked me.

I heard a laugh I recognized from one of the shower stalls. Outside it,
on the floor, sat a pink Prada bag.

"Baby!" I said. "Can I use your phone?"

*I need to tell my therapist your brother is going to rape Karen as payment for
amphetamines.*

The shower door popped open. Baby was naked, back to the wall,
finger between her legs. Her other hand scratched her lower lip. Jack
stood against the opposite wall, watching her.

"If you can find it in my bag," she said, and under her breath, she
added, "bitch."

Jack snapped the bag away and held it out of my reach.

"Jack," I said, holding out my hand, "a minute. It won't take a
minute."

"You called me a nerd when we were in the nuthouse. Who's the
nerd now?"

"You're still a nerd, Jack. Own it. Now give me the bag."

"If I'm a nerd, what are you?"

"I'm a prude and a rat." I reached for the bag, but he snapped it away.
Baby still danced in a shower stall with her fingers between her legs.

"Kiss Baby, and I'll give you the phone."

"No."

"No?" Baby asked. She acted as if I'd just stuffed Santa back up the
chimney.

"I'm just not in the mood."

I could have explained there was someone in my life I didn't want to
hurt. That kissing another human being would jeopardize a relationship
that already wasn't supposed to exist. But I didn't have the energy, and I
wanted the phone.

"Never mind," I said. There were a hundred phones on the other side
of the door. "Baby, when you're done here, I just want to talk."

"About?"

"Your brother."

She shot out a little laugh through the thick soup of her high. "You talked enough."

I shot a look at Jack, who had put the bag down and was rubbing black stringy tar out of a little glass jar.

"He's going to be embarrassing. I can take it all back. Say I lied. But I need a meeting with your dad."

She smiled. "You Drazens all have daddy issues."

"Open," Jack said. She opened her mouth, and he tucked a bit of tar between her gum and lower lip.

Baby continued, "Every time Warren fucks someone else, it's one less time he fucks me."

I absorbed what she said but didn't have time to react before I was fed the image of Jack putting his tar-coated finger between her legs. She gasped. Groaned. Her eyes went wide, and she cried out then came with a shriek.

"Holy *shit!*" she said then thrust her hips forward and came again.

"I tell you what," Jack said to me. "For the purpose of scientific inquiry, I didn't see you take a drink yet. I want to see how this stuff works on clean blood." He scraped the jar of the last of it. "You give this a shot, and I'll make sure my uncle gets you a meeting with Daddy Chilton. He's in town until Tuesday morning, I think. Then he's filming in like Zululand or something."

Baby was still in the throes of ecstasy.

"Was that safe? To put it on her clit like that?"

"No clue. It works on membranes. I'm experimenting with adding a little K before I go wide. Come on."

Jack actually could get the meeting through his uncle, who was a studio head and a big player in the Hollywood old boys' network. And he could get it soon.

"You better come through, or you're going to be the sorriest nerd in California," I said.

Baby groaned and slid down the wall.

"Open up."

"You're putting it where everyone else does," I said. "Lip only."

I opened my mouth. He wedged his finger in the front and slid it across.

"I always liked you, Fiona." He took his finger out.

"I never disliked you, Jack. But I'm starting to."

I had more to say, but my thoughts were drowned out by two things: Baby screaming "Make it stop, make it stop," then clenching, thrusting, pushing against the wall, and my brain flooding with an explosion of endorphins. I had the most unmotivated sense of well-being and bliss I'd ever experienced. This was more than an orgasm. More than emotional happiness. More than a feeling of safety and joy. It wasn't like coke, where I felt *like* God, or LSD, where I thought I *saw* God.

I became one with God in a blinding eruption of love.

I couldn't even feel my body.

I was trying too hard to get out of my skin to engage a sound or feeling. It was like blacking out without the blackness. Losing consciousness without sleeping. Being engulfed in a light so bright it wasn't visible.

This drug was blunt force trauma to the soul.

A quiet voice in the light said, "Never, ever do this again."

At the end of that thought, I became aware of my face at the top of my chin, where the gum curved into lip. It itched a little, then like mad, growing into a fury of tingling deep inside the muscle.

When I scratched it, I tipped, and something in me said I shouldn't fall over, whatever I did. I became aware of weight on one elbow, and realized I was on my hands and knees. Lifting a hand to scratch had thrown off my balance.

I got up on my knees and clawed my chin.

"Fiona! Get down!"

The voice sounded like a stereo turned down then up then down really fast.

A blue light cut through the black light.

Then a red light.

And a blue light.

And the sound of a *whop whop whopping* helicopter.

Deacon, who shouldn't have been anywhere near that rooftop, had a voice that reminded me of feeling safe and right when I felt most vulnerable. I opened my eyes. Or maybe they were already open and I decided to use them to see.

On my right, just below me, Deacon raised his arms. "Get down. Just get down."

On my left, a twelve-story drop onto Sunset Boulevard.

"Baby," I said. "Is she okay?"

"She's fine."

The music had stopped. An ambulance was parked outside, flashing its lights, and the paparazzi were huddled across the street with their black Cyclops eyes looking at me.

"You're lying," I said. The itch in my chin was furious.

"Come down, and we can talk about it."

"I'm scared."

"You don't have to be," he said.

"I can't stand up."

"Fall. I'll catch you."

I tipped a little to the right, then more, and fell into white sheets on a thin mattress with a white light humming over me.

Chapter 96

FIONA

MY GUMS FELT as if they were on fire, and my spine hurt between my shoulder blades, all the way up to my neck. I felt as though someone was pinching the top of my hand, but when I opened my eyes, I saw the IV bag hanging over me, and I knew where I was.

I took a deep breath.

Something rustled. To the right and at the foot of the bed. My senses were back, and I smelled him there. I hadn't placed his scent before.

"Has anyone ever told you that you smell like the air before it rains?" I said.

He didn't answer.

"I'm sorry," I continued.

"Me too."

"I can explain."

I moved my hand. It wasn't tied down. I touched my chin and pressed at the cleft where it met my lower lip, relieving the itch in my gums.

"I'm sure you can."

I hitched myself up on my elbows. I was in Westonwood blues. He was in a tan suit and blue tie, his elbows on his knees and his arms draped between them as if fully engaged in something he didn't understand. Loving me.

I felt like a clown.

"What were you thinking?" Elliot asked.

"That I was taking a cab home."

He smiled and looked at the floor.

"I didn't go with Deacon," I said. "He showed up there."

"I know."

"How do you know?"

"He told me he didn't bring you, and he's a lot of things, but he's not a liar. And also, I followed you."

"Elliot!"

He put his finger to his lips to remind me that no one should hear. "That makes me an asshole. Fine. But I thought you might pull a stunt to get back in here. And here you are. Well done."

I flopped back down. "I had a completely different stunt planned."

I put my forearm over my eyes to cut the light. I saw the night in a flash. The pool. The roof. The locker room.

"Baby," I said.

"Yeah?"

"No." I moved my arm away and stared into the light. "Baby Chilton. Is she all right?"

"I guess. You were the only casualty. You're all over the news."

"I don't give a shit about that."

I didn't. Baby was all right, at least physically. That mattered to me. I'd had nothing to do with her episode in the shower, but I felt responsible somehow. I was sure Jack had put the tar on her pussy to show off to me what it could do.

Elliot stood over me, blocking the light. I wished he'd put his hands on me, but he had a sort of detachment about him, and I felt ashamed of what I'd done. Again.

"So what's the deal? Am I fifty-one-fiftied again?"

"You checked yourself in."

"I did?"

"The paramedics gave you a choice: the ER or a mental facility. And here you are. Outpatient probation broken." He put his hands on either side of me and leaned in, blocking out the light, the room, everything. "Now, how am I going to keep you away from Warren Chilton?"

"You're not."

"I'm passing you to another therapist."

"Obviously. Since you're fucking me."

"I want you to leave Warren alone. Give him enough rope to hang himself."

"Am I a disappointment?" I asked.

"I knew what I was getting into with you."

I put my palm on his cheek. He hadn't shaved, and the roughness under my hand was pleasantly tactile. "I asked if you were disappointed."

"I'm not going to lie. I should say 'thank you' and walk away right now. I'm surprised at myself. I'm a sensible guy. I think things through, and anything that's too risky—I don't do. But you woke something up in me. I was dead. My life was dead. Then you came, and I feel God in you. I hear him in your voice. The crazy shit you do… he speaks to me. I don't know how long I'll last on a roller coaster. But all I want right now is for you to get out of here so I can experiment with your body."

"Will God keep talking to you if I stop doing crazy shit?"

"I hope I find out soon."

I didn't want to promise him anything. Promises were for children and people who weren't worthy of trust. So I didn't say a word to him, but I spoke to myself.

I promised myself he'd find out what it was like to be with sane Fiona. Not normal Fiona. Not staid, conservative Fiona. Not a Fiona who made all the least risky choices and didn't break any rules. That Fiona didn't exist, and trying to create her wouldn't do shit but make me miserable.

But he could get to know sober Fiona. Straight Fiona. Faithful Fiona. I could work hard, stay monogamous, and still be the force of nature he saw God in.

In his ocean-colored eyes, I saw my own potential. With a little work, I could become those things for him and, more importantly, for myself.

Chapter 97

ELLIOT

OBVIOUSLY, I had no interest in emotional self-preservation. I couldn't
even bring myself to consider leaving her.

I was crazier than she was.

I'd seen this type of thing go bad, read the case studies, talked a few
dozen couples through nightmares of drugs, alcohol, and unpredictable
behavior. I didn't understand why anyone would put themselves
through what those people put themselves through, but I counseled
them anyway. I'd been the perfect example of ignorance. I didn't know
what made them love each other because I didn't understand love.

And that was why I didn't feel threatened by the fact that Deacon
Bruce was in my Westonwood office. He loved her. I got it. I had as much
compassion for him as I had for myself.

"Mister Bruce," I said, closing the door behind me.

He was sitting in the leather chair by the window as if it was his
office, not mine. He wore a dark suit and white shirt open two buttons,
revealing a leather string tied around his neck. A bone-colored pendant
in the shape of a cornucopia dangled from it. "You need to let her go."

"I can't." I started for my desk but stopped. I didn't want to sit behind a barrier. I put my files down and sat across from him. The light from the window behind him kept his face in darkness and must have exposed my every expression.

"You're the one managing her probation."

"Not anymore."

He didn't make a move. He was pure control, and I wondered for the first time why he needed to regulate Fiona. I saw his cracks and knew his secrets in that moment. His life was out of control, and without her, it spun away.

"You found her in a weakened state, and you took advantage of your position." He spoke as if broadcasting the news. All facts. "She came here, confused and willing to hear whatever anyone said. She idealized you, then you found a way in. You used tricks like hypnosis. You manipulated her vulnerability. For what? What's your game? Are you her therapist or her lover? Because you know as well as I do that you can't be both."

And in those few words, I was on the defensive.

"You need to let her go," I said, turning the subject away from the lines I'd crossed.

"You don't have the tools to give her what she needs. You're weak. If you loved her, you'd take care of her. You'd do what she needed you to do." His voice was absent jealousy or venom. He spoke as if we were two men with a common interest, and his was superior.

"It doesn't work like that. She needs to make her own life."

"You're going to let Warren Chilton rape her again?"

The "again" was loaded. It implied I'd let it happen the first time. I tamped down my desire to defend myself. I didn't have to. I hadn't done anything wrong. I hadn't failed, even if I felt as though I had.

"You thought I didn't know who did it or where it happened," he said. "She told me last night, before the ambulance came for her. She was raped under your care, and now I'm supposed to roll over and let you have her? You underestimate me."

"What do you think I should do? Arrange her release? What caseworker in their right mind would put her back in a police cruiser to go home after she was found on a twelve-story ledge, fucked up on a designer drug? Or I should find a way to get Chilton out so he can continue his psychotic spree in society?"

"She is your priority. Not society."

"It's all my responsibility. All of it. I don't get to pick and choose."

He sprang up and stood over me. "That's the problem."

I wouldn't be cowed. I wouldn't be intimidated. Not every decision I'd made had been perfect, but I'd be damned if I would be told I didn't love her the right way.

I stood. He was two inches taller, and I was over six feet.

"The problem, Mister Bruce, is that you've done nothing but baby her. You've continued the damage her parents did. Your boundaries are constructs. They don't give her the power to make the right decision. You don't let her fail because you design failures that are irrelevant and you train her behavior to mold into your world, not the real world. You fucked this up. You fucked it all up. You took a woman who could have figured her life out, and you turned her into a pet who couldn't wait to run away as soon as you left the gate open."

I thought he recognized the truth in what I was saying. Or maybe I needed to believe that. But he seemed to soften just a little, enough for me to continue.

"You need to let her be," I said.

"So you can take her?"

And there, in its full and splendid glory, was the reason therapists shouldn't fall in love with their patients. It muddied the waters to thick paste. I lost my ability to advise both Fiona and her enabler. Neither could trust me.

"You know what's right. Just do it." I opened the door. "Let me figure out what to do with Warren."

He stepped toward the doorway but stopped long enough to say, "I'll figure out what to do with him. Here's what you do. You understand that she's mine. You understand that what you did was wrong, and you go back to your God and ask for forgiveness. You do not stand in the way of what she needs, now or ever, because I will expose you. I won't have to lay a finger on you to destroy you."

And with that, he strode off as if taking care of Chilton was his responsibility.

What a fucking mess.

Frances made her way down the hall, passing him. She gave him the once-over, head to toe, then nodded, smiling, and turned her head as he walked by.

"Chapman," she said before I could close the door, "I want to talk to you."

She slipped in, and I shut the door behind her.

"Who was that?" she asked, sinking into the seat Deacon had just vacated.

"You want his number?"

"Jealous? You're cute too. I'm just used to you."

"He wants Fiona Drazen released to his care."

"And? Do you have a recommendation?"

"A few days observation."

She held up her file. "By someone else, apparently."

"I wasn't able to help her before—"

"So you're abdicating? That's not like you. As a matter of fact—"

"I haven't gotten anywhere," I said.

"Are we still talking about her therapy?"

"What does that mean?"

"I've been doing this a long time. I've seen nearly a thousand kids come in and out of this facility, and I've managed dozens of doctors. I've seen how they stand with each other. How they talk. I've seen you and the Drazen girl in the same room, and what I see is that you're too damned handsome for your own good—"

"Frances, really?"

"Tell me what's going on."

"No."

"We could get in a lot of trouble," she said.

"You won't."

"Besides the core ethical ickiness."

I crossed my legs. "Are you making an accusation?"

"I'm prying directly into the place where your business intersects with mine."

"There is no such place."

"I sense you're deflecting." She crossed her legs to match mine and upped the ante by crossing her wrists over her knee.

"You must have been amazing in session."

"I was. And you're still deflecting."

"I came to you with a serious problem," I said. "Fiona was raped by Warren Chilton on the grounds of this facility. What did you do? You took me off his case, and he's still walking around like he owns the joint. Let's address that core ethical ickiness."

"He denied it."

"Welcome back to the nineteen-fifties."

"Please"—she waved as if there was nothing there—"give me a break."

"Tell me what Rob Chilton's people said about Warren's habits. And I mean habits. Fiona's not the first or last. You know it. They know it. Is the Chilton Foundation putting a new wing on the place? Paying double?"

"Enough." She straightened her legs and leaned forward. "The matter is under investigation." She stood. "Until the authorities come back with something to nail him, like actual evidence, there's nothing I can do."

I stood and walked toward the door. "This has been such a fun little chat. Was there something you wanted?"

"I enjoy the hell out of you, Chapman. I'd hate to see your career end over a little ickiness."

It was doomed to end over something. Old age. Exhaustion. Death. Might as well be love.

Chapter 98

FIONA

"THIS IS like déjà vu all over again," I said.

Frances smiled with an undertone of superiority then slid the papers across the table.

"I bet this happens all the time, actually."

"Everyone's different," she said noncommittally. "Some people need to do this a couple of times. Sometimes we have to switch methods. Try new things."

I scribbled my name on familiar forms. "Such as?" I was just making conversation.

"We're putting you in a group session," she said.

"Okay."

Whatever. I could do a group. Not a big deal. I didn't feel as if I needed to have Elliot in a room to myself. He and I could wait. We were solid.

"We'll do everything possible to keep you away from Warren Chilton."

My blood froze, and I stopped signing.

"But you have to meet us halfway," she said. "Stay where you belong. We closed off the holes in the fence back there, but you guys are smart. I'm sure there are more little hideouts. Stay away from them. I've scheduled you for different mealtimes, but you're to steer clear of each other in the halls and everywhere else."

"You're making it my responsibility to stay away from my rapist?"

"I'm asking you to participate in preventing it from happening again. You asked to be here. I'd be happy to transfer you to a different facility."

I had no recollection of asking to be at Westonwood. It must have seemed like the best option at the time, or the best way to get to Warren. My stoned self was far braver than my sober self. Time would tell if she was any smarter.

The option to switch out did have its appeal. Starting clean and participating, as she said, could be very productive, yet it felt like running away. I had business to attend to here.

"Is Jonathan still here? I don't have to avoid him, do I?" I tried to sound non-threatening, but I'd somehow poked her, because she smiled again.

"No. He's been asking for you."

I dotted the last i on the last form and pushed it back to her. "Great. Thank you."

"The MD is going to look at you in an hour so we can review your medications."

"I'll be ready," I said.

I left the office fully-charged, the exact opposite of angry. I didn't forget Warren for a second, nor did I forget what my brother needed from me, but I felt as if I was in Westonwood for my own good, and I could make something of it.

Chapter 99

FIONA

WESTONWOOD HADN'T CHANGED. I had. Through the lens of my time outside, most of which was spent without drugs or sex, Westonwood seemed more hopeful a place, sunnier, brighter. I walked the halls looking for Jonathan and talked to a few people I'd seen before, but I didn't get a sense of where he could be during the free hour.

It wasn't until the lunch break was nearly over, and I was sitting on a bench by the basketball courts, that I saw him loping toward an errant ball. He saw me, scooped up the ball, and dribbled toward me. Had he gotten taller? He looked as if he'd crested six feet in his weeks at Westonwood, and though he was as graceful as ever, he treated his limbs like new attachments. I swelled with protective warmth.

"I knew you'd be back," he said, throwing himself into the seat next to me as if he were indestructible.

"Nice, you had such faith in me."

"You didn't look ready when you left." He spun the ball on his finger, whipping it around until the black lines blurred.

"How was your hangover the other day?"

He popped the ball up and caught it. "How did you know?"

"You called me. Presumably on Warren's phone?"

He neither confirmed nor denied any of it. He flicked the surface of the ball, making an echoey pinging sound. "What did I say?"

"You asked for money."

He shook his head and spun the ball on his finger again. My brother was brilliant but an avoider of things that made him uncomfortable. Eventually, he'd probably avoid me altogether. Might as well get on with it.

"You know who I saw last week?" I asked. "Mindy and Baby."

He kept spinning the ball. No reaction.

"They asked about you."

"Say hi for me if you get out."

"Jon?"

"Yeah." He didn't stop with the ball.

I wanted to shove it down his throat. Instead I just clapped it between my palms and held it. "They had a lot to say about you."

He looked at me for the first time. "What's that mean?"

"I don't know what your relationship with Rachel was, or if it involved you fucking other people. Or if you're a cheat or what. I don't know. But nothing you do is private."

"I'm not a cheat."

"Good. Hold on to that. I heard them talking about stuff I didn't even want to envision."

He shrugged. It wasn't a denial that he'd fucked half of Hollywood, but it wasn't an admission. That was fine with me.

"It's not easy being whatever it is we are," I said. "And we hang out in our own circles so we don't have to explain ourselves. Like why we never fly commercial or why we don't… whatever… cook a meal because why should we? But look at Margie. She's almost normal. I think she's got it right. She's, like, in the world, you know?"

"Yeah, well, old money fucks old money. Sometimes it fucks new money. There's a reason for that shit."

Rachel hadn't had much in the way of money, and in his adolescent mind, staying away from the likes of her equaled staying away from middle-class girls.

"Warren fucks Baby. How about that for a reason to stay away from them?"

He twisted his face until he looked as if he was wearing a blender.

"I know," I said. "It's fucking gross. She told me as much. I have no idea how consensual it is, but she flipped it off. And they have a younger brother, so I don't even want to know."

"I'm going to be sick."

"You did fuck her, didn't you?"

He put the ball on his knees and put his forehead to it. "I thought we had problems."

"We do. But I think you should avoid him. I don't want that brand of crazy rubbing off."

"I can't believe you'd even suggest that shit."

"He's fucking crazy. No more booze. Don't take anything from him. When you called me… I know rohypnol when I hear it."

"Man"—he leaned back—"I don't even remember any of that. Woke up in a padded room."

"Did anything hurt?"

He looked at me with those emerald-green eyes, the sounds of inmates playing basketball behind him. I should have paused before asking or maybe couched the question.

"Such as?" he asked.

"Anything unexpected."

"My arms from trying to get out of the straps."

We stared at each other for a second. Then two.

"Why?" he asked softly.

"Because Warren made that call, I was able to get someone here to put you in solitary. You're welcome. Stay away from him."

"What did he do to you?"

He'd find out soon enough when he got out and the news was the news. But all was silent in Westonwood, and I had to continue to protect Jonathan the same way I protected Deacon. But I couldn't say nothing.

The bell rang. It was time to get to our business.

"It doesn't matter." I stood. "He's not an appropriate friend. That's all."

"Thanks, Mom."

I snapped the ball away. "I'll leave that to Margie."

I threw it at a hoop, missed by a mile, and took off for the main building.

Chapter 100

ELLIOT

I WATCHED her talk to her brother on the side of the basketball courts and felt the connection between us. The rope had heft and drag, as if it was as real as the nose on my face. I was done denying it.

So what to do about my work?

Frances had been very clear about her suspicions. Her conversation had almost been a warning salvo that I had to make choices, and they'd have consequences.

How long could I tread water and do both at the same time? The rules were clear. A therapist could see a patient two years after the therapy ended. I had no chance of waiting that long. And with Fiona's public persona, I had even less chance of keeping it a secret for two years.

The bell rang. My session would be here in seconds. A young woman with profound feelings of isolation was going to sit across from me, and she needed my full attention. On the basketball court, Fiona took a shot at the hoop and missed before she trotted into the building I watched from.

"I'm sorry I'm asking for something again," I said softly to no one and the only one who mattered. "I love my work. I don't want to lose it. I'm not trying to be transactional. I need some help figuring this out."

No answer. At least not in the form of the clouds parting and a bearded guy telling me to get my shit together, deal with the consequences, and trust him.

"I trust you," I said, and I meant it.

I took a breath and let the worry go so I could do the job I loved.

Chapter 101

FIONA

I PUT my Westonwood blues back on. The doctor had run through his
examination quickly, focusing on the blood work and sparing me
another pelvic. He was bald but for a few strands on top of his head, and
his hands were bulbous and creased. He asked for a rundown of what
he'd find, and I gave him the list without apology. I wasn't defiant or
brazen. I wasn't contrite either. I didn't owe him an apology. I owed him
a list of the drugs I'd taken in the past week. When I told him what I
remembered of Jack's description of the tar, he looked at me over the top
of his glasses.

"Ricin?"

I shrugged. "It was loud. It was *ricinus something.* He might as well
have been speaking another language."

"He was." The doc made a note and left the nurse to finish.

She took blood, my temperature, checked my reflexes. The arm band
squeezed so tight to get my pressure, I thought blood would never
circulate through to my fingers again. The doctor had come back to listen
to my heartbeat and left me to get dressed.

I thought I'd gotten through to Jonathan. Nothing like grossing someone out to make a point. I'd have to remember that. Of course, Warren still had one over on my brother, and he would try to make my brother pay for it.

I didn't know what to do about that.

The nurse directed me to the doc's office. It was richly painted in greens and cranberries, like a year-round Christmas theme. I threw myself into the upholstered chair, leaving the wooden one in front of his desk empty.

"All right, well…" He cleared his throat. "Most of this will take some time to get back, but we did a quick run on a couple of things. You've been sexually active?"

"Yes." *Duh.*

He looked at me over his glasses. "You're pregnant."

He could have shocked me more. Like if he'd said I was growing a furry tail or a penis. Or if he'd said I was actually the love child of Whoopi Goldberg and Bruce Lee.

"I have an IUD. Those are, like, one hundred percent effective."

"No," he said. "You don't."

"What?"

He held up a piece of typed paper with a signature on the bottom. My signature. "We checked you when you came in the first time. Weeks ago. The IUD had passed its expiry date, and we removed it."

"What? How did I not feel that?"

"You were medicated. It doesn't hurt to remove anyway."

"Was I stoned when I signed this?" I snapped the paper away from him.

"No. You signed the next day."

I'd signed off on understanding this the first time I was released, an hour before I got into Deacon's car. Well, crap. Crap crap crap. I'd always been careful. I'd never had to have an emergency D&C. Never took a morning-after pill. Never missed a period.

"Wait. Doesn't it take weeks for the tests to know?"

"Blood tests can detect pregnancy days after conception."

What the hell was I supposed to do?

And what had I done to my body in the past week?

"Is it okay?" I asked. "I smoked. And there was that thing I took last night—"

"Two nights ago."

"I don't even know what it was. Did I hurt it?"

And did it matter?

And whose was it?

"We won't know until you get a CVS at twelve weeks. The meds you're on aren't contraindicated, but I'm lowering your dose."

Jesus Christ. I didn't know who the father was.

Another item on the list of things that may or may not matter.

"Would you like to discuss your options?" the doctor asked.

How long had I been staring at that paper?

"No," I said. "Not right now." I didn't think I could discuss options until I'd absorbed what had happened.

"All right. If you want to use the phone to tell your family, I'm sure it's allowed."

I walked down the hall, crossing the cafeteria. I saw Warren sitting next to the ping-pong table before I saw Jonathan hitting the ball back over the net to someone I didn't know. Warren made eye contact with me, his expression flat and charmless as if he never felt a thing about anything. Then he smiled, and I realized I'd seen his true self in that unguarded second. Just emotional emptiness he had to fill every single minute of every single day.

Jonathan's back was to me. He dropped his paddle and shook his opponent's hand. Warren and I were still bound by our stare, his vacant smile, the breakneck swirl of guilt and shame over a bean of a baby. I wondered if he could see inside me, but I knew he couldn't. I was having feelings, hot and cold, up and down, a broken narrative of thoughts spitting out waves of anger, joy, confusion, helplessness. He'd never had an emotion. Not about anything. He couldn't see mine. He craved my feelings, fed on them, was so curious about them he'd rape me to create them.

I hadn't chosen what to do about the baby, but when I walked away from the cafeteria, it wasn't because I was afraid for myself. I had another person to protect.

Chapter 102

FIONA

I SKIPPED DINNER. Skipped rec time. Skipped talking. Skipped thinking. Went to group session in the afternoon because it would be noticed if I didn't, and my feet hurt from standing by the window.

I couldn't get a space on one of the Herman Miller chairs, so I sat next to another girl who had her hands in her lap. She bounced her knees as if they were fully gassed-up pistons. I didn't want to talk to her or the four people across from us. They had ennui, depression, a case of the existential blues. Too much tickle and not enough slap.

And guiding us through all of this was Brazilian blowout. Dr. Deanna.

"Yesterday, we talked about Quentin's last night out before he came here, and his feelings of—"

Good times.

Could I eat the organic, locally grown, handmade crackers? Was starch bad? Was there too much salt? Was I even keeping this thing? Never mind who the father was, how was I qualified to be a mother?

"We've had some very productive discussions, so—"

Did I have to tell the father? Would I tell both of them? Neither? Would I just get rid of it and smile happily at Elliot and pretend I didn't have cause to see Deacon ever again?

"But first, I wanted to make sure we all know—"

And then what?

And why?

"Would you like to introduce yourself to—"

Did I have something better to do?

Was I broke? Orphaned? Sick?

Did I have nothing at all to offer a baby?

"I have something to offer," I said to myself but loudly enough that Deanna thought I was speaking to her.

"Go on," she said.

Six sets of over-privileged eyes stared at me in varying shades of curiosity and distrust. I hadn't wanted to speak. I was just going to say hello and go back to my room to brood. But they expected something from me now, and it wasn't to feed their egos or entertain them but to help them.

"I…"

Swallow.

"I have a lot to offer. I'm a good friend. A good sister. I protect people who are important to me. I can teach someone about the world, about what to expect. I can help them avoid my mistakes. I'm honest with people even if it hurts me. And I'm funny sometimes. And brave." I sat straighter, because I felt the truth in that one. From bone to skin, I knew it was true, so I repeated it.

"I am brave."

Chapter 103

FIONA

I SLEPT. I didn't know if it was the meds or the after-effects of Jack's stupid tar shit. But I left session without elaborating or speaking again, and I went to my room and slept.

When I woke, I knew something for sure.

I had to tell Elliot and Deacon.

I was keeping the baby, and I had to tell them. If I was brave, and I was, then that was what had to be done. Toying with any other options was cowardly shit, and I didn't do cowardly. Not any more.

Decision made.

I saturated the sheets with relief, melting into the bed, soaking the pillowcase with silent tears. I mourned my old self. My long reign of fuck yous. The broken record of highs and lows. I wept for the youth that should have killed me, the unabashed hunt for pleasure, the search for meaning in pain. It was all over, and I was glad to see it go. I was committed to leaving it all in the past and terrified I wouldn't make it.

But brave bitches do what they have to do.

I got up, showered, took my meds, and walked the halls without looking one way or the other. Just paced my ass over to Elliot's office before his first session.

The door was closed. It was too early, and I had to be out of my freaking mind to try to talk to him in here. Was I trying to ruin his life? Going to see him, telling him I was pregnant, what did I expect? He'd either make too much physical contact or none at all, and we'd both be ripped apart.

Get it together.

I didn't want to ruin his life. I had to do this myself. I had to contain both my anxiety and my unreasonable joy. One had to be managed and the other made managing it difficult.

But what about Deacon? He had a right to know as well. In the years we'd been together, we'd never discussed the possibility of children. Would he tell me to get rid of it? I wouldn't if I didn't want to. I didn't need anything from him.

The flip side, of course, was that he might do the less surprising thing and ask for a life with me. I stood on a stone path in the back of the main building and wondered what that would look like. I took the life with Elliot I'd imagined and inserted Deacon. Deacon making eggs. Deacon picking up the kids. Deacon having guests for dinner.

Jesus Christ. No. That wasn't working.

He could be on a ranch in Montana. He could teach the kids to care for the horses and manage the hands. He could teach retribution. Vengeance. Bullies would disappear in the night and be found hanging from the town flagpole in the morning.

I rubbed my eyes.

I didn't need either of them. But I was tied to one for the rest of my life.

A nice long line of flake would really help me get control of this. I laughed at the thought. I was crazy. The last thing I should be doing was snorting. I'd probably damaged the baby forever as it was with Jack's stupid tar shit.

Fuck it. I couldn't talk to either of those guys. Not good for my mental health. What was I supposed to say? *Blah blah pregnant blah blah might be yours might not?* Westonwood was the best place for me.

I was so deep in my thoughts, I wasn't looking where I was going, and I bumped right into Warren. In the sunlight, I could really see him. His tight curls had gotten fuzzy and grown out, and his skin had more grey than pink in it. He must have seen me coming and stood in one place until I ran into him just to see what I'd look like when I recognized him.

"Get the fuck away from me," I said.

"What's with you? Telling people shit? They got everyone on lockdown. Hired half a new staff. You fucked it up for everyone else."

"No, I fucked it up for *you*. You're a fucking psychopath."

"Want to know the best shit about being a psychopath?"

"Fuck you."

"Not caring that other people think you're a psychopath."

"Hey," a voice called from down the path. One of the new security guys. "You two."

Warren and I each took a step backward.

"You all right?" the security guy said to me.

"Yeah."

He stared at Warren until he backed up. My nemesis was apparently losing the war of public opinion in crazyland county. Warren looked into the faces of others to see what he felt about himself, and if he saw something besides admiration, I could only imagine how he'd react.

"Come on, Miss Drazen," the security guard said. He indicated the door back inside. "Your sister's here."

Chapter 104

FIONA

MARGIE LOOKED SHAKEN to the core.

She didn't, really. She wore a custom-made charcoal grey suit and heels that were just this side of sensible. Her red hair was back in a low twist, and every lash had a reasonable amount of mascara. But her world had been rocked. I knew it as soon as the door closed behind me and she spoke.

"Hello." She hugged me.

I held her for dear life, but it felt as if she leaned into me for support rather than the other way around. She led me to the chair next to her, the same ones we'd sat in the day I was released.

"What's wrong?" I asked.

"I'm here to ask about you. What the fuck happened?"

"I was stupid. That's all. I was trying to get to Warren through his family."

She tilted her head left then right, as if stretching her neck. "It doesn't matter."

"Really?"

"None of it does. Nothing. There's nothing we can do to him or any of them. The rape kit was inconclusive. He's going to walk."

"What did the prosecutor say?"

"Bought and sold. He dropped it. I'm sorry. And we have nothing." She popped open her briefcase. "Our father is on a downward trajectory. The money isn't there. It's tied up. I can't even discuss it. And the Chiltons are waging a PR war to protect Warren's directing career. They put him in the same ward with you, and they're fighting any separation because it makes it look like he's guilty, which he *is*." She slammed her hand on the table. "We have no tools. Not above board. None that play by the rules. And this—"

She put a folder in front of me. Man, she looked like hell.

"I don't know how to make this right for you," she said. "Not yet…"

She stopped herself, sniffing back a sob angrily, and indicated the folder.

I opened it. "Oh."

Irving's pictures faced me. They were works of art. Depictions of a woman in bone-deep pain.

"I made a promise to myself," Margie said. "I'm not relying on the law to protect this family."

"You're a lawyer." I flipped through the pictures. Five. I was in varying stages of pain and nudity. My heart broke for myself.

"Warren is facing consequences," Margie said. "By any means necessary, Fiona."

I turned away from the pictures and looked at her. She had thin damp lines of mascara under her eyes, and her lips were set in a determined line.

"We're making a new name for ourselves. No one fucks with us. When they hear Drazen, they're going to feel nothing but fear. No one's going to hurt you again." She slapped the folder closed. "First thing is stop this from publishing. I'll sneak into Condè Nast and break kneecaps myself if I have to."

My finger traced the outside of the folder, and I set it straight with the edge of the table. "I think we should let it publish."

"They're going to drag you through the mud."

"I don't care. You do what you have to. I… did they tell you?"

"I'm going to assume they didn't."

"I'm pregnant."

I'd seen a cartoon once where the character's face turned to ice, cracked, and fell off in a cute little pile of cubes. Margie's face froze like that, and I waited for the cubes.

"It's not Warren's," I said quickly.

"How do you know?"

Wasn't she there for the rape kit? Didn't she hear my testimony? Maybe not. She wasn't looking right at the affected area for the kit and she'd been out of the room on a call for part of the conversation with the female cop. My god. Did I really have to say this? Was I that brave?

I made myself look casual about it. "He only raped me anally."

Ice cubes to blow torches.

"I'm going to kill him."

"It's fine, I just—"

"Literally. Kill. Then destroy that family."

"I just want to focus on this right now, okay?" I said. "I can't worry about tearing his guts out, which yes, I still want to do. I have to tell the two men who could be the father. I have to stop wanting drugs so bad. I need new friends who don't party. I have to have a life. I don't have the energy for anything else."

She took my hands in hers. "I can't let it go."

"I'm not saying I can either. But it's too much. You figure out the retribution and let me know."

"So you're keeping it? The baby?"

"Yes."

"Daddy's going to shit."

"Fuck him. He'd shit either way."

"That's my girl."

"I need you to get Deacon in here. I don't want to tell him over the phone."

She nodded. "You got it, little sister."

Chapter 105

ELLIOT

I SAW Fiona Tuesday and Thursday in the halls or in the common area. I watched her talk to her brother and a few friends she'd made. We exchanged cordial words. I kept an eye on Warren. I dropped in unexpectedly on the weekend to do paperwork so I could make sure she was all right. I spoke to the staff about keeping her and Warren separated, because even if none of the patients knew about Fiona's accusations, the rest of the world did.

A constant state of stress and emptiness followed me everywhere. I cancelled a session with Lee because I couldn't stand her judgments. She would be right. I had no right to touch a patient, and I didn't care anymore. My right didn't come from a board of ethics. It came from God.

In the hallway right before the staff meeting, I saw her alone. She stood framed in the perspective of the hall, the vanishing point on the horizon. Thirty feet away, she faced me, and as far away as she was, I knew something had changed about her. She didn't buzz. She hummed with the universe in a wordless harmony.

I let my mouth shape a single word without sound. "Soon."

A smile curled one side of her beautiful mouth. She continued to breakfast, and I went to my staff meeting.

"Good morning," I said. Last one there. How long had I been staring at Fiona? I would have to be more careful.

"Chapman," Frances said in greeting, checking my name off the list.

We were all here. Three licensed therapists, two MDs, and three administrators.

"Two incidents this week," Frances said.

I pulled out the reports. One incident involved Chilton. In the other, he was suspected as an instigator. He was indeed using the abundance of rope to hang himself.

"He's acting out," Deanna said. She took his sessions. "The thing with the Drazen girl is upsetting him."

"He's incapable of feeling upset," I said.

"He needs to know his voice is heard in here," Deanna said. "He's being kept away from activities because of an accusation. It's hard on him."

"What's he taking?" Frances pored through his file.

A discussion ensued where they talked about him as if he were a normal person with *feelings* that needed to be managed and a chemical makeup that was like everyone else's.

"What about Paxil?" I interjected. "Get control of the outbursts."

"Contraindicated for suicidal side effects," one of the other therapists interjected.

"In depressed patients," I said.

"Anger is a form of depression," Deanna said.

"Not in his case. He's frustrated. Different."

"I think it's okay," one of the MDs said, not looking up from his agenda.

"Done," Frances said, checking it off her list. "And we're separating him and Fiona. Sorry, Deanna. We'll let them mingle in a week, but the Drazen girl's bound to be emotional and unstable."

"Why?" I asked too fast. I cleared my throat. It didn't look as though anyone had noticed.

"She's pregnant and on med reduction."

Every nerve ending in my body fired a signal to my brain to stop what it was doing. Don't react. Stay still. Look down. Blink. Produce spit. Breathe. Swallow. Fucking breathe.

They moved on to other subjects. I stared at the way my pencil wove through my fingers. I placed it at a forty-five degree angle to the edge of the paper, which was at a ninety-degree angle to the edge of the table.

Blink.

Clear fog from eyes.

Don't think about it.

Pregnant.

Is she keeping it?

Shut up.

Is it mine?

Forget it until you're out of this room.

Does it matter?

I want it. I want it.

We flipped the page, and as I placed my pencil at the exact angle that gave me some measure of aesthetic control, I saw where the tip landed. The visitor list.

Deacon Bruce. Wednesday. 9am.

The pencil broke between my fingers.

"I need to come in on Wednesday," I said.

"We're not doing schedule yet," Frances said, tapping the agenda. She addressed the MD. "Now, the Roberts kid. We've seen improvement…"

I held myself together the rest of the meeting. I left after the standard post-meeting discussion, and I went to my office. I had session in fifteen minutes, but my heart was pounding. I was sweating. My face was on fire.

Jesus fucking Christ.

I want to thank you.

But I don't know if I can.

I want it I want it IwantitIwantit.

"God, I hate this." I said to the heavens. "I want to talk to her."

And I couldn't. I couldn't.

Could I?

If I did and lost my license, any good I was doing with anyone would be wiped away. People who needed me on Alondra would be abandoned. Patients in Westonwood I was making progress with would be left with fucking Deanna, who had no talent and too much ambition.

"Can't. Be patient. Jesus, I want to talk to her for five minutes."

The need was physical. Chemical. Every cell in my body pulled toward Fiona. I wanted to tell her I wanted her. Wanted the baby. Wanted us in every way. My insides felt bigger than my outside. Soon, they'd shred me and I'd be nothing but my desire.

My hands were on the arms of the chair, and I looked at the blank space six inches in front of me.

"Get through today. People are counting on you. She's okay. You're okay."

I took a breath and stood. The window looked out on to the garden. Warren walked east with a younger kid at his side. Fiona walked in the opposite direction, alone. I clenched my fists when they passed. Nothing happened. They didn't even look at each other. I released the tension from my fists. I almost turned away in relief until I saw Warren spin around and point at Fiona's back with one hand and grab his crotch with the other. She turned as if sensing something, and he blew her a kiss with his hand still on his junk. She walked away.

Keep her away from that animal.

The edict came clothed in my father's voice, and I never disobeyed my father.

<hr>

Chapter 106

<hr>

FIONA

I STARTED HATING THE WORD "PREGNANT." The juiciness of it. The way it stuck in the mouth. The weight of the shame I was supposed to feel and didn't. The silence I knew I'd hear after I said it.

I couldn't sleep Tuesday night. I heard every bump and thump. My room was on the top floor, and at one point during the night, it sounded as if someone was doing the tango on the roof. The crickets outside were extra loud, their song unimpeded by the thick glass. The squeak and splash of a mopping bucket came from the hall around midnight.

Then silence.

I listened to the sound of my heartbeat. My breaths. Felt every inch of my body against the sheets and clothes. The air had weight. It smelled of bleach and oranges. The mint in my mouth was swallowed into the lingering taste of dinner.

I didn't feel sorry for myself. I felt called to do something I hadn't considered in my rush to put things inside my body. I let that purpose fill me in the empty space of the night. Breathed it in. Let it sit. Breathed junk out.

I lost count of how many hours I was awake, or how many breaths I took. Time on the clock wasn't important. Only the lightening of the ceiling as the sun rose mattered.

It was Wednesday. It was the day I took matters into my own hands.

FRANCES OPENED the door to the conference room, and I held my breath. Deacon walked in. He still took up too much room. Still commanded and demanded without speaking a word. Still looked at me as if I was his and his alone.

"You have half an hour until session," Frances said, looking at Deacon then me. "Do not leave this room."

I nodded. He smiled at her. Her eyes narrowed. She found him attractive, of course. She was human. She left, snapping the door closed.

"Hi," I said in a little girl voice I didn't know I had. Shit. I'd have to buck up.

He sat next to me and scooted his chair so our knees were touching. "Kitten." He took my hands.

"Don't call me that." I couldn't look at him, but his eyes were on me. I knew it by the way my skin reacted.

"You wanted to see me?"

"You were right. I'm not submissive. Not the way I thought. Not the way I thought I needed to be."

"I think that's where a lot of your acting out came from. You can switch. I can teach you."

"Yeah. You could. I know. All that. But I don't think that's going to do it for me. Maybe. I don't have any answers. I want a fresh start. Need one, actually. And I needed to say that before saying what I wanted to see you about. Because I'm not going to be bossed into doing anything. It's my life."

He didn't speak. He just let my words hang between us as I watched how our hands looked together. I was too small for him. Too insignificant. And while that would have scared me before, now it seemed so true it freed me.

I looked at him. He was waiting. He'd put on aftershave and a clean suit so I could tell him this. Better make it good.

"The last time I was here, they removed my IUD, and I was too medicated and fucked in the head to know it." Understanding passed over his expression, and I rushed to fill in the space. "You're going to ask if it's yours—"

"Stop."

He was still a dominant personality, so when he said stop, I stopped.

"I'm asking no such thing."

"I need you to let me go."

He unclasped our hands and leaned back, elbow on the table, finger tapping his lip. "No."

"Deacon, really? What the fuck is it with you?"

"Never." He tapped his finger to make his point. "I'll never. Let. You. Go."

I let out a breath of complete and utter fucking exasperation.

"And let me tell you something." He pointed at me. "I took responsibility for you a long time ago. Now maybe you've moved on. But I don't move on. That's not my way. You are always mine, and anyone who hurts you has me to deal with."

"God, Deacon. Please. Please don't do this."

"I've done a lot wrong with you. I pushed you—"

"I begged for it."

"No." He sliced the air with his hand and spoke firmly. Stating facts. "You were put here, in this place, because of me. I'm going to fix it. I'm making it right for you and my child. Then I'm leaving. Not for me, but for you. There's nothing here for me after that."

"After what, exactly?"

He stood. I stood with him.

"Deacon, after what?"

He grabbed me so fast I didn't have a chance to blink and held my face, crashing his lips onto mine, pushing his tongue into me. I let him do it. I let him kiss me, and I returned it for the years we'd had, for what he taught me, for being by my side after all the wrong I'd done.

I gave him that kiss fully, because it was the last.

The door opened.

"Fiona," Frances said, "that'll be enough of that."

I pulled away, giving Frances an apologetic look. Behind her, Elliot walked down the hall in the opposite direction.

Chapter 107

ELLIOT

I RECOGNIZED his black Range Rover. Eighty-thousand dollar car. Clean as a whistle. It shone like patent leather and pulled light into it at the same time.

He came out of the building, squinting in the morning sun. He saw me and didn't rush. Didn't slow down or acknowledge me until he was close enough to speak without shouting.

"Doctor." He blooped the car. The locks clicked.

"Mister Bruce."

"I'm not threatened by you. At all." He opened the door to get in.

"I don't expect you to be. But I need to get her things. She's not coming back to you."

He slammed the door shut and came at me. I resisted the urge to step back.

"You let him walk around in the same building with her."

"It's not me."

"You let him continue to exist on the earth. To breathe. And not to better protect her. Not for her interests, but yours. *You* need to keep it secret. *You* need to follow your boss's instructions. *You* need to walk a tightrope, and you put her in danger to do it. If she's incompatible with your career, then you have to choose one. Only cowards want both."

He didn't wait for me to answer. He got in and slammed the door. I got out of the way so he could get by without hitting me, and I watched him go with my hands in my pockets.

He was right.

God damn if he wasn't right.

Chapter 108

FIONA

INITIALLY, I wanted to talk to Elliot to explain what he'd seen, or didn't see. I had no idea, then as I got to the end of the hall, I wondered what Deacon had meant by making it right for me. Who was he threatening exactly?

Was he threatening Elliot?

I picked up the pace. He wasn't supposed to be in on Wednesday, so he had no sessions.

His office door was ajar. I was well aware of what I meant to him while I was in here. I was the end of his career. So I didn't burst in as if I had the right to. I rapped lightly and pushed the door just a little. I wouldn't get him into trouble. We'd keep the door open so we'd be seen across the room from each other or sitting with a desk between us.

The door swung easily into the dark room. The blinds were closed, letting through thin lines in a ruled notebook of light. The desk was still neat. The chair was pushed in. The bookcases were full of the usual thick volumes with acronyms for titles.

I opened the door all the way.

The couch where he'd hypnotized me was where it always was, squat and satisfied in its glory.

Framed diplomas checkerboarding the wall. California Board of Psychology dot-dot-dot squiggle-squiggle. Who had I been then? The same girl? Didn't feel that way. Jumping over that desk to strangle him for suggesting I'd stabbed Deacon was a million years away.

Maybe he'd left for the day. Maybe he'd seen me with Deacon and split. Maybe he'd just gone to Alondra. Maybe Deacon was going after him tonight. Maybe tomorrow. Maybe he'd implied he was going to tear Warren apart and Elliot was safe.

I turned that over in my head on my way to the common area with its soothing video of flowers and fields. I had the group thing in fifteen minutes, and I couldn't talk about anything that was on my mind. Again. I saw someone I knew in the cafeteria, and I got into the food line. The bell for lunch had rung a few minutes before, and my stomach was ready.

"Hey, sexy," came a voice so close to me, I heard it just as I felt the body attached to it. Fucking Warren.

"Get away from me," I hissed and went to a table.

Over his shoulder, I saw Elliot watching us. He didn't look right. I had a second to wonder if he'd seen me with Deacon before Warren opened his stupid mouth again.

"Your brother and I are partying on the roof tonight." He threw himself in a chair two spaces away. Far enough away to say he wasn't touching me. "Wanna come?"

He said "come" with a slither.

Jonathan clapped Warren on the back. "That shit you said? Baby's a liar."

"Always has been," Warren added with a wink, and Jonathan sat between us, slapping down his plates. "So, partying tonight?"

"No way, dude," Jonathan said, all bro-like. "Not going in the pokey again."

They laughed together, and I knew through all of Jonathan's denials, Warren made my brother feel good, as if he was a part of something. Some boy club made especially for the adolescent son with seven sisters. Was this kid ever going to be a man?

I looked between my brother and my rapist, and I knew all had been forgiven. Friends again. Nothing but a little roofie-laced scotch on tap for later.

"Don't do it," I said to Warren.

He just smiled. Behind him, an orderly rushed to us. He was going to pull Warren away from me. I wanted that. I wanted him as far away as possible, but I also wanted him incapacitated for my brother's sake.

I didn't have time to think too deeply about what I was doing, but I wasn't in some thoughtless rage either. I wasn't blinded by firing glands or rushes of emotion. "Jonathan, did I ever tell you what Warren did the day I left? Why I looked kind of off?"

"What?" he asked, poking his fork into his meat.

Warren tilted his head, as if wondering where I was going with this. One eye narrowed. "What *I* did? You mean what *we* did?"

Of course that was the tack he was taking. I didn't have time for his shit. I couldn't allow Warren to meet with Jonathan until I'd told my brother what he was dealing with.

I very coldly stood and pivoted behind my chair. I moved it, feeling its weight. The orderly behind Warren slowed down since it looked as though I was moving away.

I breathed and lifted the chair, quickly calculating how to swing it so it didn't hit Jonathan. There was a scream, a tray clattering. I breathed and brought the chair down on Warren's head. It bobbed, and he tipped off his chair, splayed on the floor.

I grabbed a fork and jumped on him.

In the tunnel vision of violence, I saw that I had enough time to gouge out his eyes. I could see the path of my hands and smell his blood as it splashed on my face. It would feel so good. So good. The last drug I'd ever need.

I raised my arm to make my vision a reality. I could practically smell his psycho fucking blood. Aggression took up most of my brain, leaving no room for logic.

I was pulled away before I even touched him. Furniture clattered and squeaked.

I made a show of resisting, but I had no intention of going anywhere. I called his name. I kicked someone. Got away. Got caught. Flooded with endorphins and adrenaline, I saw Warren being helped up like a victim. A sad, sorry victim who wouldn't hurt a fly, but there was enough blood going down his face to ensure a trip to the infirmary. Maybe an overnight stay.

I felt a pinch in my arm as they shot me with a trank, and my last thought was… as successes went, this wasn't too bad.

Chapter 109

ELLIOT

I WASN'T KIDDING myself into thinking I was Deacon Bruce. The man had a core of quiet violence I would never develop. Whatever he had in his head to do to keep Warren away from Fiona was probably more than I was capable of doing, or getting away with for that matter.

But what I was doing wasn't working.

Once Fiona was subdued and Warren taken to the infirmary, I went to my boss's office and closed the door.

"Doctor," she said dryly.

"You need to do more to separate Fiona Drazen and Warren Chilton."

"I hear. She's really a bag of tricks."

"He was standing close to her, whispering in her ear. She has PTSD from what happened. Her reaction was totally within the norm after what he did."

"Allegedly did."

I put my knuckles on the desk and leaned over it. "He needs to be in a high-security facility. Westonwood runs one in Salton Sea."

"Yeah. No." She pushed her chair back and laced her fingers over her

452

rib cage. She seemed too smug, too relaxed for the conversation. "No criminal conviction, no Salton Sea."

"If you won't do something, I will. This place is a really juicy story for the *Times*. Psychiatric resort for the rich? They'd love to shred you."

"You don't give a damn about your job at all, do you?"

"No. I don't."

"All this for a patient? A single patient?" She raised an eyebrow, tapped her finger against the top of her hand.

"Every patient counts."

"Tell me something. Everyone else is fine with how we're handling it. Why are you throwing yourself in front of this?"

"Am I the only one who cares?"

"In what way?" She crossed her legs. She was waiting for me to admit the whole thing. Frances was wasting her time as an administrator. Given the right circumstances, she could crack a man open with her posture from ten feet away.

"I don't think it matters," I said.

But it did. Betrayal mattered. I was denying Fiona three times before the cock crowed. Frances would question me as long as I'd let her, and I'd continue to say she was just a patient until the very edges of my soul were blunted into the shape of renunciation.

"Say it, Chapman. I'm getting bored."

"I'm in love with her. And you can save me the countertransference speech."

She leaned forward. "I wouldn't waste my time."

She swung her computer screen around. *You* magazine's website had posted a picture of Fiona and I talking over buttercups in a Koreatown coffee shop. In it, I held her hands as I told her it was all going to be all right.

"I just wanted to hear you admit it," she said. "But what we have going on here is enough to lose your license over. From what I can see, this was what you wanted the whole time. So congratulations."

"You need to separate them."

"Or what? You're going to tell everyone? With your credibility shot to hell? Now you're just a disgruntled ex-employee. I'll let you go to your office and pack up while I inform the board."

She turned her computer back and typed. I backed toward the door. I had a lot to say, but no patience for the answer.

"You know," she said, "when I was at Loyola, they had a date rape problem they didn't talk about." She glanced at me long enough to say, "Jesuits," then went back to the screen. "Big secrecy game. Like the Opus Dei, those guys. And it didn't occur to me that someone I went on a date with wouldn't get the signals for no—like a struggle or biting. I mean I liked the guy. Right? We're in my parents' basement and I'm trying to rationalize two things. I liked this guy on one hand. On the other, he's hurting me. Even during it, I made excuses for him like, 'He's choking me, so I *can't* say no,' and 'Maybe I should have said it louder when he started, but I was afraid my parents would hear because he wouldn't...'" She stopped typing, sniffed, cleared her throat. "Just *do that*. Right? I must be mistaken somehow. And when I went to the school clinic the next day, you know what they said?" She made eye contact as if she expected an answer but kept talking before I could give one. "They said, 'You'll get over it, Frances. But he's a shining star. It wouldn't be fair to ruin his life over this. One. Incident.'"

I let the story hang there for a moment, fermenting in the sour air between us.

"I'm sorry." I had an arsenal of right things to say in that situation. It was part of my training. But she knew my weapons of compassion better than I did.

She cleared her throat again and opened her drawer. "I always leave these on the desk." She tossed a ring of keys in front of me. "Anyone can grab them. I'm told it's going to get me in trouble one day."

She went back to her work. Was this a trap? The story, the keys, the pantomime of looking away?

"I'm glad you love her," she said. "You both need it. Now get out of here."

She must have hit a button or something, because the door opened behind me. Bernie, the orderly, put his hand on my shoulder. I quietly took the keys and let myself get hauled away without thanking her.

I HAD a couple of boxes of things I'd managed to grab with security's supervision. None of my files on my patients came with me. Books, diplomas, a few knickknacks.

I pulled over a mile outside the facility, while still in the quiet wilds of Palos Verdes, and took a deep breath.

Well, that was fun.

I'd associated losing everything for Fiona with loud noises and some kind of physical pain. I'd accepted it. Knowing better did nothing to reduce my mind's commitment to the image of a hammer coming down, being hurled off a cliff, breaking bones, and a shame so all-encompassing that strangers would see it a block away. My left brain I knew that if I lost everything, I wouldn't cease to exist. But I couldn't imagine anything after it, and the fear had come from the black hole I'd be sucked into afterward.

Elliot Chapman was here a minute ago. Now he isn't anywhere.

But I was breathing. I was sitting in my car with a normal heart rate. The birds were singing, the leaves rustling, and the world was turning the way it always did.

I wasn't afraid for my existence at all.

I was afraid for Fiona. She was stuck in a ward with a vengeful psychopath, and no one was watching him. I should have done something already. I should have taken care of this instead of trying to stay on the narrow path.

Well, I'd been thrown off the path into the black hole I feared.

I weighed the keys in my palm. There were about thirty, and they all looked the same.

How far was I willing to go?

The sensible thing to do was drive away, leave California, try to get a license in another state. Not get attached. Not fall in love with a patient again. Not stick my head out from behind my defenses. Any normal person would lick their wounds and slink away.

Love wasn't worth it. All the psy journals said so.

Well, the theological journals said love was always worth it. And my experience of listening to people talk about their relationships said otherwise.

He stole his brother's girlfriend because he couldn't live without her.

She betrayed her husband because she fell for another man.
They broke the law to defy parents who stood between them.
He stayed by her through her manic phase.
Poverty.
Pain.
Sickness.
Death.

I'd heard love transcend all of it and never believed it. Not until she came. Fiona put it all into place for me. She made all the stories make sense. All the reckless, senseless, bold, beautiful, risky, irresponsible, brutal, and selfless acts I'd heard about but never understood came into focus through the lens of love.

This was past wanting her. Past possessing her. Past fucking her or protecting her.

How far was I willing to go?

I was willing to be self-destructive, negligent, brave, audacious, and stronger than I ever believed possible.

But I wasn't willing to be stupid. Intentional failure wasn't acceptable, so there was a bigger question.

How far was I *able* to go?

I let the weight of the keys pull my hand down, and I closed my fingers around them.

Nothing to lose really. Except her crazy ass.

I slipped my phone from my pocket and found the numbers I needed, took a deep breath, and dialed the first.

Chapter 110

FIONA

THE QUIET WOKE ME. Isolation. I opened my eyes. It was neither dark nor light. Every corner and ridge was equally lit in a flat, colorless white. That meant it was nighttime. During the day, it was brighter so your circadian rhythms didn't get cocked up.

They'd put me in a straitjacket even though I hadn't been resisting.

"Fuckers," I whispered but didn't mean it. Not really.

I shouldn't have been surprised. This was what they did. This was the good news. I didn't know why I hadn't thought of it sooner. Now they'd separate us like they meant it.

I just laid there looking at the little camera eye in the center of the ceiling.

No one came. I couldn't have been in too long. My arms didn't ache, and I wasn't hungry. I didn't have to pee or anything, but hours went by in my mind. I listened for Elliot's voice in my cells, the smooth one he used for hypnosis. The one that suggested strongly. The exact opposite of Deacon's Dominant voice, which commanded as if he had already been obeyed. Two sides of the same coin, those voices and the men who breathed them.

I closed my eyes and touched Elliot's body, tracing every bone from toe to head with my fingertips. He had Deacon's face, with its stark blue eyes and unforgiving jawline. And they melded together into one man I'd hurt irrevocably with my selfishness and immaturity.

"God," I whispered, "I know you're there. I don't want to mess up anymore. I don't want to be a fuckup. It's hard. Too hard. And it hurts everyone. I can't live like this. I'm tired of being alone. Alone and thinking no one understands. Elliot says you don't make deals, so I'm not going to make a deal. I'm just going to say, I see you there, and when I'm about to fuck up, I'm going to think of you and do better."

I said that prayer over and over, changing it slightly, repeating words until they flowed and it became my breath.

Change. My way of thinking, my way of speaking, walking, breathing. I was going to believe I could change until everyone else did. In my bones, I knew the higher power I was talking to existed, and it believed in me.

Chapter 111

FIONA

THEY'D MOVED me to a proper isolation room with a bed and toilet. I
was there for three days. Frances came to talk to me about Warren, and I
told her clearly and intelligently why I'd hit him with a chair. She
nodded and didn't say much. A new therapist named Sol came in to say
hello. I was back to private sessions when I got out, and not with Elliot.

Probably for the best.

I got the sense that things were happening outside the door, but I
didn't ask about them. I just asked myself what I was going to do with
my life when I was out.

I was good at partying, being seen partying, and making other people
want to be me. I didn't know if that was something I should spend the
rest of my life doing. Not with a baby coming. I'd never cared if I was
terrible at everything I tried, but being bad at motherhood wasn't an
option. I couldn't fail. That wasn't allowed.

When they opened the door and walked me to Sol's office, I'd come
no closer to a solution to the problem.

Sol indicated the chair across from his desk, and I sat. He was almost completely bald, portly, with thick glasses. His wedding ring squeezed his finger, and I wondered if he could get it off if he tried.

"Miss Drazen," he said with a slight New York accent, "nice to see you again."

"Nice to be out."

"I bet. Do you want to tell me how you're feeling?"

"Sure. I'm, uh. I have this headache from being inside too much, and my joints feel kind of numb. I want to go for a run or something."

"Do you want something for the headache?"

"No. I'm okay."

He sat back and laced his fingers together over his belly. "I read your file. You're a very interesting young lady."

"Thanks. Not feeling real interesting right now."

"You're what I call a 'truth teller.' A fascinating personality type."

"I've been lying to myself for a long time."

He smirked and nodded then pointed his finger. "That's the root of your suffering, I think. But first, I need to tell you what happened while you were in isolation."

"Is my brother okay?"

The words came out before I even thought about it. He was the only thing I cared about in this mess, and I hadn't even realized it until I asked about him first.

"He's fine." Sol smoothed his pants, brushed something off his knee. "There was an incident on the grounds here."

"Who?" I wasted the question. I knew exactly who it was.

"Warren Chilton. He was found behind the garden where the creek is fenced off."

I knew he was watching my reaction closely, so I tried not to cheer internally. "Found?"

"It's a little gruesome."

"Tell me anyway."

"He was hanging from a tree. He's paralyzed from the neck down."

I blinked back my reaction and failed at hiding my shock. He was alive? Was I relieved or disappointed? Both? Some other third thing that had just released a twist in my gut I'd forgotten? "That's too bad. I just wanted to hit him with a chair."

"Really?"

"No. I wanted to break his head with a chair. Or whatever. I wasn't too picky about what I broke. Wow," I said, realizing he was alive and his dick wouldn't work. I almost laughed and cried at the same time, but ended up doing neither.

He nodded. "Wow is right. I know you and he have a history. You're going to hear a lot of rumors in the rec room. The police are taking this very seriously."

"I'll do a little truth telling." I shrugged. "I'm glad I was in isolation, because I wanted to do much worse to him."

"I'm glad you were in isolation too. This way, we can turn this lying to yourself around and get you out of here without interference. You ready for that?"

"Yes. Yes, I am."

"Good. I'm approving you to be deposed by the LAPD, and we'll get to work first thing tomorrow. You'll still have group starting this afternoon."

I stood, ready to take it all on.

Chapter 112

THE COPS ASKED me how much I hated Warren, and I didn't hold back. They couldn't put me away for hating the motherfucker, and apparently I wasn't the only one. They asked about Deacon. I told them he was in Eretria as far as I knew. They asked about Elliot. I told them to ask Elliot about Elliot. I hadn't spoken to him since I was back in Westonwood. They asked if Warren had been suicidal and if he'd been into breath play or asphyxiation with me, as if he and I were "into" anything together.

They let me go with a warning that they might ask more later. It was lunchtime, and all I wanted to do was run to Jonathan. When I saw him down the hall. I broke into a gallop and jumped into his arms.

"I heard," I said into his shoulder.

"You don't know half of it," he said into my ear then dropped me. "It's good to see you. Really good." He shook his head.

"Are you all right?"

He put his arm around me and guided me through the food line then to a small table where Karen sat alone. I kissed her cheek and sat. She had a plate in front of her with slices of cantaloupe. Jonathan dropped into the chair across from me.

"Do you have to eat that here?" she asked Jonathan, pointing at his steaming plate of protein with her fork. "It smells disgusting."

In answer, he speared a slab of meat and potato and shoved it into his mouth. Karen sighed and dropped her eyes to her plate. She cut the tiniest sliver of melon with a steak knife and put it in her mouth without letting the tines touch her lips.

"How is it?" I asked.

"Not bad."

I looked at Jonathan then back at her.

"You're eating," I said.

"Don't make a big deal about it, or she'll stop," Jonathan said around a mouthful of lunch.

"Okay." I poked at my plate. "It's good to see you guys. Good to be out."

"Now that he's gone," Karen said softly, "it's better in here. Like I can breathe and think at the same time."

I nodded. We ate in silence, air heavy with all the things I wanted to know. I kept glancing at my brother and my friend.

"I noticed the cracks in the ceiling for the first time last night because I wasn't sleeping in a ball." Karen swallowed a paper-thin sliver of melon as if she were swallowing an entire beefsteak tomato. "I thought, wouldn't it be cool to have a georgette scarf with those cracks in it? Such a nice print. And then last night, I thought about how Warren was hanging. All twisted and tangled up like he was fighting his way out. That's what they said. It was so complex, and I thought… ropes. A print of ropes on a scarf that when you tied it, the print was straight, but when it was flat, it was like Warren. Twisted."

"That's a plan," I said.

"He was hanging by the throat for three hours and didn't die. Just a broken neck," she said as if continuing the same conversation, glancing at me sidelong. "Because of the way he was snarled."

I swallowed my food with effort. "What else?"

Karen and Jonathan glanced at each other. Jonathan smirked.

"The whole camera system was on the fritz," Jonathan said. "They think Warren did it because he met me on the roof."

"No."

Two letters one syllable for, *Tell me you didn't do it. Tell me he didn't do it to you. Tell me you weren't involved.*

"He was passed out up there," Karen said, tilting her head toward Jonathan.

"Fuck you," he replied then turned back to me. "We had a few drinks."

"I told you not to," I growled.

"I had my reasons."

Three days had gone by, and in my brother's green eyes were another few years of maturity. A few more decades of experience in seventy-two hours.

"What did you do?" I practically spit the question in half whisper, half growl.

"I'm just a stupid kid," he said flatly. "He roofied me." A little smirk touched his lips, and he didn't break my gaze.

"And Nortyl'd himself pretty good," Karen said. "Without that, I don't think he would have tried to commit suicide. Westonwood's in big trouble for leaving that stuff where a patient could get to it."

My gaze didn't leave Jonathan's.

"He didn't try to commit suicide," I said.

"The Nortyl wiped his memory of everything that night but the need to die," Jonathan whispered "die" with a pop, as if pulling the trigger on the word.

He'd fooled me, and maybe everyone. He'd never been Warren's friend. Never believed him, at least not during my second turn in Westonwood. He'd known what Warren did to me—maybe from Margie, maybe from the rumor mill—and had kept it to himself until he could do something about it. The face I saw over the cafeteria table wasn't sixteen years old. It was a hundred and sixteen.

"You're scaring me," I said.

"I was passed out."

"Alibi notwithstanding, asshole."

"You know what was weird?" Karen said, still intent on the

cantaloupe pieces. She was really making a dent in them. "They fixed the holes in the fence after we left. And there were no new ones. The paramedics spent ten minutes looking for keys then just cut their own hole. No one can figure out how he got back there." She scrunched her face up as if she was sick. "Oh. I have to lie down."

"You're not going to puke, are you?"

"No. It'll pass. I just…" She didn't finish but got up and went for the couches, leaving my brother and me alone.

I held up my hand. "Open pledge."

He held up his hand. "Open for yes or no questions."

"You don't get to dictate what you answer."

"I was passed out. I went up for a drink because I was mad at you and I didn't believe you. He gave me mine. He drank his. We had a few laughs. I forget the rest. Cameras went back on an hour later, and I was still there. Passed. Out. Ask the cops. Pledge closed."

"No! You're leaving stuff out!"

He stood and scooped up his tray. "I love you, sister."

The bell for afternoon sessions rang.

I grabbed his arm before he could walk away. "Jonathan. Who got to you?"

"You did, stupid." He kissed my cheek and strode off.

I was supposed to be in group session in five minutes, but all I could do was put the Nortyl and the complex knots together with Jonathan getting Warren out of his room when the cameras were down. Pack that all in a bong and smoke it, and even with the hundred holes in the story, it added up to one thing.

I was loved by a team of smart, shrewd, criminally-inclined vigilantes.

But I was loved.

If I denied that any longer, I was calling them all liars. And if I denied I was worthy of it, I was convincing myself they were delusional and stupid.

I wasn't lying to myself anymore. Not about that.

Chapter 113

FIONA

RUMORS ABOUT WARREN were vicious and horrifying. I could tell the truth from the lies, because every detail traced back to someone who loved me.

LIE: Warren was practicing autoerotic asphyxiation.

TRUTH: The knots were so tight they broke skin.

LIE: Warren had been given Nortyl for bipolar disorder.

TRUTH: The rope he'd been tied with wasn't from anywhere inside the institution.

Bottom line: Warren had been in a state of soul-ripping, mind-blunting pain when he broke his neck, and he woke up dickless. That was all I needed to know.

I didn't try to get out. Didn't strategize the right things to say or do. No tricks. No games. Without Warren around, a calm fell over crazytown. No one was taking off-script drugs or paying for favors in blow jobs. Mark got let go a week after Warren was wheeled away, and couple of guys in security were let go quietly. A PA confessed to getting him pills but swore he never doled out Nortyl. No one believed him.

Sol stayed around. Deanna stayed. There was a rumor Frances had to fight for her job. Elliot was gone.

I knew he was waiting. I told Sol I had someone. He was from outside my world. He was loyal and decent. He set the right path by example, not force, and he loved me. Crazy as it was, he loved me. Of all the world's gifts, that was the greatest, and I wasn't going to decide I didn't deserve it. Only he could decide that, and if he said I was good enough for him, I wouldn't argue otherwise.

Except when I did. Old habits died hard, but they died.

"Your brother's getting out in a week," Sol said from behind his desk.

"I want to to wait for him."

"That can be arranged. Why?"

"I want to walk him out. And this way we can share a ride."

"I didn't know carpooling was so important to you."

"There are ten of us. Think about it. The Drazen Carpool can probably wean the US off foreign oil."

He shifted forward. "Besides running the biggest carpooling organization in the country, what are your plans when you leave here?"

"Get lunch?"

He cleared his throat, which was code for, "I get the joke now answer the question."

I looked out the window. The sky was a flat blue. A black speck of a bird shot across it and was gone. "I think I need help. Deanna talks about meetings. I know the ones in Hollywood. Big celebrities go, and they're not treated any different. No one notices." I brushed the velvet pile on the chair until it was all the lightest color. "I need new friends anyway. The ones I have are nuts."

"You might need a job."

I laughed. Right. I'd been cut out of Drazen money like an infection. "Yeah. I don't know. I can sell the condo and a car and invest in something."

"Such as?"

"I know a guy who makes excellent designer drugs."

"Fiona," he scolded.

"I'm joking." I joked because I didn't have an answer. I didn't know what I wanted to do, but I wanted him to know I was thinking about it. I took my life seriously, even if I didn't have the answers. So I riffed on a pebble of a notion Karen had left for me. "Maybe something with scarves and clever prints." I moved my hands around as if spooling an idea around them. "I don't think making stuff is my thing, but I'm good at people. People who make stuff. Like that. And I can wear the scarves out to parties. Calmer parties. The ones people with babies go to. Be seen. Get photographed. You know, that-do-that-I-do."

"It's a start," he said. "Risky, but I guess your family won't let you starve."

I laughed. I thought of Karen, how she wouldn't starve if she had something about herself to love.

Maybe this wasn't a bad idea.

Chapter 114

ELLIOT

I GOT to the Westonwood parking lot before Margie Drazen. We had a
cup-of-tea bet going on about whether she'd make it first from Beverly
Hills or I'd make it from Torrance. I cheated and left twenty minutes
earlier than I said I would. She pulled in right behind me.

"What time did you leave?" she asked as she walked from her
Mercedes toward my shit Honda. She had tall paper cups in each hand.

"Seven ten." Admitting it made me a lousy cheater.

"You beat me fair and square." She handed me a cup.

"We were starting at seven thirty."

"I left at seven."

"See you in hell." I took a sip of my tea.

I'd just gotten done with an overnight at Chino State, where I usually
waited for something to happen then felt grateful when nothing did. On-
call crisis counselor was the only job I could get with my license being
under review. It had been three months, and another three years could
go by before I would be off probation. The board never approved of my

relationship with Fiona, but I was clear she was the first and the last, and I wasn't giving her up. They called it "lovesickness," and I had to laugh. I was sick, and they were sick, and everyone who ever touched love was most certainly terminally ill. We all died from this disease of love.

"What color did you decide on for your office?" I asked.

"Green for money."

Margie had left her job and started her own firm. She said she needed freedom to pursue her own interests. Like getting Deacon Bruce on a plane in the middle of the night. Like pressing the license review board in my case. Like delivering a set of keys to the director of a mental institution without being seen. Or aiding Declan Drazen in the expensive backhand dismantling of the Chiltons' business. Bit by bit, movie by movie, relationship by relationship, Margie and Declan were moving the pieces on the chessboard to block, sabotage, and break the family. I didn't have details, only the knowledge it was happening, and the news. Charlie Chilton had lost a huge directing deal in the previous week, and all permits for their half-built house had been rejected.

I pitied them. Their son would never recover. But I was just a man. They were in denial over the danger their son posed to other people, and he'd targeted someone I loved. My compassion had limits.

"They're coming," Margie said, putting her cup on the hood of my car.

Jonathan exited first and held the door open for his sister.

She was as breathtaking as ever.

Her strawberry hair bounced when she walked, her chin tilted upward when she saw us, and her body was the most perfectly fuckable thing to ever grace the earth. When she smiled at me and picked up the pace, I couldn't help myself. I ran to her. She was worth running for. Worth every loss in my life. Worth stepping outside the law. Worth living, dying, and everything in between.

She fell into me, and we became arms and lips and hands. Breath and movement. I tasted her, felt her, understood in the way she moved that she and I were connected, and nothing had changed for her in the months we were separated. Even when she pushed herself against me and I felt the extra curve in her belly, nothing had changed.

"You've never been fucked like I'm going to fuck you," I whispered.

I felt her shudder in my arms. Warm and pliable, sharp and twisted, fuck her was the least of it. I was going to love her brutally and unconditionally.

Forever and ever, amen.

Chapter 115

FIONA

WE SAID our good-byes and hurled ourselves into Elliot's car. He took off down the winding road through Rancho at the speed limit. It was warm, so he wore a button-down shirt and slacks without a jacket. I saw his body move, the way his fingers controlled the wheel, the flicking of the wind in his sandy hair.

He didn't say anything. No small talk. No dirty talk. His ocean eyes stayed on the road.

"You've been working out?" I asked.

"It helps redirect my energies."

I put my hand on his knee. He took his hand off the gear shift and clasped mine.

"We have a lot to talk about," I said.

"Yep."

I had phrased the next part in my head a billion times. I didn't know if I'd bring it up right away, but I didn't expect the car ride to be the best time. The fact that he wasn't looking at me would make it easier.

"I'm going to have a baby."

"If it makes it easier for you, I already knew."

"It does," I said. "I don't have to talk you down from shock."

"How are you feeling, by the way?" He turned to me for a second. "They wouldn't tell me anything, and Margie just said 'fine.'"

"No morning sickness or anything. Just hungry." I cleared my throat. "I did get this test done a couple of weeks ago."

"Yes?" he asked.

"I was worried because I did some partying, and she seems okay."

"She?"

"It's a girl."

He squeezed my hand and smiled. God, this was going to be hard.

"They had to put this needle in, and they tested the DNA also, and here's the thing. I was with you, but also, God I hate this—"

"Fiona—"

"Shut up. It was a transition period. There was no crossover. Once it was you, it was you, and it's not a big deal to me but…" I ran the rest together without punctuation. "But in the time this baby was conceived I was with both of you and if you'd let them get a cheek swab we'd know if it was yours I'm sorry but I don't think it's fair for you not to know."

He laughed.

"What's so funny?'

"You."

"Why?"

"Because you think I give a shit." He glanced at me to check my reaction then looked back at the road. "I will never, ever give you a cheek swab or anything else to prove this baby is or isn't mine. You can leave me tomorrow, and I'll claim that baby girl."

I crossed my arms. "I don't know if I'm relieved or annoyed."

"You don't have to be either."

Then gently, as if turning into his own driveway on any other Tuesday, he turned onto a dirt road, followed until it went left, and stopped.

"Where are we?" I asked.

"Alone."

He fell onto me, lips and tongue on mine. Hands up my shirt, taking skin that hadn't felt a man in too long, he cupped my breast and twisted a nipple that needed it so badly, I groaned and cried out at the same time.

"Right here," he said. "I'm taking you right here."

I didn't know how we did it. The Honda had no room for two adults to become one twisting, curling, half-clothed mass of flesh. But against all the odds, against even the laws of physics and logic, we did.

Epilogue

FIONA

THERESA, for all her pearl-clutching and airs of civilized grace, wound up with a devil. He was as handsome and charming as the devil, too. Dark eyes and hair. Full lips. Bit of a Roman nose but not too much. The eyelashes, a defining feminine feature on most people, actually set off a masculinity so intense he seemed as likely to pour from the wine bottle he held, as break it over someone's head.

"Okay," he said with an Italian accent. "Red then. A chianti."

"I'm fine," I said. "Thank you."

He blinked, apparently incredulous. Behind him, the doors opened onto a guest-filled patio and, beyond that, a flowering olive orchard deep in Temecula.

"You're eating," he said. "You have to—"

"Antonio!" My sister Theresa broke in, wedding dress trailing over the tile floor. Good thing it was a huge kitchen. "She doesn't drink. Get off her case."

Bottle in one hand, glass in the other, he spread his arms as if he was the innocent victim of a foreign culture. *"Perche, no?"*

Theresa plucked the glass and wine from him and kissed him. "Get her some water, would you?"

"*Come vuoi tu, Capo.*" He kissed her back.

A guttural sound of flat disgust came from behind me. I jabbed Amanda in the sternum. She exhibited every single annoying trait of adolescence, but being grossed out by kissing and sex? Not annoying.

I didn't want my daughter to be a sexless wonder. I wanted her to be liberated and enjoy her body, but one less thing to worry about was one less thing to worry about.

"I have water, thank you." I tapped my glass with my spoon and the population of the kitchen joined in.

I'd discovered this old Italian tradition within an hour of arriving. If the guests tapped their glasses, the couple had to kiss. I winked at Amanda, and she rolled her eyes. They were blue. Shocking blue. A blue like I'd seen on a face only once before. She was tall and had jet black hair without a touch of red. I wondered if she was my daughter sometimes, especially when her report cards came in looking like every key on the teacher's computer was broken except the letter A.

In response to the clinking glasses, Antonio and Theresa kissed like the newlyweds they were. He whispered something in her ear, and her knees bent a little. Sexual liberation came late to Theresa, but when it came, it came hard.

"Gross," mumbled Amanda, turning a deep shade of red. "Are you going to let Alex see this?"

Alex was our ten-year-old. A pure-strain ADHD case with a joyful laugh and enthusiasm for just about everything. He had sea-green eyes and bright red hair. Completely unaware of social norms, he pushed between Antonio and Theresa to get to me. They separated, laughing.

"Mom!"

"Can you apologize to Aunt Theresa and Uncle Antonio for pushing them, please?"

He spun around. "Sorry!" Then he turned back to me.

I bent my knees to get on his eye-level. His shirt was already untucked and his jacket was probably under a rock somewhere. He could have survived a week on the hors d'ourves stuck to his tie.

"Uncle Jonathan says he can teach me to pitch, and I'm a lefty, so he said I can prob get on any varsity baseball team in the world if I can pitch, and he'll teach me!"

"All right. You can start after the Thanksgiving break."

"No! Today! He says today is as good a day as any and it's only an hour or something out in the orchard please please please.

"You're wearing your good shoes."

He didn't have time to answer before Jonathan appeared above me with a bag of oranges. He'd grown tall and strong and saved the Drazen empire from insolvency right out of grad school. An insolvency the press attributed to Daddy's non-existent drinking problem. It was easier to say Declan Drazen was a drunk than that he'd spent almost every dime taking down Charlie Chilton. Daddy didn't care if the world thought he was a drunk, as long as they didn't know what he really did.

"So what?" Jonathan said. "It's pitching. He's not going to ruin his shoes."

David, my sister Sheila's twelve-year-old, handed Alex a lefty glove with a ball in it. "Had it in the car."

Alex made a pleasepleaseplease face. I loved the fuck out of that kid. He loved doing things. Sports. Art. Writing. Tag. Dungeons and Dragons. People. Overall, he loved people, and I knew he cared more about spending time with his uncle and cousin than he cared about his curveball.

"Is your wife all right without you?" I asked Jonathan.

His wife, a stunning musician with a smart mouth, was about eight minutes to giving birth, and he doted like a mother hen.

"She's surrounded by half of Naples. I can't even get near her." He slung the bag of oranges over his back. "We'll be over that way." He pointed at some vague place out yonder, toward the setting sun, beyond the tables and people dancing.

The three of them took off without another word from me.

An Italian dance had begun out in the yard, and Theresa was hoisted above the crowd like a lily bouncing on the water.

Amanda sat to the side, all in black, a puss on her face that would freeze oceans.

"She's still sulking?" Elliot's voice came from behind me.

"Yeah."

He touched the back of my neck and ran his finger across my shoulder. He knew the exact right amount of pressure to make me forget everything. "You should let her go," he said.

"I can't discuss this anymore."

"But she and I can." He turned me around so I faced the kitchen. It had emptied out, so there was nothing to distract me from his ocean-green eyes. They'd earned some lines at the edges over the years. He'd gotten more impossibly handsome with age. "So she and I win."

"No, you don't." I smoothed the front placket of his clerical shirt. He'd finally done his discernment for the Episcopal priesthood and gone back to spiritual practice. It had been a long, hard slog. Eight years. But at the end of it, he was a new man.

"How about this?" he said. "If you admit the real reason you don't want her to go to Nambia, we'll make other arrangements for next summer." I was about to say she wouldn't be safe when he held up his finger. "The real reason. You know she's safe with Deacon. He'd burn the entire continent down before anything happened to her."

I bit my lips then told him the real reason, which he was damned well aware of. "He'll see her, and he'll know. And she'll know."

"Know what?"

"She's his."

"She's mine. She's always been mine."

"Can we stop kidding ourselves? Please?"

"I don't care about her DNA. I really don't. I've been her father for fifteen years, and he's been a pen pal. When she wanted to sell Girl Scout cookies, who sat in front of the grocery store all weekend? When she wanted to play basketball, who coached the team? When she got her first period, who ran out to get her supplies? Me. She's mine. And she's going to go there and fall in love with the adventure and worship her Uncle Deacon like everyone else, but she knows she's mine."

"What about him?"

"I wouldn't worry about him." He'd always been so confident about his earned paternity, as if things being unimpeachably right in his world made them right everywhere. He was a believer in truth, and his one overarching truth was always that his family was whomever he claimed.

"How's that?"

"I can take him in a fight." He put his arms around me and put his lips to my forehead. "For my family, I'll take him and a hundred like him."

"Men," I grumbled, putting my head on his chest. "Wait. I won the bet. Now that I admitted the real reason, she can go to Monterey next summer."

"You don't want her to, now that you've said the truth out loud."

He was right as usual. Voicing my fear had taken the power from it. Amanda craved adventure and travel. I couldn't hold her back much longer.

"What did I ever do to deserve you?" I asked.

"You let me love you."

"Is that all?"

"Yes."

I turned my back to him, and he wrapped his arms around me, burying his lips in my neck.

"Worth it," I said.

Out on the flagstones, Antonio and Theresa danced. He held her, and when he looked up, our eyes met. He said something to Theresa and she protested, but he pushed her away and bounded up the steps and through the crowd to the sliding kitchen doors.

"You don't drink wine?" he asked through the screen, as if being dry at a wedding was an impossible concept.

"Sixteen years sober, Antonio. You didn't notice? I've known you six months already."

"Do you have any fun at all?"

"Yes," Elliot answered. "That's my wife's job."

Antonio cocked his head.

"I'm seen having fun," I said. "Didn't Theresa tell you anything?"

"I didn't understand it, I admit."

Elliot let me go, leaving a hand on my neck.

"I find designers. I invest in them. I take them out. People talk. We build a business."

I couldn't tell if he was impressed or doubtful anyone could make money doing something so silly.

"Do you dance?" he asked.

I had to think for a minute. It had been a while. "Yes, as a matter of fact, I do dance."

Antonio slapped open the screen door and addressed Elliot. "I will never get used to a priest having a wife. But, do you mind if yours dances with me?"

"Not at all." He took his hand off my neck. "Be careful with her. She's the most valuable thing I have."

"I will treat her like a precious flower," Antonio said when I took his arm. "But she may have to hold me up. I've had too much wine."

Antonio walked me out to the clearing where a crowd danced under the setting sun. At the edge of the orchard I could see Jonathan kneel next to my son to show him how to hold a baseball, and my nephew pitched oranges against a tree trunk. To my right my daughter pouted because I hadn't told her that yes, she could go to Africa next summer, and behind me, Elliot watched as I danced with my brother in-law. My sister danced in her wedding gown. Margie spoke urgently to my parents. My brother's wife waddled to the bathroom.

We were connected. All of us. By the gestures of our hands and the tones of our voices. By our intentions, our actions, our loyalties, By our willingness to sacrifice for one another, we were joined by the ropes of our love and held fast by the knots of our hearts.

I was among my people, and I was worthy of them.

Where do you go from here?

Margie Drazen.
Two rock stars.
One bed.
A family with devastating secrets.

Find out how she became the Drazen Fixer.
Trust me. You won't see it coming.

CLICK HERE TO DOWNLOAD THE SIN DUET BUNDLE TODAY!

—

*GET on the mailing list for deals, sales, new releases and bonus content - JOIN HERE or **text cdreiss to 77948***

My Goodreads fan group is called CD Canaries: join the group!

Facebook fan-run group, go here. Most fun, guaranteed.

Facebook fan page is here. I run this, and it's for official news and announcements.

I'm on Pinterest, Tumblr, Twitter and Instagram with varying degrees of frequency.

My email is cdreiss.writer@gmail.com.

Also by CD Reiss

The *New York Times* bestselling Games Duet

Adam Steinbeck will give his wife a divorce on one condition. She join him in a remote cabin for 30 days, submitting to his sexual dominance.

HIS DARK GAME

Monica insists she's not submissive. Jonathan Drazen is going to prove otherwise, but he might fall in love doing it.

COMPLETE SUBMISSION

Fiona Drazen has 72 hours to prove she isn't insane, just submissive. Her therapist has to get through three days without falling for her.

FORBIDDEN

Margie Drazen has a story and it's going to blow your mind.

THE SIN DUET

Her husband came back from the war with a Dominant streak she didn't know he had.

The complete Edge series

EDGE OF DARKNESS

Contemporary Romances

Hollywood and sports romances for the sweet and sexy romantic.

Shuttergirl | Hardball | Bombshell | Bodyguard | Only Ever You